Quarter-finalist in Publisher Weekly's Booklife Prize

Triple Winner at The BookFest Awards for
Fantasy Action & Adventure
Fantasy Dragons & Mythical Creatures
Literary Science Fiction & Fantasy

# Praise for
# Dragons Unremembered

"Of course, in this era, there will be immediate comparisons to George R.R. Martin's Song of Ice and Fire series, but this felt much more reminiscent to me of the work of Anne McCaffrey and her Dragon Riders of Pern series, such is the feel and classic storytelling on display."
— *Books That Make You*

"The author has created a complex story line nestled against stunning worldbuilding. The plot is rich and meandering, but laser-focused on the details for discerning readers. Dragons Unremembered is a foreign and complex world, and the author is able to recount its history and culture through narration and dialogue, rather than long, descriptive passages—a potent way to set up the story while still engaging readers. The book hums with diverse characters and a vibrant, multilayered setting, and the creative storytelling flawlessly immerses readers in the plot. Readers will glean insight into he main players through their words and actions, and the large, varied cast is most effective when reacting naturally to the tense moments in the story. 9.75 out of 10"
— *Booklife Prize*

# Dragons Unremembered

## Volume I of The Carandir Saga

# DAVID A. WIMSETT

Dragons Unremembered
A Cape Split Press Book

TM

Published by arrangement with the author

Printing History
First Printing 2018
Second Printing 2022
Third Printing 2025

ISBN 978-1-7775745-6-7

Background - ID 26234778 © Algol | Dreamstime.com
Warrior - ID 136466522 © MerryDesigns | Dreamstime.com
Dragon - ID 1333514462 © Warpaint |Shutter Stock
Map designed by Glendon Haddix | Streetlight Graphics, LLC | www.streetlightgraphics.com

Used through arrangement with the artists

For my son, Ronald

**Other Books by David A. Wimsett**

Half Awakened Dreams: Volume II of the Carandir Saga
Covenant With the Dragons: Volume III of the Carandir Saga
Beyond the Shallow Bank
Beyond the Shallow Bank: Illustrated Edition
Something on My Mind
Unintended Consequences


**Children's Picture Books with Joanne Fouchard**
Santa is a Cat
The Ant and the Magician

# ACKNOWLEDGEMENTS

It is said a novel is a long piece of writing with mistakes. This second edition corrects mistakes found in the first edition. The book has also been extensively restructured to make the prose more dynamic and align them with the rest of the series. Sections have been added, removed and reorganized to improve the flow and meaning. I thank my editor,Nancy Cassidy, for helping me improve the novel.

Since its inception, many people have read and offered suggestions. The late best-selling author, Leonard Bishop, was instrumental in pointing out how to address nuts and bolts problems. The members of Leonard's weekly writing group continually pushed and encouraged me. Leonard is sorely missed. Ann, Jeff, Glenn, Bruce, Anna and Ed gave both literary and moral support. The members of the Squaw Valley Community of Writers workshops helped me to polish the book. Most importantly, I thank my son, Ronald, for his patience and understanding.

David A. Wimsett
Nova Scotia
September 2022

# Monarchy of Carandir

TO THE
NORTH CONTINENT
(DISTANCE UNKNOWN)

← TO THE WESTERN OCEAN

N

TO XINGLAN →

## THE GREAT RIVER

PORT OF RASCALLA

PORT OF FELLANT

UTA MTNS.

TO AU →

RASCALLA

PERET RIVER

THE PALACE

OLD KEEP

METH

VARDA RIVER

VARDA MTNS.

DESAN

LENTAR RIVER

RIVER NERA

PONTALARA

FELLANT

### WESTERN BARONIES

### EASTERN BARONIES

THE EER

THE LENA

RIVER RESPA

KAR RIVER

EASTERN SWAMPLAND

SHENAN RIVER

LUSAR MTNS.

NEMTANKA RIVER

LAKE HASP

LAKE SHENAN

GELALAN

MENTARO

## KINGDOM OF KARAKEN

TO HURA →

SOUTHERN DESERT

TO TAQUAN →

# PROLOGUE

*The Monarchy of Carandir*
*Barony of Rascalla*
*Two Thousand five Hundred and First Year of Avar the Great*

Nur's lanky frame swayed in the flat bottom boat as he peered through swamp vegetation on the eastern edge of the barony of Rascalla. The nineteen-year-old's light clothes were soaked from heat and humidity. "I don't see anyone, Willa."

Willa, Nur's twenty-four cousin, crouched in the rear of the boat. The bangs of her short cut hair dropped across her forehead below the wide brimmed hat she wore. "I wish my parents had never agreed to visit your family in this backwater land. Meth is safe. No one harasses you in the capital."

A stern look came to Nur's features. "Rascalla is not a backwater. Baron Dek keeps the peace. Those men must be smugglers. I've just never heard of any of them coming this far north."

"Well, they have. What were they doing in those heavy, red robes and hoods anyway? They had to be sweltering. And to have them threaten us just because we were gathering turtle eggs. Did they think they owned that little island?"

"Well, we got away."

"And left Tib."

"Your little brother shouldn't have run off."

"He was scared."

"So was I, but I had the sense to run to the boat."

The sound of swishing rippled across the stagnant water.

Nur looked through the vegetation. "Shh. I see them."

Willa's voice rasped in a whisper. "Are they coming this way?"

"No. They haven't seen us." Nur's mouth opened in a gape. "Father of Dragons, they've got Tib."

Willa sat up. "What are we going to do?"

"We'll follow their boat and see where they take him. Then, we'll pole back and have my father alert the garrison."

"Your father's gonna skin us alive."

"Stop thinking about yourself for once. Just pray to the dragons they don't hurt Tib."

Nur poled the boat with care not to make a sound.

The other craft picked up speed and moved ahead. Soon, it faded into mist.

Willa sighed. "We've lost them."

They heard wood scrape against rock.

Nur poled in the direction of the sound.

The hazy outline of an island emerged from the mist. An empty boat lay beached on its bank.

Willa pulled on Nur's arm. "Let's go back for your father."

"We have to make certain it's them."

"Are you mad? They'll catch us too."

"I'll land behind those reeds."

A square, three-story tower appeared out of the haze as they approached. Nur put in at a muddy bank and they crept up to the keep.

Willa ran her hands along the stone wall. It was smooth and free of any lichen or moss.

They entered and found no trace of Tib or the men from the boat. The second and third stories were also empty. They climbed to the top and looked all about. The island was deserted.

Willa scanned the ground. "There must have been a second boat on the other side of the island."

"Most likely. Let's get back."

The caution Nur and Willa initially felt evaporated as they walked back down the stairs.

Willa removed her hat and wiped her forehead. "I still don't understand why you left Meth to come back here. At least in the capital there's life and excitement. I've never been so bored in my life."

Nur's lips curled up in a sardonic smile. "Being hunted by mysterious men isn't exciting enough for you?"

"That's not the kind of excitement I meant. You remember what Meth's like."

"I rarely left the vaults of the Kyar beneath the palace. My time was spent in lessons and learning spells. I just didn't like the monastic life, so I came home."

Willa scoffed. "Magic spells. Ha! More like parlor tricks."

"The Kyar and the Daro hold the last remnants of magic after the wizards left. They keep records of the past, a past most people have forgotten."

"A bunch of old men reciting nonsense and old women concocting ointments and useless potions."

"There are plenty of young Kyar and Daro. They may not have the power of the vanished wizards, but their magic is real. I've seen it work."

"Wizards. Nonsense. They're as fake as Jorondel and Ilidel, the supposed father and mother of dragons."

Nur scowled. "Are you saying the magical crown of Carandir doesn't keep the dragon Baras confined?"

"That so called evil dragon is just another myth. Come on. Do you honestly believe in dragons and wizards?"

Nur hesitated for a moment. "Well, yes. I do. I may have left my studies with the Kyar, but my faith in Ilidel and Jorondel has never wavered."

Willa laughed. "You have to be joking."

"There're powers beyond us. You can't deny that."

"I'm a city engineer. I'll deny anything unless there's proof. Ilidel, Jorondel and Baras are folklore, symbols of good and evil."

"The Kyar's vaults are filled with uncounted books and scrolls chronicling the Dragon Wars and the beginnings of Carandir."

"But who wrote them?"

Nur raised an eyebrow. "What about Avar the Great? Do you deny he subdued Baras with the power of his crown before he founded Carandir?"

"Oh, he established Carandir all right. That's actual history. Saying his crown was magical is ridiculous. He was just the first king. The crown is an artifact, not a talisman."

Nur frowned. "You've never stared into the eyes of the dragon-crested crown. I have. There's something about it."

"Stop living in your imagination and look at the real world." She ran a hand across the stone wall next to her. "For instance, who put this up in the middle of nowhere?"

"It's probably been here since the Dragon Wars. Before they vanished, the wizards used such strongholds to imprison demons."

"More ancient lies."

Nur turned his head toward his cousin in a slow movement. "Well, a lot of people in the east hold faith with the dragons. You need to be more careful of what you say out here."

Willa raised her hand. "Shh."

They moved behind a column and peered down the stairway to the first floor. A section of wall stood open like a door. A hooded man in a crimson robe emerged. He pressed five stones in a pattern. The door closed and he walked out of the keep.

Nur and Willa moved down the stairs with caution.

She peered into the swamp. "Whoever he was, he poled his boat away. Let's get out of here."

Nur inspected the wall. "I remember reading something about this. A pattern of stones act as a key."

"You want to open it? Those men could be inside. Let the Militia handle this."

Nur pressed the stones in the same order as he saw the robed man do. "Tib might be locked inside."

With an audible snap, the secret door opened. A rough-hewn corridor led down. Torches were spaced along its wall. Each gave off light without heat or smoke.

Nur remembered reading about red-robed men and torches that gave off neither heat nor smoke. He felt a vague sense of dread as he led the way inside.

Willa shook her head, then entered.

As soon as both cleared the threshold, the door closed behind them.

They descended and rounded a bend. Below was a large cavern. Dozens of men in red robes stood before braziers where smoke rose from fires.

One man sat on a throne with a hood pulled over his head.

Fifteen-year-old Tib knelt next to the throne.

Two other men held him by the arms.

The man on the throne spoke words that were lost in the cavern.

Tib moved his head from side to side.

Nur pointed back the way they came.

Willa stood still as if paralyzed.

Nur shoved her.

She backed away a pace, then turned and ran up the steps with Nur close behind.

A tall, young man in the blue and white uniform of a Carandirian naval officer came down the steps. With relief, Nur recognized him as Lieutenant Petstra, an adjunct to the senior staff.

Nur breathed in short gasps. "Lieutenant Petstra. Thank the dragons. Someone's captured my cousin."

He looked behind the officer and saw three crimson-robed men on the steps.

Petstra drew his sword. "Walk back down the stairs."

Nur and Willa came to the cavern floor where they were grabbed and forced to kneel beside Tib.

Nur looked up at the throne where an emaciated man with pale skin sat beside a brazier. A sweet, thick stench permeated the air.

Petstra knelt. "Lord Reshna, more intruders."

Reshna pointed to Nur. "I sense wizard magic. Who sent you to spy on the Barasha?"

A shock of terror ran through Nur. He told himself this was impossible. Every book and scroll he'd ever read told how the Barasha were destroyed by the wizards.

Those tales said the dragon Baras himself taught this group of men sorcery to work minor spells with potions and chants. When the dragon wars began, Baras showed the men how to bind demons and force the spirits who had joined him to perform true magic in exchange for living souls. Those men took the name Barasha, servants of Baras.

Tib gave a whimper.

Willa stared up at Reshna, her face ashen.

Nur forced out words in a stammer. "No one sent us. We were only hunting turtle eggs."

Willa shook. "We won't betray your secret. Let us go."

Reshna addressed Petstra. "Were you successful in the palace?"

"Yes, Lord Reshna. I was made privy to many secrets. The queen has conceived twins, as you foresaw. I spoke the incantation to hide the second child from all examination."

Reshna leaned back into the throne. "We have but to wait until the birth for confusion or corruption. I will now call upon our master."

He looked to Tib. "That one."

Tib was dragged to the brazier next to Reshna's throne.

Two Barasha priests held him.

One slit the young man's throat as he screamed.

The other cast yellow powder into the victim's face.

Tib gave a gurgling cry as blood splashed the burning coals.

Nur tasted bile and fought not to vomit.

Barasha priests chanted in unison.

The smoke of the brazier twisted and congealed to form a round, green body. It was half the size of a person with short, clawed hands and no legs. Its head consisted of just a mouth with jagged teeth.

The demon's voice was shrill. "Who summons me?"

"I, Reshna, Lord High Priest of the Servants of Baras. I will speak with my master."

The smoke wavered, then congealed again. "I will not approach the power of the crown with the dragon crest fashioned by Jorondel and the will of creation breathed into it by Ilidel."

"You took the offering. You cannot refuse."

"None can stand before the spell."

"Others before you have opened his mind to me. Will you suffer the wrath of Baras? He dreams only of hatred. For now, those dreams are consumed with the generations of Avar. Do you wish his attention as well?"

"What care is it to me? He will sleep for eternity."

"No. The crown itself will release him."

"Impossible. Only Avar's heir can remove it from the crystal sphere."

Reshna poured red powder into his hand and held it up to the demon. "It has begun."

The demon examined the powder. "It will cost two more souls."

Reshna pointed to Nur and Willa.

# BOOK I

*The Barony of Fellant*
*Western Carandir*

# CHAPTER ONE

Dek, Baron of Rascalla, studied the soldiers and courtiers assembled around the large table. He sat in the council chamber of Etera, Baron of Fellant in western Carandir, and gauged each face for signs of who would support the king and queen if civil war erupted in Carandir.

Next to him sat Haram Avar, King of Carandir and descendant of Avar the Great. At the age of forty, the monarch was a year younger than Dek.

The baron squirmed uncomfortably in a chair too small for his muscular frame. His dark beard itched, but he refrained from scratching it.

The room was silent. Dek looked past the king to Araney, thirty-seven-year-old Queen of Carandir and daughter of Etera. The fingers of her right hand rested on her belly, now swollen near to term with pregnancy.

Araney leaned forward. "Father. Do you desire to bring civil war to threaten your own grandchild who I carry?"

"It's not I who threatens the monarchy, daughter. This obscene game has played for two generations. I won't have it inherited by a third. The council must be purged." Etera looked directly at Dek. "The king must remove these descendants of traitorous shop keepers, this *New Nobility*."

Etera's long, flat nose reminded Dek of a hatchet ready to fall. He half rose from his seat. Though Etera spoke the words softly, everyone in the room knew the insult they carried. New Nobility. Uncouth. Usurpers.

Etera's line extended to the formation of Carandir. Dek's lineage ran back just two generations to a time when Haram's grandfather elevated the heads of six powerful merchant families to nobility and created baronies for them.

The heat of rage burned on Dek's face as he returned to his seat with his eyes riveted on Etera.

Haram gave Dek a sideways glance, then looked across the table. "Baron Etera. You will accompany us to the Port of Fellant and sail up the Great River to the palace at Meth with no more than twenty-five retainers, there to meet in a council of all eighteen, equal baronies."

"Majesty, I'm not prepared to travel to Meth or any other city at this time. If there must needs be a council, the twelve true houses may meet here in this chamber."

Araney's voice cut across the room, clear and controlled. "Father. If you do not ride before the morning ends, I will withdraw from this house."

A chill ran down Dek's back at the proclamation. His horror was reflected on the faces of all in the hall, except for Haram.

Etera looked to Haram, then to Araney. "Without a house you forsake your own legitimacy, daughter; your own noble status. How can you expect to bear an heir to the throne without parentage yourself?"

"I am queen. I require no further legitimacy."

"If you deny your lineage, you deny your right to the throne."

Dek watched as Haram leaned against the arm of his chair as if he were enjoying a fencing match.

Araney held her gaze on her father. "Any questions concerning my child's legitimacy must be answered by the full council. But, know this, father. Even were I denied the throne, I would rather withdraw and raise my child as a commoner than see this monarchy torn apart by pettiness and greed."

Haram stood, clasped his hands together and touched them to his forehead. All assembled came to their feet and touched their foreheads as well, for this was the sign of the covenant with the dragons and showed respect and reverence for Ilidel and Jorondel, Mother and Father of Dragons.

Haram took Araney's hand. "We will have your answer before brightnail, lord baron."

A trumpet sounded. Captain Yetig, commander of the king's guard, drew his sword and held it upright. His jet-black hair was cropped short and his goatee beard and mustache neatly trimmed.

Dek knew if there was trouble, Yetig was the one who would get them out of it. He found the captain openly ambitious and sometimes arrogant. Still, Yetig was the best officer Dek had ever known. Other commanders held back the desert raiders from Karaken in the south. Only Yetig drove them back across the border and regained territory stolen centuries before.

Captain Yetig led a procession of guards followed by the king and queen.

Behind them walked a man wearing brown robes of coarsely spun material and a woman clothed in emerald green robes. Other than white rope belts around their waists, neither wore any adornment.

To see them for the first time, Dek might have thought they were no more than fifty. Yet, he knew each had lived for well over two centuries.

The woman was Mistress Telasec, eldest of an order of women healers called the Daro who tended the sick of both body and heart.

The man was Master Orane, chief of the Kyar, an order of male scholars who studied the scrolls and books left behind by the now vanished wizards.

The Daro and Kyar had been taught these skills by the wizards who vanished eons before.

Last to leave was Dek. He bowed formally to Etera who clenched his jaw and narrowed his gaze. Dek smiled and left the chambers.

Outside, he moved quickly down the hall. "Master Orane."

The Kyar scholar stopped.

Dek looked around to make certain no one else was close. "Did you expect that?"

Orane shook his balding head. "I didn't, though I'm certain the king did. It can be the only reason the queen would agree to travel this far from the palace so late in her term."

Dek liked Orane and Telasec from the moment he met them. Each worked together to hold faith with the dragons. As with most of the Eastern families, Dek held deep faith in them, unlike many in the western lands. Yet, even without this, Dek found Orane bright and witty, quick to laugh and easy to talk with.

The two men reached the chambers set aside for Dek and his entourage. Guards dressed in the brown and tan uniforms of Rascalla stood at attention.

Dek looked up and down the hall before he spoke. "Do you think Etera will answer in time, my friend?"

Orane looked to a south facing window. He overlapped his thumbs, spread his fingers and aimed them toward the zenith. The sun shone between the second span of fingers from the left.

This was an ancient way of telling time. Starting to the left of the little finger, there were five spans to the morning, five to the afternoon, five to the evening and another five for night. By long tradition, mid-day was called brightnail and the midpoint of night darknail.

The exact length of a span varied with the seasons as the days lengthened or shortened. More sophisticated sand dials and water clocks were introduced long before that divided the day and night into twenty equal parts. Yet, the periods they measured were still referred to as spans and many people continued to use the old ways.

Orane lowered his hands. "Baron Etera has two spans to decide. The queen has placed him in a difficult position. He worked very hard to become grandfather to the heir. It's a prize he won't relinquish easily. Excuse me. I must prepare for travel. Farewell." He moved down the hallway.

Dek entered hid suite.

Seven Rascallans busied themselves within the confined space of the common room.

Dek was certain the cramped quarters were an intended insult by Etera.

The baron's steward, Penta, bowed. There were streaks of gray in his hair. "Refreshments are prepared, my lord."

"Thank you. Bring them to the inner chamber along with the dispatches. Then pack everything for travel."

"Yes, my lord."

The refreshments and dispatches were brought to an even smaller room barely large enough for a bed and desk. A single, narrow window cast dim light into the space.

Dek lit an oil lamp as Penta set out wine and fruit.

The baron broke the wax seal on the leather pouch and poured papers out onto the desk. He muddled through the mundane matters of merchants suing each other and petitions for offices.

One report noted there was still no news of Nur, the young man who disappeared in the swamps with his cousins eight months earlier. His father was a prominent merchant and Dek knew the family well.

This brought his thoughts to his wife, Jea, Baroness of Rascalla, and their infant daughter, Mirjel.

He was about to put the documents away when he found a note written in Jea's elegant hand.

*Dearest,*

*Trade is brisk. There hasn't been a single caravan raid since you left. The treaty with the Sinkarakans seems to be holding. I miss you so. Mirjel pulled herself up last week. She coos and babbles. I think she actually said a word. I wish you were home. Hurry back. Love from both of us,*

*Je*

Dek ran his fingers over the paper, then folded it and tucked it into his jerkin.

A knock sounded, followed by Penta's voice from the other side of the door. "My lord. The king bids you attend him."

Dek walked to Haram's chambers, accompanied by two guards.

He was met at the door by Captain Yetig. "My lord baron, the king bids me to escort you into his presence." The words implied Dek's guards were to remain outside.

Inside, Haram sat in a padded chair with a goblet of wine in his hand. He had removed his doublet and reclined in breeches and a linen shirt whose laces were undone. He motioned to a decanter on a table. "Please, have some wine, Baron Dek. That will be all for now, Captain."

"As you command, sire." Yetig bowed and left.

Dek poured himself a goblet of wine.

Haram walked to a sphere of crystal an arm's length in diameter. It rested atop a wooden box carved with the images of dragons. On the front panel of the box was a small drawer and above it a keyhole. Within the sphere was the crown of Carandir, which always accompanied the monarchs, even on procession. This was a steel cap with a gold band around its base and four vertical bands of gold to divide it into quarters. Across the front was a silver crest formed in the shape of a dragon as it leapt into the air. The body was long and sinuous. The wings appeared to be as sheer as lace.

Haram ran his hand over the crystal. "What is the crown, Dek?"

"It's many things, Highness; a symbol of Your Majesty's authority, a reminder of your lineage, the central…"

"Yes, yes. I know all the official definitions. But what is it really? To you?"

Dek looked at the crown, then back to the king. "Carandir itself, my lord, the breath and life of the monarchy and all who dwell here. It holds at bay the great evil and delivers the prosperity we know."

Haram smiled. "There are some who would call you a fool for expressing such antiquated ideas."

Dek felt his face flush. "Did His Majesty summon me here to do so?"

Haram poured more wine. "Far from it. You were asked to accompany us on this mission because you do know what the crown truly stands for. You are highly respected in the council among both the Eastern and the Western houses."

Dek noticed Haram used the polite distinction for the merchant families. "I have no influence with Etera, Majesty."

"Nor does anyone else, except the queen. It was a terrible gamble for Her Majesty to travel so late of term, but know this. Queen Araney conceived and will carry out the threat to withdraw from the house of Rascalla."

The king sipped his wine. "There are five souls in Carandir we trust without question; Araney, Telasec, Orane, Yetig and you."

Dek sank sat his goblet on a table and bent to one knee. "Majesty."

He felt Haram's hand on his shoulder. "Arise, Baron of Rascalla. This is a time to speak frankly. We must have the full support of the Eastern houses. Etera holds much sway in the council. With the Eastern houses united there will be enough support to quell a rebellion."

Dek saw a terrible weight reflected in the king's face. "Does His Majesty expect civil war?"

Haram gave a half-smile that fell into a frown. "Carandir has become a nation consumed with greed for wealth and power. Thoughts of the monarchy and the good of its citizens are lost to many. People will do anything when a nation loses its moral bearing. Evil can never be defeated, Dek, only contained.

That takes never ending vigilance. The strength of Carandir is in the faith we all hold within ourselves. That faith is being tested in our time."

A knock sounded.

Haram looked up. "Enter."

Yetig entered and saluted. "Majesty, Mistress Telasec requests your presence."

Haram laced up the shirt and threw on his doublet. "Make ready to ride, Captain."

"As you command, Majesty."

Haram left Dek and Yetig alone in the room.

Dek ran his hands across the crystal sphere. "Do you believe in the power of the crown, Captain?"

"I don't understand your question, my lord."

"Do you believe in the wizards; the dragons; the magic of the crown?"

"I'm a soldier, my lord, not a Kyar or Daro. I serve the Crown. Others will have to answer questions of religion."

Dek poured himself more wine. "Yes, you serve the Crown, but you agree with Etera when he says there should be only twelve houses in the council."

Yetig held himself at attention, looking neither left nor right. "My loyalties are to the king and queen if that's what you are questioning. If you're asking my political views, I have none. A soldier can't afford them."

Dek took a generous sip. "Oh, I don't doubt your loyalty, Captain. Still, everyone has an opinion. Tell me, if you'd served the king's grandfather, how would you've handled the merchant uprising when they shut down trade and marched in the streets?"

Yetig faced Dek with the right edge of his lip turned up. "As I would answer any traitor, with steel and blood, my lord." Yetig gave a shallow bow and left the room.

Etera stared out the window toward the sun as it approached brightnail. His chief minister, Yapell, stood behind him.

The Baron slapped a fist into his palm. "Araney was always headstrong. I should never have indulged her as a child. If only her mother hadn't died so young, Araney would have been raised more gentile as befits a young girl."

"You've done well, my lord. She's queen, an equal partner on the throne."

"She forgets her duty to her father. I thought she'd act in the best interest of her family, instead of betraying me. What counsel have you, Yapell?"

"You must travel. She doesn't make idle threats."

"I know this well. Still, I won't walk blindly into Meth and cede my goal." He paced back and forth. "Many friends owe me favors. The king thinks to outflank me but he's made enemies. I hear their whispers. If I organize the true houses behind me, I can force his hand to nullify the New Nobility and expel the foreigners who infests our nation. The royal army can't stand against all the rightful baronies of pure Carandirian blood."

He stopped and looked to Yapell. "Send word to all my allies before they can be summoned to the palace. I need support in the capital to eradicate the New Nobility. Tell them to be ready for war."

Word came to Dek that Baron Etera would ride to Meth. He was allowed thirty retainers instead of twenty-five as a consolation to his pride.

The queen was tended by Telasec and Mistress Seben, a senior Daro, who joined Vera in the royal carriage. Haram chose to ride on horseback, as did Dek. Etera traveled in an ornate carriage drawn by four horses. The company departed at brightnail.

Whereas the palace at Meth stood next to a bustling center of commerce, Etera's stronghold was surrounded by league upon league of fields and orchards, the true might of Fellant.

The royal procession moved north past grand estates and small farmhouses. They reached the city of Pontelara where citizens turned out from slate and thatch roofed houses with streamers and garlands to cheer the monarchs.

They left the farmlands behind and entered a thickly wooded forest of oak, ash and birch. Dek breathed in the fresh scent of the forest air, so different from the humidity of Rascalla near the Eastern swampland.

Scouts fanned out ahead, behind and to the side. Yetig moved up and down the line. The blue coat and white breeches of his uniform shone brilliantly under a clear sky.

Dek considered how best to approach the six Eastern houses. Though they shared common interests, some still thought of themselves as competing merchants instead of nobles.

Quib, Baroness of Mentaro, would be the most trouble. She was a woman who saw no farther than the last caravan and was not above dealing with smugglers. Dek suspected the bulky baroness was allied with some of the tribes who inhabited the southern regions of the swamp.

These conducted raids on Carandir soil. They were war like and territorial. Even before Carandirians settled the lands near the edge of the swamps, the southern tribes raided the villages of their peaceful northern cousins.

Many people, particularly in the west, referred to them as swampers and considered them to be dim witted savages.

The name they called themselves was Sinkaraka, which meant people of the root in their tongue. Short and thin, with reddish hair, slightly olive skin and hazel eyes, it was uncertain where they originally came from. A small number of Sinkarakans were nearly as tall as many Carandirian.

Caravans passed unscathed through Quib's own lands while those that traveled just outside her borders sometimes suffered heavy losses. Quib called the raids bad luck. Still, her troops were never able to capture the raiders once they crossed into her territory.

The procession approached the foothills of mountains whose tops were shrouded in clouds. The party wound its way up a series of switchbacks to a pass. The ground at the summit was damp.

Dek looked out across a wide valley. The road continued down the other side to skirt in and out of the forest as it headed north toward the swift flowing Lentar River. Northeast, he saw an overgrown road obscured by trees and brush. He hadn't noticed it when he rode toward Etera's stronghold.

The ground became wetter. Dek looked back to Queen Araney's carriage and hoped the wheels wouldn't get stuck in mud.

An advance scout galloped back to the column. "Highness. The bridge is down."

The king raised his hand for a halt. "Captain Yetig, guard Her Majesty. Lieutenant, bring two men. Dek. Orane. Ride with us."

The lieutenant and his men led them around a bend to the south bank of the Lentar River. A sturdy wooden bridge had spanned the wide waterway only two days before. Now, all that remained were stone piers on either bank. Silt and boulders filled the water. Trees along the bank were scarred and broken.

Orane dismounted and inspected the ground. "I would say the bridge was washed out in a storm."

Dek inspected the pilings. "There was no sign of such a deluge at Etera's stronghold."

"The weather can vary dramatically between valleys in Fellant."

"We should have had some sense of a storm this big." Dek looked upstream. "Perhaps the river's become silted and we can ford."

He walked along the bank. The farther he got from the bridge piers, the less damage he saw.

Something bright caught his eye. It was a swatch of red material snagged on a thorn bush. He examined the cloth, then tossed it aside.

Dek returned to the king and reported his findings.

Haram surveyed the destruction. "Let's get back to the others."

They rode back and formed a council.

Etera shook his head with a barely concealed smile. "The bridge will have to be rebuilt, Highness. We can return to my estates and send engineers."

Yetig stepped forward. "Majesty, It would require a month or more to reconstruct this bridge. We must take the longer overland route."

Dek rubbed his beard. "Highness, I'm sure I saw a road going off to the northeast as we descended the hills. Orane, do we have any maps of this region?"

Etera chuckled. "Don't bother, Highness. I know the road Baron Dek speaks of. It's not been used in centuries. In my youth I traveled down it for a while to see what was there."

Haram looked to Dek, then Etera. "Does it cross the river?"

"It was overgrown then. It must be impassable now."

The king's voice took on a sharp tone. "Does it cross the river?"

Etera bristled slightly at the king's sharp tone. "The trail winds through the forest, Highness, and reaches an abandoned keep on the river's banks. There was an old bridge there. The path bends back and connects to the main road beyond the river."

"Then we shall take that road and see."

"Highness! If this bridge is thrown down by some force, what chance is there for the other? Let us be sensible. Captain Yetig's estimates are wrong. My engineers can have the bridge rebuilt in a week. It's the only choice."

Haram thought for moment. "Let us convene in half a span." He walked away from the council as Dek and Etera continued to argue.

Telasec followed the king. "Highness. It was dangerous to bring the queen at all. Taking her down an unknown road places her in grave peril. If we follow Captains Yetig's advice she could give birth before reaching the palace. It would be best if she returned to her father's stronghold until the bridge can be rebuilt. You could go on ahead."

"I have weighed this and fear for her welfare as well. We must reach Meth quickly. I am certain Etera maneuvers in the shadows in preparation to strike. Araney is my greatest strength. Her voice in the council is respected. We must attend the council of baronies together. If she returns with Baron Etera, more blocks will be placed in her way until she gives birth in Fellant. The opposing baronies would claim the child and gather strength to topple the monarchy."

Telasec made the sign of the covenant.

Haram returned to the council. "We will take the overgrown path."


The old road was as bad as Etera reported. They cleared brush and cut trees. Yetig and his men were forced to push the wagons forward several times when they got stuck in vegetation and mud that clung to wheels and boots.

At the third span past brightnail, the sun descended toward the horizon. Cold dampness grew as low fog cut off visibility.

Dek's horse plodded on as it pulled one foot from the mud, then another.

Yetig appeared out of the mist. "Highness. My men reached the river. The bridge still stands, though it must be shored up before any can cross. As Baron Etera said, there is an old keep just off the road."

Haram looked up to the growing twilight. "It's too dark to work tonight. Repairs will have to wait until morning. We will take what shelter we can in this stronghold."

Dek was only able to see a few paces through the fog as he rode forward. A high stone wall appeared without warning. They reached an arched opening. He saw rusted hinges from a gate that had rotted away.

The baron dismounted and walked his horse through. The walls were as thick as three people standing side by side. He rubbed his hands over the weathered rocks, which were smooth and free of any lichen or moss.

A courtyard appeared. It was once enclosed by a wall whose stones were toppled in many places. The remains of what might have been barracks or stables stood in one corner. A three-story tower of stone rose in the center. Though the top level had fallen into decay, the bottom two appeared to be intact.

Haram cast his gaze around the scene. "Etera and Dek, your troops are under the command of Captain Yetig tonight. Yetig, form what parameter you can on whatever embankments remain. Telasec, prepare a place for the queen inside the keep. Orane, come with us and…" the king stopped in mid-sentence as a voice sang in the forest.

> *I've toiled now beneath the sun,*
> *A hard day's work is finally done,*
> *But one stop first I have to make,*
> *To find a house this coin to take,*
> *For vow I've made, e'er sky doth pale,*
> *I'll drink some good brown country ale,*
> *Hey la la dee dee da,*
> *Hey la ley;*

It was a drinking song heard in taverns and inns across Carandir.

A short man stepped between rubble of a gap in the wall. He wore brown breeches and a green jerkin. His dark hair flowed out from beneath a woolen cap. Draped around the back of his neck was a deer's carcass.

Captain Yetig shouted, "Hold. What is your business here?"

The man dropped the deer, drew a bow and crouched low. "Stand back, thieves. You'll not have my supper tonight."

The narech stepped in front of the king. "Archers, fire a warning."

Carandirian archers let loose a volley in a circle around the intruder who dropped his weapon and raised his hands. "Can't we talk this over? There's plenty for all of us."

Two soldiers seized the man.

Yetig towered over him. "Who are you?"

"Who wants to know?"

"Answer my questions in the name of the king."

"Of course. I'm certain His Majesty sent you out personally to speak with me this evening."

Haram leaned forward in his saddle. "Let us say it is more of a chance meeting."

The man looked up. His defiant expression changed to one of recognition. He dropped to one knee and bowed. "I meant no offense, Highness. I'm a poor trapper. I thought you were brigands after my pelts. Please forgive me."

Etera shoved a soldier aside and glared at the man. "Trapper? Poacher! These are the king's lands. By what right do you trap his majesties game?"

The man looked up at Haram with his hands held together. "Please, Highness. I catch just enough to make a modest living, no more."

The king smiled, then laughed. "We mean you no harm, master trapper. What is your name?"

"Tanant Maltey, Highness."

"Then let us feast on our royal deer you have so conveniently shot for us. Captain, have some men help Master Maltey with the kill. Orane, speak with us."

Orane looked back to Malty as he and the king walked away. "Is it safe to trust this man, Majesty?"

"Certainly not. Yetig will keep him in check. Send two messages by terec, one to the captain of our ship and the other to Narech Waser in the palace. Explain our delay and our expectations to reach the port. Let Waser know Etera rides with us."

"As you command, Sire."

Haram walked away to the queen's carriage.

Orane went to the rear of a wagon whose bed was filled with a wooden box large enough to ride in. Two younger Kyar scholars sat within. They wore the same type of roughly spun robes as Orane.

The chief Kyar motioned to some cages. "Leesad, hand me a terec."

The young man retrieved a small gray bird.

Orane held the terec before him and stared into the animal's hazel eyes. The bird stared back without blinking. Orane formed the king's message to Narech Waser in his mind.

The rank of narech was held by the supreme commander of the Carandir army and navy. Waser served as such from the time of Haram's father.

When Orane finished the message, he traced a path in his thoughts for the bird to follow. He imagined the Great River, the body of water to the north where the king's ship lay in anchor. It flowed from an unknown source in the east to the distant ocean in the west. The river was so wide it was impossible to see the far bank, even after months of sailing.

The land where Carandir sat was known as the South Continent. Legend told if a ship sailed far enough north it would cross the river and so come to the North Continent and the legendary city of Amblar. None knew for certain, for no Carandirian had attempted that crossing for thousands of years.

Orane's vision flew eastward along the tall cliffs of the southern bank. A break appeared. It led to an immense body of water named Lake Hasp. This extended deep into the mainland to the south.

Within the lake, the cliffs tapered into plains. On the western shore of the lake sat Meth, the monarchy's largest city. It boasted a busy shipping port and was the capital of the Barony of Lanteler.

His mind rode past the docks and wharves. He looked north again to the hills. Off the lake's shoreline, where the cliffs remained tall, was a pinnacle of stone. It rose like a rock arm thrust up from the surface of the water. On its tip was the royal palace with its tall towers, white walls and arched bridge, which connected it to a high plain of the mainland.

The palace grounds were the size of a small village with a perimeter wall running around the edge and many buildings inside. There were residents for scribes and bureaucrats, stables, barracks, storehouses and two tall, flat roofed towers, between which sat the great audience hall.

His vision soared into a window of the south tower, past gardens where grew every kind of tree and flower found in Carandir.

He pictured Waser, past seventy, tall and thin with white hair. "To him," thought Orane, "Take the message to this man."

The terec's eyes changed from hazel to green, an indication it received the instructions. Once released, a terec would travel through wind and rain, day and night, pausing only to feed, until it delivered the message.

The terec darted into the sky.

The chief Kyar sat on a stool in the wagon and closed his eyes in exhaustion. He could have formed an image of Waser's face and allowed the bird to seek out the narech. A terec thus impressed was able to fly anywhere without further direction, even to a place the sender had never been. Such releases without detailed directions could take months.

He stood up and set about impressing the second bird.

Inside the keep, two soldiers made a bed for the queen near the hearth. An apprentice Daro named Seben brought cushions from Araney's coach and arranged them. A fire was lit. Warmth spread throughout the room.

The haunches of the deer were set to roast and a barrel of ale tapped. When the meat was cooked, Maltey helped carve, placed a piece on a plate and handed it to a soldier. "This is a tender piece. You should give it to the queen."

They all ate a merry meal for the circumstances.

Mistress Seben fluffed a pillow while the queen ate.

Telasec placed her hand on Araney's forehead. It was warm with a glisten of preparation. "How do you feel, My Queen?"

Araney finished her portion of venison. "Strange. I can't say how."

Haram knelt at her side. Though he gave a confident smile, Telasec saw the concern on the king's face.

He took the queen's hand. "It's not the feather bed I promised you tonight."

Araney smiled back. "Just a pleasant adventure." She closed her eyes and took in a sharp breath.

Telasec checked her pulse. "Do you feel any pain, Highness?"

Araney breathed in gasps.

All pretense at joviality dropped from Haram. "I won't leave your side."

Araney gave a cry.

Haram turned his head sharply. "What is it?"

Telasec wiped sweat from Araney's forehead. "The queen's in labor, Highness." She was amazed as the birth was not due for weeks.

Telasec made the sign of the covenant. "Ilidel, Mother of Dragons, guide our sovereign through a safe birthing."

# CHAPTER TWO

Telasec spoke the words of a spell passed down from the wizards millennia before. She timed the queen's contractions as they grew more frequent and intense.

Haram held Araney's hand.

Telasec wiped the queen's forehead with a damp cloth. "Push again, Highness."

Araney panted and gave another push. A baby boy emerged. Blood covered the child, soaked the cloak Araney lay on and splattered Telasec's arms.

Mistress Seben cut the umbilical cord.

The infant's cries resounded throughout the keep.

Everyone cheered at the birth of the heir.

Telasec felt the infant's life radiate from his soul, pure and untouched.

The queen cried out as another contraction came.

Telasec handed the child to Seben as, to her surprise, a second babe, also a boy, emerged from the womb. Every examination she conducted showed only one child.

Again, she felt vitality surge through her as she held the second infant. He appeared to be identical to his brother.

Then, another sensation came, an icy wave that ran down her fingers as she'd never experienced at a birthing.

The babes were brought to their mother to suckle. Araney inspected the first born, then his brother. Until she put them to her breast, they were unclaimed and without birthright.

In the time before Avar, mothers sometimes rejected children born with missing limbs or bent backs. Such a one would never grow to farm the land or tend the herds and so would be left to die in the wilderness.

Avar abolished the practice, but from long tradition, mothers still checked their babies before they allowed them to suckle.

Araney took the infants to her breast. "I'm so tired, Mother Healer."

"Rest, My Queen."

Seben took the heir from Araney and sang a song as she rocked him.

> *Sleep my baby,*
> *Safe and warm,*
> *You shall never,*
> *Come to harm."*

> *Don't let the Sarte,*
> *Give you fright,*
> *For they will not,*
> *Have you tonight.*

The babes were wrapped in warm cloaks. A blue ribbon was tied around the wrist of the firstborn before he was handed to Haram.

The king cradled his son with a wide grin on his face. "He is magnificent." Haram rocked his heir and walked over to the other babe nestled in Araney's arms. "And look here. A second child as a bargain."

Dek thought of how it was over a month since he last saw his daughter, Mirjel. He asked himself what kind of world they might leave these children. Would they be able to watch their own families grow up or be lost in petty squabbles and the constant threat of conflict?

The baron looked to the crystal sphere. Within it, the silver dragon shaped crest of the crown shone even in the dim light. One of Yetig's sergeants, pike in hand, stood at attention beside it.

The soldier's body tensed and fell to the stone floor.

Maltey stood behind with a bloodied knife in his hand. The trapper opened the drawer in the wooden pedestal, reached inside and removed a silver key whose handle was forged in the shape of a dragon.

Dek drew his sword. "Carandir, to the crown."

Yetig formed a phalanx of soldiers in front of the king and queen, then led his remaining troops across the room.

Orane followed.

Before Maltey could insert the key in the hole, the metal glowed first red then brilliant white.

Dek smelled the stench of burning flesh.

Maltey screamed and dropped the key. With his injured hand cradled in the other, he ran to a wall and pressed several small stones on its surface. A section swung open. As soon as he entered the secret door, it closed behind him.

Baron Dek reached the wall and pounded on it.

Orane ran his hands along the stones. "There's a catch mechanism."

The Kyar's fingers pushed in on one small stone, then another. When he pressed three stones simultaneously, the secret door sprang opened.

Dek charged down a flight of stairs.

Yetig and his soldiers followed.

At the bottom was a long corridor lined with metal doors. Maltey knelt in front of one. Beside him was a discarded vial and pouch. He now wore crimson robes that were the same color as the swatch of fabric Dek found next to the river. A leather pouch was secured around Maltey's neck with twine. He winced as he clutched a rabbit with the burned hand. In his other he held a knife. Two geometric designs were traced on the ground with yellow powder.

Maltey sliced the rabbit's throat.

Blood splattered the symbols as the Malty recited an incantation.

The door rattled.

Dek's skin tingled.

Orane shouted, "Back up the stairs. Quickly."

Fiery pain shot through Dek's head. He cried out and stumbled back as the metal door distorted outward in the form of a clawed hand. In the chill air, Dek saw Maltey hold tightly to the charm around his neck.

The cell door burst open. A dark whirlwind emerged into the corridor.

Dek felt the warmth of his body sucked away as the formless creature advanced. The Baron bounded up the stairs two steps at a time.

At the top, he pointed to Seben, "Take the babes. Flee this place."

The Daro healer scooped the infants up, one in each arm.

Dek knew he was pursued by a demon. He'd read how such places existed in Carandir; remote caves and fortresses where spirits who followed Baras were imprisoned by the wizards eons before.

The demon burst through the door.

Two soldiers attacked.

The whirling creature lifted them from the floor, snapped their necks and dropped their bodies.

Dek heard a crack and dropped to the floor as a large timber sailed overhead and crashed against the far wall.

He regained his footing and saw a soldier flee the keep with one of the infants in his arms.

Seben handed the other babe to a second soldier who followed his comrade. The healer helped the queen stand.

King Haram ran to the crystal sphere and picked up the dragon shaped key. This time, it didn't glow or grow hot. Only the true and rightful sovereigns of Carandir, king or queen, were able to touch it without suffering harm.

He inserted the key and turned it.

A horizontal line appeared around the middle of the crystal. The top of the sphere hinged open like a box.

Before Haram could take the crown, he was seized by the demon.

It dragged him into the center of the room and shook him as a wolf might do to kill its prey. Then it hurled the king aside.

Haram struck a wall and fell to the floor.

Near the hearth, Seben supported the queen as the two women hurried toward the door.

The demon made for them.

Soldiers blocked the monster's path.

The whirlwind threw them aside like straw in a storm. When the demon reached the two women, it raised them off the ground.

Dek heard a wet crack as both their heads flopped to the side and their bodies went limp. He ran to the king. "Majesty, can you hear me?"

Haram opened his eyes.

Dek saw a dazed look on his king's face. A flicker of motion caught Dek's vision as Maltey, still in his red robes, made for the open sphere.

The king spoke in a near whisper. "Dek, take the crown. Confine the demon."

"How, Highness?"

Haram started to speak, then fell to the floor.

Dek ran to the crown and saw his movement now attracted the demon.

Maltey reached the sphere first.

Dek was there an instant later. He grabbed Maltey from behind and pinned the man's arms to his sides.

Maltey stomped his heel on Dek's toes.

The baron gritted his teeth as he held tight.

The demon moved closer.

Dek felt the room grow cold.

Maltey's lips turned up in a cruel, half smile. "I'll enjoy seeing your face twist as the demon rips your soul out."

"You'll die too, dog of hell."

"Baras protects his servants."

Dek spied the pouch dangling around Maltey's neck. He seized it and ripped it away.

Maltey's face became white. He screamed and thrashed.

The baron held tight to the pouch as he pushed Maltey away.

The demon reached the crystal sphere.

Dek prayed to Jorondel.

He was never able to say later if it was divine intervention or the magic in the pouch that saved his life. He only knew the whirling cloud touched him, surrounded him and did him no harm.

His foe was raised off the ground.

Dek turned away as the demon dismembered Maltey's body. He looked up for a moment to see see his adversary's arms broken and twisted in dozens of places as they dangled like the entrails of a slaughtered sheep.

Dek dropped the pouch, grasped the crown with both hands and placed it on his head. His voice boomed within the keep. "Back. Vanish. Be gone."

The whirlwind dropped Maltey's body, then moved toward Dek.

The baron searched for whatever secret would activate the crown's power. "Jorondel protect me." He reached for his sword, knowing it would not stop the demon. Still, he could think of nothing else to do.

Haram's words from that morning came to him. What was the crown? He remembered answering it was Carandir itself. Was it in the land or the army? No, Carandir's strength was in the never-ending faith of its people and all the ideals set out by Avar and the dragons.

The world around him fell into focus. He saw the demon not as a whirlwind but as a nine-foot-tall, hairless wraith with long talons for fingers and a mottled gray complexion.

Dek didn't so much hear or see things. He knew them. He knew the king was badly hurt yet still lived, and the queen had departed this world and journeyed to the Dragons' Halls.

He now understood how to shut the demon away in a cell beneath the keep. The baron expected instructions. Instead, he was immersed in the memories and experiences of ancient kings and queens; their dreams, hopes and fears. To Dek, it seemed hours passed. Yet, in human terms, it took less than a heartbeat.

In his mind, he saw the demon walk back down the stairs to the dungeon.

The creature hissed and spit and clawed at the air. Still, it went.

Orane followed.

Onward Dek drove the demon, past the shattered door into a new cell. He formed the locking magic in his mind.

The demon slammed itself against the cell door with a resounding bang. Dust fell from between bricks. The door vibrated. The attacks grew weaker as the demon slipped back into limbo and there was silence.

Orane inspected the empty vial and the writing on the floor. "I've seen these symbols only once, in a scroll held secret from all but a few of my order. It was written by the Barasha in the demon tongue. I can't tell what was in the vial. I'm certain its contents induced the queen's labor prematurely."

"Maltey said Baras protects his servants, the Barasha."

"It must have been a wishful boast. Though he obviously found a copy or fragment of a scroll, he can't be a Barasha priest. The wizards wrote clearly of the foul order's utter destruction."

Orane wiped away the symbols in the dust before he led Dek up the stairs.

The wounded were brought to Telasec. The dead were reverently lain in the courtyard and covered with cloaks. Araney's body was placed in her carriage.

Dek walked to the crystal sphere. He now knew the power of the crown to defeat any army or foe. There was no need to convene the Council of Baronies to settle the dispute between east and west. It was possible to command Etera and Quib to do as he chose. He need not stop with Carandir. No force could stand before him. King Dek. Lord of the World. "Even the dragons will bow before me."

It wasn't so much his own blasphemy that shocked him. It was the realization of how easily the temptation of corruption came. The crown now sat like a weight upon his head. He was certain Maltey intended to break the holding spell and release Baras. Would he have been able to surrender the crown afterward?

He glanced over to Haram. The two men's eyes met. Dek took the key, which didn't burn him while he wore the crown, and dropped it in the drawer which snapped shut. Then, he removed the crown, placed it inside the sphere and closed it. The crystal sealed itself whole once more.

The baron looked back to King Haram who nodded and fell unconscious.

Dek made the sign of the covenant.

Etera approached. His voice wavered as he spoke. "My daughter is dead."

Dek bowed, "I'm sorry, Etera."

Etera either ignored or didn't hear the condolence. "The king may not survive the day. For the first time in the history of Carandir there's a threat to the succession."

"Has the heir died as well?"

"Both babes live. The ribbon tied around the heir's wrist fell off in his crib. The Daro healer who handed the babes to the two soldiers was killed and neither of the men knows which child came from which crib."

"Father of Dragons."

Etera summoned Orane and Telasec to join them in council.

Orane studied a leather-bound manuscript whose pages were yellow with age. "There's no reference in the books I brought that reveals a method to discern the true heir short of the test of the dragon key. Of course, there're voluminous scrolls and books in the upper archives, as well as untranslated manuscripts left by the wizards in the deep vaults."

Dek paced the floor. "Let's press a finger of each babe to the key now to see which can suffer its touch. We can surely pull their hands back before they're hurt."

Orane shook hi head. "I'm afraid that won't work. The heir can't take the key before the king's death."

Telasec looked to the corner where Haram lay wrapped in a cloak. "That time may come soon. The king took much hurt from the demon. His life drains quickly. I fear I lack the power to keep him from the Dragons' Halls."

They all made the sign of the covenant.

Orane closed the book. "And even if the king died this moment, there's no way to tell which is the heir before the age of twenty. Until then, it'll burn the hand of any who take it."

Dek felt as if he was sliding down a hill of sand. "There must be some way around such a dilemma. What if an heir dies before twenty?"

"The magical birthright passes to the heir's eldest child. If there's no issue, lineage flows to the eldest niece or nephew. Neither Haram nor Araney have either."

"Not a brother or sister?"

"No. Jorondel and Ilidel, in their wisdom, made this so to prevent a sibling from taking the crown through assassination."

Dek looked to the crystal sphere. "I can well see someone driven to murder for such a prize."

Etera picked up the book and leafed through it. "What if the twins and the king die?"

The Kyar shrugged. "I don't know. In all the history of Carandir, there's always been a living heir. A regent was appointed when an heir was not yet twenty. Still, there's never been a question of lineage."

Etera snapped the book shut. "There is now and I should be that regent. I'm their grandfather, their closest kin"

Dek jabbed a finger toward Etera. "You'd poison the minds of the brothers against the Eastern houses. If the king can't designate a regent, the full council must."

"The council will debate until we all fly to the Dragons' Halls. We must decide this now."

"Without the full council's support any proclamation you make will be meaningless. The baronies will split into factions, each claiming one prince or the other."

Etera stood. "Then you have no choice but to support me in this, Dek. The alternative is civil war."

The company settled into sleep. Telasec kept a vigil with the king. She'd worked magic most of her life. Still, the demon's cold rage drained her.

The door to the courtyard opened.

A guard entered.

Telasec saw the night sky through the opening. It was coal black with pinpoints of stars.

Inside, the only light came from the banked fire in the hearth. It cast enshrouded pools of darkness.

The guard woke another soldier who collected her gear and went outside.

The first man crawled into his own bedroll and fell asleep.

Telasec slipped into slumber for an instant. The exhaustion, the darkness, the glow of the fire, all worked to create a waking dream.

A ball of mist no larger than a pebble appeared in the center of the room.

Telasec dismissed it as an aberration of too little sleep.

It grew to a disk the size of a person.

A figure in robes and a hood stepped from the mist. The stranger walked to the cribs and touched the chest of one of the newborns.

Telasec snapped awake and sounded an alarm.

Sleeping soldiers jumped to their feet and drew their weapons.

The intruder moved both arms in a circular pattern to become enveloped in dense fog. The mist lasted for only a moment. When it cleared, the stranger was gone.

Telasec and Orane ran to the twins. On one of the infant's chest was a small mark. When examined closely, it resembled a leaping dragon.

Telasec rubbed her finger over it.

Orane 's face reflected confusion. "Is it dye, Mistress?"

The Daro healer shook her head. "No. The skin blemish is true. This is magic beyond any I know."

Dek ran his finger over the mark. "What does it mean? Is it the sign of Ilidel and Jorondel or Baras?"

Etera 's gaze narrowed. "It might be a sign to guide us, or mislead us. What color were the robes, Mistress Telasec?"

"It was too dark to tell"

A moan came from the other side of the keep.

All four ran and knelt at the king's side.

Haram's voice was weak. "Speak truthfully. What bodes for me?"

Etera began to answer, then stopped.

Dek leaned forward. "The Daro have no power to heal the hurt the demon wrought. You die, My King."

Haram closed his eyes. "And Araney?"

Dek held back tears, though his voice cracked. "She awaits you in the Dragons' Halls."

The king looked into Dek's eyes. "I knew, yet I had to hear. You are the Crown's truest servant, Baron Dek, to speak so honestly."

Telasec told Haram of the confusion in which the twins could not be distinguished, and the mysterious visitor who left the dragon mark.

It was evident to Dek the king forced what strength was left to him. "Listen now to the last decree of Haram Avar, Monarch of Carandir. Name the child with the mark Ryckair, for faith, and his brother Craya, for hope. Etera. Dek. We name you co-regents, to hold power over all other baronies until one of the twins can take the dragon shaped key and claim the crown."

Haram's voice became a whisper. "Dek, you have been greatly loyal to us."

"I serve the Crown, my liege."

"Yes, we saw you with the crown and know your choice. We owe you a great debt. Name a boon and it is yours."

Dek looked to the others. "My liege, if you so command, I request my infant daughter, Mirjel, take as husband the brother who suffers the touch of the key to become king, and so make her queen."

Etera's face flushed red. "How can you take advantage of His Majesty like this?"

Haram raised his hand. "Dek but obeys our command. Master Orane, let it be recorded that Lady Mirjel Rascalla, daughter of Baron Dek and Baroness Jea, shall wed the next king of Carandir and become queen of the realm. Let this union bind Western and Eastern houses alike into one council."

"It is done, Majesty."

Etera's body shook slightly as he clenched his jaw.

Haram's face relaxed. "I have often dreamed of rest, Dek, and have never known it." He closed his eyes as his breath grew shallow, then stopped before his body fell limp.

Dek rose and made the sign of the covenant. "Rest at last, Majesty, and may the dragons protect us all."

# BOOK II

*The Palace at Meth*
*Eighteen Years Later*

# CHAPTER ONE

P rince Ryckair Avar knelt at the edge of the fencing ring. Heavily quilted pads covered his arms, legs and chest. He wore a helmet and visor. In his hand was a blunted practice saber.

He watched his brother, Prince Craya, kneel at the other side of the ring. The dragon mark on Ryckair's chest began to burn and itch again. He gritted his teeth. *Father of Dragons*, he thought. *Not now*.

Yetig raised and arm, then dropped it sharply. "Fence."

Ryckair pushed himself up. Craya was on top of him before he was able to stand. Ryckair just managed to raise his blade and deflect his brother's blow. He fought to concentrate as the burn of the mark intensified.

Ryckair had never won a match against Craya. It was clear his brother inherited their father's skill with the sword, not he, and Craya seized every opportunity to taunt his brother over it.

A trickle of sweat slid down Ryckair's forehead and into one eye. He blinked to drive away the sting.

More than anything, he wanted to win just once to stop th-e taunts. He wasn't a poor swordsman. Craya was so much better, and not just at fencing.

Though Telasec thought them identical twins at birth, each boy grew to become distinct.

Craya's dark, handsome features drew attention from ladies of the court who vied to dance with him at balls and banquets.

This was not so for Ryckair. He was ordinary to look at with sandy blond hair. This alone caused him to be eclipsed by his brother.

As well, Ryckair carried the dragon mark. Some considered it to be a sign of good, others of evil. None wished to be too close to it.

Ryckair parried a blow and searched for an opening to riposte. He found none.

Craya lunged.

Ryckair only just deflected the attack.

The itch on his chest struck again. It began the previous year as a gentle tingle. When he told Orane about it, the chief Kyar said it was nothing to be concerned about, though he offered no explanation. The tingle intensified to an incessant itch and finally to the wretched burning he now felt.

He tried to force his mind to concentrate on the match among the buzz of conversation from the young officers who urged the princes on. The uniformed men and women formed a circle around the two princes.

Most were light skinned, an inheritance from their forbearers who came from the North Continent thousands of years before with Avar the Great to establish Carandir.

The features of some were dark with densely curled hair. These were the descendants of immigrants from Hura, a tropical nation to the south on the shores of the Western Ocean.

Others whose ancestors once lived in the far eastern country of Xinglan, had pale skin, flat facial features and mono-lidded eyes with epicanthal folds.

A few had the light brown skin of people who inhabited the low desert regions to the southeast.

Some of the officers showed characteristics of all four groups.

It was apparent Craya could win at any time. That no longer amused him. The new sport was to see how hard he could make his brother work before the final touch.

Ryckair spied Yetig as he watched the brothers from the sidelines. At nearly fifty, he moved with the grace and agility of a man half his age. His jet-black beard showed no sign of gray. There was always a sense of excitement and impending danger about him.

Over the years, he rose in rank from captain of the king's guard to narech, replacing Waser who died six years after the twins' birth.

Craya lunged and landed off center.

Ryckair saw an opening. He arched his blade around Craya's defenses toward a touch and felt a shot of thrill at the look of surprise in his brother's eyes.

Craya beat his brother's sword aside with a desperate slash, then dropped and rolled into Ryckair's legs. The blow knocked Ryckair to the ground. Craya was up in an instant, his blade within inches of Ryckair's throat. "Yield, brother. Call me sword master to all present."

Ryckair struggled to no effect.

Craya laughed. "You spend too much time in the Kyar's vaults and lack the practice a king requires. Now you must do penitence. Lick my boot, brother dear." Craya put his foot in Ryckair's face.

Ryckair grabbed it and shoved Craya to the ground. He jumped up and raised his saber. Craya gave a howl of rage and got to his feet.

Narech Yetig's voice cut across the combat. "Hold."

On command, Ryckair pulled back.

Craya pushed forward.

Ryckair barely raised his blade in time to parry a strike to his head.

Yetig grabbed Craya by the wrist. "I said hold. In this yard I rule."

Craya shook himself free. "It doesn't matter. I still won."

"No, Highness. I award this match to Prince Ryckair."

At first, Ryckair thought he misheard. Then, a wave of excitement washed over him.

Craya confronted Yetig. "I had him beat. In a real battle he'd be dead."

Yetig collected the fencing sabers from the brothers. "You committed one fatal error, Prince Craya. Instead of finishing your enemy while he lay on the ground, you taunted him. A soldier has no such luxury in, as you say, a real battle. Any hesitation allows your foe time to form a plan, as Prince Ryckair did when he grabbed your boot."

The thrill of victory ebbed as Ryckair saw the humiliation on Craya's face. He hadn't wanted to win a match as much as put an end to the taunts. "I didn't have a plan, Narech Yetig. I simply acted in desperation."

"Desperation is sometimes the best plan in battle, Prince Ryckair. Remember that, both of you. The lesson is ended."

Yetig left the field.

Ryckair called after him, "Craya really won."

Craya shoved his brother away. "I don't need you to defend me." He stomped off the field.

A sour pit formed in Ryckair's stomach as he remembered a time when they played together as boys and shared secrets.

He returned to his chambers in the north tower where servants helped him bathe and change into white breeches and a blue doublet. His steward handed him a simple silver circlet unadorned with neither jewel nor image. Ryckair placed it upon his head.

Two guards accompanied Ryckair down the tapestry-lined corridor that connected the north tower with its living quarters to the south tower where the administration of the monarchy was housed.

In the middle of the corridor on the west wall were a set of wooden double doors carved with the reliefs of dragons in flight.

On the east wall were two sets of stairs.

One led up to the halls of the Daro on floors above where the healing women taught their arts and magic. Many of the Daro also resided there, including Mistress Telasec.

The other gave access to the vaults of the Kyar delved deep into the pillar of rock the palace stood on.

The double doors were the private entrance to the royal audience hall. Ryckair paused for a moment, then entered.

Light streamed through a vaulted ceiling made of crystal. Several doors used by courtesans and servants lined the north and south walls. At the west end was the public entrance, a set of tall, double doors whose tops formed arches.

Ryckair stood on a raised dais where the two thrones of Carandir stood. Ahead of him, down the north and south walls of the hall, were eighteen wooden boxes, one for each of the noble houses. They were separated from one another by waist high walls. Ryckair always thought of them as miniature fortresses.

At the foot of the thrones, encased inside the crystal sphere, was the crown.

He walked down the steps and stared into the eyes of the dragon crest. They terrified him. Craya was better suited to rule Carandir. Still, he feared the key might chose him. This was a thought he hid from everyone, even Orane, to whom he confided his greatest secrets.

The prince thought about Baron Dek's daughter. Her people had come from Au centuries before. It was one of the walled city-states east of the swamps. They followed strict codes of ethics that included customs suitors were required to obey for arranged marriages.

The twins hadn't met her and were not even allowed to see her or images of her until she was presented in court with a chaperone after the boys reached the age of twenty. Although practices of her family became tempered after they settled in Rascalla, they still maintained more conservative views than the majority of Carandirians.

His grandfather once met Mirjel when she was a young girl. Out of respect for Dek's traditions, he gave no report.

Ryckair stepped back into the corridor and walked down the stairs to the Kyar's vaults.

His guards took up position outside.

At the bottom was a metal door with no adornment. He passed a hand over the surface. The door swing inward and he stepped into a corridor whose walls were constructed from large blocks of stone. Each fitted perfectly, even after thousands of years.

Crystal globes supported by silver brackets lined the corridors. Their soft light generated no heat. Orane once told Ryckair they were one of the last relics left by the wizards before they vanished. None were able to explain how they worked or create them again.

He reached a wooden door and knocked.

Orane's voice filtered from within. "Enter."

The chief Kyar looked up from a set of papers. The flicker of a fire in the hearth shone off his balding pate.

He laid the papers on his lap and smiled. "Highness, what a pleasant surprise. Come in. Have some kan."

Kan was a spicy, invigorating drink brewed from ground herikan root. Orane grated some into two mugs and added water from a kettle that hung by a hook of the hearth.

Ryckair took a sip. "Thank you, Master Orane. I thought I might be able to work on that passage from the *Kura Kar* before supper."

"Epic poems before meals? I'm not sure how that will affect your digestion. Besides, why spend time on that old sonnet? It's been a part of popular folklore since Avar's time."

"I've been working with several Kyar to translate a newly discovered version I found in a small book hidden inside a cut out cavity of a larger volume. It gives a very different account of a meeting in a north continent forest between King Gotenag and his enemies."

Ryckair and Orane enjoyed their kan and talked of the day's events. The prince described the duel he won and how he hoped it would end Craya's taunts.

Ryckair sat his mug down. "He would have won in a real fight. He's better than me. I felt guilty, like I'd taken something away from him. He wasn't just angry, he was hurt. I could tell. You probably think that sounds foolish."

"Not at all, Highness."

The prince gazed into the fire. "We used to be close, Master. We always wanted to go everywhere together."

"I recall."

"Do you remember when Baron Dek brought us little statues of mounted riders?"

"They were made of silver, weren't they?"

"Yes. My horse had a ruby on its forehead and Craya's had a sapphire. We were just nine. I polished my statue every night and imagined riding off in search of adventures.

"I had an archery lesson one day. Craya got both statues out. He dropped mine and knocked the rider's head off. When I came back, he said, 'Ryckair, if I did something terrible, something really awful, would you still love me?'

"I answered, 'Of course.'

"He said, 'Forever?'

"I said, 'Yes, forever and ever.'

"Then he held up the headless statue.

"All I wanted to do was hit him. I remember how I clenched my fist. He waited for me to strike. His eyes showed fear, as if he thought he'd lost my love. My hands shook. I couldn't hurt him.

"I said it didn't matter and went outside. No one was in the stables when I pounded my fist against a hay bale and shouted." Ryckair smiled. "It scared the horses."

"Do you think the win today will stop the taunts?"

Ryckair lowered his head with a sigh. "I hate it when he humiliates me in front of the officers. I really wanted to win. It felt empty when he looked at me with such hatred in his eyes, like I didn't have a brother anymore."

"Are you certain it's hate and not avarice for the crown?"

The fire hissed and popped. Ryckair closed his eyes and leaned back into the chair. "Never a crown can split apart, to sit upon two heads. The victor needs hide a smile. The other tears not shed."

"So, you read Feena after all."

"The poem always seemed like nonsense before. Now it's too clear."

"Do you desire the crown?"

Ryckair stood and stared into the flames. "I've been afraid to speak of this, Master. It's eating at me. Craya's more suited to be king. He's a better soldier and commander. I don't deserve to wear the crown."

He expected Orane to lecture him on duty and the foolishness of his fears. Instead, the Kyar poured more kan. "The crown is a terrible weight, yet the key will choose who's fit to rule. Nothing can change that."

The prince sat back down. "This may sound cruel. I never missed my parents when I was young. Mistress Telasec was like a mother and you a father. Now, it's as though something's gone. I think about my parents at night, especially my father. It's like I have a hole in me, right in my chest. Craya's the only family I have left. Now, I'm losing him."


Craya sat at a desk within his private audience hall in the north tower. It overlooked a parade ground below. His anger had cooled enough for him to think of revenge.

He called out, "Ackella."

A tall, blond Carandir army lieutenant entered the room and bowed.

Craya motioned to a chair. "Take some refreshment."

Ackella reclined on a divan and filled a golden goblet with wine. "How may I serve Your Highness?"

"Where's my brother?"

Ackella wiped his mouth with his sleeve. "With Orane, Highness."

"The Kyar." Craya picked up a lesson book, slapped it rhythmically against his palm, then threw it across the room. "Books are for fools. Remember that. What about Yetig?"

"He examines reports of attacks in the swamplands."

Craya stood and stared out a window to a parade ground below. "How could he humiliate me in front of the officers like that? For years, I've studied his drills, read his papers, even emulated his commanding walk."

He turned to the Ackella "Who do you serve, Yetig or me?"

"I serve you, Highness. The narech I placate."

The prince said, "As I've known well over the last year. You're my eyes and ears in this palace. Ryckair's stepped too far. I want his movements constantly watched. Report everything he does, everywhere he goes, everyone he talks to."

Ackella tilted his head. "I am your servant, Highness."

Baron Etera's suite of rooms in the north tower of the palace overlooked Lake Hasp. The floor was covered with rugs. Tapestries filled with scenes from the hunt hung from walls. A window overlooked Lake Hasp.

Five other nobles sat in chairs; Barons Gilyon Eel, Refran Ulata, Keysta Tesar, Womb Petala and Baroness Luja Shenan, all from original houses.

Etera stood and walked to a window that overlooked Lake Hasp. "In two more years, we'll know who's king."

Baron Womb sipped wine. "If Prince Craya takes the throne, It would only take a little flattery to turn him to our cause of a land for pure Carandirians free of the New Nobility and foreigners."

Gilyon smiled. "Vanity and pride have always been his weaknesses."

Keysta shook his head. "What of Baron Dek's daughter? She'll try to influence her future husband to keep the New Nobility. She'll share his bed."

Etera continued to stare out the window. "I met her as a girl. She's more interested in clothes and horses. It won't be difficult to distract and control her."

Refran stroked his beard. "I agree we could influence Prince Craya. What if the key accepts Prince Ryckair?"

Gilyon laughed. "Does anyone here still believe that legend?"

Etera spun around. "It's not a legend. I've seen it. Only the first born will be able to hold the key."

A hot breeze blew in through the window.

Luja tilted her head to the right. "How do we turn Ryckair to our cause? What does he want?"

Gilyon poured more wine for himself. "To be a Kyar, it would seem. The boy has no confidence. He denied his win today. Could we offer him a monastic life if he abdicates in favor of Craya?"

Refran took a long breath and exhaled. "It would be risky. Once he tastes power, he might like it. As well, he's dedicated to tradition and could see it as his duty to rule. He spends an excessive amount of time with Dek and is sympathetic to the New

Nobility."

Yapell opened the door. "My lord, Narech Yetig requests your presence at a meeting with Baron Dek over the raids in the east."

"I'll attend him shortly."

Yapell bowed and left.

Etera scanned the assembled nobles. "Any more thoughts?"

Keysta raised an eyebrow. "We could kill Ryckair and let the succession move forward."

Etera dashed across the chamber floor and shoved Keysta against a wall. "You will never entertain such again. He's my grandson. No matter what plays out, he'll not be harmed. Is that clear?" He looked around the room. "Is that clear to all of you?"

He left.

Keysta rubbed his shoulder. "I'm only thinking of Carandir."

Luja gave a sly smile. "As we all are. The usurpers must be removed before the royal bloodline is tainted. If the Rascallan becomes queen it matters little whether Craya or Ryckair is king. Baron Etera thinks for his family. Bold actions are required before either prince is wed."


Several weeks later, Dek and Etera crouched together behind brush on an outcrop above the swamplands in Rascalla. It was a span before dawn when they saw a line of torches move out of the swamp.

Dek pointed to the ground below them. "There, do you see them, Etera?"

Etera yawned. "Yes, Dek, I see them. What does it prove? They might be poachers."

"There's nothing to poach in this part of Rascalla. Captain, send two scouts to follow them at a distance. I want to know where they go and who they contact."

"Yes, my lord."

Dek hoped Etera would believe his own eyes after dismissing calls for help on the eastern border. "The wealth of Carandir disappears across the swamps and goods come in without paying duty because there're not enough troops to stop it. The smuggling is nothing compared to the caravan raids."

"Caravans are private ventures. They need to pay for their own protection."

"They hire guards. It's not enough. We need more garrisons and troops here."

Etera yawned again. "The treasury is not endless. There are many demands upon it."

Dek looked up to the sky. "Father of Dragons. Money is spent on new baths in Nemtanka, repairs for roads to hunting lodges in Shenan and changes to the color of drapes in Tesar, all Western baronies."

"These expenditures were approved by the council."

"It's time the council approved some expenditures in the east. The garrisons will be built if you make public your intention to support them. How long do you think I can keep this alliance together if you ignore the smuggling and the raids?"

Etera gave a sigh. "How much?"

"Thirty thousand gold crowns."

"You're joking."

"That's what it will take."

"I can't convince the western houses to approve that kind of money. I don't see how I can get ten."

"We need at least three new outposts and two garrisons. If we can provide more bases where caravans can find sanctuary, they'll have protection clear through."

"What's wrong with the troops the Crown already placed here?"

"There's nothing wrong with the troops other than the fact they are spread too thin. We know the smugglers are helped by some of the Sinkaraka."

"Then we'll send soldiers into the swamp to hunt them down, burn a few villages and teach them a lesson."

"No army can hope to defeat them in their swamp. A battle there would be suicide. Besides, many Carandirians profit from the smuggled goods and would warn those involved, not the least of whom is Baroness Quib, even though she hides her involvement."

"I find it hard to understand how near savages with stone axes and crude bows can threaten a modern army. Jorondel's blood, they're just swampers."

Etera's use of the derogatory term grated on Dek's ears. He was born in Rascalla and lived near the Sinkarakans all his life. "Most of them are peaceful. They gather those turtle eggs you're so fond of. Only a few from the south take part in the raids and smuggling. It's obvious they're supplied with modern weapons by someone else."

"Who?"

"No one knows. That's what I need the troops for."

"Perhaps I can convince the western houses to support fifteen."

"You might as well not bother. It'll take twenty-five at the least."

"Eighteen."

"Twenty-three."

"Twenty."

"Very well. Twenty." It was the figure Dek decided on before he approached Etera.

False dawn grew. Mists rose from the wetlands that stretched eastward to the horizon. Carandir only laid claim to lands bordering the swamps and recognized the authority of the Sinkarakan tribal leaders. Still, some Carandirians expanded into tribal territory. This prompted the raids on caravans.

Etera stood. "We've seen all we can here. Let's find some breakfast and a hot bath."

They reached one of the few royal garrisons along the eastern border just as the sun broke. It stood on a flat plain near the walled city of Desan whose gates were still closed against night raids. There were two caravans camped outside the garrison walls that had arrived too late to enter the city.

The Carandir army was always focused south on the Kingdom of Karaken, a nation that conducted constant skirmishes across a border whose boundaries had been in dispute for centuries. The problems in the swamplands were considered an eastern matter.

The fortress gates opened.

A Carandir officer led twelve soldiers out. He saluted. "Captain Amar at your service, my lord regents."

Etera dismounted. "Why is Colonel Herrik not here to greet us?"

"The Colonel was called away to a raid, Baron Etera. She assigned me to attend you."

Rascalla held a tenuous relationship with the royal garrisons, as did all the Eastern houses. The company in the fortresses consisted of Carandirian regulars. Their orders were to protect the interests of the baronies, yet those baronies had no direct control over them.

Dek frowned. "What raid is this, Captain?"

"A farmhouse, lord, a quarter span's ride to the north. A report came of an attack last night by Sinkarakans."

Dek look north. "I find that difficult to believe. Sinkarakan raids always involve caravans. They've never attacked a settlements. Take us to this farm."

Etera glared at Dek. "We've been lying in dirt without food for over a span. Captain, have a full breakfast prepared and a hot bath drawn."

"Get back on your horse, Etera. We both need to see this."

"I'm not going any farther than this garrison."

"Ride, Etera!"

Etera took a step back, looked at Dek, then mounted his horse again. "This had better be something quite horrendous."

"Pray to Jorondel it's not."


After a short ride, they stood before eight burned out houses arranged around a central well. Dead livestock lay strewn about the yard. Broken fences marked the edge of the farm. Grain waved in the humid breeze.

Colonel Herrik, a tall woman with short cropped hair, bowed. "This is an unexpected honor, my lord regents." She pointed to white sticks driven into the ground. "All the bodies were removed for burial. We marked where each one was found. The stakes are numbered. This report has detailed descriptions."

Dek took the scroll. "Are there any more copies of this?"

"I'm afraid not, my lord. We have few scribes here and little time to write the original reports, let alone copy them."

Dek referenced each spot as they toured the farm and examined where the victims were found. The nauseous smell of rotting livestock threatened to overwhelm him in the damp heat.

They made their way across the common yard to a ring of stones. In the center of the circle was a white stake. The stones were blackened as though scorched by a hot blaze.

Dek pointed to the scroll. "The report says a burned body was found in the pit."

"Yes, my lord."

He rolled the scroll up. "Everything here's odd. This pit's the oddest. The Sinkarakans don't mutilate bodies in any attack."

From a broken fence post Captain Amar called, "Sir, there's something here."

Caught on a picket's splintered surface was a scrap of crimson material.

Dek's mind flashed back eighteen years to the demon's attack at the keep in the Fellant forest. He felt chill in the summer heat. "Father of Dragons."

Etera sneered. "Will you make sense?"

Dek ran his fingers over the red cloth. "It's the same weight as the robes Maltey had worn. Several of Master Orane's books reference men who wore crimson robes and performed rites of human sacrifice to call demons. Those men were Barasha priests."

"What did you say?"

"I said Barasha, Etera, like Maltey."

Etera spread his hands and looked up at the sky. "In the name of all the dragons and wizards, you drag me out here without breakfast and start spouting nonsense about long vanished sorcerers. Orane told you they were destroyed by the wizards. The sun's addled your brain."

"You saw the demon, Etera. If you'd stood next to Maltey while it pulled him apart, you'd know I'm right. Before he died, he said, 'Baras protects his servants.' The Barasha."

Etera put his hands on his hips. "Chase shadows if you wish. I'm returning to the garrison." He stomped off across a field of waist high wheat.

Five paces out he jumped back with a shriek.

Dek ran through the stalks of grain, followed by Colonel Herrik and Captain Amar.

They stared at what was once a human being. The body lay face down. The head was twisted around backwards. The arms and legs were bent at the elbows and knees. Flies swarmed over exposed flesh.

Dek took in long, measured breath. "I've seen that look before. It was on Maltey's face as the demon tore him apart."

Etera stared at the corpse with his mouth open in a gape. "Colonel Herrik, No one is to know of this. Burn the corpse personally. Speak of this to no one." He turned to Dek. "You will have your full thirty-thousand."

# CHAPTER TWO

Ryckair often spent entire days working on manuscripts within the Kyar's vaults. No one disturbed him, not even Orane. The prince became consumed in scrolls and tomes that as he read about vanished lands, lost cities and people from long ago.

It was several months since he won the fencing match. He tried to make peace with his brother. Craya either gave a terse rejection with the explanation he had other things to do, or ignored him.

Ryckair's mind sometimes became too full of questions to study. He wanted to roam free through the forest to clear his thoughts. Guards accompanied him everywhere, except for the cell set aside for him in the Kyar's vaults. A year before, he discovered the solution in an ancient book.

There were secret entrances to hidden chambers and corridors, like a second palace built between the inner and outer walls of the visible one. Until Ryckair's discovery, these secret places were known only to the Kyar, who rarely went there.

It was a warm, summer day. Ryckair found it impossible to concentrate. The next morning would bring the Day of Fealty. The ceremony occurred every two years. Nobles traveled to Meth to swear allegiance to the Crown. It was a time of feasts, trade talks and political maneuvers. Each barony brought a small force of militia and many retainers, most of whom were spies. He would be confined to the upper palace for a week.

The affair was incredibly dull. The Day of Fealty in two years promised to be more interesting. Baron Dek and Baroness Jea would bring their daughter, Mirjel. Ryckair had no interest in who she was or what she looked like. He was convinced she would be his brother's bride and he could return to the vaults.

He made no noise as he left his study cell. The wizards' crystal spheres illuminated the hallway. He walked to the globe across from his door and twisted the bracket. A crack appeared in the stone as a section of wall opened.

Inside, steps descended into darkness. He lit an oil lamp and descended.

At the bottom was an immense hall. The light from his lamp only hinted at a ceiling. The far side of the hall was lost in darkness. A hearth large enough to roast five sides of beef on a skewer was built into one wall. Air blew in from unseen passageways.

Another corridor led to more steps. He continued downward. The finished rock walls gave way to rough-hewn stone. At times, he emerged into large caverns where stalactites hung precariously from the roof. Twice, he crossed rock bridges. Each spanned deep crevices.

From time to time, he caught a glimpse of a shadow or felt a chill run across his body. He knew these to be lesser spirits vanquished by the wizards. Devoid of form or substance, they moved about corridors that demons once ruled.

He reached a cave with a sandy floor. Daylight shone through an entrance. The prince stepped out onto a narrow shoreline that sloped into Lake Hasp. The rock pinnacle, upon which the palace stood, towered overhead.

He retrieved a small boat secreted behind a rock inside the cave. It was made of tarred animal hide stretched over a wooden frame. Light and stable, it was a favorite among fishers.

Ryckair folded his clothes, then placed the silver circlet and his personal signet ring atop them. He changed into tan breeches, a brown shirt and a leather jerkin before he rowed onto the lake where others fished the waters.

Just outside Meth was a cottage on the lake where a blind soldier named Gara lived. He once saved the life of King Haram, but lost his sight and half his nose to a Karaken sword. The king awarded him a large pension for his service.

Gara stabled a horse for the prince. Ryckair always spent time with the former soldier over Kan. Once, Gara asked to feel Ryckair's face. "You have your father's strong jaw and the compassionate cheek bones of your mother, my young prince." Ryckair loved to hear stories of his father and mother.

This trip they discussed the coming Fealty Day, the increase in the price of bread and antics in court.

Ryckair stood. "I can't thank you enough for keeping my horse and my secret, Gara."

"It's I who should thank you for your visits. Only old Rilen comes by any more. He just drops off supplies and leaves now."

Outside , Ryckair mounted his horse and set off down a path. It was a warm day. The air felt clean and fresh in his lungs as the weight of Fealty Day evaporated to the back of his mind.

He soon came to an intersection.

North, a road wound up to the high plain and the arching bridge that connected the palace to the mainland.

West, another road led to the Valley of Remembrance where Carandir's leaders were laid to rest since the time of Avar.

Beyond the valley stood the Dragon Mound, a set of cave-filled hills on which no bush or tree grew. The wind blew cold and biting there, even in summer. It was reputed to be the hiding place of bandits and outcasts.

Past that, the road ran through several western baronies, including Fellant where his grandfather ruled. It jogged southwest, through the baronies of Petala, Shenan and Lusar to twist over the Luser Mountains and so come to the Wild Lands past Carandir's borders.

It was reputed the road once led to the ocean where the Great River emptied into it. The remnants were overgrown and blocked by trees. No Carandirian had traveled that way in living memory.

Some said a people called the Laran lived there. Ryckair had read how they were the original inhabitants of the land now known as Carandir. They called it *Khach Ena Eer*, tree place unending in their language. After Avar freed them of the Barasha and subdued Baras, they granted the land around Lake Hasp to him and his heirs.

The texts said the Laran lived near the Carandirian's for a while and adopted the newcomers language to make trade between the two easier.

After a few centuries, the Laran announced they would travel west and asked for seclusion. Avar used the magic of the crown to obliterate all traces of the road west of Lusar.

Ryckair took the west road for a short distance until he came to an overgrown path hidden behind brush. A few steps in, a trail meandered down a low hill to a tree-lined pool. It was one of his favorite places.

A loud rustle came from above as a horse bounded over the ridge. The intruder wore a green cloak and hood which seemed odd in the heat.

Ryckair cursed under his breath.

The rider reined in the other horse and rider. "How dare you block the trail that way, you fool. We might have both been killed. Who do you think you are?"

Beneath the hood was the face of a young woman with auburn hair and hazel eyes. Small specks of green highlighted their color.

Ryckair tried to look stern. "Who am I?" He didn't want his true identity revealed. "I'm the royal forester for these woods and you're trespassing."

"I don't believe you."

"Are you saying I'm a liar?"

"Yes. Foresters have to study as apprentices for more years than you've seen."

"Well, I'm his assistant and I act in his name."

A raspy male voice sounded from above. "She has to be here someplace."

The young woman looked up the trail.

Ryckair dropped his bluster. "Are you being hunted?"

She spun around. "I can take care of myself."

Ryckair pulled on the reins of his horse. "Then do so."

"Wait." She paused for a moment. "If you truly do know this forest, take me away from them."

Ryckair's first thought was to ride off and leave this spiteful young woman to fend for herself. Her frightened eyes held him. He gave a sigh. "Very well. Follow me. Be silent." He expected a rebuke. None came.

The sounds of the men faded away into the distance. Ryckair traveled through hidden paths and over hard ground and rock to mask their passage.

They came to a clearing where a stream flowed beneath shade trees. Grass grew in the sunlight. They dismounted to let their horses graze. Both walked at the edge of the water, each looking at the ground; her hands clasped together in front of her, his straight at his sides.

She scuffed the grass with her feet. "I'm sorry I was so rude. Please forgive me. You are an excellent forester to have escaped those men."

Ryckair cleared his throat. "Actually, I'm not a forester at all. I just like to ride through the woods." He looked out over the stream. "May I ask your name?"

She turned her head. "It's better you don't. I left my father's entourage. It may be my last chance to ride alone. The guards can do little more than bring me back. No punishment can be worse than what awaits me." She looked at Ryckair. "But if they thought you aided me you might be imprisoned. I can't bear that."

He suppressed a laugh at the idea of any merchant guard reprimanding a prince. Still, he saw tenderness in her eyes that made him believe she truly cared about what might happen to him.

She unfastened her cloak and let it fall to the ground to reveal leather riding breaches and a bodice with finely stitched embroidery.

They stood in silence. Ryckair searched for something to say. "Is this your first time in Meth?" He immediately told himself how stupid he was to ask such a trite question.

To his surprise, she smiled. "This is my first big trip anywhere. The city's huge. I never imagined it was like that with all the different people and foods. I had only read about such things."

She looked to the ground. "That's a pretty flower."

"It's called nerres. If you boil the petals in water, you can make a salve that'll take the sting out of any insect bite."

"That's amazing."

He rubbed his arm. "Do you have a book?"

The puzzled expression on her face made Ryckair fear he'd said the wrong thing.

She went to her saddle bags and brought back a volume of poetry.

Ryckair plucked a nerres and placed it between two pages. "Now I will press the flower and it will remain with you always."

She smiled "That will be lovely, oh noble Knight."

He bowed low. "The service is its own reward."

They both laughed.

Ryckair looked down at the page and recited.

*The beauty of her haunting eyes,*
*Outshines the sun of summer day,*
*Then on my chest her head she lies,*
*And smiles in her special way.*

Her features softened as she took the volume back. "You have a fine voice, though I must confess I don't remember that poem. It will now be one of my favorites."

Ryckair felt himself blush. "It's not from your book. I composed it."

The silence came again. In that hush he felt closer to this nameless woman than anyone he had ever known.

He reached over for her hand.

She pulled back and looked away as her arm trembled slightly. With deliberate slowness, she stretched her hand out to meet his. They sat down under an oak, hand in hand, staring into each other's eyes.

A splash sounded from the stream. Ryckair jumped up and drew a dirk from his boot. The thin blade gleamed in the sunlight as he scanned the water for signs of the men they escaped from.

Another splash came. A large frog sat sunning itself on a rock. At Ryckair's attention, it dove back into the stream with a third splash.

He turned back to the tree to find the young woman in a fighting stance with a short sword grasped expertly in her hand. Ryckair saw the scabbard for the blade was sewn into the lining of her cloak.

He sheathed his dirk and laughed. "No defender do you need, madam. I think perhaps I should solicit you to protect my poor skin."

She relaxed her stance and returned the sword to its sheath. "Oh, brave warrior, against a horde of toads no greater rescuer could I have."

She curtsied formally. "And now, my lord, what reward would you claim for your valor?"

A flush spread across Ryckair's body. In his mind he thought, *to be with you forever*, but forced a smile. "What will you offer, my lady?"

She considered for a moment, then unlaced a blanket behind her saddle. Underneath was a sixteen-string harp as was common among troubadours.

She sat on a rock and strummed a soft melody.

Ryckair settled against the tree trunk and listened. He loved the harp and often wished he'd learned to play. The sound was dreamlike, sweet and soft, and this woman played as though she were born for it.

She strummed through old melodies he remembered from childhood and tunes just presented in court that year.

A familiar melody came, one he'd heard many times. She hummed as she played, then sang in a clear and sweet voice.

*A hunt was planned,*
*For king and prince,*
*To shoot for bird and venison,*
*So, bows were strung,*
*And quivers stocked,*
*Then chancellors, prince and king rode forth;*

*Into the woods,*
*And through the fields,*
*The merry hunt proceeded well,*
*But faithlessness,*
*And secret plan,*
*Were in the chancellors' heart that day;*

*For chancellors eight,*
*Sought royal heads,*
*Their thoughts to end a dynasty,*
*And so instill,*
*Their will and force,*
*On kingdom, lands and people there;*

*Then arrows rained,*
*A king did fall,*
*His body trampled on the ground,*
*And turned then men,*
*Of bow and shaft,*
*To slay the prince and heir as well.*

Ryckair hadn't heard the ancient lay in years. When a Kyar sung it at a festival, the prince had been fascinated by the bardic meter of six stanzas, four of four beats and two of eight.

He'd almost forgotten its story of a rebellion in which a king was murdered and a prince barely escaped assassination.

The young royal ran through the woods and came upon a magical spirit in female form called the Chyning who slept in the forest until called for by the true and rightful king.

At his approach, the Chyning awoke and offered her magic for whatever aid he requested.

One wish was forbidden. He could not ask for the Chyning's love, for she would lose her magic and become mortal.

The Chyning helped the prince drive out the chancellors who betrayed his father. All but three were killed. The remaining traitors fled.

With the battle won, the Chyning left to sleep in the woods.

The king longed for her and forgot his duties. The remaining chancellors returned and overthrew him. The king fled into the woods in search of the Chyning again.

He found her asleep in a glade. When she looked into his eyes, she fell in love and lost her magic. The chancellors ambushed them and slew them both.

> *With arms entwined*
> *Their bodies fell*
> *Upon the ground with thud of death*
> *Departed then*
> *The chancellors three*
> *Now having won their victory*

> *But no foul beast*
> *Consumed that pair*
> *For Ilidel, who's wisdom reigns*
> *Looked down upon*
> *Their faces fair*
> *And called them up unto her halls*

*Then hand and hand*
*She led them high*
.    *Into the star filled canopy*
*And there they stand*
*For all to see*
*The lovers of the evening sky*

*The kingdom now*
*In ruin lies*
*The chancellors all reduced to dust*
*But in the sky*
*The starts shine on*
*For love will last beyond the world*

When the song ended, Ryckair stood and took a half step forward.

The woman laid the harp aside and looked into his eyes with an unreadable expression.

He leaned down and placed his lips against hers. He'd never kissed anyone before and was both thrilled and terrified.

She threw her arms around his neck and returned the kiss with passion

Lost in excitement, Ryckair had no thought beyond the instant. He felt her warmth against him, took in her unique scent, heard her urgent breath. All the while, she held him tightly.

Then, she pushed him away and stepped back. Her body shook as she covered her face with her hands.

Ryckair said, "I... I'm sorry. I didn't mean..."

Her voice was again an angry fence. "Did you ever consider I may have had a life before I met you? Leave me alone. I don't need you to save me. I don't need anyone."

Ryckair stumbled back toward his horse.

She ran after him. "No, please, don't go." She bowed her head. "I wanted you to kiss me and I wanted to keep kissing you forever. I can't. My fate is sealed and we shall never see each other again."

Ryckair opened his mouth to speak.

She placed her fingers over his lips. "I know what you will say and I can't bear to hear the words." She closed her eyes. "Say instead you hate me for my rudeness."

He caressed her hair. "I would cut out my tongue before I spoke such a lie."

They held each other tightly.

At last, he helped her secure the harp to her saddle.

She mounted her horse and reached down to brush his cheek with her fingers. Without a word, she spurred her horse away.

Ryckair stood in silence as she vanished down the trail. All the while, he felt the echo of her touch.

# CHAPTER THREE

Ryckair thought of nothing but the woman in the woods as he rode back to the palace. When he returned to his study cell, his mind couldn't concentrate.

The only cheer he found was the thought Baron Dek would be there on the Day of Fealty. The baron always brought wondrous stories of the lands he visited in his travels. Ryckair delighted in the tales of foreign customs and sights.

The next morning, the prince dressed in the blue and white colors of Carandir and placed the silver circlet on his head, then entered the audience hall from the rear corridor.

Craya already sat in the left-hand throne. He wore the uniform of a Carandir officer.

Trumpets sounded. The arched double doors at the west end of the hall swung open. The nobles of Carandir marched in.

One by one, from the eldest houses to the newest, they approached the thrones and knelt to pledge allegiance to the Crown in the formal language of court. This was a carefully preserved dialect from the time of Avar that was rarely heard beyond its use in official ceremonies. Though it closely resembled the language spoken in the streets and countryside, it required concentration for those not schooled in its subtleties.

Baron Dek and Baroness Jea stepped forward. With them came a young woman whose face was hidden beneath a drawn hood. They knelt before the thrones. Dek and Jea recited together.

"*In the sight of the dragons, Rascalla pledges loyalty and fealty to the Monarchs of Carandir and their heirs for this and all time.*"

Jea and Dek rose, leaving the young woman kneeling.

Dek bowed. "*Your Highnesses. Many years have passed since the tragic death of thy parents. On that mournful day thine own father did proclaim the next king would take our only daughter, Mirjel, as his bride and queen.*"

Jea stepped forward. "*It was planned she would travel here on the next Day of Fealty to be presented in court. Given tensions at the Karaken border, we deemed it prudent for Mirjel to travel with us this year. Therefore, we bring our daughter to reside in court, that she may come to know each of thee in preparation to wed the one who passes the test of the key. Your royal Highnesses, our daughter, Mirjel.*"

After a pause, the hooded woman spoke in a barely audible voice. "*In the sight of the dragons, I, Mirjel Rascalla, pledge loyalty and fealty to the Monarchs of Carandir and their heirs for this and all time.*"

Ryckair recognized that voice. His heart beat rapidly as Mirjel raised her face to reveal she was the woman he had met in the woods the day before.

Mirjel's mouth opened as she stared up at him.

Dek and Jea stood, bowed and returned their box.

Mirjel hesitated for a moment before she followed.

Craya watched them go and noted the look on his brother's face. Mirjel was striking. Still, he had known many beautiful women in Carandir. Mirjel, however, possessed something more. There was a subtle quality to her stance and a set to her jaw that hinted at deeper thought.

Still, he was never concerned with the considerations of any woman beyond their ability to amuse him. What he found most fascinating about Mirjel was the effect she provoked in Ryckair.

Craya studied his brother and was certain Ryckair craved this woman. Here was his revenge, no matter who became king.

Dek studied the maps spread across the table of Yetig's chart room. "I don't like any of the choices. Can't they just lead some troops to the Dragon Mound and back?"

Etera looked at Dek with distain. "Every heir has led troops in a campaign before their coronation. It is traditional and practical. They need to feel what it's like to command in the real world."

Dek riffled through more maps. "Well, Karaken is out of the question. We can't put them in that kind of danger."

The hint of a smug smile spread across Etera's lips. "Then it's settled. Prince Ryckair and Prince Craya will each command a company of troops and escort a caravans to verify the northern swampers are abiding by the treaty. It'll be perfectly safe."

"After having stood at that farmhouse, how can you call the swamps safe?"

"Nothing has happened since."

Dek looked to Yetig. "What say you, Narech?"

Yetig stepped up to the table. "You are correct, Regent Dek. Karaken is far too dangerous. I also don't consider the eastern lands to be perfectly safe, Regent Etera. Nowhere outside the palace is truly safe.

"Still, the northern Sinkaraka tribes have always honored the treaty. If the Princes stay in that region and out of the swamps, the risk is reduced. Colonel Herrik is a good commander. She's well aware of the situation."

Etera rolled the map up. "It's really the only choice. In less than six months the twins reach their twentieth year and one of them takes the crown. They need this training now."

Dek shook his head. "I don't like it. Still, I don't see any other choice. Narech Yetig, how soon until the campaign can begin?"

"Preparations can be completed within a month."

Dek stepped back from the table. "The last week of autumn is usually the quietest. I hope you'll be there with a sizable force in case there is trouble, Narech."

"Of course, My Lord Regent."

Mirjel took up residence in the palace. The twins were assigned strictly enforced schedules for courting.

Ryckair tried to concentrate on his studies, but his thoughts often wandered to their next meeting. When Craya was with her, he hid in his cell in the Kyar's vaults and paced the floor.

They were only allowed to touch while having one dance at a ball. It always ended too soon and a chaperone escorted Mirjel away. This was usually her aunt, Lady Zedo.

Between balls and official receptions, the twins were allowed to see Mirjel three times a week for a span. These meetings were always chaperoned. When the weather was pleasant, they met in the gardens.

Ryckair sat on a bench next to a fountain and imagined Mirjel in his arms as they walked through the paths that wound about the trees and flowers gathered from all regions of Carandir.

Mirjel arrived, led by Lady Zedo. Behind them came Lek, Mirjel's lady-in-waiting, and a young girl Ryckair remembered as one of Mirjel's cousins, though he didn't recall her name.

The girl sang a song to herself as she skipped along.

> *Two, three, four, five,*
> *Keep the marching men alive,*
> *Seven, nine, twelve, fifty,*
> *Keep the Oola from the city;*
>
> *Left, center, right, down,*
> *Never let them find the town,*
> *Over the bridge and under the tower,*
> *There to find the morning flower.*

Ryckair recalled how one of the palace cooks would tell Craya and him the Oola would get them if they didn't stay out of the kitchen.

He rose and bowed.

The ladies curtsied and took their seats, the aunt next to Ryckair, followed by the young cousin, Lek, and finally Mirjel at the end of the bench.

Lady Zedo nodded. "Good day, Your Highness."

"Good day my lady. How fare you?"

"As well as can be expected, with the maladies of age. Oh, to be young again."

Ryckair purposefully averted his eyes to the ground. "And the Lady Mirjel?"

"How kind of you to inquire, My Prince. She is well."

He looked up, and for an instant, caught Mirjel's gaze.

The aunt sat forward and blocked his view. "Does My Prince have one of his wonderful sonnets today?"

Ryckair drew a slip of paper from a satchel.

Lady Zedo snatched it from his hand. "May I see this first? Oh, my. Oh, dear. My Prince. If it were not for my station, I might remark that this poem is most unseemly. I'm afraid the delicate modesty of the lady does not allow such."

She placed the paper in the folds of her skirt. "Has His Highness something more suitable?"

Ryckair handed another slip of paper to the aunt.

The matriarch smiled. "Yes. I like this very much." She handed the paper back to the prince. "Please proceed."

Ryckair stood.

*Flowers bright among the haze,*
*Sit within the field and flood,*
*And everywhere the cattle graze,*
*As pastorally they chew their cud.*

It was the most absurd thing he'd ever penned. He wrote it as a parody of poems popular among groups who took on names such as *The Poetry Society of Meth* or *Literary Endeavors*. He read some of these satires to Orane, who insisted the other Kyar hear them as well. They all laughed. There was no laughter in Ryckair now.

When he finished reading, Ryckair sat back down on the bench.

Lady Zedo closed her eyes and held her hands together as though making the sign of the covenant. "Oh, yes, Highness, so much more suitable. Poems should be symbolic, not blatantly vulgar. Do you not agree, Lady Mirjel?"

Mirjel barely heard her aunt as she pictured herself running into Ryckair's arms. This was Meth, she told herself. Lovers met openly here. Soon, she would be queen. The oppressive morals of her own people need not stifle her.

Her heart pounded as she pressed her hands against the bench.

Lady Zedo glared with a frown.

Mirjel remembered the family ruined when courting lovers dared exchange notes directly and the couple in Desan forced to flee to Lusar after being found alone together.

By Carandirian law, she was of an age where she was entitled to own property, enter into a contract or marry whomever she chose without her parents' consent. She certainly did not need a chaperone.

Then, she thought of her father and his position in court, both in Meth and Rascalla. She brought her hands to her lap and smoothed the fabric of her dress as she was want to do when nervous.

Ryckair rolled the parchment into a tube and handed it to the aunt. "Allow me to make you a present of this, madam."

Lady Zedo accepted the gift. "Thank you, Highness. Shall we now take kan?"

Servants brought kan and small cakes.

Lady Zedo gossiped about various people in court.

All the while, Ryckair stretched to catch a glimpse of Mirjel.

Servants collected the cups and plates.

Lady Zedo dabbed her mouth with a napkin. "And now, the young couple should spend some time alone. Shall we adjourn ladies?"

Adjourning consisted of Lady Zedo, Lek and the young cousin moving to a bench a little closer to the fountain and barely out of earshot where they stared at the couple.

Ryckair remained at one end of the bench, Mirjel at the other.

Rascalla drew its traditions from the orthodox culture of city-states in the east like Au. There, courting couples were allowed a tenth of a span, called a tespan, to speak alone, though physical contact was forbidden.

Ryckair held his body ridged. "Did Lek pass my letter to you yesterday?"

"As faithfully as all your others. That was the poem you wanted to read, wasn't it?"

"Yes. After your touch at the ball last week, I thought I was going to die when we parted."

"Don't speak of it, I pray. Ilidel, what are we to do?"

Since childhood Mirjel was prepared to marry whichever brother became king. It was her duty. She had to be brave and do her duty, for her nation, for her people, for her family. Her father told her this many times. She tried to understand.

"*But Papa,*" she once said, "*What if I don't love him?*"

She remembered how her father would often make a silly face when answering one of her questions. That time, he had looked at her in earnest. "*You are to be the Queen of Carandir, Mirjel. Queens have a higher purpose. A higher duty. You will understand this.*"

She blinked back tears now. All she could imagine was her arms around Ryckair. Being so close yet out of reach hurt her more than anything she'd known. A part of her thought it might be better never to see him again than to endure this. Then, she hated herself for the thought and hoped Ryckair hadn't guessed it.

As if he read her mind, Ryckair dared a glance toward her. "You are the love I have longed for, though I did not know it. If we were parted this instant, if mountains and oceans came between us, you would never leave my heart and I will always find you."

She nearly lost her composure. "What if Craya becomes king?"

"It doesn't matter. I'll not lose you."

She felt a shot of excitement mixed with fear. "What do you mean?"

"We will both perform our duties and we won't be parted."

She knew affairs were common where loveless marriages were arranged, some practiced openly, others in whispered secrecy. "If Craya takes the crown we will surely be discovered."

"There are secrets in this palace unknown to Craya. Will you trust me in this?"

She smoothed the fabric of her dress and saw her aunt at the edge of vision. "Yes." *Such a small word*, she thought, *yet with the power to change everything.*

The tespan ended.

Lady Zedo collected Mirjel and left.

Ryckair remained only a moment longer, then walked away. He didn't see Ackella step out from behind a bush.

The twins boarded rowing galleys at a military dock in Meth. Each prince traveled in his own vessels along with the troops they would command.

Ryckair stood at the prow of his galley as wind flowed through his blond hair. He felt a tinge of excitement at the prospect of command. All the lessons Yetig taught over the years rolled through his mind. For the first time in his life, the book learning would be tested in the real world. He knew it would be different.

The possibility of failure was clear. If he did become king, the real world would override any theory.

They landed at the port of Rascalla. Craya ignored his brother and embedded himself within the company of his troops.

Yetig stood on a small, portable platform. "Your highnesses. We'll march to the Rascalla stronghold where you'll be assigned a caravan each to escort along the edge of the swamps to trading posts. An army detachment will follow a span behind you. Don't stray from the designated path. When the caravans arrive at their final destinations, Carandir troops will escort you back to the stronghold. Should you encounter any resistance, take a defensive position and send a terec. Troops will be dispatched immediately. Mount and follow me."

A week later, Craya stood outside his command tent and eyed the swamp around him. On the third day out, he left a handful of men on guard duty with the caravan and took the majority of his forces into the swamp in search of Sinkarakan raiders to confront.

He pulled on his new beard that mirrored Yetig's. His brother tried to grow facial hair. No one could see his soft blond whiskers from more than a pace away and Ryckair abandoned the effort. Craya took this as a sign of his own superiority.

He ignored the clouds overhead and surveyed his camp. Tents were erected on packed earth at the edge of the swamp. Sentries were posted, cooking pits cleared and latrines dug.

It was an hour after sunset of a short day in late fall. Snow never touched the swamplands, yet a bitter wind blew off the Varda Mountains to the east whose peaks were dusted with an early snow fall. Gusts cut across low hills covered with stalks of winter grass, harsh and filled with burrs.

He searched for a way to use Ackella's information about Ryckair's secret. The lieutenant hadn't yet discovered what it was. Craya wasn't worried. Ackella made certain Ryckair was watched every moment, even in his private chambers. The only place his brother wasn't observed was within the vaults of the Kyar. Craya saw no way Ryckair could be of any harm locked away with those books. The time for vengeance was at hand.

He would not simply take Mirjel away from Ryckair; he would possess her in body and soul. She would desire him, plead for him, submit herself utterly to him. He'd practiced the art of seduction both in and out of court. Scandal would ruin many a family if Craya's affairs were known.

Mirjel's seduction, however, was a challenge. He had to show himself a man and Ryckair a boy. A military victory was the first step. He was convinced a display of power and glory impressed women. To Craya's disappointment, they'd not encountered a single Sinkarakan.

A flash of light scratched a line overhead, followed by the boom of thunder. Rain fell in hard, driving pelts. The soldiers on guard tightened their cloaks around their bodies. Those who were awakened from sleep rolled over in their tents and closed their eyes.

A second flash of lightning arched across the sky.

Ackella emerged from the command tent, approached the prince and bowed low. "Highness. I trust you are well this evening."

"Where are they, Ackella? Where are the swampers?"

"I can't say, Highness. Our scouts report no signs."

"Then have them sharpen their eyesight. There's a prize in that stink filled quagmire. I mean to have it."

"As you command, Highness." Ackella bowed again and clandestinely poured black powder over the toes of Craya's boots.

The prince continued to pace.

Another flash of light preceded a rumble.

Craya looked up to see someone in red robed on a ridge next to the camp. The figure yanked on the hair of a prone man, then drove a dagger into the man's chest.

A scream pierced the air.

Tent flaps flew open as the prince's troops were ripped from sleep.

The ground shook.

A crack sounded and the earth split open beneath the feet of the army. Soldiers fell into a growing crevice.

An officer near Craya slipped into the pit. She grabbed onto the root of a bush. A gigantic hand emerged, each finger the size of a person. With a single sweep, the hand seized the officer and dragged her below.

Craya turned and collided with someone. With a start, he realized it was Narech Yetig.

The narech took Craya's arm. "This way, Highness."

He followed Yetig through the turmoil of dead and dying troops. Blood soaked into the ground. Smoke rose from the crack in the earth, illuminated by a pulsating green glow.

They ascended the hill.

Craya fell to his knees and folded his hands over his face as though to pull the memory from his eyes. "Oh, sweet Jorondel, Yetig. I've never imagined anything so hellish."

The prince looked up. His heart pounded. With the exception of Yetig and four of his officers, the men now surrounding him wore red robes.

Ackella ignored Craya as he ran into the circle and saluted Yetig. "Narech, he calls."

Craya got to his feet. "Ackella."

The blond headed officer surveyed the prince as one might a disobedient child, then continued his report to Yetig.

Craya felt his cheeks burn in anger. "Ackella! I rule here."

Ackella spat on the ground before Craya. "For years I've put up with your rude and infantile actions, along with your arrogant insults. Rule? You're not fit to rule pigs."

Yetig grabbed Ackella. "Enough. He's a prince of the realm and will be shown due respect." He scanned each person of the assemblage, then looked to Craya. "If you will follow me, Highness."

"Yetig, what is this?"

"Please, Highness. Your questions will be answered in a moment."

Craya was certain it was a dream. The green glow, the earth splitting, the hand and now Yetig a traitor. Craya couldn't believe it. The narech was the most trusted officer in the Carandir military. *Lord of Dragons*, he thought, *Yetig is the military.*

They walked to the top of the hill. A brazier filled with coals sent oppressive smoke into the air. Behind the brazier was a small dais where Reshna sat on a throne. He was surrounded by a dozen Barasha priests.

A song bird from Karaken was perched in a metal cage next to them.

Yetig knelt before the throne. "Lord Reshna, I present Craya, Prince of Carandir."

He stood and looked to Craya. "Your Highness, His Excellency, Reshna, Lord High Priest of the Servants of Baras."

Bile stirred in Craya's gut. He summoned the courage to step forward. "What is the meaning of this? I demand immediate release and safe passage to the nearest Carandirian garrison."

Reshna's riveting eyes were black pools. "Prince Craya Avar, let it be known we bring you here this night to offer you the crown of Carandir."

"How do you offer that which is not yours?"

"You have always desired the crown yet fear it might not come to you. Through long years we have searched for a sorcery to defeat the spell cast on the dragon shaped key. We have succeeded."

Craya's bluster evaporated. "Spell?"

"When the next full moon rises, a Barasha priest will anoint your brother with magical powder, recite a chant and kill him. Once this ceremony is performed, you will be accepted by the key as the true and rightful heir, whether you were born first or not."

Craya always thought he would take the crown. He was stronger, a natural leader. The idea his brother might become king was absurd. He was convinced the choice had nothing to do with magic or dragons. The Council of Baronies would decide the next monarch, not some ridiculous ritual. He was certain they would select him.

Then, he considered the possibility they might choose his brother. Most of the Eastern houses, with their backwards religious fervor, favored Ryckair and his connections with the Kyar. This was especially true of Dek, who held great influence with many in the council, both east and west.

If Ryckair died, there would be no need for a choice. Craya wanted revenge. He never thought to murder his brother. There was something very wrong with the offer. "Why make me king? Why not Ryckair? What's your price?"

For an instant, Craya was certain Reshna's controlled features changed to reveal lust.

The sorcerer's composure returned. "Only this. Allow me, of your own free will, to lift the dragon-crested crown from the crystal sphere and place it on your head."

Though Craya was unable to see any harm in this, he still didn't like the sound of it. He was convinced the sorcerer considered him a fool and wondered what the Barasha priest really wanted. If Reshna thought to declare himself king in that instant, the nobles would never support him. "Do you actually expect me to let you touch the crown of Carandir? You ask too much." Craya continued to talk in the hope Reshna would reveal his entire plan.

The Barasha priest stared at the song bird. It gave an irritated chirp and ruffled its feathers. Its agitation increased. The prince slowed his tirade, then stopped.

The air grew thick. The bird screeched and jumped about madly.

Reshna held his gaze.

Yetig turned away.

Craya stared wide eyed. It took all his effort to force words past his lips. "Stop. Leave it alone."

The song bird gave a terror filled scream, a sound Craya thought no bird could make. The feathers smoldered, then burst into flame.

Reshna closed his eyes. "You will become the heir and allow me to lift the crown from the crystal sphere."

Two of Yetig's men led Craya away.

Reshna retrieved the smoldering body of the bird and held it in his emaciated hand. "Is the site prepared, Yetig?"

"Those bodies not dragged into the pit have received wounds by sword or lance."

"Excellent. Ackella, step forward."

The lieutenant knelt. "Lord Reshna."

"You have done well. Your reward will be great."

"Thank you, my lord."

"Are you prepared to play the role of the lone survivor?"

"I will be most convincing."

"Indeed, you will."

Two Barasha priests grabbed Ackella by the arms while a third gouged out his left eye with a dagger.

Yetig and six of his men escorted a wagon from the site where Craya's forces were massacred. Ackella lay in the back with a rag bandage over his empty eye socket.

Light rain left the ground damp. Yetig's horse trudged across a muddy field converted into a temporary city for the troops under Prince Ryckair's command. Soldiers saluted the narech as they stood in front of tents flanked with racks of neatly stacked pikes. Cooking fires sent coils of smoke into the air. Troops marched in formations or practiced with swords on the grass.

Yetig guided his column to the royal pavilion. Pennants bearing the dragon crest of the royal house of Avar waved overhead in the chill breeze. Four guards saluted at his approach.

He pointed to the wagon as he walked up to the tent. "Take this man to a Daro healer."

Inside, Prince Ryckair sat in a wooden chair.

Orane stood beside him.

Yetig bowed and recited the story he concocted to give the impression of a military attack on Craya's camp. "The only bodies we found were Carandirian soldiers, Highness. Prince Craya is presumed captured. Lieutenant Ackella was the sole survivor. He lost an eye and was delirious when we found him. The Daro now tend to his wounds."

Ryckair wanted nothing more than to dismiss them all. Every angry thought he ever held toward his brother now seemed petty. "Do they hold him for ransom?"

"We've received no such demand, Highness. Colonel Herrik sent scouts into the swamp. None have yet returned."

"I'll lead troops into the swamp and find him."

Yetig knelt. "Highness. I'm as shocked and saddened as you, yet we must think first of Carandir. Entering the swamp presents far too much danger to Your Royal Person and the monarchy."

"What kind of example will I set by cowering here in camp while others face death? Would my father have waited here?"

Orane placed his hand on Ryckair's shoulder. "Highness, your father was a great leader. No one questioned his bravery. Still, he never placed Carandir at risk. A tenuous stalemate exists between the baronies. If the succession is questioned further, those threads will snap. If you are the true heir, you must live to take the crown. If Craya was born first and dies, you must live to father the next heir. In either case, your safety is now paramount."

"You speak as if he is already dead."

Yetig rose. "Highness. I'll command my entire force in search of Prince Craya."

Ryckair avoided eye contact with everyone. "I want a daily report by terec."

"The last terec was dispatched to the palace this morning, Highness. None have yet returned. I'll send word each morning by rider."

Ryckair closed his eyes. "For the good of Carandir, I will stay behind. I wish to speak with Ackella as soon as he awakens."


When Ryckair learned Ackella was conscious, he ran to the Daro tent.

The former spy opened his right eye. "Highness." He held his voice faint.

Ryckair sat in a chair next to Ackella. "What happened to my brother?"

The lieutenant feigned a moan. "We tried to stop them, Highness. We killed hundreds. They kept coming. I stood before Prince Craya and they did this to me." He pointed at his eye patch. Under his breath, he cursed Yetig who let the Barasha maim him. His reward had better be more than great.

Ackella clenched his jaw and feigned pain. "They bound Prince Craya's hands and feet and carried him away."

"The Sinkarakans?"

Ackella raised himself up and looked into Ryckair's face with his single eye. "The Karakiens. We were attacked by southern swampers led by Karakien officers. They took your brother, Highness. The Karakiens. Tell Narech Yetig. He must know before rumors spread in the ranks."

Ackella dropped to the cot and pretended to pant.

Ryckair sat back. "This explains everything. A second Karakien front to draw our forces from their border. That's how the Sinkarakans in the southern swamp get modern weapons. Dear Jorondel, Narech Yetig rides into a trap."

"You must send a message to the narech by terec, Highness." He knew Yetig ordered one of his men to dispatch them all the night before.

Ryckair shot to his feet. "Yes. No, wait. There're no terecs in camp. I'll send riders."

"Highness. No one else can know of this. Not yet. If our troops learn the Karakiens now attack from south and east it'll spread panic. I'll ride. Just set me on a horse." He started to sit, then fell back on the cot.

Ryckair was convinced the lieutenant was in horrid pain. "Don't be absurd. You can't even get up."

"Then the narech is doomed." Ackella saw hesitation in Ryckair's face. If the prince sent one of his guards after Yetig the plan would fail.

He sat bolt up. "I remember now, Highness. Just before I blacked out, they intended to take Prince Craya to a patch of high ground just south of Keleta Island. Narech Yetig knows the spot. It was terrible, Highness. The last thing I remember was Prince Craya calling your name and pleading for you to save him."

Ryckair looked to the tent flap. "I'll ride to Narech Yetig myself. He's only a span away. One rider can easily overtake a column."

"You'll do this, Highness?"

"It's the only way to save my brother and the monarchy."

Ackella dropped back to the cot and turned his face away from the prince to hide a grin.


The description of Craya's ruined camp ran through Ryckair's mind as he galloped over the low hills. At the same time, there was a sense of excitement at being a part of the campaign with the knowledge of an important secret.

He crested a ridge. Yetig and seven mounted Carandir soldiers sat on their horses in a depression below. He recognized one of them as Lieutenant Petstra. Ryckair felt relief at catching up with the narech. The ride allowed time for Orane's words to sink in.

Ryckair spurred his horse forward. "Narech, I've important news for you. I had to come."

"Yes, Highness. I know."

Four of Yetig's officers seized the prince and pulled him from his horse.

At the top of the ridge two men in red robes appeared and moved down the hill. One cast his garments aside to stand naked.

Ryckair struggled. "What is this, narech? Who are these men?"

"Prince Ryckair, please understand I act for the good of Carandir. Your brother must sit on the throne to annul the New Nobility and return Carandir to stability so it can regain the greatness it has lost. I'm truly sorry, Highness."

The other Barasha priest placed a bowl to the lips of the naked man.

His body twisted as if it were a clay statue molded by unseen hands. The skin rippled down his torso, arms and legs before solidifying into an exact double of Ryckair, including the dragon birthmark on his chest.

All the stories Baron Dek told of the demon and the Barasha came to Ryckair like a whirlwind.

The soldiers wrestled the clothes from the prince and dressed his double in them. They pulled the signet ring from Ryckair's finger and placed it on the impostor's.

The Barasha priest sprinkled powder over the head of Ryckair's double, who rocked on his feet and fell into a catatonic state.

More powder was sprinkled over Ryckair. The prince felt dizzy. The world blurred.

Before he lost consciousness, he saw Petstra draw his sword and hack the double to death.

# CHAPTER FOUR

The false story of Ryckair's death preceded Craya's military column as it made its way back to Meth. Yetig assigned his elite guard to both protect Craya and make certain he remained under the narech's control.

Craya rode on horseback at the head of the column. At the rear of the procession, in a place of honor, a wagon carried the body of Ryckair's double.

Unseen by any, the real Ryckair, subdued by the Barasha's spell, lay in a comatose state in a wagon near the middle.

Officials and commoners vented their rage and repeated the rumors they heard.

*Narech Yetig rescued Prince Craya from Southern Sinkarakans armed with modern weapons,*

*Prince Ryckair killed a dozen before his body was hacked to death.*

Over and over, Craya heard voices shouting, "Filthy, murdering devils." At first he was elated with the knowledge nothing now stood between him and the crown. He imagined his coronation as the heads of foreign states knelt and paid homage to the most powerful monarch in the world. Ryckair's death was the ultimate revenge.

Yet, it felt a hollow vengeance. It wasn't enough for his brother to die. Ryckair must know Craya's power, come to embrace it even as the knife pierced his skin. There was only one way to achieve this, his possession of Mirjel before his brother died.

They rode past farmlands, villages and cities across the eastern baronies. Black pennants hung from poles, trees and balconies.

They turned south when they reached the eastern shore of Lake Hasp. After weeks of travel, the column rode into the city of Gelalan at twilight. It lay at the southern tip of the lake and was the largest port in eastern Carandir.

There were no walls around the city. It grew from a small fishing village to a major center of commerce over centuries. Goods from as far away as Au, Xinglan and Hura flowed through the stone and wooden warehouses, along with produce from fields and orchards, gold and silver from mines in the Varda Mountains, Iron from the Kar Mountains and rare items from the southern lands, including Karaken, even though trade between the warring nations was forbidden by royal decree.

The streets of Gelalan were a maze of narrow pathways. They ran between buildings up to three stories in height. Smoke from cooking fires left a haze in the air.

Craya's column bivouacked near the docks where there was little activity at night and few to ask questions. Yetig's men stood guard along the perimeter while Barasha priests watched over Ryckair. Spread throughout the company were taller southern Sinkarakans who wore Carandir uniforms.

After the onlookers filtered away, Barasha priests moved the unconscious Ryckair to the hold of a merchant ship.

The moon set a span after darknail. A bearded man in a dark cloak and hood darted between shadows. He made no noise as he moved down one of Gelalan's wharves. Creases in his light brown face revealed his origins in the desert nation of Taquan east of Karaken, as well as a life on the road. His dark beard showed traces of gray. The man scratched his wide nose and scanned the scene.

He thumped on the door of a storage building with no windows. It opened to a darkened interior. The man stepped inside and was grabbed by strong hands.

The door closed. Someone opened the shutter of a lantern. Two muscular guards held the cloaked man by the arms while a heavyset woman and two men sat behind a table. Draped over the woman's shoulders was a brocade cloak.

She half smiled. "Well, Batu Kazmere. We were beginning to think you weren't coming."

Batu shook off the arms holding him. "What's with the bully boys, Baroness Quib?"

Quib shrugged. "These are unsettled times, my friend." She motioned to the guards who stepped away.

Batu removed his hood. "I had a little trouble getting through the militia tonight. My usual contacts were nowhere to be seen. I didn't want to chance a bribe with someone new. Still, they weren't able to stop me from delivering these."

He cut a slit in the hem of one sleeve and removed six iridescent stones, each the size of a pea. With a dramatic flair he placed them on the table in front of Quib.

The Baroness picked one up and studied it. "By Ilidel's wings, Karaken fire gems. Magnificent. How did you get these?"

"With great difficulty."

"I can imagine." Quib handed the stone to another man. "It makes me all the sadder to say that I can't handle them."

"They're the highest quality stones and worth a fortune."

"They would be if I could sell them. With the mayhem over Prince Ryckair no one in Carandir will touch these."

"Mayhem?"

"His murder."

"What're you talking about?"

"You haven't heard?"

"I rode directly up from the desert."

"I see. Well, it seems a large host of swampers armed with modern weapons supplied by Karaken attacked and slaughtered a Carandirian column. They hacked Prince Ryckair's body into pie meat. Pity. I had a hefty wager he'd become king."

Batu was Carandirian, even if he lived outside of the law. A sense of disbelief rose inside, then fury. "When did this happen?"

"Over three weeks ago. It's a great nuisance for trade. The army's checking everyone, even me. Perhaps, especially me. I'm surprised you got through. That's why, as pretty as these are, I can't take them."

Batu leaned on the table. "We had a deal. I have debts to pay."

"Oh, I understand your plight. If only you had brought me something more negotiable..." She looked at the fire gems again. "I'd have to take these east of Au. I don't know how I'd get them across the border. The carrying charges would eat any profit."

"Then give me an advance until things cool down."

There was a loud pound on the door, followed by a forceful voice. "Open in the name of the Crown."

One of Quib's men grabbed Batu while the other opened a trap door in the floor. The Baroness and her companions dropped through. Batu was thrown to the side. The guard jumped down the hole and pulled the door shut behind him.

Batu tried the handle. The hatch was bolted from the other side.

A battering ram smashed against the outer door.

The smuggler looked up. The ceiling vaulted into a pitched roof with rafters spanning the room. He jumped, grabbed one of the beams and pulled himself up, then moved to the gable end of the building directly above the entrance.

The door gave way. Three town militia stormed into the room, followed by a Carandirian army lieutenant.

The officer went to the table and picked up the fire gems. "So, that's what he was carrying."

A corporal pulled on the ring of the trap door.

The lieutenant placed the fire gems in a pouch. "Don't bother. They're gone by now. Well, at least they didn't get away with their booty."

The soldiers continued to inspect the room.

Batu pressed his body against the gable. His foot slipped and scraped across the wooden beam.

The captain looked up.

Batu dropped from the rafters and ran from the building. He darted in and out of alleys with the militia close behind.

He rounded a corner and found his escape blocked by walls directly ahead and to the left. To his right, the wharf opened out onto Lake Hasp. The smell of tar from the pilings permeated the air.

He retrieved two daggers, one from each boot, then ran directly at the far wall. With a high jump, he drove both daggers into the wood and pulled himself up as far as he could. He drew the blade in his right hand from the wood, jammed it into the wall a little higher and pulled himself up. He did the same with the knife in his left hand and repeated the action as he steadily climbed to the roof.

The militia appeared below.

Batu laid flat against the tar covered rooftop and listened.

A voice echoed from below, "He must have jumped in and swam or he's under the wharf. Shine that lantern out there. You two, get down and inspect the pilings."

Batu jumped to the next roof with a steep pitch. It was difficult to keep his grip. He crawled to the peak and down the other side.

Another leap brought him to a building whose roof cantilevered over the wharf. A merchant ship was moored next to it. Stiff breezes blew from the west. The vessel rolled in the water. The spars of the masts moved in toward the building, then away in a rhythmic undulation.

A voice came from below, "The captain wants us to check the roofs."

There were a dozen buildings between Batu and the city. The ship continued to roll. He timed the movement of the masts and leapt.

His hands caught canvas of the furled main topsail. He crawled along the spar and looked down. There was no one on deck. He moved to the mast, climbed down the standing cordage, lifted the edge of a tarp covering one of the hatches and eased inside.

There was no light. From a flap in his cloak, Batu took out a candle and a small vial of oil with a cork stopper. He dipped the candle wick into the oil, then struck a flint. The spark caught and the candle gave off steady light.

There was nothing in the hull except a long, narrow box. Batu decided to hide inside until the militia abandoned their search. He pried the lid open with a dagger.

Inside lay Ryckair. Filthy rags covered the dragon birthmark on his chest. Batu had never seen any of the royal family in person or even a portrait. He thought the body a corpse until he noticed the rhythmic signs of breathing.

He stepped back and bumped into a Barasha priest.

The sorcerer threw powder into Batu's face.

The smuggler's vision blurred as he fell unconscious.


Prince Craya's company circled the south end of the lake, then headed north along the western shore. With Ryckair removed from the procession, mourners were allowed to approach the body of the impostor and give further credence to the prince's supposed death.

The column traveled for four weeks before Meth appeared through morning mists. They headed for the wide bridge over the Peret River.

Craya felt a sick pit in his stomach as he worried his betrayal might be discovered.

He considered breaking free of the column and galloping to the palace to tell his grandfather about Yetig's pact with the Barasha. Baron Etera would know what to do.

Craya's horse reached the bridge.

Bells rang out. Flowers filled the lanes. The people of Meth flooded into the streets from inns and shops and stables and smithies. Voices rose with cheers. They came to welcome home their prince. News of his arrival spread. A great crowd stood along the south wall of the old city.

Merchants and dock hands left their work to greet the procession. Men waved feathered caps. Women tied bright ribbons to the garlands in their hair to replace the black ones they'd worn since the reports of Ryckair's death. Sounds of merriment echoed from white stucco walls as the company rode forward.

Craya raised his hand and brought the column to a halt. The mists thinned, then cleared. North past the city's walls, Craya beheld the two tall towers of the Palace of Carandir atop the tall panicle of rock.

Horns echoed from its lofty parapets. Craya imagined they announce, "The prince has returned. The succession is assured. The monarchy is safe."

Tears came to his eyes. He looked about as people cried his name. Pride swelled in him. This was his rightful place. He was meant to be their king. They all loved him. Mirjel would love him.

He waved as he led his company through Meth to the palace.

No notice was taken of a trading vessel at a Meth wharf. None were there to see Narech Yetig walk down a gang plank.

Behind him came Reshna and three Barasha priests.

A closed, horse drawn wagon approached. The animal halted. The driver cracked a whip. The beast became frantic but didn't move.

Reshna raised a hand, cast powder into the air and spoke a command in a language Yetig had never heard.

The horse's eyes glazed over before it moved forward.

A chill crawled up Yetig's back. He saw how the sorcerer's power grew each day. Though he still needed the Barasha, he knew if he didn't kill Reshna soon, he might not be able to.

The narech signaled to the ship.

Sinkarakans carried two narrow boxes down the gang plank and set them on the dock.

Yetig opened one of the lids and inspected Ryckair. The prince's eyes were shut and his breath shallow. At the next full moon, he would breathe no more. The narech regretted the prince's death. He liked the young man. Yet, if the New Nobility were to be eliminated and Carandir made strong again, sacrifices had to be made for the good of the monarchy.

The two boxes were placed in the rear of the wagon. The Barasha priests climbed in after them. A heavy sheet of canvas was drawn over the back.

The narech Yetig sat up front next to the driver as the horse moved off toward the palace.

Mirjel watched from the window of her chambers in the north tower as Craya and his column filed across the bridge into the main parade ground. The funeral wagon followed behind.

When her father reported the news of Ryckair's death. The words were like a far-off wind. When he finished, she smoothed the fabric of her dress, thanked him and walked to the window of the tower room to stare blankly out to the west.

Sitting again at the same window, she knew she should rejoice in Craya's safe return. If the key accepted his touch, the crown would pass peacefully to him. If not, he would father a child who would take the crown.

In that case, she would not be the mother of his child. The pact between King Haram and her father would be void if Ryckair had been the heir. She didn't know where she would go or what she would do. She only knew for certain she would not marry Craya.

Mirjel sat on a stool next to the fireplace. She took the harp she played for Ryckair the day they first met into her hands. Her fingers ran across the strings. She played no melody in particular. The music flowed from her in sad tones and echoed throughout the chamber.

Then, she sang the words of an ancient tune whose origins were unknown, even to the Kyar.

Her voice was weary at first. As she sang, it gathered strength.

*Cross lands unknown my love has flown,*
*To halls for warriors fallen,*
*And ne'er again shall he kiss my brow,*
*Or hold my hand most gently,*
*On dragons' wings he flies away,*
*May Ilidel protect him,*
*On dragons' wings he flies away,*
*And I must wait to hold him;*

*Such is the fate of those who wait,*
*For all who ride to battle,*
*We chop the wood and tend the hearth,*
*To guard our hearts from breaking,*
*On dragons' wings he flies away,*
*A somber hall he comes to,*
*On dragons' wings he flies away,*
*And still I watch the fire;*

*And now the troops return from war,*
*My true love's horse is unmounted,*
*I cry his name, no answer comes,*
*His voice is ever silent,*
*On dragons' wings he flies away,*
*May Jorondel receive him,*
*On dragons' wings he flies away,*
*And I am left to mourn him.*

Mirjel stood the harp upright and stared at the wall across from her for nearly a tespan.

Her breath became ragged. She threw her hands over her face as tears finally flowed.

It was a span past dawn. Mirjel and Lady Zedo sat on a bench in the gardens as they waited for Craya.

Mirjel was consumed with Ryckair's memory. She wished only to sit in her chambers.

Her aunt insisted the courtship resume.

Though Ryckair never spoken ill of his brother, Mirjel saw Craya through unfiltered eyes. She watched him closely since her arrival and heard stories Lek brought from the servants. Craya was a cruel bully and womanizer who lied and cheated without remorse to get what he wanted.

The prince arrived, accompanied by six Carandir soldiers.

Mirjel found this strange. The brothers always instructed their guards to wait at the entrance of the gardens during courtship.

Craya bowed and spoke in the formal court language. "*My Lady, I grieve with thee and for thee. I have lost a brother and thou a prince. Please, allow me to comfort thee as I may.*"

Lady Zedo bowed her head. "*The lady doth thank thee for thy gracious concern, Highness.*"

"*Then, madam, we will hear such from the lady herself, as it is she we address.*"

The aunt glowered.

Mirjel smoothed the folds of her dress. "*I thank thee, fair sir, for thy concern, yet no more comfort do I ask than that which be granted thy people. Mine is but a single grief and theirs the tears of many.*" It sounded like something Craya wanted to hear. The words were forgotten by the time they left her lips.

Craya took a step forward. "*This may be. Yet even in sadness we must needs think of our wedding.*"

The aunt placed herself between Mirjel and Craya. "*Thy wedding shall be a lovely ceremony, Highness.*"

Craya's face reddened. He dropped into the common tongue. "Madam, we are not in the habit of speaking through one of our subjects."

Lady Zedo continued in formal Carandirian. "*Highness, proper etiquette must needs be observed.*"

"Enough has been observed."

"*Highness, please.*"

Craya signaled to an officer. "Captain, it seems the Lady Zedo has taken ill from the sun. Assist her to her chambers. Make certain she's not disturbed."

The aunt's mouth opened wide in disbelief. "*Highness, the lady must needs a chaperone.*"

With a wave of his hand, Craya indicated the guards behind him. "These soldiers are chaperon enough."

Lady Zedo was led away.

Craya sat beside Mirjel and returned to the formal court language. "*And now, Madam, to a wedding of king and queen.*" He gave a smile that seemed more a leer to her.

Mirjel shivered. What kind of cruelty was Craya up to? "*There be yet the matter of the key, my lord.*" She started to stand.

Craya put a hand on her knee and forced her back down."*What of keys? Legends only. I am the heir. I will be king.*"

Mirjel knew it was best to remain silent, yet something inside made her press back. "*If indeed thou doest truly pass the trial, then king thou shalt be.*"

Craya smiled again. This time coldly. "*We hear a certain hesitation in thy voice. Tell us, if my brother sat here next to thee and poor Craya lay in state, wouldst thou still insist that he pass this test of the key?*"

"*Highness, I pray. Give heed to things private that should not be asked of another.*"

"Private?" His speech fell into common Carandirian. "Not so private as you assume. Things like letters, love poems, all passed in secret by your loyal lady-in-waiting? You must think me blind as well as stupid. I know everything about you and Ryckair, even how you planned to meet secretly and conduct an affair behind my back. You thought yourselves so clever."

She fought to remain in the formal tongue. "*Your Highness'words are a puzzle.*"

He made ready to strike her.

Mirjel moved her hand near the dagger secreted in her bodice. By long tradition, women from Rascalla carried such weapons to protect their virtue.

Craya lowered his hand. "Don't patronize me. I've too many eyes and ears in this palace. My agents followed Lek everywhere she went. She unwittingly revealed all of your secrets. Remember that when I'm king."

Mirjel answered in the common tongue. "If the key accepts you, then you will be king and my duty will be to wed you."

"Duty! I don't want your duty. I'll rule the most powerful nation in the world. I must have a queen to rule with me and love me as a husband. It's my destiny. Even Ryckair knew it, though he was fool enough to think he could have you when I took the throne."

She slapped him. "Love you? I despise you. The thought of you sickens me, let alone you're touch. It'll never happen. The key will reject you as I do. Ryckair was the true heir. Anyone with eyes can see it. Yes, I loved him. I still love him. As for you, you're not fit to rule pigs."

Craya's jaw tensed at the same insult Ackella had used in the Barasha camp.

He grabbed her arm. "You've no idea what's happening. It's just a game to you. Well, let me tell you something of the real world. No ghost will lie between us in our bed. You'll become my queen and sit at my side and bear my children, all for your precious Ryckair."

His manner became calm and controlled, almost detached, which scared Mirjel more than the rage.

He snapped his fingers.

Two of the guards stepped to either side of Mirjel.

He rose. "Follow."

They passed sculptured hedges and fountains set before the high windows of the ballroom. At a break in the shrubbery Craya threw open an iron gate and led her down a damp alley to a door set in stone. He shoved Mirjel through.

She found herself on the landing of a spiral staircase.

The guards remained outside.

Craya lit a torch, then closed and locked the door behind him.

They descended to a cavernous room where several dozen men loaded wooden barrels onto carts and wheeled them through a large opening to another chamber. She recognized them as Sinkarakans, even though they wore the uniforms of Carandir soldiers.

Craya pulled her down a passage lined with iron doors, each with a small viewing slat set at eye level. The air was near choking with torch smoke.

The prince stopped in front of one of the doors and placed his torch in a metal bracket. "Now, my dear, I've an old friend for you to meet." He opened the slat in the door.

Mirjel peered into the gloom. At first, she saw nothing in the dim light. Her eyes adjusted and she recognized Ryckair lying on his back, chained to the floor.

The light where they stood was dim. Mirjel was certain the Sinkarakans couldn't see them. A set of keys hung from Craya's belt. She drew the dagger from her bodice, spun around and sprang on him.

The point of her blade was aimed at Craya's throat as she flew into his chest and knocked him to the ground.

He clasped his fingers tightly around her wrist and tried to deflect the dagger.

She lay on top of him as she bore down with all her weight. The blade moved forward until The tip of the dagger pricked Craya's flesh.

He howled.

Three Sinkarakans charged. They pulled Mirjel back. One of them gave Mirjel's wrist a sharp twist.

She cried out in pain and released her grip.

The knife fell on Craya's chest. He grabbed it and seized her by the hair.

She tried to pull away.

The Sinkarakans held fast.

She spit in Craya's face. "Go on. Finish it."

He traced the point of the dagger across her throat, up her chin, her cheek and around her eyes before he threw it into the darkness, jerked her head forward and slapped her hard across the face. "Put her on her back."

The prince rolled on top and pressed his lips hard against hers.

She tried to knee him to no effect. Still, she fought on.

Craya stopped and pulled back as he panted. "No. I won't deflower my prize yet. That is a pleasure I'll save for our wedding night."

He stood and addressed the Sinkarakans. "You can release her. Go back to your duties."

The Sinkarakans left.

Mirjel jumped up and pressed her back against the wall. "I'll cut out your heart while you sleep."

He shook his head. "You won't hurt me. Nor will you reveal anything of what has happened here. Tell me, how often has your father spoken of the Barasha?"

Mirjel stared at him.

Craya laughed. "He was right. They've risen. But they're not the all-powerful devils your father makes them into. They're as mortal as you or I. Still, they can call upon powers to end the strife in Carandir forever. Narech Yetig and I have come to terms with them."

"You're mad."

"No one's ever been saner, or more aware of what he wants and how to get it. What do you want? Ryckair's life? Four days from now, as the full moon rises, the Barasha will kill him in a magical ceremony to guarantee I'm the heir."

Mirjel looked to Ryckair's cell.

Craya raised his hand in a gesture of assurance. "They need not have their victim. Consent to become my queen, of your own free will, and Ryckair will live. I'll order him marooned on an island, safe from the sorcerers. Each year I'll allow one letter between you, so you may be assured he still lives. As long as you submit, the Barasha will never know where to find him and the letters, along with his supply of food, will continue."

She shook her head. "They'll consume you Craya, along with the rest of Carandir. Don't you realize who they are, what they mean to do?"

"Of course. They mean to have the crown. I, however, will crush them as soon as I become king. They think they play with a child."

"No child. Simply a stooge."

"The Barasha do my bidding. I'll take the crown whether Ryckair lives or dies. Don't think he's protected by brotherly love or magical spells. If not for the superstitions of bureaucrats, I'd march into the throne room and take the key right now. My brother can die at any time. It doesn't really matter how."

Craya slapped the viewing slit closed. "Imagine a Barasha priest as he sprinkles powder over Ryckair's head and shoves a blade into his heart. So quick. No pain. No suffering. Done and over in an instant. Almost humane. Not like some other kinds of death. Not like being ripped apart by wild boars, for instance."

He fondled her cheek and throat. "Have you ever seen a pack of them attack a man who is strapped down, my lady? A most visceral scene and possible to arrange this very moment. In the cell next to Ryckair is a Rascalla boar. I'm certain you're familiar with them. I can let it through to have its sport."

"Even you won't kill your own brother like that. No one can do such a thing."

Craya tore open the cell door, shoved Mirjel inside and shouted an order into the darkness. A small gate rose jerkily at the far end of the cell.

From beyond came the unmistakable cries of the Rascalla boar, a foul beast with a tough hairy hide and long straight tusks. Standing as tall as a person's thigh, they hunted in packs and fell upon mounted riders, pulling down both rider and horse and killing them with their tusks and ripping teeth.

Mirjel saw a flat snout push under the gate.

Craya pointed to his brother. "Watch the legs, that's where it will attack first. They like to make certain their victims don't escape." He gave a cackling laugh. "Of course, this one can't."

The door crept up a finger's width. Mirjel saw the pointed tusks. She imagined them spattered with gore as they tore into Ryckair's side. In her mind she heard his screams, saw him arch his spine and throw back his head, felt the torment and imagined his contorted face, searing pain the last thing he knew of life.

Mirjel breathed rapidly. "You can't do this."

"It's in your hands."

"Stop this insanity."

"Be my queen."

"Craya!"

The creature pressed its head into the cell.

Ryckair stirred.

Mirjel closed her eyes and screamed, "Yes!"

Craya shouted another order. The gate stopped. He shoved Mirjel against a wall. "Yes, what?"

"Yes." Her words were garbled from tears. "I'll remain silent. I'll give myself. Just let him go, Craya. In the name of all the dragons let him go." She slid down the wall to the stone floor and wept.

Craya's hands shook. He chuckled at first. The sound grew in intensity until it blasted out in maniacal laughter.

He composed himself. "Seal the gate."

Two Sinkarakans with large clubs entered Ryckair's cell and beat the nose of the boar until the animal retreated into its pen beyond the wall. The gate dropped into place. The Sinkarakans left.

Craya straightened his clothes. "Now, My Queen, we will share the joy of our betrothal with my dear brother before his departure." He took hold of her arm. "To complete the effect, you'll tell him you always loved me, never him. Do you understand?"

Mirjel hung her head. "Yes. Anything. Just have it done with."

Craya placed a small berry in his brother's mouth.

Ryckair opened his eyes and blinked.

Craya made a mocking bow. "I trust you slept well, brother. It's been a long journey."

"Where am I?"

"We're in the old prison complex. Don't you recognize it?"

"What am I doing here?"

"I'll let you discover the answer. You were always so brilliant in such matters."

Ryckair's head cleared. The attack in the swamplands flashed in his mind. "Dear Jorondel, the Barasha have risen." He looked up at Craya. "You can't have joined them. I don't believe it." Ryckair tried to sit up and quickly found the limits of the chains holding him.

Craya knelt. "Believe, brother. Yetig and I will use the Barasha to purge the New Nobility and expel the foreign scum who infest the land. We'll make Carandir great again. Then, we'll destroy the sorcerers. As for you, there's a long voyage in your future. I've brought a visitor to see you off." He returned to his feet. "Come forward, lady."

Mirjel walked into Ryckair's sight. Her eyes were averted to the ground.

Ryckair saw bruises on her face. "What have you done to her?"

"Done? Why brother, I've only the most honorable of intentions toward the Lady Mirjel. You see, we are to be wed."

Ryckair let the chains go slack. "Craya, turn aside from the Barasha. You seal your death as well as mine with this pact. You loved me once, brother. You know I have never stopped loving you."

Craya wavered. From the past he heard the laughter and tears of two small boys as they held each other and shared secrets. He saw the truth of the Barasha's web for an instant.

"Fight them, Craya."

The image of the crown came to Craya's mind. He threw Mirjel to the ground near Ryckair's head. "Tell him. Tell him who you really love, who you have always loved."

Her voice was low and flat. "I love Craya. I've never loved you."

Ryckair fixed his gaze on her. "Look at me. Let your eyes tell me this."

She raised her head and tried to form words.

Ryckair pulled on his chains. "Say it!"

She covered her face with her hands. "I can't. I wanted to buy your life with a lie. I love you too much. I'll always love you. Forgive me. Ilidel forgive us all."

She reached out to caress Ryckair's cheek.

Craya shoved her away before her fingers bridged the gap. He smiled at Ryckair. "Yes. I think I like it better this way. My victory is complete, brother, and it feels so grand."

Ryckair tried vainly to sit up. The sleeping spell returned. He fell back into an unconscious stupor.

Craya dragged Mirjel out of the cell and slammed the door shut.

A lieutenant from Craya's personal guard saluted. "Highness, we've located a suitable ship, the *Sea Dragon*."

"Very good." He wrote out a message. "Take this note to the captain of the ship. Have my brother secreted aboard. He's to be left on an island in the Western Ocean with one year's provisions, unhurt and in good health. No one's to know my brother's identity. Is that clear?"

"Yes, Highness."

"You'll say nothing of this to anyone, even Narech Yetig."

"Yes, Highness."

Craya turned to Mirjel with a smile. "You see, my dear. I'm a man of my word."

She remained silent.

The lieutenant looked at the paper with the orders. "What of the other one, Highness?"

The prince opened the slat of a second cell and peered in.

Batu laid unconscious on the floor.

Craya stroked his beard, took the orders back, wrote a change and folded the paper.

The lieutenant dripped hot wax from a candle over the seam.

Craya pressed his signet ring into it. "Take this man along with my brother. A prince, even in exile, should have a court."

# CHAPTER FIVE

Craya ordered his personal guards to move Mirjel and Lek to chambers higher up the north tower. The windows and a balcony faced out on Lake Hasp with no view of the rest of the palace. Tall Sinkarakans in Carandir uniforms stood in the hallway outside.

All contact with her family was cut off. Mirjel couldn't imagine what Craya told her father.

After the guards left the room, she gathered breeches for herself and Lek. The women knotted bedding together in a long rope.

Mirjel stepped out onto the balcony where a wrought iron railing overlooked the water. The pinnacle of rock upon which the palace stood descended thirty stories where waves from Lake Hasp brushed against rocks. Two levels below was another balcony.

Mirjel secured one end of the makeshift rope to the railing and tied a fire poker to the other for weight before she lowered it. A stiff breeze blew the sheets back and forth across the face of the tower.

It took three attempts before the poker settled on the balcony below. Mirjel climbed over the railing and down the sheets with Lek behind her.

From above, Mirjel heard her lady-in-waiting's labored breath. "Lek?"

Lek halted with her eyes closed and a tight grip on the sheets. "I can't move."

"We're almost there. Slide down to the balcony."

"I can't."

Mirjel climbed up and pressed her head against Lek's feet. "I'm here."

Lek pulled her feet up and floundered as she fought to retain her grip. "Don't touch me. Sweet Ilidel, I don't want to die."

"Can you climb back up?"

"I can't move!"

"Lek, we have to go down." Mirjel thought. "Put your foot on my head."

"I can't see."

"Just do it."

Lek lowered her leg until her right foot rested on Mirjel's head.

"Good. Keep pressing down on my hair. Don't open your eyes." Mirjel lowered herself with care.

Lek followed. Her foot never lost contact with Mirjel's head.

Mirjel felt as if a span passed before they reached the lower balcony. She held onto the sheets and crouched down so Lek could keep contact with her head. When Lek's waist was below the railing, Mirjel moved aside.

Lek fell to the balcony and curled into a ball.

Mirjel cradled the young woman in her arms.

Lek shook. "I'm so ashamed, lady. I've never been so high. I don't know why I spoke so. Forgive me."

Mirjel stoked Lek's hair and kissed her forehead. "You're very brave. We'll rest here for a while."

When Lek recovered enough to stand, they opened the door and moved down the empty hallway.

The two descended a servant's staircase to an empty corridor.

They came around a corner and surprised a patrol of Sinkarakan guards in Carandir uniforms.

One had sergeant's stripes on his sleeve. He clutched Mirjel by the arm. Another seized Lek.

Mirjel bit the sergeant's hand.

He yelped and released her.

She grabbed the hilt of his sword, thrust the blade into the side of the Sinkarakan holding Lek and led her in a charge down the corridor.

The others fled the other way.

The sergeant shouted after them. "Come back here, cowards." He spoke

Carandirian with no trace of an accent, indicating he'd learned the language early as an apprentice in a human community.

Mirjel tried handles of doors she passed. All were locked.

Lek  pointed to a set of stairs. "These lead to the gardens."

A tall Sinkarakan opened a door ahead of the women and stared, then drew his sword.

Mirjel released Lek's hand and ran with full force.

The Sinkarakan swung at Mirjel's head.

She easily parried the blow.

He had some training but it didn't match hers. Still, he was muscular and exhibited great stamina.

Mirjel was certain the others would be on them in moments.

The Sinkarakan showed no sign of slowing.

Mirjel let her opponents blade clash against hers, then pulled back.

The Sinkarakan's sword continued down toward the floor.

Mirjel cut into his wrist.

He dropped the sword and cradled the wound.

She turned to take Lek's hand.

Five Sinkarakans stood in the passage. One held a knife to Lek's throat.

The sergeant took a whip from his belt. "Drop your weapon or she dies."

If she were alone, Mirjel would've charged. It was impossible to reach Lek before the guard slit her throat. She dropped the sword. "I'm the daughter of the co-regent. Let me pass."

The sergeant gave a short grunt. "Prince Craya offered a hefty reward for whoever's fortunate enough to prevent your escape."

"Craya will flail the skin from your bones if you touch me."

The sergeant focused his gaze on Lek. "No one will touch you, Lady Mirjel."

Two of the Sinkarakans slammed Lek against a wall. A knife stroke ripped open the back of her bodice and shift.

The Sinkarakans held Lek while the sergeant raised his whip and raked it across her back.

She screamed and tried to pull away.

Five times the whip tore into Lek's flesh until a voice shouted, "Enough".

Narech Yetig marched down the hallway with a squad of Carandirian regulars.

He yanked the whip from the sergeant's hand. "What are you doing?"

The sergeant placed his hands on his hips. "Orders from Prince Craya. All acts of sedition are to be dealt with at once."

Yetig seized the Sinkarakan by the throat. "I issue orders in this palace. They don't include flailing defenseless courtiers."

He looked to a young officer standing beside him. "Lieutenant. Have them taken to the parade grounds. Strip them of their uniforms and give each ten lashes. Dump them at the Karaken border."

The condemned Sinkarakans pleaded for leniency as they were dragged off, saying the desert would kill them.

Lek was placed face down on a litter.

Yetig watched as she was carried away. "Her wounds are superficial. They will heal quickly. With proper treatment, they may not even scar. Many a soldier has taken worse."

Mirjel slapped him. "Lek is not a soldier."

Yetig held himself stoic. "She'll know justice for the hurt she's taken. Her tormentors will be dealt with as traitors."

"And what about the other traitors in this palace?"

He towered over her. "You play at matters that far exceed your depth, Lady Mirjel. I alone have the courage to save Carandir. I don't wish you harmed. That's not necessary to achieve my goals, but be warned. I act for Carandir first and will sacrifice my own life and that of anyone else for my monarchy. You'll now return to your chambers."

One of Yetig's men placed his hands on Mirjel's arm.

She shook herself free and walked regally down the hall.

Six soldiers fell quickly in step around her.

Yetig stared after her. "Lieutenant, assign members of our own troops to guard Lady Mirjel."

"Is it necessary sir? After all, she's merely a woman."

Yetig surveyed his junior officer.

The lieutenant swallowed hard. "What I meant sir, is their escape was simply lucky. They're scared now. What can they possibly do?"

"I remind you, lieutenant, a woman brought you into this world and I assure you a woman can remove you from it. Never underestimate any enemy.

He regarded Mirjel as she rounded a corner. "You are certainly wrong about one thing. Lady Mirjel is no mere anyone. In her is the courage to make Carandir great again. Had she been born queen a century before, there'd be no need for the Barasha or the weak willed Craya. This is a woman of danger, Lieutenant. A woman to be watched. See to the guards. I must report to Lord Reshna."

He walked to the south tower where a set of double doors were guarded by four sentries.

It was once a chart room where battles were planned.

Now, the interior was dark and smoky, the maps were gone, the cases dismantled, the space filled with couches, tables and braziers. Thick drapes blocked all sunlight.

Reshna sat in a high-backed chair and stared into a metal bowl from which smoke rose.

Yetig knelt.

The sorcerer took a handful of powder and threw it into the embers. A hiss issued from the brazier as clouds swirled into the oppressive air. Reshna raised a hand. The smoke dissipated. "Prince Ryckair is aboard a ship. Why is this?"

"Meddling of Craya, Lord Reshna. He's bargained his brother's life for the attentions of Lady Mirjel. I regret to report she has learned of our plans through him."

"That is of no consequence. Ryckair must die by the ceremony."

"He shall. I've sent Commander Petstra to deal with Craya's bumbling."

Reshna studied the smoke. "Excellent."

Yetig had promoted Petstra over the years for meritorious service. The narech was shocked when he learned the man was a Barasha priest, yet saw a way to use him, though he wondered how many other officers held such secrets.

He bowed to Reshna. "By your leave."

Reshna raised a hand. "Yetig."

"My lord?"

"You despise Craya, don't you?"

"He's a fool, yet he is useful."

"Do you also despise me?"

"I serve the Barasha, whose presence serves Carandir."

"Yes. So, you do. Go now."

ℬ  ✚  ℛ

The *Sea Dragon* sailed west on the Great River, far from sight of land. Unlike the rowed galleys found along the banks, this was a true sailing vessel built for deep water.

In a compartment of the hull, Batu opened his yes to darkness. His head felt as if he'd woken from a terrible drunk. Pain shot through his head and his teeth ached. He flexed his arms and legs, which were unbound.

A vertical hatch opened. Batu turned his head away as Petstra entered with a lit lantern. Two men followed.

In the dim illumination, Batu saw a body on the deck. He recognized it as the man in the box of the merchant ship.

Petstra hung the lantern from a hook and took a leather pouch from a satchel as he inspected the sleeping Ryckair. "He must be brought top side and revived just before the full moon rises tonight. Once he's anointed with powder, I'll recite the enchantment and kill him. No harm can come to him until the ceremony is complete."

"Aye, sir. What about the other one?"

"Dump him overboard when you return."

Petstra left the lantern on the hook, led the other men out and closed the hatch.

Batu shook Ryckair. "Hey you. Wake up. Everyone's gone crazy."

Ryckair lay face down. Batu didn't see the dragon shaped birthmark glow for an instant as the prince awoke.

Batu tuned Ryckair over. "What's going on?"

The prince stood. "We're aboard a ship heading for the open ocean and a deserted island, I fear."

"Neither of us are gonna reach any island. I heard them talking. You get murdered and I get dumped overboard."

"I assure you, I'm worth far more to my brother alive."

"Look, I don't know who you are or who your brother is. All I know is there were three men standing over us sharpening knives. We've got to get out of here."

"I won't argue with that." Ryckair walked unsteadily to the hatch and found it locked. "We're obviously under sail."

Batu grabbed Ryckair by his ragged shirt. "Enough games. Who are you?

Why do they want to kill you?"

"You don't know?"

"Should I?"

"I'm Prince Ryckair."

Batu rolled eyes upward. "I'm locked in a hold with a madman and a ship full of murderers."

"I'll explain later. We have to steal a launch. Have you ever rowed?"

"I've never been over water deeper than the Peret River."

The hatch rattled.

Ryckair whispered, "They'll think us still unconscious. Do you see any weapons?"

"No. Wait." Batu bent down and retrieved a large rock. "Ballast."

Ryckair picked up a second rock. "Good." He blew out the lantern.

The hatch swung open. Petstra's men stepped in. "Demon's blood, the lamp's gone out."

With sharp blows, Ryckair and Batu took the sailors down and made for the hatch.

A jar reverberated throughout the ship. Desperate shouts filtered from above. The hull resounded with a second shock. Water burst through a crack.

They ran out the hold into a dying sunset. Another crash came. Both men were thrown to the aft deck.

Ryckair looked up to see the long, sinuous form of a massive water snake. The beast's girth was as wide as a cart. Its scaly brown body towered above the ship. On its back, just behind the head, rode a human shaped form with the head of a fish. The human-fish creature carried a cross bow in one hand a shimmering cloth in the other.

Ryckair made the sign of the covenant. "Jorondel's blood, the Sarte."

Eight more water snakes with Sarte riders circled the floundering vessel. The crew did battle with arrows, slings and catapults that flung chains heated in boiling oil. Only the latter showed any effect on the scaly hides of the snakes as the chains seared scales and raised blood.

The monsters continued to batter the hull. Sailors fell overboard from decks and rigging. Many were swept under the great bulk of the snakes and drowned. The riders maneuvered their water mounts toward the others and threw their shimmering cloths at the victims. As each cloth struck the water, it formed a spherical bubble that encased the struggling sailor. The bubbles bobbed on the waves for a moment, then disappeared beneath the surface.

Batu dropped the rock he was still carrying. "That's it. I've had enough." He ran aft.

Dead and dying men and women lay everywhere.

Another lurch threw Ryckair off balance. He tumbled forward over a low railing and down onto the main deck.

Commander Petstra faced one of the snakes. He shouted over his shoulder. "Don't just stand there, fool, find a bow." He looked behind him and saw the prince. "You."

Petstra looked to the east just as the tip of the full moon rose over the horizon. He threw the leather pouch. It struck Ryckair. The prince was coated in red powder. Petstra raised his sword and charged.

Ryckair grabbed a sword from a fallen sailor's hand and deflected the sorcerer's blow as the Sarte continued their assault.

Petstra recited a spell in a language Ryckair recognized as the demon tongue.

The commander maneuvered Ryckair toward an abandoned catapult. Fire still blazed beneath an iron kettle filled with boiling oil.

Block and tackle fell from the rigging above and struck Ryckair's sword arm.

Petstra slashed at the same instant.

Ryckair's sword was knocked from his weakened grasp.

The commander finished the incantation and thrust his sword toward Ryckair's chest.

Another blade swung between the two men and deflected Petstra's blow. The commander lost the grip on his weapon and it fell back.

Ryckair saw Batu, sword in hand.

The prince shot to his feet and ran full force into Petstra. He knocked the commander against the kettle.

Petstra's left arm was immersed in the boiling oil up to his shoulder. He screamed and fell to the deck.

The prince and Batu ran up an aft ladder. A boat with four sets of oars hung from the stern.

Batu halted, his face ashen. "I can't swim."

Ryckair shoved the smuggler in, jumped onboard and lowered the small craft to the river. He took up one set of oars and manoeuvred away from the destruction. "Grab the other oars and row with me."

The ship listed to port. The bow protruding into the air as the aft hold filled with water.

Ryckair and Batu rowed with all their might to escape the sinking vessel.

The snakes and riders paid the small boat no heed as they moved to round up the sailors who dotted the surface.

Ryckair pulled hard on the oars. "I think we're safe. Why did you come back?"

"I guess I have an affinity for madmen. Besides, where was I gonna to go?"

The prince laughed. "What's your name?"

"Batu Kazmere. I'm… Well, let's just say I'm a discreet purveyor of goods upon request. Now, who are you, really?"

Ryckair's ragged shirt was ripped in the fight.

Batu stared at the birthmark. He reached out and touched it, then pulled his finger back. "How can this be?"

A crack came from the stricken ship. They watched as the bow upended to stand near vertical for a moment before it slid beneath the waves.

Batu stood up, as though a higher elevation might bring back the vanished sight. "Great Father of Dragons."

A water snake burst from the river and capsized the launch.

Ryckair surfaced as one of the transparent cloths descended on him. It wrapped around his body and he felt as though he would suffocate before the fabric puffed out to form an air-filled bubble.

He bobbed on the surface of the water.

Batu was encased in a similar bubble next to him.

A tug came from below. He looked down to see a line ran from his bubble to a snake.

A jerk threw him back against the side of the membrane as the bubble was pulled beneath the water.

# CHAPTER SIX

The hasty preparations for Craya's coronation shocked Dek. By long tradition, there should have been a month of feasting and celebration. Instead, the barons and baronesses were ordered to assemble with no more than fifty retainers. Only five of these were allowed in the royal audience hall. There was no time for Baroness Jea to travel from Rascalla. The line of courtly lords and ladies was canceled. Worse, a serious diplomatic blunder was committed when Craya failed to invite a single foreign noble.

Most worrisome of all to Dek was his inability to see his daughter or even hear from her.

Craya's steward said Mirjel was busy preparing for the ceremony.

The prince himself avoided contact all together.

As the nobles filed in, Dek searched the hall for some sign of Mirjel and caught the merest glimpse of a figure behind one of the thrones.

Craya sat on the left-hand throne surrounded by his personal guard. Orane and Telasec stood next to the crystal sphere that encased the crown. The barons, baronesses and the few retainers allowed to them sat in their boxed seats along the north and south walls.

A fanfare of trumpets sounded.

Craya rose and stood before the crystal sphere.

Orane and Telasec opened the drawer in the pedestal together and recited a liturgy in the formal court language. *"Oh, high and mighty lord, receive now thy birthright. Take the key and accept into thy care the dragon-crested crown of Avar the Great, first monarch and protector of the land, for each…"*

Craya snatched the key from the drawer and held it aloft. *"I, Craya Avar, by right of birth, declare myself Ki…"* A sharp ache tore down his arm. *"King of Cara…"* The key became molten hot. Craya screamed and dropped it.

Reshna pushed forward from behind a curtain. "Fool! Your brother lives."

The key struck the marble floor. A blinding flash engulfed the hall, followed by a boom. Courtiers were knocked from their feet. Those sitting in the closest boxes were blown against their low walls. The Eastern houses at the far end of the hall were less affected.

Dek found himself blinded for only an instant. He rubbed his eyes and regained his sight.

Craya knelt before the crown. It was still encased in the crystal sphere. He held his hand and screamed in pain.

People shouted as they ran about, fell to the floor to flail in pain or lie motionless.

The key had vanished. Only a scorch mark where it fell to the marble floor was visible.

Dek saw the figure he spied earlier was his daughter.

Mirjel was shielded from the blast by the back of Craya's throne. She spied her father. "Ryckair lives. Craya and Yetig have betrayed us to the Barasha."

Dek drew his sword. "Rise Carandir. Rise and defend Prince Ryckair, the true heir."

The Eastern houses and their handful of troops charged the thrones.

Baroness Quib remained behind, then slipped out of the audience hall unnoticed.

Panicked screams resounded from the walls and the crystal ceiling above.

Dek reached Etera's box near the front of the hall. The aged baron sat stunned. Blood seeped from his mouth and nose.

Dek took Etera's hand. "Can you hear me?"

Etera breathed in hard gasps. "Rally Carandir, Dek. Go."

Most of the baronies who charged forward were from the Eastern houses. Many of the western families remained in their boxes. Some seemed still too shocked from the explosion to move. Others appeared to only feign hurt. A few seemed too terrified to think.

Five western nobles, Gilyon, Refran, Keysta, Luja and Womd, took up arms against Dek. They were joined by Sinkarakans who charged from the rear of the audience hall.

As Mirjel ran down the steps of the dais, she passed Craya.

He whimpered as he held his scarred hand. The glittering jewels of a ceremonial dagger sparkled on his belt.

The memories of the dungeon, of Ryckair's banishment, of Lek's whipping, combined to drown out the combat around Mirjel. She wondered how long it would take to pause and kill Craya.

The din of battle snapped her attention back to the present. Telasec lay unconscious on the floor next to the crystal sphere. Mirjel realized she could either save the Daro healer or kill Craya.

She ran past the prince and knelt at Telasec's side. "Can you hear me?"

Telasec opened her eyes.

Mirjel raised her from the floor.

The two women half walked; half ran toward Baron Dek.

Reshna recovered from the flash and surveyed the room. The Sinkarakans were a frightened rabble as Dek and his handful of professional soldiers swept through them. He heard the clink of chain mail and knew Yetig's men were just outside. Still, he and Craya might be overrun before reinforcements arrived.

He grabbed one of Craya's wounded guards by the hair and slit his throat as he chanted a spell and cast powder into the air.

A wall of flame erupted between Reshna and Dek. It consumed Baron Keysta and the Sinkarakans near him before the blaze burned itself out.

A green haze formed above the ash. It floated in place for a moment, then expanded toward the nobles.

Dek raised his hand for a halt.

One of Etera's guards laughed. "Come on lads. A little fog won't stop us."

Dek grabbed the man by an arm. "No, get back. Everyone, flee the hall."

The soldier shrugged Dek off and charged. When he reached the mist, the guard screamed as his skin bubbled and dissolved away with a sickening stench. Within moments, nothing remained but his sword and armor.

The mist cut Mirjel off from her father. He often described the demon Malty summoned. Until this moment she'd doubted it.

Dek maneuvered the loyal nobles and their troops away from the haze. The group broke into a rout as the formless demon gained on them. Those nearest it were overtaken and consumed.

Mirjel looked for another way out. Behind her, Orane stood shakily. She pointed to an empty box and ran to it while supporting Telasec.

The chief Kyar followed.

By the time they reached the low wall, Telasec was able to stand and move on her own.

Mirjel dared a peek over the edge.

The mist continued to advance toward her father. Sinkarakans and humans ran about in panic as Yetig's troops charged into the hall in full battle gear.

Mirjel slid back down. "What now?"

Telasec pointed to a servant's entrance on the south wall. "The kitchen. We'll gather whoever we can to make a dash for the bridge to the plain and hope we can cross in the confusion."

The three of them skirted the walls of the hall. As they passed a fallen guard, Mirjel took his sword.

The door took them to a corridor that led to the hallway between the towers. Orane stopped at the stairs to the Kyar's vaults. "This is as far as I go."

Mirjel gripped the hilt of the sword. "They'll be here in moments."

"I must seal the books away. My life is insignificant compared to the knowledge the Barasha would destroy or the secrets they could discover. No arguing. There are places in Meth where you'll be safe. Mistress Telasec knows them. Go now." He made the sign of the covenant and rushed down the steps.

The two women started off.

Mirjel stopped. "Lek. She's still in my chambers."

"You can't go back for her now, child."

"You know what the Barasha will do to her if I escape." Mirjel hefted the sword in her hand. "Take whoever you can to Meth. I'll find you." She ran down the hall.

Mirjel came to the ornately carved archway leading to the foyer of the north tower. She peered around one of the pillars.

Two armed Sinkarakans stood at the foot of the grand staircase.

She sprang and raked her sword across the belly of one.

He bellowed and slumped to the floor.

The second Sinkarakan raised his blade.

The first guard's body lay at the foot of the stairs. Mirjel maneuvered her opponent toward his fallen comrade. When they stood next to the dead guard, she cut quickly to the left.

The Sinkarakan was thrown off balance as he tried to parry. He slipped on the blood of the dead body and fell.

Mirjel raised her sword to strike. It felt heavy. Her arm shook. She dropped the weapon and fought for breath as her eyes watered and a rancid odor wafted through the air. It seemed as if a red gauze descended over her eyes. Her arms and legs felt frozen.

She looked up.

Reshna stood next to several Barasha Priests.

He turned to them. "She is yet needed."

Mirjel fell unconscious.


Dek led as many as possible out into the parade ground where the Carandir army waited to greet its new king. Though Yetig commanded these men, none knew of the Barasha and all were loyal to the Crown.

Etera stumbled.

Dek knelt at his side.

The older baron waved him away. "Leave me. Save yourself. Save Carandir."

"Save your breath." Dek picked Etera up and carried him.

Colonel Herrik was puzzled at the rout.

Dek shouted for the army to retreat.

The Colonel, thinking he signaled for help, ordered her troops forward.

The mist emerged through the door. It swept through the Carandir troops. Soldiers and horses were inundated and consumed. In less than a tespan, most of those standing on the parade ground were dead.

Dek raised his voice above the roar of dying soldiers. "Sound retreat. It's sorcery we fight here. No force of arms can stand before it."

Dek lumbered forward as he carried Etera toward the arched bridge. The disorderly rout from within jammed at the gate. Only a trickle escaped.

The various troops of the baronies not permitted in the hall or parade ground were encamped on the high plain adjacent to the palace. Each force awaited the return of its nobles from the coronation.

As people streamed across the bridge, Lieutenant Semco, an officer in Etera's militia, grabbed a soldier by the arm. "What has happened?"

"Death comes." Mad with fear, the soldier ran on.

Semco signaled to his troops. "Some deviltry is at hand. To the palace."

Etera's militia charged. They pushed the escaping Carandir troops back into the parade ground.

Dek tried to halt them to no avail.

Other captains, fearing their own nobles were in danger, pressed forward. Many were caught in the cloud and destroyed.

At last, the blockage at the gate prevented any more from entering. The mist emerged out over the bridge. Troops and horses died, unable to move aside in the press. The demon halted at the edge of the plain.

Dek lowered Etera. A great part of the army and navy were assembled at the palace for the coronation. Only a handful of soldiers were stationed at royal garrisons, largely on the border of Karaken, and only a handful of sailors were left to secure the ships. Most at the palace and many of the troops brought from each barony had perished.

Etera opened his eyes. "I was a fool, Dek. For twenty years the nation was in danger and only you saw. Haram was right. You're the Crown's truest servant."

"Come now, Etera. You'll turn my head and spoil what little modesty I have."

"No jests, my friend. I'll be dead soon. Promise you'll find Ryckair and drive the Barasha out."

"I swear it Etera, in the names of all the dragons."

Seven surviving royal houses, west and east, gathered around them.

Colonel Herrik and a thousand Carandir troops formed a defensive position.

Etera raised an arm, "Dek is now the sole regent. Follow him. My dying wish is for Western and Eastern houses to live together in peace."

Each of them swore it would be so.

Etera took Dek's hand. "Forgive me." His voice faltered and he died.

Dek made the sign of the covenant. "All debts are forgotten, old friend."

One of Dek's officers rode up. "What stopped the mist, my lord?"

Dek got to his feet. "Who can say? Perhaps it can't leave the presence of he who called it."

"Then let's mount a counterattack."

"No. This is a thing beyond our power to fight. I'll send terecs to the ships at anchor and those who remain in royal garrisons. We'll pull back to the western forests beyond the Dragon Mound.

He addressed all the survivors. "Send terecs to your strongholds. All families and servants are to mount and ride from Carandir. Have them find sanctuary anywhere except Karaken." He prayed Jea would be able to reach safety in the eastern city-states where they still had strong family ties.

"Command all troops to reach the Lena Valley in Fellant by the swiftest means. We're defeated here. Still, there's hope. Prince Ryckair lives. In him is the power of the dragons. We'll seek for him wherever he may be. In the meantime, we and all who remain loyal to the Crown will harass the Barasha and those who align themselves with these sorcerers, no matter what barony they come from. Let there be only one allegiance, Carandir."

At this, they all cheered.

Dek stared at the palace. Mirjel was still inside, lost beyond his grasp. "If I can't save you, my daughter, I'll avenge you," He mounted his horse and rode west.

The demon mist dissipated a span after Dek's departed.

Telasec checked for any remaining guards, then led courtiers, bureaucrats, Daro and servants from the south tower through the parade grounds and out across the bridge.

They made their way toward the north gate of Meth. Men, women and children weep as they trudged. At a point, everyone stopped as though there was no will left to go on. They looked to Telasec.

She stared back into their eyes. "I know you're all scared. I am too. It might seem there's no hope, and little can be done other than to sit down and wait for the end. Many people would do just that."

She drew herself tall. "But we're Carandirians, the descendants of Avar's people. Our ancestors faced the evil dragon and all his demons. There're secret rooms and underground tunnels. That's where we'll hide to be close at hand when Prince Ryckair returns. And return he will. So come, all of you. There's work to do and not a moment to spare for tears."

ॐ  ✦  ॐ

Orane finished the last incantation of a spell on the heavy metal door of the Kyar's vaults.

A young, dark skinned Kyar spoke with fear in his voice. "Will it hold against the sorcerers?"

"No more than a few spans, Suel. That'll be time enough."

They walked back to the central library where Kyar scholars loaded the most important books and scrolls into baskets and carried them through one of the secret doors leading to the hidden palace within the inner and outer walls.

Leesad, now a senior Kyar, bowed. "Master. The last of the manuscripts have been moved."

"Excellent."

Suel formed a quizzical expression. "Master Orane, if the Barasha can break down the vault, how will we protect the secret entrance?"

"The sorceress must be convinced we've escaped with the books after they inspect the cleared-out vaults."

Suel picked up a discarded scroll, one of many. "I thought you didn't want the Barasha to get these."

Leesad took the scroll and tossed it to the floor in a haphazard fashion. "This is a copy of some histories. It'll be of no use to them. We must make the ruse seem real."

The last of the Kyar passed into the secret passages. Orane closed the secret door, then placed his hands against the wall and wove a spell through it. "There. The Barasha will have to probe very hard to detect this entrance. Narech Yetig has replaced the guards who died in the demon attack at the palace gate. They will be our witnesses."

Unlike the Barasha, the Kyar and the Daro were able to perform some true magic without calling upon demons. These skills were taught by the wizards to better confront the Servants of Baras. Yet, the spells they worked were no more than the efforts of children compared to the power once possessed by the wizards.

Orane sat on the stone floor with an open book in his lap and chanted in a low voice.

The words droned on for a tespan before the air glowed with a blue light.

Orane's voice rose in pitch and tempo.

The Kyar scholars slapped their in unison.

Outside, the guards at the gate heard  the charge of horses and saw eighteen wagons filled with Kyar and books barrel down upon them.

The captain at the gate pulled a pin to drop the portcullis. It fell a hand's width, then froze in place.

Guards fired arrows. They struck the wagons but failed to hit any of the Kyar. The wagons charged over the bridge and onto the plain. Soldiers mounted horses to give chase. Before they reached the gate, the portcullis freed itself and crashed down to block their way. The wagons with the Kyar rushed into the western forest.

Soldiers watched them disappear into the woods. They never saw the wagons fade away into mist once they enter the forest.

Deep within the secret palace, Orane closed the book and looked to the other Kyar. "It is done."

Reshna returned to the throne room. Craya was taken to his chambers and the wound on his hand treated by one of the Daro healers who hadn't been able to escape the palace. Reshna gave the healers' comings and goings no more notice than he did the kitchen staff. Though the power of the Daro came from the wizards, it was a power to heal and mend. The Barasha measured all things by the power of force alone.

The Kyar, however, he feared. Their magic surpassed his own unless he called upon a demon. He had broken the spell on the doors to the vaults and inspected the scrolls strewn about the floors, but looked no further, for Orane's ruse succeeded and Reshna was convinced the Kyar escaped the palace.

Dark clouds blew across the sun to cast a shadow in the hall. Reshna stared at the crown within the crystal sphere. Now he knew Ryckair was the true heir. The vanished key would call him. If the Barasha found the prince he would lead them to it. They could still kill him in the ceremony to make Craya the heir.

Yet Reshna knew the plan could still fail in so many ways. Ryckair could raise an army and take back Carandir. If he fathered a child and died, that babe would become the heir, but the barasha would have no influence over it.

If Ryckair died childless, a babe fathered by Craya would become an heir Reshna could manipulate. Any mother would do, but it would take decades and Dek might defeat them.

There was another way.

Through research and interviews with demons, Reshna learned when Avar fled in exile to the eastern city of Au, his aunt married a man whose descendants later formed the house of Rascalla. Mirjel and Craya were distant cousins.

A babe born of their union would become the heir. More, the infant would be able to take up the key at birth. Ryckair would no longer matter.

Barasha priests escorted Baroness Luja of Shenan, Baron Refran of Ulata, Baron Womd of Petala and Baron Gilyon of Eel into the hall.

The sorcerer studied them. "I am Reshna, Lord High Priest of the Servants of Baras. Why did you take up arms against Baron Dek?"

Womd bowed. "We support Prince Craya who will put an end to the Eastern houses and the foreigners who defile our nation."

"You have seen the demon. Do you not fear me?"

Luja stepped forward. "We see your great power and respect you. Are our goals for Prince Craya not the same as yours?"

Gilyon looked to the other nobles, then to Reshna. "We pledge to support you in making Prince Craya king."

Reshna examined the four. He saw a slight tremor in the hands of the barons. Luja stood motionless. "You will be rewarded for your support. The Eastern baronies will be divided among you."

He waved his hand. Another Barasha priests escorted the four from the hall.

Yetig entered and bowed. "The *Sea Dragon* is overdue, Lord. Whatever happened, they didn't have time to send a terec. A second ship was dispatched. No wreckage has been found."

"The prince may have drowned before Petstra could cast the spell. He may have escaped and made his way to land. Mount a search of the south and north continents."

"Lord Reshna. No Carandirian has stepped on the North Continent in centuries. We have no maps or guides."

"Find Baroness Quib."

# CHAPTER SEVEN

Ryckair was convinced the bubble he rode in would pop as the giant water snakes pulled it through a labyrinth of underwater tunnels. The beasts sported luminescent nodules on their foreheads. This allowed Ryckair to make out some features of the water caves. He deduced the bubbles must be made of gill weed, a peculiar plant from the deepest part of the Great River. A book described how the transparent membrane wrapped around its seed casings allowed oxygen in and spent air to flow out.

Ryckair's bubble, along with five others with only men inside, were pulled off on a side tunnel while the others with woman sailors from the *Sea Dragon* continued on ahead.

The snakes stopped and released the bubbles. They floated up and broke the surface of a pond located in an air-filled cave.

Ryckair looked down into the water. By the dim light of the snake's nodules, he saw they were positioned over a ledge. It sloped down like a rock beach and rose to a narrow strip of dry rock that ended in rough walls with a single tunnel opening.

The spheres bobbed on the water as the ropes were untied. A Sarte rider poured green fluid over the bubbles. They began to disintegrate.

Ryckair felt wetness on his legs. He caught a piece of the plant between his toes before it dissolved and swished it in the water to wash away the fluid.

Light grew from the opening. Two men with muscular physiques walked from the archway. One wore a tattered vest over filthy rags. He carried a basket with a glow root, another strange plant from the underwater world. It gave off luminance when exposed to air.

The face of the man with the vest had craggy lines. His hair was streaked with gray.

The other man was bare chested. He brandished a metal pick as though it were a mace.

Both men had dirty, tangled beards.

The fabric of the bubbles dissolved except for the small swatch Ryckair managed to save. The captives stood on the rock ledge of the lagoon. The Sarte riders turned their snakes and disappeared beneath the water.

The man with the lantern stepped forward. "I'm Lekto, chief miner. I assign all work and award all favors. You're now miners. You'll work from the time you wake till the time I call for sleep."

The chief miner raised the basket with the glow root and indicated for the new arrivals to walk through the passage. The guard stepped forward to give authority to the command.

They filed into a larger cavern. Cold light from glow roots filtered in as two cooks prepared a meal. At least fifty men sat on stones and held metal cups in their hands. They came from many lands with light skin, pale skin, brown skin, black skin, various textures of hair, rounded eyes, monolided eyes, and noses long, short and flat. All wore mere scraps of clothing. The stench of human bodies was intense.

The floor was smooth, though not level. Stalactites hung from above. Prominent in the center was a rock platform.

Another tunnel led to a smaller cavern with piles of ratty bedding.

The chief miner climbed on the platform. "Six more miners have arrived. During the next shift the Sarte will deliver more charcoal fuel and food to the cooks. Eat quickly."

The cooks handed cups to the new arrivals. They lined up with the rest of the men. The fare consisted of coarse brown bread with thick crusts, fish stew and mushrooms.

Batu and Ryckair found a rock to sit on.

They tried to talk to others but were ignored.

When they finished, Lekto stood back on the platform. "We'll work the old tunnel today. The Sarte demand copper."

A voice came from the crowd. "There's no copper in the old tunnel"

"Do You challenge me?"

"Where's the copper?"

"It's there. We've pulled much from that place. The Sarte have rewarded us with extra food and spices and twice they brought ale."

"Now they cut the rations because we don't deliver. We must work the tunnel near the fissure."

"I'm the chief miner."

A tall man with black skin leapt onto the platform. He was younger than Lekto. As with all the miners, his body was muscular. He brandished an obsidian knife. "I, Theb, challenge."

The man with the pickaxe pushed the crowd back. Lekto pulled an obsidian knife from within his tattered shirt. The two men crouched and circled each other. The crowd watched in silence.

Theb feigned a thrust.

Lekto ignored it. He took a swipe as Theb who jumped back.

Theb slashed Lekto's knife arm.

Lekto thrust for his opponent's chest.

Theb lunged and bashed his head into Lekto's gut.

The chief miner stumbled back.

Theb sprung forward and knocked Lekto down.

Ryckair expected the chief miner to fight on.

Instead, the man let his arms fall to the platform. He dropped his knife.

Theb jumped on top of him and brought his knife to Lekto's chest.

The chief miner laid back and offered no resistance.

Almost inaudibly, Ryckair heard him say, "Free."

Theb pushed the knife deep into the chief miner's heart.

Lekto gave a shudder before his body relaxed into death.

The victor took the tattered vest and fastened it around himself. "I, Theb, am the chief miner. We work the tunnel near the fissure."

ஒ  ✦  ஒ

The Stronghold of Rascalla stood on a plain of rolling grasslands and farms with the tree covered Uta Mountain to the north. Those peaks extended east nearly to the swamplands less than a day's ride away, then turned north toward the river.

The grounds were walled with gates to the east and west. Many buildings and a large tower keep were set within, along with a pleasant garden where Baroness Jea sat on a bench.

A terec landed.

She expected good news about the coronation and her daughter. Instead, her hands shook with the story of the Barasha and the Demon.

*Flee at once*, came Dek's thoughts through the bird. *Colonel Herrik sent a terec to alert the garrison. They'll evacuate Desan. Find refuge in Au. Try to raise their help to confront the Barasha.*

Jea's chest went cold with the thought of her daughter trapped by the sorcerers. Her voice cut across the garden. "Penta."

The steward ran to her side. "Baroness."

"Gather everyone inside and outside the walls. We must flee to Au. Your master's been right all these years. The Barasha have risen."

There was much complaining among the courtiers. Some gathered trunks of cloths and chests of gold and jewels. Penta told them to leave their finery and sew jewels into the garments they wore.

Jea stood on a chest. "Quiet, everyone. A danger approaches that will kill us all. We may never return here if we even survive. Sorcerers will bring demons and death. Food is packed for a journey to Au where all of us have family. Everything else is forfeit. Prepare to leave within three spans."

In the Carandir garrison, Colonel Herrik's terec landed next to Captain Amar. He called the troops together and repeated the message. "Lieutenant Bisa, lead the force into Desan and take control of the city in the name of the Crown. I've been ordered to take troops and personally escort Baroness Jea to safety."

When Captain Amar arrived at the stronghold, a train of people, escorted by the Rascallan militia, meandered out of the eastern gate.

Penta tried his best to organize everyone.

Captain Amar saluted. "Baroness Jea, I've been ordered to accompany you and your party safely to Au".

Jea watched horse drawn wagons and carts filled with couturiers and their belongings. "Thank you, captain." She shook her head. "They're moving like a rabble. We need to reach the docks. Those who can fit on galleys will be rowed to Au. The rest will walk over the hard ground north of the swamp."

"Allow me to stop and organize the march."

Amar halted the procession and brought them into a single column for easier protection. He inspected the wagons and carts. In spite of Penta's instructions, he found cloths, paintings, statues and strong boxes.

Lady Zedo commandeered two wagons for her finery and made her servants walk beside them. People complained and cried as the garrison troops threw the extra baggage to the ground.

Amar placed his horse soldiers to either side and to the rear of the column. The militia were interspersed with the garrison troops. They moved out at four times the pace.

They came to the swamps sooner than Jea expected. All the while, she glanced behind in search of the Barasha.

The cliffs along the eastern side of the Uta mountains reached nearly to the swamp. A narrow strip of road led to the port.

Deep shadows formed as the sun sank.

Amar called for a halt to prepare supper.

People stepped out of wagons to stretch their legs and rub sore muscles. Cooks lit fires and prepared food.

A flash of light exploded ahead of them. Screams fill the area. In the ghostly light were three Barasha priests mounted on horseback and a force of Sinkarakans.

At their head rode Baroness Luja.

She gave a twisted smile. "Leaving so soon, Jea? I hoped you would stay and welcome me as the new lady of Rascalla."

The Sinkarakan soldiers charged. People fled back to the south. Some ran madly into the swamp. Others stood numb, unable to move.

Jea threw back her cloak to reveal the scabbard of a sword sewn into it the same as Mirjel's.

Captain Amar drew his blade.

Amar's troops formed a wall between the civilians and the attackers.

The Sinkarakans were no match for a highly trained, battle-hardened force.

Jea and Amar ran toward Luja.

Two of the mounted priests rode forward and grabbed one of the servants.

The man struggled and tried to break free.

The third sorcerer dropped powder over the servant, spoke a chant and sliced the terrified man's throat.

Overhead, clouds gathered in the nearly black sky. The air was suddenly chilled. A blast of wind shot down onto the Carandirian and Rascallan troops. They and many of the civilians became encased in thick ice. The rest fled south in a rout.

Jea grabbed Amar's arm. "We can do nothing here. Into the swamp."

The captain and Jea waded through a bog of shallow channels, deep pools and small bush covered land masses that pushed up above the water.

Ten paces out they were lost to sight, though they heard the splash of the Sinkarakans.

She caught a glimpse of movement through the foliage and pointed it out to Amar.

A boat scraped against the small island they stood on. They readied for battle. Instead of their pursuers, they found a short, olive skinned Sinkarakan. He spoke in the native tongue of his kind. "*Baroness Jea. What brings you here?*"

Jea let out a breath. "*Horatello, my friend. Thank Ilidel you found us. We're pursued by great evil.*"

Horatello stepped onto the island. "*We must consult Alakana. The elder will know what to do.*"

Amar spoke few words in the Sinkarakan language and could only make out the word elder. "What's he saying?"

Jea smiled. "We've found help."

They boarded Horatello's flat bottomed boat. He poled the craft forward through the swamp for at least a span until they came to his village where buildings of stone stood on a large outcropping of earth.

One wooden hut sat on stilts in the water just offshore. A ladder extended to the water. Horatello moved the boat to it.

Inside, an aged Sinkarakan woman sat on a mat. Her hair was sparse and her teeth nearly gone. She rose at Jea's entry. "*May the dragons bless and protect you.*"

Jea made the sign of the covenant. "*As they may for you and your household.*"

They sat on mats. Jea told Alakana about the Barasha and Luja's attack. Of all the baronies in the east, Rascalla held the closest ties to the Sinkaraka. Dek's ancestors asked permission to settle near their lands, where other Carandirians entered the swamps with disregard to gather turtle eggs or farm small islands.

Alakana sighed. "*We know some of our people in the south formed ties with evil men. I didn't suspect they were Barasha.*"

"*We'll leave at once. Our presence endangers your village.*"

"*You can't outrun them. They must be directed away.*"

"*We're heading for…*"

Alakana raised her hand. "*Don't tell me. I can't betray you if I don't know.*" She thought for a moment. "*To the south is a special place to hide.*"

She smiled at Captain Amar. "*Do you understand?*" She pointed to her ears.

Amar returned a sheepish smile. "*Speak I little, honored one.*"

Alakana laughed. "*It's a good try. More than most would make.*"

Horatello poled them to a mound of dry ground south of the city. They carried torches in the near pitch night. A single tree stood there.

Alakana led them to one of the roots. She placed her hands on the bark and murmured words to the tree. When she stepped back, A portion of the root opened like a hatch. Inside, a stone stairway descended underground. Along the walls were set globes like those in the Kyar's vaults.

Alakana pointed down the stairs. "*This is a gift from Ilidel and Jorondel for our help in the Dragon Wars. It's a place of refuge my ancestors used when the Barasha came. It can't be detected, nor can anyone inside. Wait here until the Barasha pass. There's food and water within.*"

Jea took Alakana's hands. "*Thank you for your help and long friendship. I'd never have thought of this.*"

Alakana raised an eyebrow. "*Well, we are the people of the root.*"

They both laughed.

Jea and Amar descended. The root closed behind them. Inside, there was food and water aplenty. The room could have held the entire village. They each found alcoves and fell fast asleep.

The next morning, the root opened. Alakana stepped down. "*All is well. I told the Barasha you came to our village, which they would be able to detect, and you traveled south. All true.*"

"*I'm afraid I must impose on you once more. To reach our destination, we need a boat and provisions.*"

"*They've already been brought here. Safe trip and may the dragons protect you.*"

After weeks of eluding patrols, Jea and Amar reached the eastern shore of the swamps. Low, grass covered hills greeted them. The air felt fresh after weeks in the humid swamps.

Jea stepped out of the little boat and looked around. "I know this place. I played here as a child. My grandparents' cottage is just over that hill."

Less than a tespan later they stood on the porch of a one-story home. A flower garden grew in front.

Jea knocked.

An elderly woman with bright white hair answered the door. She squinted, then broke into a wide smile. "Je. I didn't know you were coming."

A tall, thin man whose hair was also white walked in from another room. "Je. Is that really you, little squirter? Oh, my word, it's been an age if it's been a day. What brings you to Au?"

"Grammy. Grampy. This is Captain Amar from the Carandir garrison in Rascalla. Captain Amar these are my grandmother and grandfather, Osba and Garto Lakan. Grampy once sat on the council. He and grammy both move in high circles."

Osba extended her hand. "I'm pleased to meet you."

Jea wrung her hands. "Oh, grammy and grampy. We should all sit down."

When the story of the coronation and the Barasha attack was told, Jea's grandfather shook his head. "I never liked Craya. I only met him three times. I could tell he was cruel. And Mirjel. Oh, our baby."

Tears came to Jea's eyes. "Dek said he saw her alive, but the dragons only know what these monsters have done to her. We have to put such thoughts aside for now. I must raise the council in Au to fight back against the Barasha. Their evil will consume the world. We must begin to form alliances. There are jewels sewn into my garments to pay bribes. I'll ingratiate myself with society and make friends. Then, I can present a case for aid to the council."

Amar stood. "How can I help, Bareness?"

"You've been a faithful friend to Rascalla and a dutiful officer to Carandir. Yet, a Carandir officer in the streets of Au won't be welcome."

"I'll return through the swamps and try to raise my troops."

Jea thought for a moment. "I still need your support. You'll play the part of my steward and aid. That'll be expected."

On a distant shore, violent waves pounded against a beach near a stone tower. Inside, Jarat, the last wizard, stirred from meditation.

Though she was old beyond mortal memory, her appearance was of a young woman with dark ebony skin, brown eyes and course, black hair cut short. She sat on the stone floor with her legs crossed.

Jarat heard Nissor's clawed feet scrape across the floor. She saw her impish companion at the door. Its long sad eyes looked down its yellow beak as his green, scale covered fingers held the latch.

The garat's tail swished rapidly. It gave a mournful coo.

The wizard waved her familiar into the room. "Yes, my friend, I felt it too."

A wave of repulsion ran through her body. The Barasha had returned.

When Baras was subdued, the rest of the wizards were convinced the sorcerers were destroyed. Jarat wanted to believe, yet an unsettling sense of dread remained.

Once, she stood victorious against the Servants of Baras with Kare and Senta and Fra and Lo and Pel by her side, wizards all, men and women, high and mighty.

They were gone. Unlike dragons, wizards were mortal, though their lives were measured not by years but in eons.

Jarat was the last of all the wizards that ever were or ever would be. She feared this call was her final task.

# BOOK III

*The Palace at Meth*
*Two Years Later*

# CHAPTER ONE

The Carandir Minister of the Treasury held a bound ledger in her hands as she stood before the twin thrones in the audience hall of the palace. "Highness, we simply can't raise taxes."

Mirjel leaned against an arm of the right-hand throne and watched Craya pace in front of the crown. Each time a minister reported, Craya demanded she attend, as if he wished to play at being king with her in the role of queen. Her observations were never welcome, only her presence.

Craya waved his hands in the air. "Does Carandir not have lands? Ships? Merchants?"

The minster clutched the ledger to her chest. "We have all in abundance, Highness. With the drought, fields and orchards are barren. Many ships wait at anchor. I'm unable to collect taxes from wealth that doesn't exist. We can no longer afford to support this new army of foreign mercenaries who demand payment in advance."

Little rain had fallen after the disappearance of the dragon key. Major rivers were mere trickles. Many lakes were reduced to mud holes. Only farmers near Lake Hasp were able to irrigate their fields. These alone couldn't produce enough food to supply the entire monarchy.

From the servants, Mirjel heard of mass starvation. What food there was didn't always find its way to the hungry. She discovered much was siphoned off by corrupt officials placed in power by the Barasha.

The minister approached the prince. "Highness, please. You must reduce the size of the army. Carandir will be crushed beneath its weight."

Craya seized the ledger and threw it across the floor. "Enough. The army is needed to search for traitors. If you don't want soldiers knocking at your door, find the taxes I need."

The minister retrieved the ledger and fled.

Mirjel closed her eyes. Her days now floated from one to the other like a fogged nightmare with no promise of an end. At first, she thought she might influence Craya and guide him to protect his subjects. This hope soon died. Except for her presence in the throne room, the only contact he desired was in his bed to produce an heir as the Barasha commanded. Her only conciliation was her mistaken belief Ryckair was safe on an island, for Yetig told neither her nor Craya about the lost *Sea Dragon.*

When Craya's guards brought her to his chambers, she tried to imagine it was Ryckair's touch upon her skin while Craya ran his eager hands over her. She never opened her eyes, even when he screamed, even when he slapped her.

In the throne room, Craya watched Mirjel turn her head away to stare at a wall. This wasn't how he imagined it. He knew Mirjel wouldn't forget Ryckair easily. Still, he hoped she would at least come to respect him over time, if not love him. Instead, her scorn grew daily.

On their wedding night, his blood raced as he took her virginity. He laughed with the joy of conquest. The joy soon wore off. Sometimes, he wanted to put her on a horse and send her into the wilderness after her father. Reshna wouldn't allow it. The sorcerer demanded an heir with Mirjel.

He knew Reshna had to be overthrown. Only the crown could do that. All of his thoughts were focused on finding Ryckair and the dragon shaped key.

He stared at the crest through its crystal encasement. Before the demon slaughtered the soldiers under his command in the swamp, he considered stories of magic children's tales. The mist demon drove all doubt from his mind. Reshna was powerful in a way never considered before.

He found it hard to believe the Barasha were such fools as to think he would hand the crown over to them. Once Ryckair was eliminated in their wretched ceremony he'd use the key to open the case. With the crown, Craya, King of Carandir, would destroy the Barasha forever. The people would love him. Mirjel would love him.

He dropped into the left hand throne and drummed his fingers on its arm. "You're smirking again."

Mirjel tilted her head toward the crystal ceiling. "My lord is mistaken."

"You're laughing inside."

"I'm thinking of days gone by."

He slammed his fist on the arm. "I rule here."

She turned her head with a measured pace and stared at him. "Where's your crown?"

He shot to his feet and stood over her with his hand raised.

Mirjel sat still with her eyes riveted to his.

Craya lowered his arm. "Don't mock me." He pointed to a guard. "Summon Narech Yetig."

Yetig entered and bowed before Craya. "Highness."

The prince smiled. "You see, my dear. Yetig knows who commands here. Narech, what word is there of the traitor, Dek?"

"No new reports have been received, Highness."

"Then let us hear the old tales. We do so enjoy reliving our victories."

Yetig looked to Mirjel. He wished there was a way to avoid repeating the story. He despised Craya who played games while the sorcerers grew more powerful each day.

There was no choice but to placate the cruel royal who lived in a near fantasy world. With so may troops lost to the demon mist, three quarters of his forces consisted  of bandits and pirates from as far away as city-sates and townships east of the swamplands. A large contingency were Karakiens.

The narech feared he might lose control over what was left of the Carandir army and navy and had no doubt Reshna would have him killed and replaced if the sorcerer knew this. "His lands were seized as you ordered and given to Baroness Luja. Many members of his household who tried to flee were put to the sword. Baroness Jea hasn't been found. Patrols scour the swamplands."

Mirjel had learned of the wholesale butchery from talk passed through the servants. She hoped her mother was able to find safety. Still, many she knew since birth lay slaughtered. She held her emotions closely in check.

Craya ran his hands over the crystal sphere. "Did Baron Dek try to rescue those in his stronghold, narech?"

"There're no reports of Baron Dek returning to Rascalla. He continues to raid army columns and supply caravans before his forces retreat into unknown hiding places."

Craya gave Mirjel a look of mock pity. "Did you hear that, my dear? Your father abandoned his home as he abandoned you." He laughed. "Narech, dispatch a detachment of soldiers to hunt down Dek. I want him brought back for trial."

"I counsel Your Highness to wait. His forces are well secreted. It's in Your Highness' best interest for our army to search for Prince Ryckair and the lost key."

"You mean it's in Reshna's best interest. Who do you serve Yetig, Carandir, or the Barasha?"

"I mean no disrespect, Highness. I merely wished to suggest alternatives. As always, I render loyalty only to Your Highness."

"Then dispatch the soldiers. They're to return the baron alive. I don't care what they do with the rest of his foul company."

"The soldiers shall ride at once, Highness." Yetig bowed and left.

Craya said, "There, my dear. Now you see who …" He stopped short.

Mirjel had left the hall.


Smoke from braziers curled through the oppressive air of the former chart room. In the background, chanting reverberated from the walls.

Yetig knelt before Reshna. "Prince Craya demands the army hunt for Baron Dek."

The sorcerer sat passively. "Send no troops. They are needed elsewhere. What of the Kyar?"

"We can find no trace of them."

"They are near. I feel the echo of their power." He threw powder into one of the glowing braziers. It hissed and gave off white smoke. "They are less than a week's journey from here. Scour Meth and the surrounding forests."

"It shall be done."

Reshna raised a hand. "Wait." He studied the swirling smoke. "Have the palace searched again as well."

❧ ✦ ❧

It was brightnail when Gilyon, Refran, Womb and Luja walked casually through the palace garden and stood at different sides of a thick bush. They remained standing as they looked away from each other.

Luja spoke in a near whisper. "My spies report Mirjel has not yet conceived. We still have time."

Refran's voice was muffled. "The Barasha watch her constantly. No one could reach her now."

Gilyon gave a humorless laugh. "They watch everyone."

Womb's eye scanned from left to right. "We risk being here."

Luja sat on a bench and stared at a planting of bright flowers. "This must be our last meeting together. I have a plan. Even the Barasha can't track the movement of a terec. I'll tell Reshna we can better direct the search for Prince Ryckair from our strongholds. Every day at the second span, we'll use terecs to send messages. I'll go first in six weeks and send word to all of you. You, in turn, will send a reply to each of us that day. We'll wait for all the birds to come to us. Gilyon will then send a new thought and wait for the replies before Refran and then Womb have their say. The cycle will repeat with me. It'll be slow but will protect us."

The nobles remained silent, until Womb cleared his throat. "The Barasha will never let us go. They trust no one."

Luja stood. "They will if the three of you offer your children as hostages."

Gilyon' voice cracked. "If we're found out, they'll die in horrific torment. You have no children, Luja."

"I'll offer my steward."

"He's hardly family."

Refran closed his eyes. "The fate of Carandir, a strong Carandir, is in our hands. Keysta's death reduced our numbers, yet others will join us once we move. Baroness Luja's plan is the only way. We must all make sacrifices."

One by one, they left the garden.

Baron Dek watched an armed column of supply wagons as it traveled east down a road next to the Nemtanka River. Twenty mercenaries on horseback, all men, moved ahead of the column in a loose formation while another six men rode behind. They were mostly Karakien bandits who carried an assortment of armor and weapons from many lands. Their commander was one of Luja's sergeant. He appeared to have little control over the company.

Dek's men waited behind embankments built the night before. They were designed to appear as piles of sod when viewed from the road. The barriers rose high enough to conceal shallow trenches where seventy mounted troops waited.

The baron watched through a small slit as the column reached the center point of the blind. The mercenaries plodded along with little heed of their surroundings. Two mounted Karakiens rode back and forth in no particular pattern. Only the sergeant in the lead wagon scanned the road.

Dek raised a palm.

Colonel Herrik reflected a flash of sunlight up and down the trench with a mirror. Her troops readied themselves. She flashed a second time. Archers sent a volley of arrows into the column. The Carandirians threw down the barriers. Herrik led them in a charge up earthen ramps.

The sergeant on the wagon blew a horn. Before the mercenaries could react, Herrik and her forces were upon them. It was little more than butchery. The mercenaries, accustomed to waylaying poorly armed caravans or solitary travelers, were no match for a disciplined force.

Herrik called, "Lord Regent."

The Colonel pulled back a tarpaulin at the rear of a wagon to reveal small wooden chests. She opened one. There was a treasure of gems inside.

Dek picked up a ruby. "Father of Dragons this would sustain our troops for a year." He opened another chest to find more gems.

A muffled sound came from the front of the wagon.

Dek drew his sword and crawled in.

A heavy-set person in large riding breaches and a jerkin lay face up on the bottom of the wagon. The figure's hands and feet were bound by ropes. A hood was drawn over the captive's head.

W/hen Dek removed the covering, his eyes widened. "Quib!"

Baroness Quib, a gag over her mouth, mumbled and writhed.

Dek undid the gag.

Quib coughed. "Dragons' blood, Dek. How did you find me?"

"By Chance. I never thought I'd say this, but I am glad to see you."

"Well, get me out of this."

Dek undid the bindings. "In the name of all the dragons, where have you been?"

"After the supposed coronation, I thought it best to travel. I took my retainers and some gold to Karaken where I have sympathetic contacts."

Dek raised an eyebrow. "Fellow smugglers."

Quib shrugged, "Let's just say accommodating acquaintances. After a while the gold began to run out and my acquaintances became less accommodating. I snuck across the border of my barony to a little cave where I keep a few items I seem to have forgotten to report to the Crown."

"A few?" Dek pointed to the chests. "This is almost a quarter of the Rascalla treasury. Where did you get all these gems?"

"Various places. They're light, easy to transport and most convertible. That was my problem. They have to be converted and the only places close by are Au or Karaken. Unfortunately, the Barasha sealed the southern and eastern borders after my return. I made myself look like a poor merchant and headed for Lusar to skirt the border along the wild lands and reach one of the far south nations. Alas, this sergeant wouldn't take a bribe."

Quib crawled out of the wagon and rubbed her wrists. "What have you been doing, Dek?"

"Something more noble."

"I don't doubt that."

"We raid caravans like this and hunt the Barasha."

"With a force this size you could have a comfortable life in one of the southern lands. I hear Hura's very nice. Pleasant sea breezes along the warm, equatorial beaches."

"I imagine you'd like to be released to do so."

Quib winced. "Something like that was my general plan. Of course, it's a great burden carting these chests around. Slows you down. That's how I got caught. I could distribute some of them among you and your troops and take a share south with me."

Dek stared at her.

Quib shrugged, "No, then?"

"As regent, I claim this treasure in the name of Carandir, to feed the loyal troops and buy weapons."

"You've no right. I always knew you were an officious, self-righteous old maggot. These chests are mine. No matter what you may think about the way I acquired those gems, they belong to me. Besides, what're you fighting for? There is no Carandir now."

Dek grabbed Quib's arm and pushed her against the wagon. "Never say such a thing again, Quib, Baroness of Mentaro, noble of Carandir. You've sworn an oath of fealty to the Crown and the heir. Desertion is treason. Look around and see how traitors are dealt with."

She grimaced. "All right. You can have the jewels. But who's the heir? Not Craya, and Ryckair's dead."

Dek stepped back from Quib. "Ryckair lives, and he's the heir."

"We all saw the body in state."

"That was an impostor. Mirjel saw the prince alive just before the coronation ceremony."

"What proof do you have that he still lives?"

"Mirjel's word is all the proof I need."

Quib rubbed her arm. "Then let me have just one of my chests and a horse. I'm no good to you."

"I won't have you captured by another Barasha patrol to report where we are." He grinned. "You'll be our guest and enjoy all the comforts we have to offer, hard ground, cold gruel and watered wine."

Quib closed her eyes.


Yetig entered Reshna's hall and knelt. "Wreckage from the *Sea Dragon* was found washed up on a small island, my lord."

"Was anyone alive?"

"The report says one person was found."

"Bring this survivor to me."

# CHAPTER TWO

In the Sarte mine, a deep comradeship grew between Ryckair and Batu. The former smuggler was protective of the younger man, even though he admitted it was difficult to think of Ryckair as a prince.

Ryckair told Batu to treat him the same as any other miner to guard his identity from the Sarte.

Their clothes, rags when they were placed on the ship, were now mere shreds of fabric. Ryckair's shirt just covered the dragon mark on his chest.

It mattered little. They could work naked in the breezeless caverns of the Sarte where the temperature remained constantly warm.

Batu's beard, once trimmed, was now long and unkempt.

Ryckair also sported a sandy blond beard

From the moment they arrived, Ryckair and Batu explored the warren of caverns during rest periods, even after the physical labor left them exhausted.

It was apparent there were air passages to the surface or they would have suffocated. Smoke rose from charcoal cooking fires in the main cavern to vanish through holes in the wall near the ceiling. The walls were smooth and impossible to scale without rope and grappling hooks.

As they continued to search for more accessible vent holes during parts of their rest periods, they shared stories of their lives.

Batu taped on a tunnel wall. "Nothing here."

Ryckair carried a glow root. "We better get back and get some sleep. I'm not sure howm you keep going."

"Years of practice as a smuggler. Sleep can be an option."

"How did you get involved in a life of crime?"

"Oh, I don't see it as crime, more a service, and I didn't start out as a smuggler. My family were merchants. We lived in a Tequan desert oasis town on the eastern border of Karaken before my grandfather moved the family to Carandir. This was during the truce between Carandir and Karaken before your father became king. Karaken is rich in precious metals and gems, but the land is largely barren, they need the food Carandir can supply, so trade was brisk, then the Karakiens broke the peace an all open trade ceased. My grandfather couldn't stand the thought of people in Karaken dying of hunger and determined to help those in need. That's how we became smugglers, though never in arms or secrets. My father inherited the business, then I did."


One morning, Ryckair clasped his hands over Batu's mouth as he shook him. "Quiet. The others are still asleep. Theb was summoned to the lagoon by the Sarte. Something important must be happening."

Batu opened his eyes and sat up.

The Sarte rarely spoke with the chief miner. When they did, it was only to retrieve ore and bring more food and cooking fuel.

The prince hoped the meeting between Theb and the Sarte would be brief so they could get back to the caverns. If they were late, he and Batu would miss their only meal before a weary day's labor.

They wove their way through tunnels until they came to a small fissure on a wall they discovered in one of their searches.

They paused long enough to jump, catch the tip of a ledge and pull themselves up in a single movement. Years of work in the mines built powerful muscles on both men.

The roof of the crawl space dropped lower and lower as they moved forward. At the end, a crack allowed them to see and hear into the space where the water of the Great River joined the cavern system.

Theb stood next to the lagoon.

The Sarte emerged from the water.

Sweat on Theb's black skin glistened in the light of the glow root. He knelt.

"Masters."

The Sarte leader spoke in a guttural tone. "We seek a man among you with a mark."

"There are many men with many marks, exalted one."

"This mark is unique. It appears as a dragon that rises in flight."

"I haven't seen this mark, my lord. The men rarely undress and never bathe. It may be hidden beneath filth. I'll have them wash and look for such a mark."

"He is to be held for us, unharmed. Your life is forfeit if you fail."

Theb touched his head to the stone floor. "I remain your servant."

The Sarte walked back to the water.

Ryckair rubbed his finger across the dragon mark on his chest.

He and Batu scooted back out and ran toward the habitable area.

Ryckair's mind flashed images of every section of tunnel or cave he and Batu explored. There was no place to hide.

As soon as they entered the cavern, the other men began to stir. Without getting close, it was hard to tell one from the other. Theb didn't ask names.

The men ambled into the larger cavern used for meals. Two cooks stood behind boiling kettles and dished out the morning meal.

Ryckair moved forward to receive his ration. The shorter cook ladled fish stew into Ryckair's bowl and dropped a thick piece of bread on top. Three mushrooms bobbed to the surface, a lucky treat.

He and Batu sat in a corner away from the glow roots. Ryckair pushed the mushrooms down and let them float back up. His eyes wandered to the smoke from the charcoal. Like the mushrooms, it rose up toward the ceiling. "This is maddening. There's our escape. All we need is rope."

Batu snorted. "You might as well ask one of those water snakes to crawl in here so we can climb up its back."

Ryckair stopped and stared at Batu. "Of course. What a fool I am."

He was cut off by Theb who climbed up on the platform that Ryckair learned was called the talking stone. "We'll work the left mine today. When we return, meet at the pool where you'll strip and bathe both your clothes and your bodies."

The company retrieved their pickaxes from the sleeping area and walked off toward the tunnels. Theb held a glow root in his hand as he led them through passages. Four more lights were distributed throughout the group.

Ryckair took one. He and Batu lagged back to the rear.

Theb and the rest of the men rounded a corner.

The prince covered the glow root and grabbed Batu by the arm. They stood in the darkness. The others took no notice of them.

Ryckair led Batu back to the living area at a run. "Were you able to see anything when the snakes carried your bubble through the caverns?"

"I sometimes saw walls as we passed."

"My bubble dropped to the bottom of the tunnel once, just before we came up in the lagoon. I saw patches of vine like plants. It seemed unimportant at the time. I forgot about it until you mentioned the snakes."

"Even if you could use the vines like ropes, there's no way to reach them that far underwater."

"I still have the piece of breathing membrane I saved from my bubble. If I hold it over my mouth, I might be able to dive down and cut a vine free."

The two men made their way to the pool.

Ryckair stripped off his tunic and walked bare chested down the stone ledge that sloped into the water.

The current beneath him looked calm. He knew it changed constantly from the ride with the water snakes. If he drifted past this area, he might rise to find himself trapped at the roof of the underwater tunnel.

Batu held the glow root over the lagoon to cast as much light as possible into the water. He waved to signal his confidence.

Ryckair placed some stones in his pockets for ballast, clasped the membrane securely over his mouth and jumped in.

The shred of bubble allowed him to breathe. He kept steady pressure through the membrane and controlled his impulse to gulp air. The light, which seemed so bright in the cavern, barely penetrated the water. His best hope was to use the feeble illumination as a return marker.

By the time he reached the sandy bottom it was utterly dark. Ryckair felt for the plants. The floor of the lagoon sloped down and became rocky. He searched with his right hand and used the left to hold the piece of breathing bubble over his mouth.

There was only gravel. It was hard to hold the membrane in place. He was about to abandon this first try when his hand came across the stalk of a water vine. He smiled, then stopped when water seeped around the edge.

With a deep breath, he took the gill fabric away from his mouth and stuffed it into his breeches. From his belt, he retrieved an obsidian knife and used its glass sharp edge to saw at the leathery plant. It took only a moment to sever the stalk.

He pushed the knife into his breaches behind his back and grasped the vine. With the membrane secured again, he dropped the rocks from his pocket and swam up. The faint light of the glow root was just discernible.

The prince surfaced.

Water washed the filth from his body. The dragon mark on his chest was clearly visible.

He drew in a sharp breath.

Batu knelt.

Theb stood over him with a pick axe. "Come up from the water. Hold your arms out."

Ryckair dropped the vine and raised his arms. The knife was still tucked in his breaches out of site. He gauged how close he had to get before striking.

Theb raise the axe. "Stop."

Batu shot to his feet.

Theb was taken by surprise and swung the pick wildly.

The tip drove into Batu's leg. The smuggler grabbed the handle and yanked it from Theb's grasp as he fell to the stone floor.

Ryckair grasped the knife and sprang.

The two men circled one another.

Ryckair searched for a weakness in his opponent's defense. The prince feigned a jab to the left and thrust toward Theb's belly.

The older man was ready for the move.

Ryckair found the chief miner's fists clamped tightly around his wrist.

Theb kicked Ryckair in the groin.

The prince's fingers opened and he dropped the knife.

Both men dove and reached the blade at the same time. They wrestled on the floor. The knife was knocked farther away.

Theb lay atop Ryckair. The chief miner put his hands around Ryckair's throat.

The prince slammed his fists against both sides of Theb's head.

Theb released his grip and arched his back.

Ryckair rolled over on top, grabbed the knife and pressed it against the chief miner's throat. In his mind, Theb became his treacherous brother, Yetig and the Barasha.

To Ryckair's surprise, the chief miner offered no defense. This intensified the prince's hatred. He wanted Theb to feel terror, know the sins he was about to die for, weep and beg for mercy.

Ryckair shouted, "Say something."

Theb dropped his hands to his side. One word came from his lips. "Free."

The memory of Lekto came to Ryckair. He asked himself if death was the only freedom anyone would find in the mines of the Sarte. *If the air holes prove impassable*, he thought, *will I become the new chief miner to deal out life and death?* The prince stood shakily and stared down at the prone figure. With a cry of rage, he threw the knife across the cavern.

Theb looked up at the young man who should have killed him. For years he lived in a waking dream of death. Numb was all he knew. Numb was all he sought. He no longer knew joy or sorrow, hope or grief.

He got to his feet. This man with the mark the Sarte sought was just another miner to him. He took no notice before. Now, he studied the other's stance. There was an air of command, and more. He stared at the dragon mark that so resembled the symbol of the house of Avar. "Who are you?"

Batu rose on one elbow as he clamped his hands over the wound on his leg. "He's Ryckair Avar, Prince of Carandir, son of King Haram and Queen Araney."

Theb fell to his knees. "Forgive me, Lord. Forgive your humble subject."

The change in Theb shocked Ryckair. The swaggering stance and authoritative glare were gone. The skin around the chief miner's eyes sagged. His hands shook.

Ryckair placed a hand on Theb's shoulder. "What's your lineage?"

"My father is Imara Reaka, Highness, ship's master of the *Nemtanka*. My mother is Yetal, senior scribe in the palace. I was first mate on the royal brigantine *Lion*, lost now more years than I know."

"Will you join us and escape from this place?"

"There's no escape, Highness. We're dead beyond death."

Ryckair raised Theb to his feet. "Take heart Theb Reaka, son of Imara and Yetal. We *will* escape from this place today and walk once more as free men beneath the sun."

They carried Batu back to the eating cavern.

Theb gave him a brew to drink. By the time the others returned from digging in the mines Batu was able to sit up.

Ryckair stood on the talking stone and surveyed the listless men in front of him. "Escape. To feel the cool breeze of the upper world on your face again. We need only scale this wall."

The men stared at him blankly. None moved or spoke.

A staccato tap sounded from the passage to the lagoon. Six Sarte armed with spears walked into the cavern. The humans moved aside as the fish men marched to the speaking stone. Their leader pointed to Theb. "You have failed to bring the prisoner to the appointed meeting place. You will die."

The leader looked at Ryckair and the mark. "You will follow us."

Theb stood silent. The other men bowed their heads.

The old fear returned to Ryckair. He was no leader. He'd be taken, Theb would die and the rest would remain in the hellish confines of the mines. He knew nothing of the world outside his books. Craya would know how to inspire them.

The thought of his brother filled him with fury.

He jumped from the rock podium. "Kill the Sarte." He grabbed a pick from one of the men and sunk it into the head of the Sarte leader.

The other miners exploded into a frenzied melee fueled by the release of pent-up hatred for their captors.

The Sarte tried to defend themselves. Their weapons were too long and unwieldy in the close-quartered combat that ensued.

Five of the human miners fell. Each was replaced by five more who swung their picks like battle axes. Within moments the fight was won. The Sarte lay dead upon the cavern floor.

Men who hadn't cheered since being entombed in the mines cried themselves hoarse with shouts of joy and victory. They laughed and hugged and danced with the elation known only to those who faced certain death yet lived.

Miners carried Ryckair on their shoulders to the talking stone.

All eyes turned to him as they cheered uncontrollably.

The prince raised his hands. "I'm Ryckair Avar, Prince of Carandir, a prince with no court, no army, and likely no power left in this world. I know you hail from many nations. An evil has risen that will destroy all. The followers of Baras have returned. Their goal is to release their master who will spread horror and death to every land. I ask you to follow me and fight under the banner of Carandir to restore freedom to the world. Our enemies are many and powerful. Yet, against greater terrors heroes have risen and won. Who will join me?"

A barrage of "I will" and "Carandir" echoed in the cavern.

The prince saw the men stand taller and walk with greater bearing.

Ryckair, Batu and Theb formed a privy council.

Theb was named narech.

The vine Ryckair dropped was augmented by dozens more. These were attached to the handles of picks. Men threw them like grappling hooks to catch on the edges of the air holes. Others scaled the wall. While a team worked at carving a passage through the air holes, the cooks gathered provisions.

The work continued past their normal mealtime. Just as the cooks returned from the lower caves, the digging party broke through and found a cavern where a gust of fresh air circulated.

The crew was recalled and the cooks prepared a great feast. The stew was rich and the mushrooms large. Food was carried to the men who stood watch at the pool lest the Sarte return unbidden.

At the end of the meal, they gathered their possessions and ascended the vines. The climb was high, though not difficult for men used to digging through rock.

A net was fashioned for Batu.

Ryckair looked down to the floor of the cavern. The bodies of the Sarte were sealed in one of the abandoned tunnels and the miners who died in the battle were reverently entombed in another. All the glow roots, picks, clothing and food were hauled up.

He raised the vines and coiled them neatly. The only thing left behind was a perfect mystery for the fish men.

Ryckair walked through the short tunnel and emerged into an immense space whose bounds were beyond the light of the glow roots. They stood on a six-foot-wide ledge carved into the face of a cliff that rose to unseen heights on one side and dropped to unknown depths on the other.

The prince turned to Theb "We must begin to conserve everything. No one is to eat or drink, except at designated rest times. Prepare a schedule."

He led the men up the path.

Light from the glow roots sparkled off the surface of the rocks. It reminded Ryckair of sunlight reflected off dew of a spring morning.

He quickened his pace not knowing if true escape lay ahead.

# CHAPTER THREE

Ryckair and his men walked at a brisk pace. Theb called for food and rest based on his best reckoning of the cycle from the mines. Picks were distributed among the men along with the spears taken from the Sarte. Ryckair kept one of the obsidian knifes.

When they halted, the prince posted guards ahead, behind and along the edge of the path to keep sleeping men from rolling into the abyss.

At one stop, Theb leaned against the wall of the path. "Tell us a story, Highness. Remind us of the world above once more."

"An epic tale of love and battle," said a man with no teeth.

Ryckair thought for a moment. "I've read many such epics in the vaults of the Kyar. There's one from the most ancient of days in the north continent, a time before Avar crossed south over the Great River."

A balding man turned from his watch on the ledge. "Highness, It's well known the north is a desolate waste, settled for a time by Carandir after Avar defeated the evil dragon."

"That's a popular misconception. The original home of Avar the Great was the city of Amblar on the Western Ocean of the North Continent. He took a host and settled on the south continent, then moved his capital to Meth."

Ryckair leaned against the rock wall. "This story is from a very old sonnet about two lovers, Stamered and Catio. Stamered was a prince of a mountain tribe and Catio a princess of a rival coastal people."

*Beat the wings, beat the wings,*
*A dove emerged from branch on high,*
*And in the cool spring forest air,*
*Stamered, prince of mountain people,*
*Cocked a shaft with careful aiming,*
*But never did that arrow fly,*
*For on a hill, in radiant view,*
*Sat Catio, the Princess fair,*
*Upon her pure white riding mare;*

*He paused his stallion silently,*
*And came upon the hill with stealth,*
*Lest the lovely maiden there,*
*Be a spirit kindled free,*
*Living as a doe, to bolt,*
*When the hunter comes in view,*
*Yet Catio saw not of him,*
*Lost was she in sorrow grieving,*
*For her brother dead in battle;*

*Upon his knee Stamered fell,*
*And cried aloud his love for her,*
*And Catio in turning quickly,*
*Saw the young man, fair and gallant,*
*And her heart went out to his,*
*Joining there within the forest,*
*Buttercups he gathered for her,*
*And with them made a chain of petals,*
*This to be her wedding garland;*

*Yet doom was laid upon these lovers,*
*For battle loomed between their tribes,*
*And Catio did not suspect,*
*That in the combat fought last eve,*

*Twas her own love, Stamered prince,*
*Who slew her only brother dear,*
*And Stamered knew not the man,*
*Whose heart his sword had pierced that day,*
*Catio's brother, Peetdeley;*

Ryckair paused and rubbed his eyes. "I'm afraid I don't remember the rest of the words. The lay continues to describe how Catio discovers Stamered slew her brother. She leaves in anger and rides her white mare into the forest. Stamered is so overcome with guilt and loss he comes before the main hosts of the warring armies and tries to halt a charge, only to be slain by his own father who doesn't recognize his son.

"Catio realized Stamered didn't kill her brother for want of murder. It was out of the unreasoning hatred between their families that infected them all with blood madness.

"She rode back and reached the plain just as the two hosts clashed. In horror, she watched as Stamered fell in his vain attempt to stop the battle.

"Filled with grief, she rode her horse off a cliff into the ocean.

"Stamered's body was taken to the beach and a funeral pyre lit. No flame touched his flesh, for a great wave came from the ocean, lifted his body and carried it out to sea. Those closest to the fire said that the white foam took the shape of a lovely maiden on horseback."

Theb 's eyes watered. "It is a sad tale, My prince."

"Yes, yet it is a hopeful one. Out of that day the two kings grieved the loss of their children together and ended their war. From the union of these people, the north monarchy was formed to eventually produce Avar the Great who contained Baras and brought about Carandir."

Ryckair and his party continued on the path along the cliff face. Batu's wound healed with remarkable speed. He was able to walk using one of the Sarte spears as a cane.

After the tenth sleep time, they encountered a waterfall. It cut across the ledge and blocked their way. The water dropped from an unknown height, flowed across their path through a trough five paces wide and fell with a deafening roar over the ledge. A bridge once spanned the water. All that remained were crumbled stone piers on either side.

Batu shouted over the noise of the torrent. "It's too wide to jump."

Ryckair hefted an axe in his hand. "We'll use the picks as grappling hooks with vines tied to them the same as we did in the Sarte mine."

It took three attempts before a pick blade snagged between two boulders on the far side. Ryckair secured the other end to the pier on his side and started across hand over hand.

Batu followed.

One by one, the men crept across.

The last three started.

When they reached the center, the vine snapped and they fell into the surge.

One man was dragged over the waterfall.

The others clung to the vine as they thrashed about.

Ryckair cupped his hands and shouted above the crash of the falls. "Stop twisting. Get a firm grip and move toward the bank"

The blade of the pick the vine was attached to cracked. It was dragged along the ground before it caught against another rock.

The climber nearest the edge lost his hold and was swept into the water and fought his way toward the bank. The river was too strong. He was pulled over the edge.

The last man scurried up the vine to safety. He fell to his knees and made the sign of the covenant, all the while praising the name of Jorondel.

Ryckair stood at the edge of the water.

Batu said, "There was nothing you could've done."

The prince continued to stare.


Six more sleep periods came. Provisions were running low. Batu's leg healed and he no longer needed the spear to walk, though he had a limp.

The trail plunged into a narrow trough whose top rose beyond the reach of their lights. After another sleep period, the canyon ended at a rock face with two tunnel entrances. The left passage continued on level while the right slanted down.

The prince conferred with Batu and Theb. They chose the left tunnel. Within a hundred paces, the company came to another split in the road with three passages. The center one climbed up while the others continued on the same level.

They took the center road with the idea it was best to continue up.

The company soon came to a small chamber. A spherical bulge protruded from the rock face directly across from the entrance. Two passages ran off to the right side of it and the others to the left. All of them continued on at the same level.

Only the first dozen of them were able to fit inside.

Batu raised an eyebrow. "We seem to have found a maze."

Ryckair studied the room. "This place reminds me of something from a book." He looked back to the entrance. "There were guards here. I'm certain of it."

The old song Mirjel's cousin sang in the garden so many years before came to mind. "This is the place from the Oola song. The tunnels were a defense. First two, then three, then four. That's how you knew you were on the right path" His vice echoed in the space as he recited.

> *Two, three, four, five,*
> *Keep the marching men alive,*
> *Seven, nine, twelve, fifty,*
> *Keep the Oola from the city;*
>
> *Left, center, right, down.*
> *Never let them find the town,*
> *Over the bridge and under the tower,*
> *There to find the morning flower.*

The balding man stepped forward. "I know that song, Highness. My mother sang it to me."

Batu frowned. "The Oola are just an old ghost story."

The prince looked up the right passage. "So were the Barasha. We've come up into one of the mines of the North Continent. There are more verses to the rhyme, but I can't remember them."

One of Ryckair's men in the rear of the company screamed and fell. An arrow protruded from his back.

Ryckair pointed to the man who knew the rhyme. "Guide them out. We'll follow."

The company streamed through the guard room. Arrows rained from behind. Three more men fell. A Flicker of torches were visible down the passage.

Batu, Theb and Ryckair stood guard.

The prince inspected the large bulge in the chamber wall. "It's a plug. Check around the side for a release mechanism."

Arrows bounced off walls as Theb and Batu searched for a latch.

One sailed through the entrance and sunk into Theb's right ankle. He clenched his teeth and continued to probe.

Two humanlike figures entered the chamber. Not quite as tall as Ryckair, each had muscular arms and large protruding jaws. They were covered in thick hair. Their snarls showed rows of sharp teeth.

One held a spear.

The other carried a stout wooden club with finger length metal spikes.

The prince swung his pick and caught one with the spear on the side of the head.

The Oola flailed as it fell dead to the floor with the tip of Ryckair's pick caught in its skull.

The prince was dragged down with the creature.

The second Oola swung its club.

Ryckair managed to roll away from the blow.

The spikes ripped into the body of the first Oola. Blood and gore spewed across the floor.

Ryckair kicked his attacker in the stomach.

The blow would have winded any human. The Oola grinned and raised its club for another strike.

The prince dove into the Oola's legs.

It toppled forward and struck its head against the rock floor, then staggered back to its feet in a daze. The Oola bared its teeth and slammed its fists into either side of Ryckair's head.

The prince reeled back and fell to his knees.

The Oola dropped its club and charged with clawed fingers extended.

There was a click.

The boulder hit the floor and rolled toward the tunnel.

Ryckair jumped to the side just as the huge stone passed.

The cracking of bone followed as the Oola was crushed. The boulder lodged in the entrance to block any further attack.

Ryckair ran to Batu and Theb. "That'll stop them for now. I'm afraid they'll be back soon."

Theb steadied himself against the wall. "The arrow's stuck in a bone. I can't walk."

Ryckair examined the wound. Blood oozed across Theb's dark skin. The prince remembered stories of how the Oola poisoned the tips of their arrows. He snapped off the end of the shaft and tore off a scrap of his shirt for a bandage. "We'll carry you."

"I'll only slow you. Kill me, Highness." He fainted.

Batu picked Theb up and headed for the archway. "Just what I needed, another madman."

They followed the route of the song and hoped the rhyme led true. No sound of pursuit followed. Ryckair offered to carry Theb. Batu said he was no burden, though the prince clearly saw that his friend still limped.

At another chamber, five passages led out. One of them continued up while another dropped down and the rest remained level. They took the downward path.

Ryckair was relieved to see the steady light of glow roots ahead as they dashed from the tunnel.

The other men stood on a ledge. Below was a vast plain. Above, stars shone against an evening sky. His lungs took in cool, fresh air.

Only fifty-one of the men from the mines remained after the Oola's attack. Ryckair was surprised they didn't show the joy of having escaped.

He looked down to the plain and saw thousands of torches carried by as many Oola. The creatures could've obliterated the humans, yet they waited.

In the distance, a bridge tower stood at the edge of a deep gorge. Across the chasm were the ruined remains of what was once a great city.

Torches parted at the rear of the plain to make way for a palanquin carried by six Oola. They stopped in front of the ledge.

An Oola taller than the others stepped out. Massive arms and legs showed the scars of many battles. On its head was a crown made from fragments of human skulls.

It stood, hands on hips, and looked at the men.

Ryckair was certain it was grinning.

The huge Oola pointed to a spot just behind the palanquin. It spoke in a snarling voice. "*Krash. Garack. Harch Narack Kalaketan.*"

Shouts rose from the Oola who took up a chant, "*Narack. Narack*"

They piled wood in a ring. A man Ryckair thought killed in the tunnels was dragged forward. His feet and hands were bound. Three arrows pierced his body.

The wood was set ablaze as the rhythmic chanting continued. The wounded man was tossed into the center of the inferno. His screams rose to a crescendo before they were cut off by the hoarse cheers of the Oola.

The Oola king leered at the prince.

Ryckair grabbed a pick from one of his men, leapt from the ledge and landed on top of the creature.

The force knocked the monster down.

Ryckair drove the pick deep into the creature's chest and drew his obsidian knife.

The Oola king clawed at the axe.

Ryckair sawed at the king's neck. The blade was sharper than any barber's razor and as hard as steel.

Blood gushed in a fountain as the Oola king flailed. The dragon mark on Ryckair's chest glowed brilliant blue. With a sharp snap, he twisted the Oola king's head from its body.

The other Oola cowered back.

Ryckair held the severed head by its hair as blood dripped to the ground. "Follow me."

The men fell into a column behind the prince.

The Oola gave way before the glowing dragon mark and the head of their fallen leader.

Two of the creatures lunged.

Ryckair shook the head and repeated the chant, "*Narack.*" He thought the word had something to do with fire. Whatever the meaning, it struck fear into the Oola.

The men reached the tower at the edge of the chasm to discoverer there was no bridge, just a duplicate tower on the other side.

Ryckair examined the bridge pier. "Seven, nine, twelve, fifty. Keep the Oola from the city."

Seven what? Did those in the city throw down the bridge to save themselves?

Batu pointed to nine stones set in the wall.

Ryckair pushed on the seventh one.

With a crash, a portcullis dropped and closed off the tower from the plain.

This broke the trance over the Oola. They charged the iron bars and clawed at the gate in a frenzy.

A boom resounded from the chasm, followed by the grind of metal on metal.

Two metal slabs rose from the sides of the canyon walls as a drawbridge whose roadway folded down rather than up. There was no physical connection between the two halves.

The Oola howled at the sight. Some scaled the side of the tower and tried to come around the stone walls. Those who attempted slipped on the smooth rock and fell into the abyss.

When the two sections met in the center, the men ran for the other side as the portcullis fell in under the weight of the Oola.

Ryckair threw the head of their fallen king into the path of the charging creatures.

A few paused and were trampled by the Oola behind.

The prince reached the other side with the Oola right behind.

"Twelve, fifty, twelve, fifty. Morning flower." He spoke the words aloud as he searched for their meaning. Along the edge of the landing was a low wall. On it were stone reliefs in the image of nerres flowers with petals in full bloom. The prince's mind flashed to his studies of botany. "Of course! Nerres was originally known as the morning flower."

Batu pointed to the wall. "There must be fifty."

Ryckair ran to the twelfth relief from the bridge. He pressed on the stone flower. Nothing happened.

He pried his fingers between the stone and pulled.

Again nothing.

He tried to remember the last verse. Walls. It was something about a wall. He wondered if the words referred to something on the wall or behind it. Safe behind them sounded familiar. It suddenly came to him.

> *Face east, search low,*
> *Till you find the one you know,*
> *Safe behind the city wall,*
> *Twist the petals, watch them fall.*

Ryckair took hold of the flower and twisted it.

The two halves of the bridge fell down and away as they slid back to rest within the chasm walls.

Screaming Oola dropped into the void.

The men cheered as hundreds of the hairy creatures fell to their deaths.

This last defeat broke the Oolas' spirits. They dropped their torches and fled from the plain.

A flash of brilliance erupted in the east.

They all stood in awe as they soaked in the first sunrise they'd seen in years.

Each fell to their knees and made the sign of the covenant.


The prince led his men into the deserted city. The air was chill. He sent scouts to look for shelter and anything they could make into clothing.

Theb didn't regain consciousness and developed a fever.

Ryckair was certain the arrow was poisoned. "I'm going to find some water so I can at least cleanse the wound."

Ryckair walked around the perimeter of the outer wall. It once enclosed a grand city with wide avenues and fine buildings. He imagined the marketplaces and fountains, the people bartering in the streets, the lively music of lutes and harps. The buildings were now rubble.

He climbed a set of stairs to the top of the west wall and heard an unfamiliar rumble and crash. It repeated rhythmically. When he reached the top, he stared with his eye open wide.

Before him stretched a wide, sandy beach. Waves rolled in and out along it. He knew it was the Western Ocean, a sight Ryckair had read of but never seen. He stood mesmerized by the force of the water. The Great River and Lake Hasp were a part of life. The sight of so much water moving in and out left him dizzy, as if a wave might reach up and take him at any moment.

Set into the wall was a round tower. Steps led to a solid wall where a door should've been. There were no windows. It was difficult to tell exactly how high it was. It seemed to rise and fall as he moved.

A chill ran down his spine as he recognized it as one of the wizard towers. There was a square tower in the Carandir barony of Barta. Baron Dek took Craya and him to visit it once.

The prince mounted the steps and touched the stones of an artifact as old as the Dragon Wars.

He left the tower and walked to the north wall. Just outside the city to the north was a river. It flowed toward the sea. Acres of reeds grew on its banks. He scooped up some water in a skin and hurried back. The other men returned to report several sheltered places to sleep but little else of use in the city.

Ryckair sat the bundle down. "How many men can make rope and weave baskets?" Most were sailors and knew the arts. "Good. There're more reeds than we can ever use along a river outside the city. We'll settle on one of these shelters, then weave ourselves clothes and boots. First, let's go to the river and bathe the filth of the Sarte and the Oola from our bodies."

Theb was settled in the cellar of a building. The chimney of a hearth was cleared and a fire lit. It soon became comfortable inside.

The men went to the river in groups and washed themselves. On their return, they brought back armfuls of rushes. Many, including Ryckair, used obsidian knives to shave their beards.

Batu ran his brown hand over his facial hair. "I've worn this since I was a youth. I'll just trim it as is the tradition of my people."

The men set about weaving the reeds into mats of different sizes. Loose grass was quilted between some. These were assembled in layers for pants, boots and jerkins that offered surprising protection from the cold. Mats for beds and a door were also woven.

The cooks returned with herbs, roots, mushrooms and berries. Ryckair identified several plants whose green leaves were edible. From these they made a fine dinner with dessert. The cellar was warm and pleasant by the time they ate their meal.

Batu rubbed his hands in front of the fire. "Ah, that's nice."

The prince popped a berry into his mouth. "Yes, I'll sleep tonight. Tomorrow we must plan. I need to determine what poison the Oola used."

"I've knowledge in this, Highness. More than a few have tried to slip something in my drink. There're ways to detect what poison is being used."

"Even if we can find an antidote, it might be weeks before he's ready to travel."

"We can make a litter and carry him."

"It's not just Theb. We all need time to see the world above ground again. This is a new land. There may be new enemies. You and I must drill the men until they act from instinct. I don't doubt their bravery, however most are merchant sailors with no soldiering experience."

At this, Batu chuckled. "I'm no soldier myself, Highness. The fact is, I've spent as much time as possible avoiding them."

"That's why you're qualified to train them. After all, you've studied military tactics to avoid capture, trained others to infiltrate territory and even how to fight. There's more soldier in you than you know, or perhaps would like to think."

Batu laughed. "And when we've trained our band of men, where do we march to?"

Ryckair stared into the fire. "Carandir. We make war upon my brother." Mirjel's face came to him along with a deep sickness in his heart.

Batu scratched his beard. "It'll take ships to cross the Great River."

"We have enough sailors. They might be able to build them."

"Well, we certainly can't buy any."


They gathered herbs and flowers. Batu prepared a white paste and spread the mixture over Theb's wound. The paste became dark purple.

"It's poison, Highness, and almost certainly comes from a mushroom. I'd say, by the color, it's Spotted Death Mask. They grow in caves and tunnels."

"Thank Jorondel you learned this art."

"It may do Theb little good. The poison's deadly. I know of no cure."

"I read something in a book. It was, oh what was it?" Ryckair looked at the door. "Yes." He left the cellar and returned with a handful of nerres, some thistles and a mushroom.

The prince combined the ingredients with some water in one of the metal eating cups and worked it into a runny liquid.

Batu eyed the concoction with suspicion. "How do we get him to drink it?"

"We don't. It has to reach the poison in his blood directly." Ryckair placed the cup on the fire. "We'll boil the remaining liquid off, then grind what remains with stones until it is a fine power."

"How does it get into his blood? Do we make a cut and pour it in?"

"The flow of blood would just wash it out. We'll make a pipe with one of the reeds and blow the powder up his nose. The medication will be absorbed. It's a technique used by the Daro."

A span passed before the liquid boiled off to leave behind dried lumps.

Batu washed off a slab of stone.

Ryckair used a rock to grind the dry substance into a powder. He placed it inside the tube of a small reed, positioned it in Theb's nostril and blew hard.

Theb awoke several days later. He looked around the room where he lay on a reed mat. "Have the Sarte come. Is the ore ready?"

Ryckair helped him sit up. "There're no Sarte, my friend. We're free."

It was nearly a week before Theb was able to stand. Ryckair told him of the escape from the Oola and how they found the city. Theb seemed confused and asked several times what had happened.

Over the following week, his wits returned. He worked with Ryckair and Batu to create plans of attack and defense for every possible situation their men might encounter.

Though Ryckair never gambled or drank with the young officers as Craya did, he absorbed military studies. From books assigned by Yetig and others found in the vaults of the Kyar, he read of battles and strategy.

Ryckair drew his officers, sergeants and corporals from those who served in the navy of several lands. He gathered them on an open space in front of the shelter. "We've escaped to walk once more above ground. Now, you must prepare the men to fulfill the oath taken in the Sarte mines. Every day, you'll drill them until the exercises become second nature. Together, we'll march on Carandir and gather those still loyal to the Crown before we confront the evil we've sworn to defeat."

Theb nodded. "I will follow you anywhere, my prince, but what tactics do we train the men in?"

"We must be ready both for battle in the south and any foe we find here. You'll have to teach the merchant sailors how to wield weapons for defense and attack. They must learn military discipline. We can't leave this place until they're trained to act without hesitation, no matter how long it takes."

# CHAPTER FOUR

In the palace at Meth, Mirjel sat motionless in her chambers.

Lek boiled water in the hearth and made kan for her mistress.

A Daro healer entered. "Highness, the spell is complete. As suspected, you carry Prince Craya's child."

Mirjel closed her eyes. "Dear Ilidel."

It was frustrating for Gilyon, Refran, Womb and Luja to hold a conversation via terec. Messages crossed and new comments were made.

This didn't matter to them. They would do anything to prevent the birth of Mirjel's child before she could introduce her blood line into the royal family.

Over several days, a plan was formed.

Mirjel stood on the balcony of her bed chambers on a starlit night. She listened to waves wash against the base of the rock pinnacle below. Even though there was no sign of pregnancy, she held her hand over her belly.

She no longer saw Craya. He was often drunk and ignored official duties. It fell on her to met with the ministers and hand out orders to keep the bureaucracy running. No one questioned her authority in the daily operation of the palace. However, the Barasha made it clear this authority didn't extend beyond.

Lek brought kan and a small cake. "You must eat, Highness."

"I'm not hungry, Lek."

"At least have some kan. Think of the child."

She thought of little else and was certain the Barasha intended to raise the babe, though they might use her to nurse the infant. Terror oozed through her as she wondered if the Barasha would kill her and Lek, or worse, once she was of no further use to them.

A knock came at the door.

Lek opened it a slit.

Baron Refran stood in the hall.

Lek stepped back and curtsied. "How may I help you, my lord?"

"I wish to speak with Princess Mirjel on urgent business."

Lek looked to Mirjel who nodded.

Once inside, Refran ran across the room and pushed Mirjel out onto a balcony that hung out over Lake Hasp.

She jammed her thumbs into both his eyes.

He cried out and released her as he held his hand over his face. "Where are you?"

Mirjel stepped back and bumped into the railing. A thud sounded.

Refran ran in her direction.

She she took two steps forward and dropped flat.

The baron tripped on her body. With a scream, he tumbled over the railing to the lake below.

Mirjel panted as she stood.

Lek ran to her. "Mistress, are you hurt?"

"No."

"Why did he attack you?"

"I don't know. He couldn't have been sent by the Barasha."

A mechanical click sounded in the room.

Mirjel reached for her bodice knife, only to remember Yetig's guards confiscated all her weapons. "Lek, stand behind me."

A part of the wall next to the hearth swung open.

Mirjel saw a stairway. Her first thought was a trap set by Craya and wondered if he had sent Refran to kill her. He was cruel enough. When he wasn't drunk, he wandered the halls of the palace. Sometimes he berated her to the servants and struck any who defended her. More often, he simply stood alone against the walls and muttered to himself.

Lek put her hands to her mouth. "What shall we do, Highness?"

Orane's voice came from the darkness. "Princess?"

Mirjel watched in disbelief as the chief Kyar stepped through the secret doorway. "Master Orane. How can it be? You escaped across the bridge. The servants saw it."

"It's a long tale, Highness. You'll hear it in full. For now, we have much to do."

She ran forward and took his arm. "Oh, Master. Is it really you?" She made the sign of the covenant with tears in her eyes. "Thank Ilidel."

Orane turned to Lek. "You must do something very brave and dangerous. Stay here and pretend your mistress is resting. Let no one enter until she returns."

"Yes, Master Orane."

"Now come, Highness."

Orane led her down the stairs and through many passageways until they came to a set of rooms where Kyar scholars sat at desks. Books and scrolls were everywhere.

Mirjel looked around in amazement. "What is this place?"

"Part of a complex of forgotten rooms and corridors from early versions of what people now see. The Kyar alone are aware of this palace within the walls and under the foundations of the visible one. We work in secret to combat the Barasha and smuggle food from the kitchens through hidden corridors."

Orane told her about the deception at the bridge and how the Barasha were convinced they escaped. "They looked for us and saw what they expected, so they assumed we left."

As they descended, the smooth rock walls gave way to rough-hewn stone. Mirjel didn't realize she retraced the very path Ryckair took on the day they first met.

She and Orane reached the cave entrance at the base of the rock pinnacle. A man stood next to a fishing boat. They climbed in and the fisher pushed the boat into the water.

There was no moon. Mirjel looked up to the palace and realized it was impossible for anyone looking over the parapets to see them in the dark.

The fisher rowed toward the docks of Meth. Mist swirled across the face of the water. Soft, muted points of light became visible as they neared the city.

The boat slipped under a pier. At its land end, several wooden slats slid aside to reveal a hidden dock beneath. At its end was a stone wall with an iron door.

Orane knocked on it with a staccato rhythm.

It swung open. Four armed men stood inside. They led the way down a torch lined corridor to another door.

Inside, Telasec sat at a table with an oil lamp.

Mirjel ran across the floor and threw her arms around the healer's neck. They all laughed and cried and touched one another to make the meeting real.

Telasec placed her hand on Mirjel's belly and asked about her health.

They drank kan and told small tales as they forgot, for the moment, the horror of the Barasha.

Mirjel put her mug down. "I wish we were able to talk all night. Lek can't keep the Barasha at bay forever."

Telasec patted Mirjel's hand. "You must make ready to flee the palace before the child is born, whether Ryckair lives or not. Our situation is more dangerous than we thought. Orane has cast many spells and one of them revealed a dark secret."

Orane told Mirjel about her distant relationship to the house of Avar and how the babe she carried would replace Ryckair and become the heir at birth.

Mirjel brushed the fabric of her dress. "I knew they intended to take the child, though this news fills me with dread." She stared into the lamp. "I can't leave yet. There's work to complete."

"What can be more important than the child you carry?"

"The people of Carandir. Each day many starve while huge shipments of food are sent to the army. Most is wasted or spoiled. I've been able to issue orders to divert a portion of it to markets and granaries. I know some of this gets to the people, yet local magistrates steal a good deal and sometimes no one knows the grain is there."

Orane squinted. "How do you create orders that no one suspects?"

Mirjel opened a pouch and produced Craya's signet ring.

The chief Kyar stared at it. "He'll discover this for certain."

Mirjel shook her head. "No one has any idea I possess the ring, least of all Craya. I took it months ago as he lay in a drunken stupor in his chambers. He's never looked for it. With this ring I am Carandir, at least as long as my decrees go unnoticed by the Barasha."

"What about Yetig?"

"He's too busy scouring the country for the dragon shaped key and my father. The daily administration of the palace is kept up by bureaucrats with no idea of what happens beyond their own desks. So long as I'm careful to move only small shipments, they'll never suspect."

Telasec thought a moment before she spoke. "This is important. It's also dangerous. If they take the babe, all is lost."

"I realize this. You must give me a poison that'll kill me and the babe I carry if I'm discovered. Give me enough for Lek as well. I won't have her taken by the sorcerers."

Orane and Telasec looked at each other.

Telasec's face was drawn. "I understand your need to help, child. I see the starvation every day. The stakes are so high if you fail."

"I want to live." Mirjel's words became ragged and tears formed in her eyes. "I want to see Ryckair again and hold him. I'm queen in all but name and queens have a higher duty. You will give me the poison and we'll save the people for as long as we can. The Servants of Baras will never have my baby. By all the dragons I swear this."

Telasec bowed. "Yes, Highness."

"Our spies can help," said Orane. "If we know when grain's diverted, we can intercept it and distribute it to those in need."

Together, they finalized a plan. Mirjel would send a message to Orane when grain was shipped. Telasec would take care of the rest. When there was enough grain for the winter, Mirjel and Lek would make their escape.

Mirjel placed the signet ring back in its pouch and said farewell to Telasec, then she and Orane left for the palace.

A deep sense of relief flooded her as the boat moved across Lake Hasp. Then, the dread returned as she fingered the pouch with the two vials of poison Telasec gave her. She wrapped her cloak tightly around herself.

Mirjel secretly diverted shipments of food from the army storehouses around Meth.

Telasec distributed them to the needy across Carandir.

The princess calculated how much grain was in the last shipment as she was rowed across Lake Hasp to another meeting. Her pregnancy was nearing the second term and the movement of the boat left her nauseous.

When they reached the secret meeting room under Meth, Orane helped her to a chair. "Highness, you've fed many who might otherwise have starved. We must now end the shipments of food. It is time to leave."

"I just need a few more weeks before there's enough food secreted away to last through the winter."

Telasec shook her head. "Highness, please. If we delay the Barasha will take the babe."

"The Barasha won't have my child. Lek and I carry the poison at all times. To flee now will bring starvation to whole cities. None can take my place in court."

The door flew open.

Six armed Carandir soldiers walked into the room, followed by Narech Yetig.

# CHAPTER FIVE

Yetig bowed formally. "Good evening, Your Highness."

Mirjel forced herself into the outer composure she used in court. "Am I to be spied upon like a common servant, Narech Yetig?"

"I've neither the time nor patience to banter with you, Princess. Your secret meetings have been known to me for weeks." He took a rolled parchment from his doublet.

Mirjel recognized it as the order she issued that morning.

He placed it the table. "I know all your secrets."

She knocked the parchment to the floor. "Then kill us now and have done with it."

The narech removed his gloves. "That presupposes I've come to kill you." He sat in one of the wooden chairs and motioned for his men to close the door. "Princess Mirjel, I bring you the throne of Carandir."

Mirjel laughed. "Tell your Barasha masters they'll have to find their sport elsewhere."

"I play no game." He snapped his fingers.

One of his men stepped forward and placed four silver goblets on the table. Another poured wine.

Yetig raised one of the goblets. "Join me in a toast to formally seal our bargain." He pushed another goblet across the table toward Orane.

The chief Kyar sat still. "We make no bargains with sorcerers. We're

Carandirians, sworn to defend the Crown."

Yetig slammed his fist on the table. "As am I, blind fool."

Orane stood and slapped Yetig.

The soldiers reached for their swords.

Yetig held them back, then fell to his knees. "I beg forgiveness, ancient one. I spoke in haste and intended no disrespect. I, too, am Carandirian, sworn, as are you, to defend the monarchy from all enemies, both without and within."

He looked up. "Once we were a proud people who held sway throughout the world. For three generations, Carandir has lost both territory and prestige after the traitorous concessions to the New Nobility."

Mirjel placed her hand over her swollen belly. "Need I remind you, Narech Yetig, I carry the blood of the Eastern houses, as does the child in my womb. Rascalla has always owed allegiance to the Crown; not to traitors; not to the Barasha."

Yetig stood. "I owe no allegiance to the sorcerers. When they first came to me with their plot, I knew, in time, they would grow too powerful for me to control, so I feigned none. Their path walked beside mine, to replace the government with one that will return the nation to greatness. They've fulfilled their purpose."

The narech set. "Master Orane, your books have secrets to bring about the Barasha's defeat. I know you and the other Kyar hide beneath the palace with them. Don't worry. Reshna suspects nothing. Your trick at the gate was most convincing. I'd have never known were I not high up in the southern tower to see your phantom wagons charge through a closed portcullis my men saw as open."

He turned to Mirjel. "As for the grain diversions, Highness, I've had to cover your blunders. Several clerks were dispatched to the Dragons' Halls when they discovered your plot."

Mirjel wanted to scream and strike Yetig until her fists were bloody. He'd made fools of them all. Worse, people died because of her mistakes.

Instead, she smoothed the material of her dress. "And when the Barasha are removed, what keeps you from removing us? Why offer me Carandir?"

"Craya's more inept than I imagined. On the other hand, you, Princess Mirjel, have ruled in his stay as a queen of old. I know the babe you carry will become the heir at birth. While you act as regent until the child takes the crown, I'll use our armies to extract the tribute due a mighty nation. You'll have ultimate power and I'll be your servant. Carandir will regained its position in the world."

"And if I choose to execute my servant?"

"So be it. You'll be set on the course I began. I'll die with honor. However, I believe you'll find me more useful alive."

"Craya's still the legal ruler."

"Many fatal accidents occur each day. Everyone knows he drinks too much. He could slip on a stair or balcony. It's a simple matter to arrange."

"A simple matter?" She hated Craya and dreamed of his death. Yet, to discuss it so coldly sickened her. "What of my father?"

Yetig paused. "That's a more delicate question. At the moment he's an outlaw and holds neither rank nor property. However, he'll be the grandfather of the heir and, thus, accorded special privileges. That will not, regrettably, include political power. This assumes he's not killed by the army that now hunts him."

Her mind focused on the question whose answer she most feared. "And Ryckair?"

Yetig took in a long breath. "Prince Ryckair is presumed dead."

"How could you know such a thing? Craya had him marooned on an island in the ocean away from the Barasha."

"The sorcerers had nothing to do with this. The Sarte attacked the ship His Highness was aboard before it reached the island. The Barasha contacted the fish men. Reshna asked them to look for a man with a dragon mark on his chest. They reported finding no such prisoner in their mines. He must have drowned in the river along with many of the crew."

Mirjel forced herself to show no outward expression of emotion, even though Yetig's words ripped through her. "How long have you known this? Why wasn't I told this before?"

"Reshna ordered the information suppressed. Even Prince Craya is unaware his brother's fate."

Mirjel smoothed the fabric of her skirt. "I wish to confer with my council."

"As you desire, Highness. My men and I will wait outside." Yetig rose and led the soldiers into the hallway.

Orane stared at the closed door."Yetig betrayed the Crown once. He can't be trusted."

Telasec spread her hands wide. "We must think of Mirjel and the child she carries. Yetig may offer us time to defeat the sorcerers."

They debated both sides as Daro and Kyar often did in their search for a common answer.

Mirjel looked to the floor and spoke in a whisper. "What if Ryckair escaped? He could return."

Telasec put her arms around Mirjel. "We both know how you love him, child. We also know it hurts deeper than bone to have him gone like this. You've shown more than courage with your grief. You must think of yourself now and of the child you carry. That rogue, Yetig, is right about one thing. You've run the affairs of a nation plagued with drought and famine and sorcerers. It's as much as any monarch can claim, back to Avar himself, as Ilidel is my witness."

Mirjel sat for a long time and stared into the light of the oil lamp. She made the sign of the covenant. "We'll accept Yetig's offer. It gains the hope of time. I can't see what will come, for even the next sunrise is unknown. We must do as best we can for Carandir, whether Ryckair returns or not."

Yetig was called inside. They toasted their new alliance.

Mirjel raised her goblet and held back tears as she pictured Ryckair's face in her mind. *Forgive me, my love*, she thought, *be you alive or in the Dragons' Halls*.


Au was surrounded by a wall with two gates to the north and south. The majority of the city overflowed its walls and spread across the land to encroach on farms and orchards.

Jea attended many balls and parties. She spoke pleasantries and gave compliments. The culture of Au was far different than that of Carandir. Men owned most of the businesses. The few women in commerce inherited their holdings from dead husbands. They were expected to bequeath them to a male relative upon their death.

The entire council was male and always had been. There were no female militia members or bureaucrats.

Jea used this fact to flatter the men she met. Her reputation for charm and grace spread. She became the most sought-after guest.

In the background, Amar diced and drank with many men, especially councilors Tradas, Dobeta and Giltom. The fortune Jea brought was considerable. Amar could afford to lose often. He cultivated the reputation of a fun-loving man who enjoyed sport.

The captain was once posted to the palace and watched the subtle but effective techniques of influencing others. Through flattery, and a little bribery, he convinced several councilors to support a cause Jea would present. He offered no details. The councilors promised to do so as they continued to take Amar's money.

Months passed. At the end of a dice game, Amar scooted two gold coins across the felt to Councilor Dobeta. "Wait until next time, my friend." He laughed. "My luck has to change."

When the others left, Dobeta took Amar aside. "I wanted you to know the council will send a request to meet Baroness Jea. She should be prepared next week."

Amar bowed. "Thank you. I'll tell her."


Jea stood before the council of Au with Amar at her side. "My Lords, I bring grave news that threatens all including Au. The Barasha have risen and intend to release Baras."

There was a rumble as she described the coronation, the demon cloud and the attack on Rascalla.

"This darkness will consume the world. We who hold faith with the dragons must rise together and fight the sorcerers before they release Baras to spawn a new Dragon War. Carandirians who are loyal to the Crown need your support. Please, commit your militia."

Naston, head of the council, held a patronizing stare. "Your description of the demon at the coronation is disturbing, yet trade continues. The council is aware changes have come to Carandir, though only a few captains and crews know of this. They've only spoke to the council about it. The situation is not general knowledge. We don't interfere with the affairs of foreign nations, especially when profits are good. The Barasha pay well. Even if they gain access to the crown, the chronicles only say it formed the subduing spell. There's no mention of a spell to wake the evil one. Most scholars believe

Baras will sleep for eternity."

Giltom was visibly shaken. "Still, if the Barasha decided to take control of Au as well, it would threaten our people and stifle commerce."

Naston was unmoved. "We can sue for peace and appease the sorcerers. It's written others did so in the past."

Tradas spoke sharply. "And the tomes say the Servants of Baras betrayed their word."

Dobeta's voice trembled. "To call a demon is a force we're unable stand before,"

Naston sat back in his chair. "Why should we start a conflict when it could threaten trade? The cost would be horrendous. We'd have to make the Barasha's presence public knowledge. No merchant would agree to new taxes when commerce is so good."

Another councilor leaned forward. "With all due respect, Baroness Jea, should it not be Baron Dek here before us today? It's not the habit of this council to entertain talk of war from a woman who should be tending her own business."

Jea kept her composure. "My husband fights the sorcerers. If this council fails to act, the Barasha will indeed march on Au and seize your wealth. They know only terror and power. No land is safe."

Naston stood. "All in Au hold faith with the dragons. They've always protected us. We need to take this under advisement. You'll learn our decision soon."

The next week, a minor clerk came to the cottage. "The council has chosen not to act on your petition for military aid to Carandir at this time." The clerk left before Jea could say a word.

She sat on a divan. "I feared this all along. The council has never seen beyond short turn profits. They live in the past and fear anything then think threatens stability."

A knock came at the door.

Amar admitted a man with pale skin and mono-lidded eyes with epicanthal folds.

Jea was introduced to him at several parties as Ambassador Exor from Xinglan, a monarchy located to the far east on the southern shores of the Great River.

Exor bowed. "Baroness, may I speak with you?"

Jea indicated a chair.

Exor spoke in a soft voice. "Councillor Dobeta confided in me about the decision to deny Carandir aid. I was disappointed. They don't see the threat and think the coming terror will pass them by. Millennia ago, my ancestors stood against Baras and suffered greatly. We've not forgotten the courage of Avar. Please, allow me to escort you to Xinglan. I believe you'll find a different reception."

"Thank you, Ambassador."

The next day, Exor arrived at Jea's grandparents' house in a horse drawn carriage.

Her grandmother hugged her. "Be careful, dear." She stepped back to dab her eyes.

Jea's grandfather enveloped her in a hug. "We'll do what we can to convince the council. Don't give up hope. Fight on. You've always been brave and smart. You'll find a way."

She and Amar traveled north over low hills to the docks of Au. Men loaded and unloaded goods to and from ships.

They boarded the ambassador's galley.

The rowers fought their way upstream. Unlike the banks of the Great River near Meth with its tall cliffs, barren plains spread along the bank east of Au.

Wind blew in gusts and picked up dust. Everyone covered their noses and mouths with brightly colored bandanas.

Each night, Exor hosted Jea and Amar to supper. The food was unknown to her with vegetables, meat and fish cut into small, bite size portions. Forks were supplied to Jea and Amar. Exor picked up the food with two sticks held between the crook of his thumb and his middle finger.

She took a bite,. "Ambassador, this is delightful."

Exor smiled. "I'll relay your compliment to the cooks. It's simple fair."

Captain Amar laughed. "Simple? I can't imagine what banquets are like in your country."

Over a month later, a peak appeared on the horizon. It extended to the banks of the river.

As they approached, Jea saw openings cut into the rock.

Fishing boats dotted the river. In one, men and women pulled nets filled with fish into their boat and sang a call and response work song together.

> *Haul in the net,*
> > *The fish are jumping;*
> *Haul in the net,*
> > *Their silver scales shine;*
> *Haul in the net,*
> > *The deck is filling;*
> *Haul in the net,*
> > *Tonight, we will dine.*

The galley docked at a stone pier.

People walked along paths carved into the mountain. Some went in and out of openings.

Exor raised an arm toward the mountain. "Welcome to Xinglan."

They walked into an enormous cavern. There were paths, fountains and parks illuminated by sunlight that came from openings above capped with crystal the same as the audience hall in the palace. Whole buildings of many stories were carved in the stone. People wandered the underground streets.

Exor guided Jea and Amar. "Quarters have been arranged, baroness. I've send a petition for an audience with our queen."

"Thank you, Ambassador, for all you've done."

On the north continent, Theb oversaw the daily drills of the men as they were marched in columns and dispersed into squares. They moved up hills, down hills, through the river and between buildings. Squads attacked each other in mock battles. Bows were made and arrows fledged to augment the picks and spears. After ten weeks of drills, the men moved with the precision of a military unit.

The first flurries of snow dusted the ground. Ryckair considered wintering where they were. He decided it was better to march as far east as possible and prepare for an assault on his brother in the spring. They could hire themselves out to raise funds for passage by ship, if any in the north would traverse the Great

River to Carandir.

On a brisk, sunny morning, Ryckair led his men through the east gate of the city. This was little more than a gap in the crumbled walls.

The clothes and boots they wove from reeds and grasses offered unexpected warmth against the cold.

A well-marked road took them up a hill. Tall grass poked above the snow. At brightnail, they approached the summit.

Ryckair looked back to the plain where the city stood. To the south was the ravine separating it from the Oola hordes. North, the nameless river flowed into the ocean.

He continue up the hill when he spied a group of men on horseback. Ryckair signaled to Theb who formed the troops into a line with the spearmen in front, those with picks behind them, and the archers in the rear.

The horsemen halted several paces away. One of them rode forward. He was dressed in rough animal hides and sported a tangled beard.

Ryckair moved his hand near the obsidian knife strapped to his side.

The man eyed the prince, then looked over to Ryckair's men, and finally back to the prince. His speech was modern Carandirian with a thick accent that rolled each pronunciation of the letter *r*, gave emphasis to the first syllable and long emphasis to the vowels "I have never seen the like of your men.".

"We're travelers. Tell me, friend, where can we find the nearest settlement?"

The man smiled with yellow teeth, many of which were missing. "You must come from very far away to ask such a question."

"We do."

"Then you seek in vain, friend. There are no settlements here, only the hills and the Oola and the city of ghosts, which you were either very foolish or very bold to enter. It is death to do so."

"We seem to have survived."

The ruffian laughed, then hardened his features. "Drop your pitiful weapons and form a line. You will make fine slaves." He drew a sword.

Ryckair neither spoke nor moved.

The brigand gave a raspy cry and spurred his horse forward. The rest of the outlaws charged.

The bandit leader reached Ryckair and slashed.

The prince dropped to the ground and rolled to one side.

The slaver overextended his cut as he tried to strike the prone Ryckair and almost lost his balance.

Another mounted man came up from behind and tried to run the prince down.

Again, Ryckair waited until the horse was almost upon him, then jumped to the side opposite the attacker's sword arm. As the horse passed, he pricked the animal's hindquarters with his dagger.

The mount reared up. Its rider was thrown to the ground.

Ryckair drove his blade into the man's chest, then pulled the sword from the slaver's hand.

The brigand captain charged full on the prince.

Ryckair mounted the dead slaver's horse and rode straight for the bandit leader.

The two men exchanged blows as they passed.

When the rest of the outlaws reached Ryckair's men, Theb raised an arm, then snapped it down.

The spearmen dropped to one knee and secured the ends of their weapons in the ground.

The archers let fly shafts.

These struck three of the charging attackers.

The rest drew their swords and spurred their horses on.

The archers fired a second volley.

Four more slavers fell.

The remaining outlaws pulled back and regrouped, surveyed the scene for an instant, then galloped away.

The slaver chief slashed at Ryckair, then fled after his men.

The prince pulled up on the reigns. "Excellent, men."

A woman's voice spoke in the same heavy accent as the brigands. "Yes. Truly Outstanding."

Ryckair looked up to the ridge of the hill to see at least two hundred mounted soldiers. Some carried pikes, others bows. All wore swords strapped to their sides.

A young woman with long red hair and green eyes sat on a horse at the head of the column.

# CHAPTER SIX

The prince raised one hand.

His men stood still.

The red headed woman gave a signal. A quarter of her troops rode in pursuit of the brigands.

She walked her horse forward. "We have pursued these slavers for several days. You have killed many and delayed the others, a remarkable feat for a beggar army. Normally, you would be rewarded, yet you have broken our most sacred law and entered the forbidden city."

"We're unaware of your laws."

"Silence! You stand as trespassers upon the Kingdom of Dharam. I am Shara, daughter of King Masalta and general of his fifth royal army. By what name are you known?"

"Ryckair, Princess Shara."

She laughed. "Address me as general. It is the title that pleases me best for it is earned. Of what land do you come?"

"From many lands, general. We escaped from the mines of the Sarte and fought our way through the Oola."

She considered this for a moment. "Then dismount and unarm yourselves. You and your men will march with me, Ryckair of many lands. Your crime of trespass can be judged by King Masalta alone."

Mirjel sat in her chambers as Yetig held a parchment and slammed his fist against a table. "Madam, it is perfectly acceptable to intercept shipments to remote outposts. They have no way to know when the ration's been cut. These diversions come from the city militia. The Barasha would've had news of it before evening."

"People are starving."

"How many more do you think will starve if your diversions are discovered?" He threw the orders Mirjel issued onto her writing table. They bore the seal of Craya, Prince of Carandir, though, as always, it was Mirjel's hand that held the signet ring.

Yetig refastened his doublet. "I was able to intercept this, though it required a clerk to be dispatched to the Dragons' Halls."

Mirjel closed her eyes at the news of another life ended. In the weeks since Yetig stormed into their secret meeting she learned how many deaths he ordered to cover up her activities. She always thought herself clever. Now, she realized without Yetig's intervention the Barasha would have discovered her plot long before.

She knew Yetig's anger was justified. The original shipment left a week early. She thought no one would notice the new order. Her cheeks flush with rage, not for the death, rather, for her acceptance of it.

Yetig adopted a gentler voice. "Your concern for the people of Carandir is noteworthy."

Long hours spent each day as the De facto head of a nation on the edge of starvation left Mirjel exhausted. She needed to talk with someone about the burden of the daily decisions she faced.

Telasec was secreted within the hidden rooms under Meth.

Orane and his brother Kyar were busy in the old lower vaults.

Mirjel certainly couldn't speak with Craya about her burden, though she still needed him to hold the figure of power while she manipulated the affairs of state. She longed to tell Craya just how much she loathed him. Yetig counseled her to keep up the pretense and speak to the prince in a courteous manner.

Yetig. She hated him for his treachery. Now, though she despised the realization, she relied on him for advice and praise. *Sweet Mother of Dragons*, she thought, *without his support I would've gone mad long ago.*

Though it pained her to admit it to herself, she admired him for his ability to turn the course of a mighty nation from behind the throne. It was contrary to her nature. An enemy faced straight on with a knife or sword was the way of her people. Still, she saw the power of Yetig's political maneuvering. He was ruthless, yet, when necessary, gentle and compassionate.

She brushed the fabric of her skirt. "You are right, of course."

Yetig tossed the parchment into the fireplace and stirred the ashes. "Soon we'll remove the Barasha."

"Yes, if soon comes in time?"

A month passed while Jea and Amar waited. They enjoyed the food and parks. Captain Amar took a particular liking to the local cuisine.

A messenger arrived. "Baroness Jea. Captain Amar. Her Majesty, Queen Quanto, summons you to an audience in one span. An escort will call for you."

Exor arrived half a span later. "It's my honor to accompany you into the royal presence."

He led them through high, double doors. The audience hall of Xinglan was resplendent with tapestries depicting hunting, fishing, battles and dragons.

Queen Quanto sat on a modest chair.

Jea, Amar and Exor fell to one knee.

Quanto raised a palm. "Rise, my guests. Ambassador Exor has spoken of your plight. Please, tell us the story in full."

Jea recounted the same tale she presented in Au. Amar provided military information received from Colonel Herrik.

When Jea finished, Quanto frowned. "It is a troubling story. We now understand why terec messages have not been responded to from our ambassador in Meth."

Quanto leaned forward. "Xinglan stood with Avar the Great when he subdued Baras. The rise of the Barasha from death comes unlooked for."

Amar bowed his head. "Great queen, if Baras is awakened, will the dragons intercede?"

"That is unclear. With the coming of Avar, the dragons gave the world to humans, though the Daro and Kyar hold some remnants of true magic and I retain some power. The sorcerer's revival endangers the Great Plan. We must withdraw and consider our options."

∾  ✛  ∾

In the palace at Meth, Mirjel made her way down the main staircase of the north tower. She planned to read reports and sign papers as usual. At sunset, guards would escort her back to her chambers. It was then she would open the secret passage and step through with Lek to escape the palace and the Barasha. Her child would be born far to the east.

Narech Yetig was away on maneuvers with the largest part of his own troops. He arranged for his men to be relieved by Craya's Sinkarakan guards. They would carry the blame for Mirjel's disappearance.

Two of Yetig's men walked with Mirjel as she descended the stairs.

Craya came staggering up from below.

Several weeks had passed since Mirjel last saw him. She was shocked by the change in his appearance. It wasn't just the crumpled and stained clothes he wore, where once he dressed in immaculate uniforms. Neither was it the filthy, uncombed hair and beard. What struck her was the hopeless stare of his eyes.

He clutched a wine bottle as he wove up the steps.

They met at the midpoint.

Craya stared at her as he swayed from side to side. He made a mocking bow. "My dear wife." His speech was slurred.

The guards moved to block him from Mirjel.

Craya waved his hands. "Dogs. Don't you recognize your master? I still rule here, in name at least." He stared at Mirjel's belly. "They probably won't even let me see it. Heir to all I possess." He raised his arms to indicate the palace. "Heir to nothing."

Mirjel forced a smile. "Good day, my lord. I was on my way to read reports on the food supply. I know how you hate to be disturbed with such trivial matters." She tried to move on.

Craya grabbed the papers from her. "I read the reports here." He swayed and nearly fell down the stairs.

Mirjel continued to hold a frozen smile.

Craya's voice erupted in an accusatory shout. "Stop grinning at me. I know what you're doing. You mean to usurp me. You and those filthy red-robed monsters."

"Your Highness is mistaken."

"Don't lie. You mock me. You whisper behind my back. You tell everyone how much you despise me and you think I don't know." He slapped her across the face.

The slap burned Mirjel's cheek. Without thinking, she slapped him back and spit in his face.

Craya gave a deep animal growl and reached for her throat.

She tried to run. Her foot slipped on the tread and she tumbled down the steps.

The guards ran after her.

Mirjel lay in a daze. She looked back up the stairs to see Craya stand in place for a moment before he turned and fled.

One of the guards send the other for a healer.

She was nauseous, then screamed as ripping pain shot through her abdomen.


Shara's troops led Ryckair and his men past rolling grasslands and into pristine expanses of forest. They climbed steadily up foothills where the green needles were covered in a white blanket of snow. Stone bridges took them over frozen streams and rivers. To the north, towering mountains rose. The column's route continued east.

Ryckair's men were free to talk among themselves, though the Dharam soldiers ignored questions. Ryckair wondered if they understood the Carandir language at all. Only Shara spoke with him in a dialect so heavy it seemed almost another tongue.

The hills became mountainous. After nine weeks of travel, they crested a peak. Before them lay a valley with a wide river free of ice. Across it stood a walled city.

Shara halted the column. "Behold, Ryckair of many lands. Kackar. Capital of the Dharam."

It reminded Ryckair of the walled cities on the eastern borders of Carandir, though larger. One gate opened to the south and another to the north. Soldiers with bows walked along the parapets.

The company crossed the river on barges and was marched through the north entrance by Shara's troops. This was secured with a heavy wooden gate and an iron portcullis.

Few buildings stood more than a single story tall. Each bore a high-pitched roof from which snow tumbled. The walls of the structures were thick with deep, inset windows shuttered against the cold. Some were constructed with wood frames. Most were made of stone and brick.

Chimneys spewed thick, black smoke. Thousands of homes and shops belched fumes from cooking and heating fires. It cast haze and left a sooty deposit everywhere.

They walked along streets filled with the filth of animal droppings and sewage. The people looked much like Shara with mostly red or dark hair.

In the center of the city was a compound. It was the largest structure, though only a quarter the size of the Carandir palace. A wall wrapped around it. Towers three to five stories tall were set at uneven intervals.

Shara delivered Ryckair and his men to a detachment of guards at the palace gates.

She saluted. "Farewell, Ryckair of many lands. Mayhap we shall meet again."

The prisoners were herded down stone stairs to a space with no windows. A cage made of iron strapping filled the area. The door only came up to their chests. They were forced to stoop as they entered. The air was stifling with the stench of urine. Straw covered the floor in damp mats.

Several spans passed before a man pushed a cart with a large kettle up to the cage. He looked very different from the people in the city. His complexion was fair. He had sandy blond hair like the prince. The man ladled stew into bowls and passed them through a slot in the cage.

Ryckair moved close to the server. "Can you understand me? Who are you? Where do you come from?"

"He is Fadella." Ryckair looked up to see Shara step down into the dungeon with two Dharam guards behind her. "They are a wild people of the north, uncivilized and untamable. Many live in the mountains around the valley where their tribes raise what they can and steal what they can't. This one can indeed understand you, though he knows the consequences of speaking to prisoners."

Shara cocked her head slightly.

Ryckair felt like a prize horse being inspected.

She motioned for the door to be unlocked. "Step out, Ryckair of many lands. King Masalta calls you to judgment."

The prince was taken to a room where roasted meats, dried fruits and pitchers of cold, fermented goats' milk were laid out on linen-covered tables.

The meat and fruit tasted almost too rich. The fermented milk was strong and heady yet refreshing on his throat.

The guards and servants left the room. Shara remained.

She took a winter berry from one of the trays and put the succulent fruit to her lips, then bit off the smallest nibble. "Ryckair." She said the name slowly as she smoothed her clothing the way Mirjel was often wont to do.

Ryckair took in a sharp breath at the memory.

Shara smiled. "Do you find me alluring, Ryckair of many lands?"

"As a great cat of prey, general, striking and deadly."

She laughed. "And now, you must be bathed and dressed to meet the king."

She slapped her hands. Two women who bore a resemblance to the servant in the prison appeared and began to strip the thatch clothing from Ryckair's body.

He held fast to them. "I can bathe and dress myself."

Shara laughed again. "Does the attention of women disturb you?"

"I prefer privacy."

"Alas, it is a luxury not offered to prisoners."

One of the serving women pulled off Ryckair's woven shirt and exposed the dragon mark.

The other servant stared, then fell to her knees as she made what appeared to be the sign of the covenant.

Both women repeatedly chanted the word, "Parili."

Shara slapped the closest. "None of that blasphemy." She inspected the mark carefully. "What trick is this?"

She tried to rub the mark from Ryckair's chest. When it didn't come off, she struck the other servant. "Dress him. Cover that mark. To speak of it is your death." She threw open the doors to the chambers. Four guards stood outside. "Take him to the audience hall when he is ready. I go to my father." She marched down the corridor.

Ryckair was escorted by guards. He noted peeling plaster on the walls and ceilings. Many tapestries were worn and dirty.

The audience hall was dark and tainted with smoke from torches set along the walls.

At the east end of the chamber an obese man overflowed his throne. He wore a heavy fur coat under an animal hide cloak. His hair and beard were bright red with flecks of gray. A golden crown studded with jewels adorned his head. A chalice rested in his hand.

Shara, surrounded by other women of the court, stood behind the throne. All wore finely groomed furs.

A man in a Carandir uniform pushed his way forward.

Ryckair gasped. "Petstra."

The commander's face was covered with scars. His left arm was missing. "Greetings, Prince Ryckair."

# CHAPTER SEVEN

King Masalta raised his chalice. "Welcome, Ryckair Avar. Long have our cousins to the south remained away. We are pleased two emissaries of the dragon-crested crown bless our court." Like Shara, he spoke a thickly accented form of the Carandir tongue.

Ryckair bowed to the king as he kept Petstra in sight. "Our cousin Dharam speaks truly. For too many years have our people been asundered."

He let his eyes stray above the king to Shara. She stood next to two other women. Her eyes slid sideways and caught his, then moved off as if to show him no special concern.

Masalta handed the chalice to a servant. "Let us continue the entertainment begun before the prince arrived. Commander Petstra was the last to weave a tale for our amusement. His, as I recall, told of a brother consumed with jealousy, who plotted to steal a crown. This traitorous prince took a ship filled with treasure and escaped. The matter would have been laid to rest were it not for the concern of the injured brother, who, after taking the crown, sent emissaries to bring his beloved sibling home."

Masalta sat back in his throne. "Does our cousin care to join with his own story?"

Ryckair noted Masalta's reference to a king. A shudder ran through him for an instant as he pictured Craya on a throne with Mirjel next to him. He wondered if this was true, or just a lie Petstra told. "A fanciful tale indeed, yet I tell another of a beloved brother seduced by evil and a treacherous officer who plotted both to steal a monarchy and murder a prince. Yet, that prince didn't die. Fate led him to his true friends."

"And what evil can overcome the reason of a loving brother?"

"That evil called Barasha."

A mumble echoed through the hall. One of Masalta's ministers whispered in the king's ear. A grave look came to Masalta's face. "Other tales have reached our ears. They seemed too fantastic to be entertained. Now, we will explore those lost tales further. Is there some sign to illuminate this story?"

Ryckair went to open his shirt and show the dragon birthmark. He stopped as he remembered the reaction of the Fadella women. Masalta might have him killed to remove a threat to his power. The prince decided to wait. "For time uncounted, the prince in this tale and the men who served him mined copper for the Sarte beneath the Great River before they gained their freedom and took the spears of their captors as proof. These were surrendered to the great and mighty Dharam troops. All proofs of sorcery were lost with the ship when it was attacked by the Sarte. Then again, it was supposed a one-armed commander also perished there. It seems he rose from a wet grave and likely carries with him instruments of dark magic in preparation for some evil deed." Ryckair looked directly at Petstra.

The commander stared back coldly.

Masalta shifted on his throne. "This is a different tale indeed. One most concerning. My own tale says there is a kingdom that trades with the Sarte and would know their spears. How then will we end this play? One story tells of sadness and a brother's love lost. The other of a darkness that consumes all it touches. Can you answer the riddle, commander?"

Petstra bowed. "As our exalted prince says, Highness, a fanciful tale."

"We do not find that adequate. This story will be held open until we have occasion to play again. For now, Ryckair Avar, Prince of Carandir, we request you honor us as our guest. "

"I thank you, cousin. Where will my men be quartered?"

Masalta gave a howling laugh that became a cough. A minister patted the king on the back. Masalta waved him away. "By the dragons' barbs, boy, you are good. Each moment I'm beginning to like you more and trust you less. There is much to be decided here. For the moment, your men will be quartered where they sit."

A squad of four Dharam guards formed around Ryckair. He saw Shara watch him. She smiled, cat-like, then turned away.

Two days later, a captain and two guards appeared at Ryckair's chambers. "We come to accompany you to an audience."

"With whom?"

"An audience, Highness. Please follow us." The sun had just set as they escorted him to a set of double doors.

Ryckair stepped into a room whose walls and ceiling were draped in fabrics of bright colors.

A pudgy man dressed in silk robes stood before another door at the far side. His face was clean shaven and his dark hair set in tight curls. He bowed low. "My name is Neesa, chief eunuch to Princess Shara. She bids you welcome and requests your presence."

He opened the door and led Ryckair into a chamber with settees, tables, pillows and rugs. Women in fur trimmed robes moved about the room with trays of food and drink. One strummed a stringed instrument unfamiliar to Ryckair as another danced with slow, undulating movements. In the center of this scene Shara, attired in several layers of colored veils, reclined on pillows.

She smiled as Ryckair stepped through the door. "Welcome, prince of the south. Will you take refreshment?"

Ryckair checked for exits as he walked across the room. "You do me too much honor."

Pillows were placed next to Shara. She motioned to a Fadella servant girl who brought a tray to the prince. "We in the north drink fermented milk. I know your southern palate prefers wine."

Ryckair took the crystal goblet. "Thank you. If only my men had such luxuries."

"It is a true general who thinks of his command. Do you enjoy the music? It is an ancient song called 'The Seduction of the King'."

Ryckair watched the dancer. "It surpasses its title."

She laughed.

When the dance concluded she clapped her hands.

Neesa hurried the women out and departed.

A hint of perfume, floral yet tinged with spice, wisped through the air. The jewels set in Shara's goblet caught the sparkle of lamp light. She sat the goblet down and rolled over to the prince. "The Sarte have brought us tales of the south from the sailors they capture. I know much of your lands. Why do you think I have brought you here tonight, Ryckair of Carandir?"

"My guess is either entertainment or intrigue."

She laughed. "Such wit you men of the south have. The Dharam are so dull. That is one reason you are here. You fascinate me; you and your beggar army marching proudly from the forbidden city. I could learn to like you very much, Ryckair of Carandir."

"And the other reason?"

Shara sat up. "I am the third daughter of Masalta. Three daughters. That was his issue. Therein is my father's greatest sorrow, for no woman may ascend to the throne of the Dharam. By tradition, whoever marries my eldest sister will fight my father in a mock duel and take the throne, whereupon he will retire to a life of leisure, a fate he is not eager to accept. Every suitor has been rejected by the Council of Ministers, upon my father's recommendation."

She walked to a set of heavy wooden shutters and threw them open to reveal a balcony. Kackar spread out before them. Above, the stars shone hazily through the smoke of the city. The choking air drove away the delicate perfume.

Shara stared at the scene outside. "You must think us barbarians, with your elegant palaces and great cities, but there is much strength in the north. Kackar can be magnificent. Imagine what the forbidden city once looked like. This can be the new Carandir. My father cannot see this vision. He thinks only to defeat the Fadella. My sisters feel likewise. The oldest will continue the line of the Dharam and my father's vendetta." She tuned back to the prince. "The throne should be mine and you will get it for me."

Ryckair swirled the wine in his goblet. "I'm hardly in a position to raise an insurrection. I have only a beggar army."

She closed the shutters and sprang onto the pillows next to him. "Then I shall give you an army that will crush my father." She brushed his chest with her fingers. "Show me the dragon mark."

Ryckair hesitated, then opened his shirt. Shara traced her finger over the spot. "Why did you hide this at the audience? It would have created a sensation and helped your claim."

"I thought it best to wait."

She stood. "To the north we are surrounded by the Fadella clans. They make war upon one another as much as upon us. Each would sell out the others for a season's grain or a handful of gold. That is how the Dharam have always kept them subdued."

A smile came to her lips. "But, if they were united, my father's army could never stand against them. With such a force, you could sweep into Kackar and take the throne. Then, as the lawful king, you would marry me and make me queen. Together, we will build a Dharam that can crush any enemy."

Ryckair laced his shirt. "I could take this conversation to your father. I'm sure you realize he'd reward me handsomely."

"You will say nothing of this to my father because I have told you it in confidence and you are not a man to betray a secret. You are honest to annoyance. Even if it were different, my father will not deliver what you truly want, vengeance on your brother. The combined forces of the Fadella and the Dharam army can give you that."

His jaw clenched at the memory of Mirjel's bruised face in the dungeon.

Shara touched his arm. "Do not be ashamed of this hatred. It is a strength that burns across your skin. Take it and mold it."

The prince walked across the room. "Even were I to agree to your plan, why would the Fadella follow me? I'm not one of them."

Shara approached, "Did you not hear what the servants called you when they saw the dragon mark? They have a legend, an ancient tale passed through more years than can be remembered. It says one will come to unite the clans as a single people. They say this one will have a mark that will be known as the gift of Ilidel. The Parili." She ripped open his tunic. "This sign. The dragon as it leaps into the air."

"Do you also believe in this legend?"

She gave a short laugh. "It only matters the Fadella believe with all their being."

Ryckair turned aside. "It's not only my brother who draws be back to Carandir. There's a woman, the Lady Mirjel. I won't abandon or betray her."

"Do you know if she still lives among the strife you describe? Petstra did not mention her."

"Petstra is a Barasha priest. His words are meaningless."

Shara outlined Ryckair's chin with her finger. "Petstra has a diplomatic pouch. If this can be secured, papers within might reveal much." She slipped her arms around his neck and pressed her lips against his, then drew back. "It is much more interesting if you participate."

He pulled her arms away. "I won't betray Mirjel."

"Will you wait to judge betrayal until you read the papers?"

Ryckair shook his head. "They won't change my mind."

It cost Shara many bribes and favors to get Petstra out of his rooms long enough for her to open the diplomatic pouch and examine the papers within. The wealth didn't matter. In a few months, she would sit on the throne and all the gold she spent would come back a thousand-fold.

In an alcove behind a curtain was a cage with five terec birds. She'd never seen one but recognized them from books she's read as a child. She wished there was a way to read the birds' minds and learn the most recent news from Meth. To her chagrin, the books said once a message was delivered to a recipient it was forgotten by the bird. She took one from the cage and hid it under her cloak before she left the room.Several papers suited her plan. They gave a clear picture of the happenings in Meth over the last months. From them, she realized the Barasha were more than legend. Though she'd seen minor magic performed by local healers akin to Daro, the calling of demons left a cold terror in her. Here was a threat to be feared. The sorcerers would not be satisfied with Carandir alone.

She considered if it would be best to abandon her plan and take the papers directly to her father. This would certainly gain favor for her. He might even name her his heir. She rejected the idea as too unpredictable, even though hers was far more dangerous.

A report of Mirjel's fall was the most pleasing to Shara. The last paragraph said the Daro healer who attended Mirjel was certain the princess would die. She chuckled to herself. "Perfect."

Then, she realized the news could destroy her plan. Ryckair might seek any means to fly to Mirjel, even if it meant his own death.

His devotion to  woman he'd not seen in years raised a strange sense of excitement, then a pang of sadness as she wondered if anyone would love her as much as Ryckair loved Mirjel.

She wished the report said Mirjel was already dead. Still, other documents had to be changed. She needed a report signed by the chief of the Kyar to confirm Craya wore the crown, something those with the right skills could manipulate. The altered copies would have to be completed by sunset so she could replace the originals before Petstra returned. She hoped he wouldn't notice the one bird was missing.

In her chambers, she donned a thick cloak and made her way down the back streets of Kackar to an alley. At a wooden door, she knocked once, waited three heartbeats and knocked four times again.

A woman appeared. Her skin was wrinkled with age. Her hair was gray. "Yes?"

"I am told you copy documents."

"Who has said this?"

"A friend with large ears and a scar on his cheek."

The woman nodded. "Come in."

It was dark inside. Thick smoke hung in the air along with acrid smells. The room was crowded with jars and pots stacked on tables or stuffed into corners on the floor. From the rafters hung baskets filled with herbs and plants. Fire licked the bottom of a blackened pot in which an unknown liquid popped as it boiled.

The old woman sat in a chair next to a hearth.

Shara stood tall. "You are the healer, Zamalatha?"

"I am."

Shara dropped the cloak to reveal her general's uniform. "You know who I am."

"I knew when you asked for this meeting. Still, I let you come. I was curious to see what Masalta's daughter wanted and what she would offer. You, of course, realize who watches over me. They wait outside this house."

"I am aware of your enforcers. I brought no one."

The healer's voice was flat. "You would not be alive now if you had. What do you want?"

"I need some documents copied and altered.."

Zamalatha extended her hand. "Let me see." She examined the papers. "How much is to be changed?"

"Only a few words on these two, a paragraph added here and a completely new report. I must have them before sunset."

"Impossible. The spell requires time to cast. I have to locate the proper herbs and parchment. It might take several days, perhaps a week."

Shara placed two gold coins onto a table.

Zamalatha examined them. "Very well. Before sunset."

Shara reached into her cloak and brought out the terec. I also want you to keep this bird. Tell no one it is here."

When Ryckair returned to Shara's chambers, the expanse of pillows were replaced by a writing desk and high-backed chairs. The subtle wisps of perfume were nowhere present.

Neesa stood in a corner with a set of papers.

Shara wore her military uniform, cold and official, yet it didn't hide the curves of her body.

She motioned to the eunuch who came forward and laid the papers on the desk.

Ryckair stared at the documents for a moment, then leafed through them.

A new, false report seemingly signed by Orane told of Craya's coronation as king after the dragon key accepted his touch and of his marriage to Mirjel.

An unaltered letter told of Mirjel's pregnancy. Another spoke of Craya's drinking and gambling. Yetig warned Petstra to clear all of Craya's orders with Reshna or himself.

Then, Ryckair held the last document. It told of Craya's drunken fit on the stairs that caused Mirjel to fall. Shara hadn't touched that part of the message except to make Prince Craya into King Craya and Princess Mirjel into Queen Mirjel. A false last paragraph was added.

> *The Daro healer tended Queen Mirjel for several days. At*
> *dawn, she succumbed to her injuries. Her spirit flew to the*
> *Dragons' Halls. Funeral plans have not been finalized.*

Ryckair read the note twice, then twice again as he searched for errors. He closed his eyes and clenched his fists. With a howl, he swept the papers from the table. "How could he? How?" Every one of Craya's cruel acts flooded through his memory. None matched this.

Shara placed her hand on his shoulder. "What is it?"

Ryckair motioned to the papers strewn on the floor.

She scanned them until she thought the right amount of time passed. "Your brother is evil and has aligned himself with even greater evil."

Ryckair's hands shook as he stood. "He's the king. The firstborn. The key chose him." The prince walked to the shutters and threw them open. "When does Petstra next meet with your father?"

"He has an audience in two days."

"And what do your spies say your father will do?"

Shara didn't have to lie this time. "His Majesty, King Masalta, will sign a pact with the Barasha. Petstra will take you and your men to Carandir."

The prince stared long to the south. "Prepare your people. We march north and raise the Fadella. I'll give you your throne, Shara. Then, I'll take the Fadella army to Carandir and avenge Mirjel."


At nightfall, Shara came to Ryckair's chambers with a thick, black woolen cloak. "Fit this over your clothes."

He followed her into the hallway. There were no guards in sight. When they reached the dungeon, Ryckair ran to the cage holding his men.

Batu put his arms through the bars. "We feared you dead."

"If we don't leave tonight that fate awaits us all."

Batu looked beyond the prince to Shara. "What's she doing here?"

"Princess Shara arranged our escape."

Theb pushed forward. "It's a trap, Highness."

Shara stood before the door with a set of keys in her hand. "If you rather, I will let my father pack you into the hold of a ship and deliver you to the sorcerers. Your prince has not told you yet. The Barasha found you."

Batu griped the bars. "I've been around scum my whole life and I know it when I see it."

Ryckair clasped his hand over Batu's. "There's much you don't know. It's not her you must trust, it's me. I'll explain once we escape"

Shara unlocked the cell. There were more woolen cloaks in a corner along with trousers, shirts, jerkins and boots.

Light snow obscured visibility in the streets. Shara led them to the stables where saddled horses waited. Each carried a pack with provisions. Blankets and tents were stowed behind the saddles. There were no weapons for the men, though Shara carried a sword. She took out the obsidian knife Ryckair used in the Sarte mines and presented it to the prince. "For luck,"

They mounted and rode into the hills. After two weeks they reached a high, snow-covered mountains of the Northland.

They made camped. The night sky was dominated by the light of a nearly full moon. To the west, a cliff of ice descended several thousand feet to a valley. To the north, the plain marched on.

Theb posted sentries. The rest of the company crawled into tents to sleep.

When dawn broke, Ryckair stepped out of the command tent and surveyed the wilderness.

Batu and Theb remained inside to study maps and charts supplied by Shara. They detailed passes and peaks, valleys and rivers. North of Kackar no roads were shown.

Shara emerged from her tent and walked across the snow with a half-smile on her face. "How fairs My Prince?"

Ryckair chided himself for finding her appealing. "Cold. The cloak feels like lace. How do you stand it?"

"You will learn. Has your Batu lost his suspicion of me?"

"I've heard nothing but your faults."

"Perhaps they are true."

He laughed. "Batu means well. He thinks only of me."

"Then I forgive him. He may hold me in kinder regard when you sit on my father's throne."

"How many of your people can I trust in this coup?"

"Before you are crowned? None. After? All."

"As I thought. Come, let's see if Batu and Theb found a route for us."

They entered the command tent. Shara put a finger on a map. "Here, just beyond these hills, lies an ice bridge. It spans this chasm where a trail leads northwest."

"How close are we?"

"A day's ride, maybe less."

Ryckair studied the map. "How wide is this bridge? Can we get the horses across?"

"In single file. I made the journey once before. If we are careful, we will cross in safety."

It was near sunset when the company came to the ice bridge. It arched over a deep crevasse.

Shara pulled her cloak tighter around her body. "We will have to go slowly. The hooves of our horse can slip upon the ice. This is the first danger. The second is each crossing breaks down the bridge so that you must move gently."

A trumpet sounded. Mounted Dharam troops appeared over a set of snow drifts. In the lead of the column was commander Petstra. The empty arm of his uniform sleeve flapped in the chill breeze. A spear was attached to a loop in his saddle. The other men brandished bows as they held their mounts in check.

Petstra leered. "I knew you had to cross here."

Shara drew her sword. "Stand back, dog of the Barasha. I am a princess of the realm and general of the army." She shouted an order to the soldiers. The bowmen kept their arrows trained on Ryckair and his men. She shouted again. Her voice was edged with anger. Still, the Dharam troops didn't respond.

The commander rode forward. "They won't obey the orders of a traitor." He motioned to a Dharam soldier who brought forward a wooden box. Petstra reached inside and raised Neesa's severed head by the hair. "I have very effective methods of persuasion. In the end your eunuch was most cooperative." He threw the head onto the snow.

"All is known to me and to your father. I carry an order signed by him. It declares all of you outlaws. You, Princess Shara, will be returned to Kackar where your father will have you hanged and you, Prince Ryckair, will be delivered to me and taken south to Carandir."

Shara shouted another order. One by one, the soldiers looked away. She sheathed her sword with a pale look on her face Ryckair hadn't seen before.

The prince opened his cloak and bared his chest to reveal the dragon shaped mark. It glowed in the twilight.

The soldiers lowered their bows.

Ryckair scanned the troops. "All here know this sign. Will any of you call down the wrath of the dragons? Petstra serves the sorcerers of Baras, I serve Jorondel and Ilidel. Choose now what authority you will follow."

The Dharam looked to each other in confusion.

Petstra hefted the spear with his single hand. "Here's the only authority to be reckoned with." He gripped his mount tightly between his legs, charged forward and threw the spear into Theb's belly.

Theb fell from his horse.

Ryckair dropped to the ground and took his friend into his arms.

Theb's eyes fluttered when he opened them. The black skin of his face contorted in pain. "Don't weep, Highness. You gave me life after years of death. I've seen the sun, felt the wind. Odd. I never truly knew them before the Sarte mines." He gave a cough and died.

Petstra rode up to the prince. "Ilidel and Jorondel have forsaken you. Plead now for the mercy of Baras."

Ryckair grabbed the commander's boot and pulled him to the ground. The prince drew his obsidian knife and placed it against Petstra's throat. "Tell them to move back."

Petstra's voice was thick with hatred. "Do it."

The Dharam soldiers moved away.

Batu disarmed Petstra of a sword, a dagger and a small pickaxe.

Ryckair dragged Petstra to the edge of the ice bridge. "You're crossing the crevasse and riding over those hills with us. If your men remain here, I'll release you. If they try to follow, I'll slit your throat."

Shara examined the arch of ice over the chasm. "We cannot take the horses."

"What do you mean? You rode across once."

"That was at night. The sun has softened the ice."

Batu looked back to the archers. "Then, we're trapped."

"We can still cross," said Ryckair. "We'll leave the horses here."

Petstra smiled. "Yes, cross into the northern winter on foot. If we don't ride you down, the night will kill you. You've lost, Prince Ryckair."

Shara began to unfasten her saddle bags and bedroll. "Nay, dog of dogs. The Dharam horses cannot cross either and you will still be our prisoner. As to the night, there are many Fadella camps."

A sneer came to Petstra's face. "They won't accept a Dharam."

"I am no longer Dharam. My father has made me Fadella."

The setting sun cast shadows across the ice and snow.

Ryckair instructed his men to use straps of leather to convert the saddle bags into packs.

They loaded them with what provisions they could.

Much had to be left behind, including Theb's body.

Shara shouted to the Dharam troops, "Whatever has befallen me, see this man is buried as befits a soldier. This boon, alone, I ask from those who have served with me."

"It shall be done," came a reply.

Ryckair handed the knife to one of the men to convert saddle bags into knapsacks.

When the packs were ready, Ryckair looked across the chasm. "How best to proceed?"

Shara hefted a back. "Once pressure is placed on the ice, we cannot let it be relieved until we are all across. I will go first, then you, followed by the other men. Petstra will cross by himself with Batu last."

Batu retrieved Petstra's sword and held the tip to the commander's chest.

The sun dropped over the mountains on the west side of the valley.

A full moon rose in the east. Its light blasted off the snow.

Shara got on her hands and knees and crawled over the arch. The ice held her weight.

Ryckair crawled after her. As his full weight bore down on the frozen arch it began to crack. Flakes of ice and snow fell into the crevasse. Ryckair and Shara held still. The ice remained stable. They moved on. Another crack came.

Batu's attention was drawn away from Petstra for an instant.

The Barasha priest slapped the blade of the sword aside, grabbed his pick and ran for the ice bridge.

The Dharam, troops charged forward.

Petstra shoved the axe into his belt, pulled a pouch from his cloak and tossed it.

The pouch struck Ryckair on the back and enveloped him in red powder.

The commander recited a chant as he hoisted the axe. When the last words were spoken, he struck the bridge.

The ice arch cracked and collapsed in on itself.

Batu looked up just as Ryckair and Shara plummeted into the crevasse.

# BOOK IV

*The Palace at Meth*
*One Week Later*

# CHAPTER ONE

Mirjel knew the baby was gone as soon as she awoke from a coma induced by the Daro. She wanted to place her hands on her belly to confirm her fears but couldn't bring herself to move.

There was no pain, no sensation of any kind. Everything was dull and hazy, except for her hand. Someone held it.

She opened her eyes to see Narech Yetig.

He sat at her bedside with his hand cupped around hers.

She fell unconscious.

When Mirjel awoke again, the pain came. It ran cold and deep through her body like a cramping void. She cried out.

Again, Yetig was there, his hand in hers.

A Daro healer brought a cup of steaming liquid. "Drink, Highness."

Mirjel felt the warm fluid flow down her throat. She almost vomited. The nausea subsided. She settled into sleep.

The next day, Mirjel awoke again and looked around the room.

Yetig lay on a couch in one corner.

The healer sat in a chair with her head bowed in sleep.

Lek sat by her mistress. The young maid smiled, then fell into sobs. "Oh, Highness, we were so afraid you would not live to see another day."

Mirjel took Lek's hand. "The babe?"

Lek averted her eyes. "The Daro could not save the child, Highness."

Mirjel felt a cold wave spread out from her chest as her fingers tightened around Lek's wrist.

The Daro healer and Yetig stirred at the sound of voices.

The healer brewed another draft for Mirjel to drink.

Lek was sent to fetch more firewood for the hearth.

Yetig sat next to Mirjel's bed.

She looked over to him. "You held my hand."

His voice came quiet. "I meant no offense, Highness."

The Daro healer raised Mirjel's head and brought a wooden bowl to her lips.

The princess sipped the medication. Before the bowl was drained, she felt the drug take effect. "Narech."

"Highness?"

"Thank you."


Mirjel slept hours into the day. The exceptions to this malaise were the visits Yetig made. Then, she woke early, bathed for a span and suffered over what to wear. Her cheeks, usually pale, took on a rosy glow and her eyes brightened.

When Yetig arrived, they sat in her chambers or walked through the gardens and talked.

Mirjel thought his only interests were battles and troops. She was surprised when he revealed a breadth of knowledge in literature, art, trade, engineering and politics. She was fascinated by his descriptions of subtle ways to influence courtiers and even monarchs.

It was a sunny winter afternoon. They strolled through the garden.

Yetig allowed himself one of his rare smiles. "Flattery can be quite useful. It can also be dangerous. Those schooled in intrigue will look for it. You must allow such a person to thwart you in some way. Then, deny defeat. Make an angry accusation you were cheated, though refrain from personal attacks. Later, let it seem you've cooled off. Give a grudging compliment for having been bested. End with a slightly concealed smile. Your adversary is now ready for you to ask your favor."

Mirjel stopped and looked at Yetig with her mouth agape. "You're talking about my father. You did that to him once."

"Twice, actually."

She laughed and pounded softly on his chest. "Fiend."

"It was only politics, Highness."

They both laughed.


In Kackar, Batu and the rest of Ryckair's men awaited news of their fate as they sat in the same cell they escaped from earlier.

Many weeks passed before a jailer stood before the cell and read from a scroll. "As enemies of the Kingdom of Dharam, you are condemned to work the mercury mines in the eastern mountains."

Batu faced death many times. Now, he felt a panicked terror as he recalled stories told by guards of men crippled and driven mad by the fumes.

He formed a plan with the others. When the guards came to get them, they would charge. Even if they were killed in their cell, it was better than dying in the mines.

Petstra appeared in the dungeon with a dozen Dharam guards.

Batu imagined his hands around the commander's throat. "Come to gloat?"

Petstra tilted his head. "I've come to retrieve you. In a gesture of friendship, King Masalta will allow you to accompany me to Carandir where you can give a full account of Prince Ryckair's death."

The commander threw powder into the cell. The prisoners slowed, then froze in place. Batu was bound and placed in a wagon. A column of Dharam soldiers escorted them as they traveled south across a snow-covered plain.

They reached tall cliffs that overlooked the north bank of the Great River. At the bottom of a winding trail was a harbor where a town hugged the cliff face. Three Dharam rowing galleys unloaded goods at the docks. Many smaller vessels dotted the water. Next to them was a Carandir war frigate.

Batu was taken onboard and chained in the hold.

On the voyage home, he listened to every creak of timber less it signal and attack by the Sarte. They didn't appear.

After a seven-week journey, the ship returned to Meth where Batu was taken to the palace and sealed in a prison cell.

Petstra knelt before Reshna. "My lord, mightiest among the Servants of Baras. I return with a witness to confirm the spell is complete. The powder was cast and Ryckair Avar died as the full moon rose."

Reshna stared at the fire in a brazier. "So, it has come to pass."

"What of the key, Lord Reshna?"

"The ceremonial death now makes Craya the heir. The key will call to him. He must be made ready. See to it."

The arrival of spring brought blossoms to flowers and fresh leaves to bushes and trees in the palace garden. Mirjel's strength returned, though the loss of her child was always present in her mind.

She and Lek practiced swordplay in a clearing of the gardens.

Yetig suggested Mirjel learn the art of fencing with a rapier. "Your father instructed you well in the broad blades. The rapier will give you discipline and balance, skills you will find useful."

Mirjel insisted Lek be instructed as well.

The two women wore breeches, thick leather jerkins, gloves and mesh masks.

She saw Yetig approach and felt the weight of the message he came to deliver.

The narech didn't hesitate. "I received news this day, madam. Prince Ryckair's death is confirmed."

She no longer saw the flowers or trees around her. Everything was a blur. "There's no mistake?"

"I spoke with a man named Batu Kazmere who was banished with Prince Ryckair in the ship. Kazmere saw…"

Mirjel threw her hands to her ears. "Stop, please. I don't want to know more. Not now."

He took her arm. "Your chambers have been prepared if you wish to retire."

Mirjel allowed Yetig to lead her to her rooms.

Lek boiled water to make kan.

Mirjel drank the hot liquid. Her gaze ran across the room. She saw nothing in particular, until her eyes fell on the harp she played for Ryckair when they first met. "I have no more tears to shed, Lek. I'm empty."

It was the first time Mirjel was out of the palace since the later stages of pregnancy. She descended the secret staircase in the palace within the palace while Lek stayed behind to tell any inquirers her mistress was under sedation in her chambers.

Once Craya became the heir, Reshna paid Mirjel no heed. She was certain he would have killed her and Lek if Yetig hadn't reasoned she could still help placate and control Craya.

When the boat reached the underground wharf, she hurried to the meeting room. Orane and Telasec were already there.

They waited a tespan before Yetig arrived and sat at the table. "I've come from a meeting with Reshna. It's taking longer than expected to sober Craya up. I thought the sorcerers would summon a demon and frighten him into submission. Instead, Reshna panders to his ego. He speaks of an alliance between the Barasha and the house of Avar to rule all the lands where Craya will be an emperor."

Telasec shook her head. "Does Craya believe them."

"I'm certain he knows they want the crown to release Baras. I think It's why he delays the search for the key. He wants time to think his way out of the trap he has set himself in."

Orane stared at Yetig. "The same trap you fell into."

He straightened his shoulders. "I acted for the Crown and admit I was wrong to try and use the sorcerers."

Mirjel leaned forward. "This is not the time for accusations. We've all done what we thought best. Let the past lie."

Telasec looked to the door. "We can't let him find the key. It calls him even now."

Orane taped a finger on the table. "He could be abducted and taken far from here."

Yetig sat back in his chair. "The Barasha would come for him. How could anyone stand before that?"

"Kill him." Mirjel's voice was flat and emotionless. "If he dies before he finds the key the crown will remain locked away, perhaps for eternity. That's the only way to confine Baras."

Shock came to Telasec's face. "Is your anger so great you would murder your own husband?"

"I don't speak out of anger, Honored Mistress. There's no other way. I must make a pretense to see him. Lek can spread a rumor among the servants. She'll say the loss of the baby and confirmation of Ryckair's death has shaken me, as they have, and I seek comfort. He will be suspicious, but his pride will betray him. "The sorcerers think I can manipulate Craya to their purposes. They'll allow no one else alone with him. I'll place the poison you gave me into a drink. I don't want him to suffer, not even now. Lek and I will leave through the secret passage and escape into the east before the Barasha discover Craya's body."

Orane's face was ashen. "You know what the sorcerers will do if you can't get away."

"Lek will come to this hideaway first. If I'm captured, I'll drink the poison intended for her."

Orane and Telasec tried to dissuade her.

Yetig stood. "Her Highness is right. She alone can hope to approach Prince Craya. There's no alternative."

Mirjel continued to issue secret orders for grain movements guided by what what Yetig taught her to conceal her actions.

She and the narech met regularly. Sometimes they conferred on trade and harvests. At other times, they just talked about nothing in particular.

One evening, Mirjel sent Lek to the kitchen. She and Yetig were left to dine alone in her chambers.

Yetig raised a glass of wine. "I toast a delightful evening, with delightful company."

Mirjel blushed. "More wine?"

"No, thank you. I fear I must be leaving soon." He smiled. "We don't want to start any rumors, do we?"

She stared at him. "Do we?"

Yetig set his glass down.

Her eyes fell to the table. "After the fall, I was certain I'd die. The one thing that kept me from screaming was when your held my hand."

"It was the least I could do, Highness."

She looked up. "No. Ignoring me would've been the least. When I lost the baby and…" Her voice faltered for a moment.

Yetig reached out and squeezed her hand.

She blinked away tears. "The Barasha no longer needed me. I was tossed aside. Forgotten."

"Many did not forget."

"They risked nothing to show me favor. You're constantly scrutinized."

"We fight for the same cause, you and I."

Mirjel smoothed the fabric of her skirt. "I know. A year ago, I cursed you." She closed her eyes and spoke in a near whisper. "Stay with me tonight."

"Highness."

"Please. I need to be with you. Everyone I ever loved is gone. The loneliness scares me more than the thought of dying."

Yetig walked around the table and brushed aside strands of hair from her face. "You spoke the truth about us. For me to have sat with you at all was a danger. For me to become your lover could be fatal."

"I don't care." She jumped up and kissed him.

Yetig returned the kiss, then took her in his arms and carried her to bed. They made love with passions unbridled.

Afterward, they lay in each other's arms.

Mirjel looked into his eyes. "I'll give you a special name, a secret name."

"I'd like that, but you must always speak of me formally lest a lapse of thought show affection outside her chambers. None can know of this affair."

The narech stayed until near sunrise. They made plans for him to return that evening. If inquiries were made, they would say they were discussing court business.

After he left, Mirjel squirmed beneath the tussled bedding. A heady exhilaration poured through her. She felt alive for the first time since the false report of Ryck-air's death in the swamplands and found herself giggling. It was as if she were watching someone else and this only made her giggle more. The thought of Yetig returning that evening brought a hot flush to her cheeks.

From the back of her mind came the image of Ryckair. She gazed into the hearth where the dying embers of the previous night's fire cooled. Did she still love him? Yes. She always would. But she'd lived with the hope of his return for too long and now he was dead.

Mirjel wasn't certain if she loved Yetig. He was a comfort and a strength she desperately needed. Perhaps she was now lost to love. Yetig was right. She was the leader of a powerful monarchy. Her actions, her thoughts, her being, had to be focused on that. All else stood in waiting. Yetig could guide her, mold her and satisfy her passions. Still, she wept for a span.

$\wp \quad \dagger \quad \wp$

Telasec pulled the scarf over her face as she crossed a street in Meth. Her destination was an inn beyond the walls of the old city. She walked through the central square with its grand fountains and marble buildings. These housed the residence and central administration for the Barony of Lanteler.

On the other side of the square, in smaller buildings of granite, were the municipal offices. Since the coming of the Barasha, Ackella resided there as lord mayor. He enjoyed sauntering about with a band of militia. They arrested those Ackella called vagrants and levied arbitrary fees and taxes on merchants.

The Daro healer avoided wide boulevards in favor of the back streets. Once, these were teeming with commerce. Now, many shops were shuttered and those still open had few customers.

She reached the city walls and crossed the bridge over the Peret River. The roads within old Meth were laid out with thought and purpose. Outside the walls, the city sprawled in a haphazard fashion into farmlands. Roads meandered between buildings large and small.

The inn she sought rose three stories tall. Next to it stood a wooden stable filled with the carts and wagons of farmers journeying to market.

She came to meet a man Orane sent to Karaken to gauge what support they might expect from the desert kingdom if open revolt came against the Barasha. She and Orane sought to build an army from many lands to fight an enemy who would soon dominate them all, even if Baras was not released.

Her contact was a man in a blue cloak and hood with a red patch sewn into it. She spotted him on the other side of the room.

Telasec cleared her throat as she approached.

He coughed twice and sneezed.

Telasec said, "My uncle had a cough like that last month."

Instead of giving the coded response, the man pulled his hood back.

Telasec found herself staring into the face of Ackella.

He sported a gold brocade patch over his missing eye.

Ten armed soldiers surrounded her.

Ackella stood. "You should be more careful when making discreet inquiries."

Orane entered Mirjel's chambers through the secret panel. "Have they made her talk?"

Yetig stood from a chair. "Not yet. She has great strength."

Mirjel made the sign of the covenant. "We have to get her out."

"Reshna has his own men guarding her."

"She can't hold out forever. The Barasha will eventually learn of our plan. Where's she being held?"

"The new prison complex."

"Master Orane, do any of the secret passages connect to it?"

"No. It's a recent addition to the palace."

Mirjel looked to Yetig. "We must form a rescue plan."

He took her hands. "You must think like a queen now. We've never been in more danger. Mistress Telasec can't be allowed to talk. There's very little hope we can rescue her. If we're unable to free her, she must die. There's no other way."

Mirjel closed her eyes, sick with the realization he was right.


A week later, Yetig pulled on his gloves as he took care not to look at Mirjel. "I can't see you tomorrow."

It was near dawn. The narech prepared to leave after spending the night. The timing of his arrivals and departures were precise. He needed to catch the cycle between hallway guards. Too many of his officers would gladly carry the news of his affair with the princess to Reshna.

In itself, the liaison would be of little concern to the sorcerer. It might even amuse him. However, knowledge Yetig conspired in secret would raise doubts. Soon the sorcerers would search deeper.

A cold breeze blew through the open doorway of the balcony. Mirjel shivered and wrapped a shawl around herself. "When will you be back?"

"I don't know."

Lek knocked once, then three times.

Yetig faced the door and halted. Without a word, he spun around and enveloped her in his arms.

They kissed with urgent passion.

As quickly, it was over.

Yetig left the room as Lek entered.

ৡ  ✦  ৶

Jea's grandfather, Garto, walked along the banks of the lagoon adjacent to the swamps. He still had a bounce in his step and his eyesight was as keen as when he was twenty.

He picked up a stone and skipped it across the water as he wondered if Jea raised the Xinglan troops. She sent a terec to say she arrived safely. No further messages followed. Both he and Osba were still angry with the council for their refusal to send help to Carandir.

When Garto sat on the council many years before, the leaders were far thinking. Since that time, the mood shifted. The councilors now sought quick profits. Their decisions were meant to please the latest whims of vocal groups among merchants and populace alike with no regard as to any ultimate consequences.

Eight flat-bottom boats appeared out of the swamp. Men in red robes sat with folded hands while southern Sinkarakans poled."

Garto ran back to the house. "Osba, we must ride to Au."

"What's the matter?"

"The sorcerers have come."

As a former member of the government, Garto had the right to call an emergency meeting of the council.

The men filed into the chambers.

Osba remained outside.

Garto scanned the council members with desperation in his voice, "The Barasha are here. They brought Southern Sinkarakans armed with swords and bows."

One of the councilors scoffed. "Old eyes see many things. Some are actually there."

Many of the councilors laughed.

Tradas was pale. "We must send the militia to stop them. We all know what they're capable of."

Another said, "Send the militia as emissaries to escort them here. We can reason with them and come to a beneficial agreement."

Garto approached the bench. "They want Jea. They've followed her here."

Naston swiped a hand across the bench. "Jea's actions are her own. We've no quarrel with the sorcerers."

The doors to the council chambers burst open.

Four Barasha priests walked in, followed by thirty-five Sinkarakans with drawn swords.

One of the priests drew back his hood "We seek Baroness Jea."

Dobeta's voice wavered. "She left. We don't know where she went. She didn't inform any of us."

Garto remained silent.

The Barasha formed a square. A Sinkarakan brought in a metal bowl on a tripod and lit coals inside it. Smoke wafted in the air.

Garto was nearest to it. He kept his features neutral.

Powder was thrown into the flames. A silver flash illumined the room.

Jea's Grandfather and the councilors grabbed their heads and screamed.

Garto fell to his knees.

Two Sinkarakans ran forward and dragged him to the brazier.

The Barasha priests chanted in low, dissonant voices.

The fire burned brighter.

A priest pulled Garto's hair back and looked into his eyes.

Garto gritted his teeth as he fought to keep his thoughts blocked.

The Barasha continued to chant louder, then stopped.

The one holding Garto let him fall to the floor, then looked to the others. "She has fled east to Xinglan."

He turned back to the council. "Au is now under the protection of the Barasha in the name of Baras. The council and militia are dissolved. We will collect all taxes and appropriate what we desire. Resistance will be met with death. We now claim these chambers. Depart at once."

# CHAPTER TWO

M irjel made discreet inquiries about Craya. She spoke in a reminiscent voice about how she missed seeing him. Everything was said in passing before the conversation moved on.

She sat alone in the gardens when five of Craya's personal guards surrounded her. "Follow us, Highness."

With no further explanation they escorted her out to the parade ground and into the throne room through the large, double doors used by the nobles and commoners, rather than through the private entrance used by the royal family.

Mirjel had not seen Craya for months. She was amazed by the sight of him.

Gone was the drunken, disheveled figure she remembered. Craya sat tall on his throne. His eyes were clear, his hair and beard closely cropped. A silver circlet rested upon his head.

Reshna stood beside him.

On his other side was Narech Yetig.

Mirjel forced herself not to look at him.

With ease and grace, Craya rose and descended from the dais. He brushed an imaginary piece of lint from the sleeve of his uniform. "It's been so long since I had the pleasure of your company."

She said nothing.

Craya stroked his beard. "You seem quiet today. Does something trouble you? Perhaps it's the weight of my signet ring you carry. Allow me to relieve you of it."

She wondered if they'd made Telasec talk. If so, there was no escape. She considered spitting in Craya's face. Instead, she handed him the ring and waited to see what he actually knew.

He rolled it around in his palm. "So many secrets." He looked to Yetig. "Isn't that so, Narech?"

"We live in treacherous times, Highness."

"So, we do."

Mirjel raised her head to meet Craya's eyes. "If you're referring to my use of your signet ring, I had no choice. The daily administration of the palace had to continue and you were incapacitated, my husband."

He studied her for a moment. "Husband, is it? Are you pining for the old days? I've heard you're lonely. Do you perhaps realize when I find the key and take the crown you'll be queen, unless there was another? Narech Yetig, draw your sword and run her through."

Yetig unsheathed his sword without hesitation and placed the tip over Mirjel's heart.

She prayed they hadn't been found out about their affair. It would be a swift thrust, she was certain, with as little pain as possible. She felt a strange calm. This was the end. There was nothing more to do. She thought of Ryckair—his smile—his touch. It seemed the right thing to do in her last moments before she joined him in the Dragons' Halls.

Craya slapped Yetig's sword aside and laughed. "That's enough amusement for today. Leave us."

Batu shivered in his prison cell. He hadn't seen anyone since the interrogation after his arrival. What little light there was filtered around the edge of a closed viewing port the guards never opened. Once a day, at his best reckoning, food and water were slipped through a narrow slit at the bottom of the door.

He heard the sound of a click and rased his head as the cell door swung opened.

The former smuggler waited for guards to enter. His body stiffened as he wondered if they'd continue the interrogation, or execute him.

After several heartbeats, no one entered. He peeked out into the hallway.

It was empty. Lanterns lined one wall. As soon as he walked out of his cell, the door slammed shut and wouldn't open.

Another cell door opened.

Batu took one of the lanterns from its bracket and peered inside.

A woman lay on a cot. She looked familiar, though he was unable to place her. Then, he recalled how people kept small portraits in their homes to ward off illness and recognized the woman as Mistress Telasec, eldest of the Daro healers.

She was unconscious.

Batu picked her up and carried her from the cell, whereupon the door closed and locked itself.

He walked up the corridor, though he was uncertain of exactly where it led. A small ball of mist no larger than a pebble appeared in front of him. It grew into a disk as tall as a person. The aberration blocked his way, then advanced. He started to run. His legs wouldn't move. The mist overtook him. He closed his eyes.

When he opened them again, he stood in a room with two beds, a table and two wooden chairs. There was a door and a hearth. A window overlooked a port town. Merchant vessels were tied up at dock.

A piece of paper and a leather pouch lay on the table next to a cooking knife, forks, plates and cups.

Batu placed Telasec on one of the beds. She took a deep breath but remained unconscious.

He sat at the table and read the note.

*Faithful Batu Kazmere,*

*Tend to Mistress Telasec as best you can until my arrival. It may be some time. Buy what provisions you need. Mix the contents of the vial with kan and give it to her. It will help. Listen for two knocks and a whistle. A cat accompanies me.*

*A friend*

His first thought was the Barasha were playing a cruel a trick, yet didn't feel like it. He opened the pouch and found fifty copper coins of a kind he'd not seen. With the coins was a glass vial filled with green liquid.

He made kan and looked at the vial. It could be poison, or worse. Still, it made no sense for the Barasha to bring them to this place to kill them when they could have done so in prison.

He poured the liquid into a mug and brought it to Telasec's lips.

As she sipped, her breath became stronger. She slowly opened her eyes. "Are these the Dragons' Halls?"

"No, Mother Healer. I can't rightly say where we are, but we're not dead." He explained who he was and how they had come to the room.

"It's the will of Ilidel." She fell back asleep.

Batu picked up some coins and went out to buy food. When he stepped into the street and saw the docks, the mystery of the coins became clear. He stared at the ships and the winding road hugging a steep cliff. This was the same port town Petstra brought him to in Dharam.

The marketplace was crowded. Everyone spoke with the same accent he heard in Kackar.

He imitated their dialect as he bought food and a sharp knife.

Nearly two weeks passed. Each day, Telasec grew stronger. Batu told her of Ryckair and their escape from the Sarte and the Oola. His voice faltered when he described Ryckair's fall into the abyss.

She told him of the secret meetings, the plan to defeat the Barasha and the alliance formed with Yetig.

Batu shook his head. "So, the key rejected Craya and Mirjel lives?"

"We all expected her to fly to the Dragons' Halls, yet she recovered."

Batu stared out the window. "Petstra must have had false documents prepared to bargain with Masalta. Ryckair would have never marched north to his death if he knew the truth."

Two knocks came at the door one afternoon, followed by a whistle.

Batu held the knife. "Who comes?"

A woman's voice came through the door. "A friend and her cat."

Batu picked up the knife before he opened the door.

Jarat stood in the hallway in her normal guise of a young, black woman.

Nissor stood next to her in the shape of a tabby cat. Then, Nissor took once more the form of a garat.

Batu grasped the knife tighter.

Telasec fell to her knees. "Mistress. Never did I expect to see one as you. Praise the dragons."

"Who are you talking about? This Barasha brought a demon." Batu backed into a corner.

Nissor cooed and cocked its head.

Jarat smiled. "Your caution is admirable, Batu Kazmere. Well-deserved is the trust Ryckair placed in you."

Batu took quick, shallow breaths. "Just who are you?"

Telasec pointed to Jarat. "Can't you see? She's of the eldest of the eldest, a wizard of Ilidel."

Jarat stroked Nissor's head. "You've seen and endured much these last years, good Batu, and you thought your part was at an end. In truth, you've been tempered for a greater battle to come. It's there you'll prove yourself or fall into everlasting darkness."

Batu lowered the knife. "If there's to be a battle, why are we here? The Barasha are in Meth."

"Yet it's here where the battle begins. I can say no more for now, lest word reach our enemies. Events move that are unseen by them. You'll be needed. Nissor will return to you as a sea bird when the time is right."


In the far northland, a young Fadella chieftain sifted through the ice and snow of an avalanche. His name was Ichary. When his father was killed in an avalanche four years before, Ichary became chief, though he had only just reached his manhood at the age of sixteen.

He sought the source of a blue glow. His father died near the place where the glow came from. He thought it might be a sign from him.

The elders of his tribe warned him not to approach it. They spoke with fear of the tumbling ice. "More will follow. Stay away from that place. It is filled with evil magic."

Ichary didn't heed their words. "Always you think me a child, yet I'm chief of the clan. I'll see what I'll see."

He dug through packed snow with a wooden shovel. Every fifth blow, he stopped to inspect the ice wall for another avalanche.

A hard stroke smashed into an air-filled pocket. Ichary enlarged the hole and peered through.

Within, still in their Dharam cloaks, were the frozen bodies of Ryckair and Shara. The young chief was puzzled by the sight of this man and woman. The Dharam never sent patrols this far north.

The woman's face was white with frost.

On the man's chest was the source of the glow, a dragon shaped mark.

The young chief reached out to touch it.

Ryckair's hand sprang to life and grabbed Ichary's wrist.

The prince's eyes shot open. "Warmth. We must have warmth to awaken."

The icy grip relaxed.

Ichary took two staggering steps back and ran to his village.

He returned with five men and a woman of great years named Sintalay who was a healer of the Fadella.

She looked inside the air pocket. "Frozen corpses, young chieftain, nothing more."

"The corpse moved."

"A shift in the ice fall."

"It spoke."

"The howl of the wind."

Ichary reached in to reveal the dragon mark, which still gave a faint glow.

Sintalay's eyes widened. "Mother of Dragons. The Parili."

"The prophecy?"

"These are no mere Dharam scouts. Fate brings Ilidel's promise to us."

The frozen pair were carried from the ice cliff to the Great Hall of Ichary's people. This was a long wooden lodge. The one room building was twelve paces wide and thirty long. There were no windows and only a single door located in the center of one wall. Two stone hearths, one at either end, blazed with fires.

Ryckair and Shara were wrapped in animal furs and laid next to one of the fireplaces. Ichary sat watch over them while Sintalay went to the other hearth to mix a potion.

She returned and poured liquid into each of their frozen mouths. Both began to breath. The frost melted from their skin, though they were still cold to the touch. Sintalay inspected the dragon mark and made the sign of the covenant.

Ryckair became aware of warm liquid against his lips the next day and woke to find himself drinking a weak meat broth.

Sintalay held a bowl to his lips. "Slowly." She placed her hands over his eyes and spoke the words of a sleeping spell. "Rest now." Her speech hinted at formal Carandirian for some words, yet lacked the heavy accent of the Dharam.

Ryckair fell into a deep slumber.

The healer moved to her other charge. Shara was not yet awake, though her sleep was normal and relaxed. Both of the strangers were now warm to the touch.

Sintalay tended Ryckair and Shara over the next few weeks. Several times, she was certain her arts had failed. On each occasion, the dragon mark glowed and death passed the pair.

Ryckair awoke fully in the third week.

Ichary helped him to sit up. The young chief described how his camp sat in a clearing surrounded by dense woods and how his people planted vegetables and wheat during the short growing season after the snow melted.

The prince told of his brother and the crown.

Ichary was amazed by the story of the escape from the Sarte and the Oola. He was especially fascinated with the ruined city. "It's like an old tale from the healers."

Shara remained asleep for two more days before she opened her eyes.

Women and men prepared a meal at the far hearth. Two men and a woman sat in the center of the lodge fledging arrows. Children played a game with pine cones and wooden sticks.

Shara rubbed her eyes. "Where are we?"

Ryckair moved next to her. "In a Fadella camp."

Sintalay brought two bowls of meat broth. Ichary carried mugs of hot Kan. After Ryckair and Shara ate, she made them stand and walk around the lodge. "The dragon mark protected you from harm."

Ichary looked at Ryckair with a sense of awe. "Truly, he is the Parili."

Sintalay donned a heavy hide parka and walked to the door. "That is yet to be decided. A mark can be made by many, even one that glows. Spring has come. The chiefs of the Fadella will gather here to pass judgment."

The next day, Ryckair and Shara donned thick hide parkas and stepped outside. Ryckair was delighted to see the sky again, though it didn't look like spring. The lodge stood in a clearing on top of a low hill. It overlooked a river valley whose waters were still frozen. Tall, snow-covered mountains rose to the north. To the southeast, the massive cliffs of a glacier slashed across the landscape.

Ryckair's breath formed clouds of frost in the air. "It seems we've found the Fadella, or they've found us."

"They are a superstitious people. We must discover what these chiefs will look for."

"They're also a closed mouth people. I've asked that very question several times. All they say is, 'You'll see'."

"And what will you do when these chiefs approve of you?"

"March on Kackar, as planned. Nothing's changed, except we've gained a great measure of surprise over your father. He won't expect the dead to attack. When we conquer the Dharam, I'll march against my brother."

"Will you not tarry in Kackar for a while to rest and enjoy the spoils of conquest?"

"Such as?"

Shara grabbed him around the neck and kissed him.

This time, Ryckair returned the kiss with deep passion. He lifted her from the snow and walked back to the lodge.

In the screened area set aside for them, they undressed and made love. When they were spent, Ryckair fell into a deep sleep.

Shara remained awake for a long while and stared at him.


Ryckair and Shara took strength from the food and rest provided by Ichary and his people while they waited for the other chiefs to assemble. They joined the rest of the clan in the evenings and listened to stories of the old days. These were often legends about people or animals from a time when the Fadella lived in warmer lands.

One evening, a storyteller arrived at the lodge. The bard was fed and given a special place near the fire. The next day he would leave for another settlement with his pack full of food and new boots on his feet.

"And that," he concluded, "is how the snow became white."

Everyone laughed, especially the children. Tiny voices echoed throughout the lodge. "Another story."

The storyteller frowned.

The children only laughed harder.

A smile spread across his face and he laughed as well. "Very well, just one more. This is the story of the ant and the magician."

He settle against the back of a chair. "In a land far away, there was a powerful magician named Tarat who lived alone in a great castle at the top of a mountain overlooking a valley.

"In the spring, he waved his hands, and the north wind ploughed the land. Next, he commanded the east wind to sow the seeds and water them. The west wind plucked weeds from his fields. In autumn, the south wind scooped the harvest.

"Down on the ground, where the winds and the rain played out their tasks, many of the creatures living in the fields were far from pleased.

"They called a meeting under the shadow of an old oak tree. There were grasshoppers and bees and birds and foxes and rabbits and all manner of beast.

"'Something must be done,' said one of the beetles who was always filled with suggestions of what other animals should be doing.

"'Yes,' said a feather-worn jay who was often bounced around by the winds, 'But what? The magician's powerful.'

"Then, a tiny voice said, 'I'll stop the magician.'

"Everyone turned to find the voice came from a little ant.

"They all laughed.

"A badger said, 'What can you do? The fox has teeth. The rabbit has claws. The bee has a stinger. What do you have little ant?'

"She smiled in reply. 'I have the best thing of all, my wits.'

"As no one else seemed willing to do anything, they all decided to let the ant try.

"'I'll need drop of honey from the bee,' said the ant. 'And the jay must fly me to the castle.'

"The a drop of honey was brought and the ant climbed onto the jay's back. In an instant, they flew up to the window of the magician's bedroom.

"'Return tomorrow morning and fly me back to the fields,' said the ant. 'Our troubles will be over.'

"Soon, the magician came home, put on his nightshirt and got into bed.

"As he lay his head down, the little ant crawled into the magician's ear and attached herself inside with the drop of honey.

"She whispered, 'I'm so tired. It's such a chore to command all those winds.'

"Now, when you hear something whispered inside your ear, even by an ant, it can seem quite loud, and because it's inside your head, you'll be certain it's your own thought.

"'Yes,' said the magician aloud. 'It is tiring. I think I'll go off to sleep'.

"'Of course,' whispered the ant, 'I've nothing else to do but sleep. It's so lonely up here on this mountain.'

"'The magician sighed. 'Yes. I wish there were people about to visit.'

"'Perhaps people from the next valley could be invited to dinner,' said the ant.

"'Yes,' said the magician. 'I'll write out an invitation right now.'

"He got up from bed and went to his desk.

"As he sat down, the ant whispered. 'The people could just come for dinner, or I could invite them to live here. They could work the fields with me and I won't need to command the winds. Everyone could share the harvest and I'd have friends.'

"Tarat jumped up and danced around the room. He almost threw the little ant out of his ear, even though she held on to the drop of honey.

"'What a smart fellow I am,' said the magician, 'to have thought of such a clever thing.'

"The magician wrote the letter and returned to bed.

"The ant crawled out of his ear.

"In the morning, the jay came for her.

"'All is well,' said the little ant.

"And indeed, people moved into the valley and farmed the land. The winds never bothered the animals again."

The bard spread his hands wide. "Now you see how a little ant overcame the mightiest of magicians."

With the story over, the children were hustled off to sleep.

Everyone else settled as well.

Shara and Ryckair snuggled beneath fur coverings in their screened space. Ryckair looked at her in the dim light of the banked fires. She was radiant.

Shara reached over and brushed his cheek with her hand.

He stared into her eyes. They called to him, drew him into her.

She leaned forward and they kissed.

He smelled her alluring scent and took her passionately into his arms as they made love.

Each night they lay together.

Ryckair worried less and less about his past life. His future was all that mattered, a future with Shara.

# CHAPTER THREE

Twenty-three chiefs of the Fadella clans assembled in Ichary's lodge. Some were dressed resplendently in furs as fine as the Dharam. Some wore simple hides. All inspected the mark on Ryckair's chest. Each chief placed a stone in a sack Sintalay passed around the lodge.

When the last chief voted, The Fadella healer held it before her. "In the time of the beginning."

The rest of the Fadella chanted, "In the beginning."

Sintalay continued, "The people lived in a land of warmth and bounty."

"Warmth and bounty."

"Fat grew the people, yet still they hungered."

"Still, they hungered."

"They abandoned the ways of the Great Plan and the names of Ilidel and Jorondel, Mother and Father of Dragons, were forgotten."

"Forgotten."

"The people worshiped their riches and gave thought to naught but taking more."

"They took more."

"Others they pressed into service by force."

"Service by force."

"Yet, the people did not share their bounty."

"Did not share."

"And oppressed the lives of those who toiled for them."

"Oppressed their lives."

"To the dragons the oppressed called with cries of suffering and pain."

"To Jorondel and Ilidel the oppressed called."

"Swift and mighty came the dragons."

"Came the dragons."

"The people cowered and wept for their sins."

"They wept for their sins."

"Jorondel's wrath pronounced this doom."

"The doom of Jorondel."

"'Your works and deeds will shatter in the wind. To lands as cold as your hearts are you banished. Naked you will flee and count the brambles and the thorns your companions.'"

"Banished were the people."

"'Nothing shall you take of the toils of others, not even the name of this place, for from this day forward that name will be confused in your mind and you will take a new name, Fadella, the Wandering Sorrow.'"

"The Wandering Sorrow."

"'For years beyond count, you and your descendants will roam, never to know your home again. Your cities will be left to decay.'"

"Left to decay."

"And there was a great wail and the people fell to the ground and bit themselves and struck their heads with their hands."

"Struck their heads."

"Then Ilidel took pity."

"The mother of life took pity."

"'Long will be the years of your exile,' said Ilidel."

"Long years."

"'Yet, I will send one who will carry my sign, the mark of a dragon as it leaps into the air.'"

"Know him."

"'The evil will be purged'.'"

"The evil will be purged."

"'From exile you will return'."

"From exile we will return."

Sintalay opened the sack and counted the stones, black for yes and white for no. "It is cast. The mark is accepted as the true sign."

Shara shot to her feet. "Then you will follow him in battle?"

"Silence, woman of Dharam. We have accepted you into our lodge, but this is not your council."

Sintalay handed the pouch of stones to Ryckair. "Count them and know the voice of the Fadella. Then, choose your path. To bear the mark but earns the right of the three trials, one for the hunter, one for the bard and one for the warrior. Each can bring death. You must pass all before the Fadella will call you Parili. You may refuse these tests and live among us for the remainder of your days. None will deny you comradeship. I ask you now, will you have these trials?"

Ryckair opened the sack and looked at the stones. They were all black. "I've suffered many trials to stand here. I'll take these last three."

"Let all now assembled witness how Prince Ryckair Avar has accepted the challenge in the manner of the true Parili. The first trial begins in the morning with the hunt of the chiefs."


Ryckair sat behind a snowbank next to the chiefs of the Fadella clans. He scanned the white meadow before him. The hunting party traveled a day and a half to reach this spot.

Ichary crouched beside the prince.

The other chiefs waited behind them, bows in hand.

A brisk wind brought flurries of snow. The breeze subsided.

A herd of large animals entered the meadow. Thick, fur hides protected the creatures from cold as they moved through the snow on cloven feet.

Ryckair was reminded of draft oxen used by Carandirian farmers, though these beasts were half again as large. Their heads towered an arm's length taller than any of the hunters. Ichary called them matula, a name unknown to Ryckair.

The largest matula bull stopped and raised his snout to sniff the air in search of a predator's scent. The Fadella were slathered in matula fat to mask their human odor. Ryckair discovered the grease carried the added benefit of keeping the cold at bay.

Ichary nodded to Ryckair.

The prince lifted his bow, notched an arrow and pulled.

Ichary raised a palm, lowered his own bow to the ground and leaned forward into it.

Ryckair tried again. This time, he lowered the bow and used his body's weight to lean into the wood. It bent with effort as he pulled the string back. He raised the bow, took aim and released the arrow. It arched high across the sky and dropped into the center of the herd.

A matula cow fell to the snow.

Panic struck the herd. Matula scattered in every direction until they blocked all movement.

The large bull gave a bellow.

The herd stopped.

He threw his head back, snorted into the air, then led the matula in a charge back along the same route they arrived by.

Before they could escape, the Fadella chiefs let fly a rain of arrows.

Two more animals fell.

The men whooped cries of victory. They charged into the meadow to the carcasses lying in the snow.

The hunters laughed and joked as they loaded the matula onto sleds.

Before the hint, Ryckair had been told nothing was wasted. The meat fed the Fadella, the hides clothed them the bones were fashioned into tools, the marrow was simmered into soup, the entrails became medicine.

Ichary had said the matula herds were spread over a wide range. Some hunts brought no game at all and others only a single kill.

With the prize of three matula on this hunt, the chiefs said the dragons favored them and declared Ryckair had passed the first trial.

The prince helped pull one of the matula onto a sled. "I was a hundred paces beyond the range of the best Carandirian bow. Yours are amazing."

Ichary laughed. "Only the Fadella have them. They're made from a very hard wood. That's why you must use your weight to bend them. They take much practice and strength to use. Such a bow lets us make a kill before the matula detect us. You're a remarkable man to have mastered it on your first try."

Ichary pointed to the smaller of the kills, then turned to Ryckair. "This will be for the sacrifice feast. By long tradition, it's the privilege of Fadella women to butcher the kills and distribute the meat and hides from a hunt. Those with husbands and children make certain their families received enough. Unmarried women are free to share their portion as they wish. From this came a saying among my people. 'Hungry as a spurned husband,' and 'Beauty fills the eye, a smile the heart, good manners the belly'".

Two of the chiefs began to cut into the smaller matula.

Ichary joined them, "The only time men are allowed to butcher an animal is to take enough meat for the sacrifice feast. This follows every successful hunt and honors the dragons for the abundance they sent. Each hunter must eat his fill and make a song for the soul of the animal, praising the prey for its cunning and strength."

A fire was lit and the feast ensued. They ate meat and drank large quantities of kan to warm themselves against the cold. Ichary, as host, performed the Ritual of Blood.

Four rocks were placed around the fire. Ichary rubbed meat from the kill on each. He then tossed the meat into the fire as an offering. "Here is the flesh given to us that we return to the dragons. Smoke and flame, we call on you to speed our offering to their halls."

He took a hide flask from under his furs and squirted a swallow of wine into his mouth. Ichary gave the flask to another chief who drank deeply. Hand to hand the wine passed.

Lastly Ena, the eldest of the chiefs, passed the flask to Ryckair.

He squirted some in his mouth and almost gagged on its coarse harshness. His first instinct was to spit it out. Instead, he forced himself to swallow with a grimace as the red liquid burned his throat.

Ena slapped him on the back. "Our young hunter prefers mother's milk to wine."

The men laughed.

Ryckair stood and held the wine skin overhead.

The laughter stopped.

He squeezed a steady stream into his mouth. The men cheered as Ryckair continued to drain the wine.

The cheers were joined by the rhythmic slapping of hands.

Ryckair squirted the last drop into his mouth and swallowed.

The hunters erupted into shouts and cheers as they patted Ryckair on the back and kissed his cheeks.

Ryckair's face burned with a flush. The sounds around him became at the same time acute and muffled. He moved his head. It seemed the insides took just a moment to catch up with the outsides.

Ichary raised his hands. "Our bravest hunter has drained the wine and so let him give a song to the matula."

The men fell silent.

Ryckair composed himself. "I will give a song to the matula who feed us." He fought with his mind to release words. "Here among the snow and…" He looked to Ichary.

The young chief said, "hills?"

Ryckair raised a finger to the horizon. "Here among the snow and hills, bravely came the matula. Bravely walked to find their fodder. Bravely sniffed the air so frozen."

"You already said bravely."

"Gallantly sniffed the air. Brave matula. Brave and…" He stopped and thought for a moment. "Raising high their mighty heads." He imitated the matula bull as it raised its nose and snorted into the air. He began to laugh, stopped, then burst into hysterics.

The other men joined him, holding their sides and laughing uncontrollably.

Ryckair contained himself. "I am sorry." He burst out laughing again.

Another chief got up to deliver his song. He failed to complete it as well. Only four hunters finished their tributes to the souls of the matula before the ceremony decayed into back slapping, imitations of persons not on the hunt whose daily habits warranted ridicule and incoherent babbling that passed as music.

The last thing Ryckair remembered was falling face down on a hide blanket.

In the morning, he wondered if someone had stuffed his mouth with matula dung while he slept. Cramps seized his stomach. He almost didn't reach the edge of camp before he vomited the majority of the previous night's feast.

Ena walked over to him. "You gave a good song last night, little hunter, though I must confess I can't remember it aright." He patted the prince on the back. "You're a hunter among hunters, Ryckair Avar. I'll let no one say otherwise. Still, next time you wish to show your hunter's soul, one swallow of wine will suffice."

Nothing but kan stayed in Ryckair's stomach. Even that required great coaxing.

Ichary gave him a root to chew on that took away the worst of the pounding in his head.

Evening fell before they neared the village. Dozens of hands unstrapped the carcasses from the sleds. They made a second feast on the carcass the hunters butchered.

Shara stood at the entrance to the lodge and waved at Ryckair's return.

He ran up and wrapped his arms around her.

They kissed until one of the children pushed on their legs to try and clear them from the doorway.

Ryckair and Shara laughed, then stepped inside the hall.

Fires blazed in the two hearths. Ryckair sat on the floor and wrapped a hide blanket around his shoulders. The other hunters entered the hall and sat near the fires.

Shara brought Ryckair a mug of kan.

He took a sip. "Thank you. I never imagined such cold, and it's supposed to be spring." He savored the flavor as he listened to the other men greet their wives.

Shara finished her mug and smacked her lips. "I'm not certain how you take it. Snow and ice have always been a part of my life, yet even I find this cold bitter."

"Soon we'll take Kackar, my love. Just two more trials."


The next day, Ryckair sat on a stool near one of the fires.

Two Fadella chiefs grabbed him from behind. Knives were brought to his throat.

Sintalay sat on a stool. "This is the test of the bard. It is written the Parili will have knowledge spanning the ages."

A healer from another clan sat books on a table.

Sintalay took one. "Here, gathered and preserved from generations now forgotten, is the wisdom of the Fadella handed down from the dragons. Each question must be answered accurately. If you fail, the knives will pierce your skin."

She opened the book and ran her finger down the page. "I ask you again. Will you continue the trials of the Parili?"

"I will take this trial."

Sintalay asked points of history and poetry, all of which Ryckair read in his studies with the Kyar. He was amazed the Fadella versions matched the books in the vaults beneath the palace at Meth.

"Name now, the sisters of Neles."

"Pare and Fito."

"What lay speaks of the battle of Tenatily?"

"The Kura Aspa."

For another span the questions continued. Ryckair answered each correctly.

Sintalay picked up another book. "The Kura Kar mentions a meeting in a forest between King Gotenag and his enemies. By what calling did the king disguise his identity?"

Ryckair hesitated. He 'd worked for months in the Kyar's vaults to translate the epic poem from a newly discovered manuscript.

The popular version said the king told his enemy he was a wheat merchant from the east. The older manuscript used the word rena, whose literal translation meant scraper. It was often applied to either a tanner or a butcher. Ryckair argued with other Kyar that the king meant butcher as a veiled threat of what he would soon do to his enemy.

He said, "Butcher."

Sintalay looked up. "The book says wheat merchant."

Ryckair felt the knives press against his skin. "Wait. That's a later translation. I found the original writings in a book within a book. It reads, '*Se matta lan rena.*' I am a great butcher.'"

Sintalay raised a hand. "Hold."

She retrieved another book from the table. A quarter of the way through she came to a place where the pages were cut out to make a hole. Inside was a second book. "Only the healers know of this hidden tome, and none know what is written within, for to read it outside of the trial is death. It is written the Parili will know of this book and the Parili alone will know its contents."

Two chiefs moved behind Sintalay and placed knives to her throat. "I will now silently read the Kura Kar in the tongue of the dragons and see if you speak correctly. If your answer is wrong, both of us will die, for it is forbidden any know the answer to this final question until it is revealed by the Parili. I ask you again, will you continue this trial?"

Ryckair had no idea as to whether or not the book Sintalay held contained the same text as the one he found in the Kyar's vaults. He asked himself if he had the right to place Sintalay's life in danger. A voice inside told him to stop. Something else said the answer was *rena*. "Yes. The king said he was a butcher."

Sintalay opened the hidden book and read in silence. She closed her eyes and bowed her head. "*Se matta lan rena*. You have passed the second trial."

The knives were withdrawn. Cheers resounded in the hall. The book was laid out for all the chiefs to read and confirm.

Shara put her arms around Ryckair. "I thought you dead."

He embraced her. "There's one trial left."

"Do not speak of it yet. Just hold me."

He pulled her close. Her body tremble against his. He remembered how Craya always goaded him for his studies in the Kyar's vaults and declared him a weakling. The thought of Craya filled him with rage. He told himself he would need that to pass the trial of the warrior.


Ryckair dressed in fur garments and gloves the next morning.

Sintalay waited outside the lodge. "This is the trial of the warrior, the last and most dangerous. There is only victory or death. I ask you one last time. Will you take this trial?"

"Who do I fight?"

"When you reach the mountain, you will know."

Ryckair looked north. "I'll take this final trial."

He set off alone with a tinder box, bow, arrows, a knife and provisions. Soon, he was out of sight of Ichary's camp with no idea of where to go.

The sky remained clear as he ascended the slopes. His only goal to that point had been to reach the mountain. When he did, he began to question what the Fadella expected of him. Was he to bring back some relic? Did they expect to see a severed head as a trophy?

Ryckair climbed for three days in search of a sign as doubts filled his mind.

For most of his life, he felt he was unfit to rule and had convinced himself the key would reject him and choose Craya.

Because of Shara's false documents, he now believed this had come to pass and Mirjel was dead. It seemed all who ever followed him were imprisoned or dead. Would he condemn the Fadella to the same fate.

It seemed so easy in Ichary's camp with their praise and Shara's urging. He wondered if he'd fooled them all, or only himself. Even if he overthrew Masalta with the help of the Fadella, what good would they be against the Carandirian army, and worse, the Barasha?

In his mind, he saw Shara as Queen of the Dharam next to him as king. He imagined a happy life with her and pictured their children as they ran through the palace at Kackar. He could make the city great, clean the filth, improve commerce. It could be a good life. He wondered if his future was in the north.

A strong wind grew as clouds gathered overhead. Snow fell, light at first, then heavy and wet.

He pushed himself up the mountain with no idea of where he was going.

His face was numb from the sting of ice pellets. The wind pulled breath from his lungs. He took a step, then another. Everything around him was a shifting gauze of white. He looked back to where he'd walked and found his own footprints covered with snow. If he died there, no one would ever know what happened.

The entrance of a cave appeared in a cliff face. He forced his feet to trudge across the snow until he was inside.

The cave continued ahead in the dim light coming from the entrance. To his right hung a curtain of matula hide. In a niche next to this was an oil lamp. His hands trembled from the cold as he lit the lamp and pulled the curtain aside to enter a chamber. Mats lined the floor. A crude hearth was carved into one wall.

Hide blankets were piled on one side of the hearth. There was wood and tinder on the other. He built a fire, removed his soaked clothing and wrapped a hide blanket around himself, then sat next to the flames.

It seemed obvious some Fadella tribe created this place as a base for hunting parties. The wood and hides were a life saver. The room became warm in a short time. After a meal of matula jerky and hard biscuits from his pack, he stretched out before the hearth and was soon asleep.

When Ryckair awoke, he was famished.

An unseen voice came from behind. "There's food and drink, young master."

The prince spun around to find an aged man with dark ebony skin whose coarse hair was speckled with gray. He wore green robes with white fur trim. Next to him stood a black hound.

Ryckair retrieved his clothes. "I mean you no harm. I found your cave in the storm and sought shelter."

The old man stepped forward. "You don't need to explain yourself. You seek the warrior of the mountain. This place has been prepared for you."

Ryckair moved his hand toward his knife. "Are you the warrior?"

The old man laughed. "No. You'll meet him in combat soon enough. I'm here to serve and guide you to the arena."

"I don't understand."

"To reach this spot takes great stamina. You're exhausted from your effort and must regain your strength before the challenge. Come. Eat."

A table along the far wall was laden with meat, cheese, fruit and mead. Two stools sat next to the table. Ryckair cut a piece of matula meat and brought it to his mouth, then stopped and examined it.

The old man laughed again. "Don't worry. The food's not poisoned. If I wished you dead, I could've slit your throat while you slept. Come now. You must regain your strength if you're to face the warrior."

Ryckair hesitated, then took a bite. It was tender and succulent as he'd never known matula meat to be. The cheeses were ripe and the mead refreshing. "This is wonderful. I haven't eaten like this in ages."

"I'm glad you enjoy it, young master. It's not often I have visitors."

Ryckair felt oddly lightened by the man's mirth. "Who are you?"

The hound came over to the table. The old man patted its head. "You may call me Maganda."

"The one who teaches?"

Maganda raised an eyebrow. "A scholar of the ancient tongue! Well met."

The old man bid Ryckair rest by the hearth while he cleared the table. When he was done, he joined Ryckair by the fire with two mugs of hot kan.

The prince took a sip and stared into the flames.

Maganda raised an eyebrow. "Your worry knits a cap on your brow."

The prince laughed at the old adage. "Does the warrior employ you?"

"No. I'm indifferent as to who wins the battle. You look as if you have a more pressing question."

"It's just, now that I'm here, I don't know..."

"Whether or not you are supposed to be? You may speak freely, for I know who you are, young Prince Ryckair Avar. There is only one who can face this challenge."

Ryckair cautioned himself to be suspicious, yet felt an unexplainable trust in Maganda. "Why have I been chosen to take this test? My brother was always better and now he wears the crown."

"You seem to have convinced yourself you're inferior, yet you have no idea who you actually are. To face the warrior, you must have faith in yourself."

"Isn't that a little simplistic? It takes more than belief in oneself to win a battle."

"I said faith, not belief."

"They're the same thing."

"Oh, a scholar shouldn't say such. The words we use are very important. What would I have to show you for you to believe something?"

"Well, proof, of course."

"And you'd be a fool to believe anything without it. What if there's no proof? What do you do then? You know nothing of the warrior. There's no proof you can defeat him."

"So, you think I'll fail?"

"Again, you don't hear the real question. More, you don't ask yourself that question. You've come all this way to face the warrior without any proof he even exists. That takes something beyond belief. Those who rely on belief would turn back"

"I'd have to believe to come this far."

"What is your proof?"

"I just know there's a trial and I have to face him. I can't prove or justify it. I just know. That's all."

Maganda smiled. "That, young master, is faith. With it, we have the strength to step beyond what we believe to see what truly is. Real power comes from faith and that comes from within us."

The fire burned low. Exhaustion overtook the prince. He settled into a matula hide and fell asleep while Maganda's words ran through his head.

Ryckair dreamed of a giant with a massive sword before he awoke with a start.

Maganda stood over him. "The warrior awaits." He handed a lantern to Ryckair and took one himself.

The old man led Ryckair deep into the mountain.

The prince held his knife in one hand and slung his bow over his shoulder.

The hound padded behind them.

The walls were covered in a sheen of ice that reflected light from the lamps.

They walked through a maze of passageways for what felt like several spans. Maganda guided him forward without hesitation.

Ryckair remembered his dream. "What does the warrior look like?"

"You shall see soon enough."

"Are you forbidden to answer my questions?"

"I may do whatever I please."

"Then tell me what weapons he'll use."

Maganda stopped. "Look into my eyes and tell me how many stalactites hang over your head ready to crash down on you."

"I have no idea."

"Better to worry about where you stand than where you might stand." The old man walked on.

Ryckair grabbed Maganda by the shoulder. "Enough of your games. I need to know what I face."

He heard the hound growl.

The old man held the prince in his gaze. "You face an angry dog somewhere in the dark who can tear out your throat."

The dog fell silent.

Maganda's features relaxed. "I'll tell you this. The warrior will carry only those weapons you bring to the combat. Nothing more. It'll be for you to determine which will overcome him." The old man smiled. "You must look to the faith within yourself."

Ryckair felt a sense of panic rise. There was too much he didn't know. The dog nuzzled his leg and he looked down to see it wag its tail.

They reached a point where a fissure cut across the floor and blocked their way. In the dim light, Ryckair was unable to see how wide it was.

Maganda held his lamp high. "The warrior awaits you in a hall of ice across the gap. This is as far as I can lead you. You must find your own way from here."

Ryckair approached the edge of the crack and peered across into the darkness. "How wide is it?"

"It's as wide as it is."

The prince walked along the edge. The chasm extended from wall to wall. He picked up a loose chunk of ice and threw it across. It echoed as it hit the other side. He was still unable to gauge how far that was. "I don't believe I can make it."

"Then, you have failed."

Ryckair peered back across the gap. He tucked the knife in his belt and held the lantern high. With a burst of speed, he ran toward the edge of the chasm and leapt into the darkness.

Exhilaration pumped through him as he sailed over the gap. There was no turning aside, pulling back or second guessing. Yet, there was no fear. His heart raced. He laughed and howled. The sound echoed throughout the cavern.

He reached the other side and slid across the floor. The exhilaration grew to ecstasy as he jumped up and danced a jig. "Did you see, Maganda? I flew like a dragon."

There was no sign of Maganda's lantern on the other side of the crevasse.

His chest itched. He opened his parka. The dragon mark glowed. He covered his chest once more and continued on with the lantern held before him.

A few paces brought him to a large chamber whose walls and ceiling were encased in ice. Several wagon size boulders littered the floor. Stalactites hung from the ceiling. In the center was a round pit whose bottom was hidden in darkness.

He sat the lantern on the floor. Light reflected off the ice to cast dim radiance throughout the space.

Ryckair spied a face on the opposite side. He ducked behind the nearest boulder and peaked over its top.

The warrior peeked out from behind another boulder.

Ryckair couldn't make out his face in the dim light. "I've come to take the challenge. How shall we do battle?"

Only his own words echoed back in reply. He notched an arrow. "Name the contest, warrior of the mountain."

Again, there was no reply.

He jumped from behind the boulder.

The warrior appeared across the chamber with a notched arrow in his bow.

Ryckair raised and fired.

The warrior matched him in speed as he fired his own shaft.

Ryckair jumped back behind the boulder. He heard a crack and looked up. A large stalactite fell toward him. He moved aside before it crashed to the cavern floor.

With another arrow notched, he looked to the right.

The warrior, bow in hand, stood before him with an arrow at the ready.

Ryckair fired again and charged round to the other side of the boulder to find the pit a few paces away.

He tried to stop.

His boots continued to slide across the floor.

He dropped to one side and drove his knife into the ice. The blade bit the frozen floor. His movement slowed until he came to a halt with his feet dangling over the edge.

The prince scampered back behind the bolder.

The warrior stood near the opposite wall.

Ryckair reached for another arrow and found his quiver empty.

He dropped his bow and ran behind another boulder. He couldn't believe how his opponent was able to follow him with such speed. Yet, as Maganda had said, the warrior dropped his bow and now carried only a knife

Another stalactite broke off and struck his arm. Pain radiated from his shoulder to his hand. He dropped the knife and fell to his knees.

He could grasp nothing in his right hand. After several deep breaths, he took the knife awkwardly in his left and stepped out from behind the boulder.

The warrior appeared across the chamber, a knife in his right hand.

Ryckair took a fighting stance. The memory of every duel he fought with his brother rolled through his mind.

He told himself he'd never actually beaten Craya. Yetig awarded the one match to him for trickery. Craya would have killed him in a real battle. His only thought was to run back to the Fadella village and live a quiet life with Shara.

The dragon mark burned beneath his parka as the warrior stared across the gap. The trial was to face him. Did that mean kill him? In the other tests he learned new skills and demonstrated his knowledge. He saw no lessons in this trial.

Maganda said to have faith. What good did that do when facing an enemy who wanted his death? Craya was king. Mirjel was dead. Everything he dreamed of was gone. None of that would be brought it back if he defeated the warrior. He couldn't even say why he was standing there.

The thought was so absurd he began to laugh.

The warrior laughed as well.

The knife shook in Ryckair's hand. He couldn't go back and face the villagers now. They all believed in him. He cursed the word. How could he believe anything?

In that instant, he knew how to win. It was foolish. There was no proof. No one would believe it. He didn't believe it. He knew it. Deep within his soul he knew what had to be done.

He dropped his knife and the warrior dropped his.

Ryckair stepped forward. "I claim victory over you, warrior of the mountain. You must match me weapon for weapon and I carry with me the most powerful of all, peace. I'll not fight you this day or any day. The battle's over."

With his hand extended, he walked around the pit to greet the warrior and ran hard into a sheet of ice. He stepped back and looked into the eyes of the warrior of the mountain. They were his eyes, his body, mirrored off the smooth ice on the chamber walls. He opened his parka and the warrior did likewise to reveal a duplicate dragon mark. Ryckair realized he fought not another man but his own reflection.

A woman's voice echoed in the cavern. "So, you discovered the secret of the mountain warrior and the only weapon that can defeat him."

The ice walls glowed. The light became more intense until it was nearly blinding. The prince shielded his eyes.

The woman said, "Come. Ryckair Avar, Prince of Carandir. Why do you cringe? You've come to know that which is dark and that which is light. Do not fear to look upon the truth."

Ryckair uncovered his eyes. Before him stood Maganda and the hound. Their images shifted to become Jarat as a young, black woman and Nissor in garat form.

He recognized the wizard and garret from images in his his earliest training with the Kyar. He knelt "Mistress, I was taught your order vanished."

Jarat put a gentle hand on Ryckair's shoulder. "I'm the last wizard. This is Nissor. For millennia I've feared the Barasha would return and waited for them. Now, I come to assist Carandir's heir."

"Mistress Jarat, I'm no heir. My brother sits as king in Meth."

"Come, there is much to discuss."

The fire in the cave where Ryckair had slept burned brightly in the hearth.

The prince sipped kan and huddled under one of the matula blankets. "Mistress Jarat, Craya took the crown."

"Did he?"

"I saw dispatches."

Jarat sipped from her mug. "Half-truths are more potent than lies."

"But there was a letter in Petstra's diplomatic pouch signed by the chief Kyar. I saw it."

"So, you believed it."

"Of course." He paused and stared into the flames. "I did believe it and assumed it was true. Petstra must have wanted Masalta to think he treated with an emissary of a king. The papers I saw were lies."

"You carry the mark of the Parili. What will you do about the lies?"

The prince rose. "I'll gather the tribes of the Fadella and march on Carandir. All these years I've thought the mark to be meaningless. I now know in my heart I'm the heir."

With those words, a great sense of purpose filled him.

Jarat sat her mug down. "An army alone can't defeat the Barasha. Only the crown can." She told Ryckair about the vanished key and the sorcerer's hunt for it. "You must find it and unlock the crystal sphere."

"Do you know where it is?"

"Finding the key is part of your quest. None but you can hope to discover it."

"Then, you don't know where it is?"

"I know you must find it or it can't be found. I've told you all I can."


When Ryckair awoke the next morning, Jarat and Nissor were gone. There was hot kan and porridge set out, along with a note.

*Defeat the Dharam first. Don't leave Masalta at your back.*
*Once you've done this, you must find the dragon key. March in*
*force to the ruined city you found when you escaped the Oola.*
*Nissor and I will meet you there.*

*Jarat*

Ryckair packed his supplies and set off. The storm broke as he started down the mountain. He turned to fix the cave's location in case he should need it again. There was no trace of it, only an unbroken cliff face.

At Ichary's village, the people stood in front of the lodge.

Ryckair looked from one to the other. "I've defeated the warrior of the mountain. I'm Ryckair Avar, heir to the Western Realm, both north and south. How do you declare me?"

For an instant he expected them to demand some token as proof.

Instead, they fell to their knees, touched their heads to the snow and shouted in unison, "As Parili and Lord."

Shara furrow her brow. "Heir to the south?"

"Petra's dispatches were lies. My brother can't be king. The key calls to me. We'll march on Kackar first and free the north of your father's cruelty. Then, we'll regain what is mine and drive the Barasha from Carandir where you will sit as queen."

"Can you be certain of this?"

"I know nothing but certainty."

# CHAPTER FOUR

A chill wind blew from the west as Ryckair raised his eyes above a snowbank to survey the walls of Kackar. Ghost-like figures of Dharam guards walked on its parapets. Though the wooden gate stood open, the iron portcullis barred entry.

Ryckair whispered in Shara's ear. "How much farther?"

"Just down this ravine."

Ryckair and Shara set off with an advance party of five Fadella. They reached a masonry culvert where foul smelling ooze dripped into a stream. A metal grate covered the entrance.

Ryckair coughed. "Will we be able to breathe inside?"

"At first, you will wish you could not. Breathe through your mouth. You will get used to the smell."

She produced a set of keys. "Let us hope my father has not thought to change this lock."

The grating opened. Shara unshuttered of a lantern. "I will go first. Keep up. If you get lost in there you may never find your way out."

The sewer wasn't quite as high as a person. They were forced to stoop as they walked through ankle deep filth.

The stench was horrendous. Ryckair and the six Fedalla warriors who accompanying him coughed. Contrary to what Shara had said, the prince didn't find the stench to diminish with time.

They came to a pit. Light filtered down through an oval hole.

Ryckair looked up. "A latrine?"

"It sits in the gate house."

They managed to squeeze through.

Ryckair cautiously opened the door and peeked into a hallway.

Shara touched his shoulder. "Those stairs lead to the gate mechanism."

"Let's hurry. If they don't see us, they'll surely smell us."

They charged up the steps. One man stood at the large wheel that opened and closed the portcullis. He reached for a horn on the wall.

Shara threw her knife into the man's neck.

He clawed at the hilt, then fell.

Three of Ichary's people grasped the wheel and turned.

The portcullis rose.

Wave upon wave of armed Fadella men and women ran through the opening. They surged down narrow streets. Townspeople slammed their shutters. Soldiers and horses died either from swords and pole arms or were trampled by those who fled the onslaught.

Ryckair ran down the stairs and led the Fadella up winding streets toward the palace. Snow gave way to freezing rain. Pelting water mixed with fine specks of ice washed off much of the muck from his clothes and left stinging pin pricks on his face.

The snow on the ground became a muddy slurry soaked in blood. Dharam soldiers and their horses slipped on the frozen streets. The screams of the dying mixed with the frantic battle cry of two armies as the prince's troops forced back Masalta's troops.

Ryckair and his men rounded a corner and ran into a volley of arrows. They faced five hundred Dharam archers.

Four Fadella were struck.

The prince pulled his troops out of range before the Dharam fired again.

Ichary and his men ran up just short of where the Dharam arrows fell. As they had against the matula, the Fadella leaned into their bows and let fly their arrows.

Dharam archers died before their commander called new orders to return fire. Their arrows all fell short.

Another flight of Fadella darts descended on the Dharam. They dropped their bows and fled.

Ryckair and his troops reached the palace. They threw down the gates. Dharam soldiers fell back as the Fadella slashed their way down corridors and through chambers.

They reached the throne room. Masalta sat alone. "I have to admit, boy, I underestimated you."

Shara raised her sword. "I shall cut off your head myself."

"I do not think your young prince will allow that, daughter."

"No daughter of yours. I am Fadella."

He studied her for a moment. "How provincial. Do you like her that way, boy?"

Ryckair brought the point of his sword to Masalta's chest. "I am Ryckair Avar, heir to the Western Realm to include the lands now held by Dharam. I lawfully claim this throne. Do you yield?"

Masalta sneered. "Dharam has held these lands for millennia. Will you have me surrender the birthright of my forefathers?"

"In the name of the dragons, yield before my troops bring their blood lust into these chambers."

Masalta stood, then dropped to his knees.

Ryckair sheathed his sword. "Declare now your loyalty and fealty to the Crown of Carandir."

Masalta bowed. "I declare…" From under his cloak, he pulled a dagger and made a thrust for Ryckair's belly.

The prince stepped aside and struck the deposed king in the back of his head with the hilt of his sword.

Masalta fell on his chest.

Shara stomped on her father's hand and snatched the knife. "Your treachery knows no end."

Ryckair raised a hand. "Hold. We're not butchers. Your father will answer for his acts."

Masalta cradled his arm. "It is broken. I cannot feel my fingers."

Ichary and his bowmen ran into the throne room.

Ryckair held up his hand. "The battle is over. Bring Sintalay to tend to Masalta's wound."

Shara seized the crown from her father's head and held it aloft to Ryckair. "You have bested my father in battle. By our law, you are now King of the Dharam. Claim your crown, my love." She placed it on Ryckair's head.

Ichary and his men cheered.

Masalta grimaced.

A council was formed to advise and aid the new king. Chief among these was Shara. They met before sunset to report the day's events and plan for the next.

Seventeen sunsets passed since the raid. The dead were cremated. Masalta and his ministers awaited judgment. Life within the city walls returned to normal with stalls open and goods sold.

Ryckair stood as he addressed the assemblage. "A greater purpose awaits. The Barasha must be defeated."

Shara looked up at Ryckair. "Let us wait at least until late spring when the high passes are clear."

"The woman of Dharam speaks rightly," said Ena. "Storms still come and a long march through snow would sap our energy for battle. As well, we need ships to cross the Great River. The Fadella are not mariners."

Shara reclaimed her title of general and selected several Dharam officers vetted them for their loyalty to the new king. Under her tutelage Fadella fighters were formed into units and trained in modern military tactics and weapons. With Ryckair's assistance, officers, sergeants and corporals were appointed among the tribes. They drilled on the plains outside Kackar's walls.

Fadella troops were sent to the prisons, work camps and mines of Dharam to free those forced into bondage by Masalta. Thousands returned to the city, most of them sick and starved. Among these were the men Ryckair led out of the Sarte mines. Less than half survived the mercury vapors. They told Ryckair how Batu was taken by Petstra.

A great reunion was held with feasting and revelry. By royal proclamation, Ryckair appointed Ena governor of the Kackar region and assigned one thousand troops to guard the eastern borders.

Ryckair patted the new governor on the back. "And remember, One swallow of wine is sufficient to show your warrior soul."

Ena laughed.

Taxes were lowered and the populace given all the rights citizens of Carandir enjoyed. The people quickly embraced their new leader.

Ryckair wondered if Baron Dek was captured by the Barasha or free to fight the sorcerers. He wished he had terecs to seek the baron with a message about his Fadella army. Petstra took them with him when he returned to Carandir.

During a meeting, a soldier entered the audience hall. "Highness, two strangers are the gate. They ask for Prince Ryckair of Carandir and being held outside this hall."

Ryckair was certain none beyond the Fadella and those inside Kackar knew he survived the fall into the ice chasm. He thought of Petstra, then, wondered if the strangers were Jarat and Nissor. The garat could take on human form if it desired. "Just these two?"

"Yes, Highness. The captain of the guard sent out a patrol. They found no one else."

Ryckair reached out to Shara who took his hand. "Bring them before us."

Fadella guards escorted Batu and Telasec into the hall.

A broad smile spread across Ryckair's face. He dropped Shara's hand and ran to embrace Batu.

Batu held Ryckair with tears in his eyes. "Never did I think to see you alive again."

Ryckair stepped back as he held Batu by the shoulders. "My dearest friend, I thought you dead at Petstra's hands."

"He had other plans for me. The Barasha soon found I knew nothing of use. I was left to rot in prison."

"How did you travel from Carandir?"

"That's a tale best told in private," said Telasec, "There are things only your ears can hear."

Ryckair led Batu and Telasec to a side chamber.

Batu checked the door. "You won't believe me. We were sent by a wizard. She and her impish companion rescued us from prison and transported us to the north continent."

"Jarat and Nissor?"

Batu's raised his eyebrows. "You knew?"

Ryckair laughed. "Not of your coming. That's a joy unlooked for. I've indeed met the wizard." He told them the story of the warrior of the mountain. "Once I realized it was my own image I fought, I knew in my heart Petstra's letters were lies and I'm the heir, not Craya. So many things have changed since we last met."

Batu 's features became grim. "Things like Shara?"

"She's changed. We've shared so much together. Shara cares about me. I love her, Batu. Without her support I wouldn't sit as King of the Dharam or command an army to challenge the cruelty of Craya."

"What about Mirjel?"

"Do you think I've ever stopped loving her? How could I? Shara is alive and Mirjel is dead."

Batu shook his head. "Did you think any of Petstra's letters were true? Mirjel lives."

Ryckair looked from Batu to Telasec.

The Daro healer nodded. "It's true, Highness."

"But the fall on the stairs?"

"She recovered and lives. More, she commands a secret network that feeds a starving nation beneath the noses of the Barasha. Much has changed in Carandir as well." She went on to tell of the conspiracy to divert grain and the alliance with Yetig.

Ryckair stared at Telasec as he drew in a breath. "Alive? Then everything Petstra said was a lie." He paused. "Did she marry Craya?"

Batu paused. "Yes, Highness. That part was true."

Telasec leaned forward. "But she doesn't love him. She loves you, and always will. You can hear it in everything she says, see it in everything she does."

Ryckair covered his face with his hands. "Oh Jorondel, what am I to do? I've held her memory for so long but I've lived with Shara through so much. I know how you feel about her, Batu. You can't imagine how much she means to me. I must think alone." He threw the door open and strode from the room.

In a secret alcove next to the chamber, Shara closed the listening slat hidden behind a tapestry. For several moments she stood silently. Then, for the first time since childhood, she cried.

❧ ✦ ❧

Shara moved along the back streets of the city with a tattered cloak pulled around her. She knocked once more at the door of Zamalatha.

The healer ushered Shara inside. "What brings you this time, daughter of Masalta?"

"I need a poison."

The healer gave a grunt. "The powerful always come to the humblest in their greatest need. So, it has been and ever shall be. Who is to die?"

"A Royal woman of Carandir."

Zamalatha retrieved a jar, took a handful of powder and dropped it into a bowl. To this she added a piece of root, some black bark and two drops of liquid. She stirred it with a twig and held the container before Shara. "Say now the name of your victim. The order of death must come from your lips."

Shara concentrated on the mixture. "Mirjel Avar, Princess of Carandir." Smoke rose from the bowl. The image of a face formed in the vapor. Shara had never seen it before, yet knew it was her rival.

The smoke cleared. Only a film of gray powder remained in the bowl.

The old woman emptied this into a scrap of cloth, tied it with a piece of twine and handed it to Shara. "It is harmless to all, save its intended victim. You must deliver it near her before the next full moon rises. After that, the powder becomes impotent. From this time until then, the poison will call to Mirjel Avar, Princess of Carandir. She will find herself seeking it, though she won't know why. The closer the poison is to her, the more desperate will be her search. When it is in her presence, she will have no thought but to consume it. Before the full moon. That is all you have."

"You must give me the terec I left with you."

Shara stepped into the alley as she calculated the moon's next cycle in her mind. She poured the poison into a small metal container and attached it to the bird's leg. In her mind, She formed an image of Mirjel's face as she had seen it in the vapor. With no idea of where Meth lay, she had to trust the bird to find the target poison's victim. When the terec's eyes changed color, she threw it into the air and watched it fly away.

Mirjel and Yetig walked past the guards who stood ridged with their eyes closed next to the entrance of the prison. The narech had slipped the potion

Orane brewed into the soldiers' tankards. They would awake in a span with no idea they'd been drugged.

He and Mirjel moved down a corridor of prison cells.

Yetig held a glass vial in his hand. He stopped and stared into Mirjel's eyes. "Are you sure you want to be here?"

She stiffened "There has to be another way."

"We both know there isn't. The potion's quick and painless. If Mistress Telasec's still conscious I'll ask if she'll swallow it. You know what she'll say."

"Why can't we take her with us?"

"She'll appear to have died naturally. Even the Barasha will think so. If she escapes, they'll know there's a traitor within the palace."

Yetig opened the door to the Daro healer's cell and stepped inside. Within a heartbeat, he returned to the corridor. "She's missing."

He opened the cell where Batu was placed. "The smuggler's gone too."

Mirjel felt a wave of relief. "The mistress has magic. She might have opened the cells and befuddled the guards."

"Do you think Reshna will believe that? It's sheer luck he hasn't asked to see one of them."

Mirjel put her hand up. "Wait."

"What is it?"

She shook her head. "I'm not certain. I thought I heard someone call my name."

# CHAPTER FIVE

Ryckair wore the crown of the Dharam as he sat on the throne. A chalice of wine sat next to him.

A gong sounded. Masalta was escorted into the audience hall by Fadella guards. Behind him came his ministers and senior officers. The guards forced them each to kneel.

Ryckair sat forward. "You come before us to answer for your crimes, Masalta."

"I answer to no one. Whatever I did in Dharam or to the Fadella I did as king. You cannot bring the law to me in these matters. I was the law."

"Enough! The treacherous attack against our royal person is enough to condemn you. Yet, this could be forgiven. It is the crime of willfully trading with the Barasha for which there is no pardon."

"Who was to believe they were really sorcerers? I made a political alliance. Nothing more."

"Nothing more? For such a small price you would turn the world to darkness?"

He stood. "Hear now the decree of Ryckair, King of the Dharam and heir to the Western Realm. We will not defile our lands with the death of one so repugnant as you. Therefore, I banish you to the desert of the far northeast, beyond the confines of the civilized world. Thorns will be your bed and brambles your road. You will thirst and hunger. The sun will parch your skin. Never will you know rest. This you will suffer until your dying day, for if ever you place foot on these western lands, our sword will end your misery."

Ryckair sat. "With you go your ministers, your senior officers, your council and all who will not swear loyalty to us. But there is another to be judged this day."

Zamalatha was dragged forward by guards.

The Dharam healer twisted and bit at their hands. "Let me go. I am a registered healer. I have done nothing wrong."

Batu handed Ryckair a stack of parchments.

He looked down at Zamalatha. "What do you know of these?"

"Nothing."

Batu pointed to the parchments. "The evidence is before you. Inquiries were made. Many were happy to reveal your true nature. I entered your house and found these. Several copies of papers carried by Commander Petstra with varying changes."

"I was asked to copy them. Nothing more."

"Copy?"

"With alterations. It is a skill I learned. No harm was meant."

"Who asked for the copies?"

"Someone I had never seen before. A tall man."

Telasec entered the hall.

Zamalatha fell to her knees. "Mercy, great one. I help people as I can. That is all. I have no formal training. My mistress taught me what she could. I know nothing of wizards or dragons."

Telasec brought her face up to within a hands width of Zamalatha's. "I see the lie in your eyes. I feel its weight in the air. Beg mercy from the king who now holds your life in his hands. I shall know the truth. Who commanded you to make these copies?"

"Princess Shara. She came twice, once before she was declared an outlaw by her farther and once after she and King Ryckair returned. I dared not disobey."

Ryckair's mouth opened in shock.

Batu pointed to Shara. "Seize her."

Two Fadella grabbed Shara and disarmed her.

She struggled in their grasp. "What madness is this?"

Batu turned back to Zamalatha. "What did Shara want in her second visit?"

The healer gasped in short breaths, then prostrated herself. "She came for a target poison for a princess named Mirjel Avar. Mercy, great lord. Princes Shara would have killed me if I had not given it to her. She sent it by terec. I saw her through my window. Do not hang me."

Shara fell at Ryckair's feet. "I had to. Don't you see. You would have run to this Mirjel if you learned she was near death and been killed by Petstra. I could not bear that. Now, you have greatness. You are the king. The note said Mirjel was likely to die. What harm did I do in predicting the inevitable? There was no time.."

Ryckair sat dazed. An empty pit dropped in his middle. This couldn't be happening, not after all they'd done and planned together. Yet, from her own mouth came an admission that cut deeper than any sword could. He forced himself to show no outward reaction, though despair clawed at him. "Zamalatha, for your sins against the dragons you are condemned to accompany Masalta into exile. Remove her."

He closed his eyes, then threw the wine chalice across the room. "How could you?"

Shara shook her head. "Do not do this. Do not let the words pass your lips. Keep them inside where they have no power; for once you release them you doom us both. You don't even know if this Mirjel still loves you as I do. I have never loved anyone before. If I lose you, the pain will kill me. "

Ryckair closed his eyes. His breath was ragged. "Shara, daughter of Masalta, for treachery I banish you with your father to the deserts of the east, never to set foot upon the western lands again."

Two Fadella guards grabbed Shara by the arms. She shook herself free, looked to Ryckair, then strode from the room ahead of the guards.


That night, a terec landed on the windowsill of Ryckair's chambers.

Instead of the usual telepathic message, a vapory image of Jarat formed before it. "You'll need aid to travel across the Great River. Use this terec to send for support from Baron Dek."

A map appeared in the prince's mind of a spot on the Great River west of the borders of Carandir.

Ryckair picked up the bird and formed a message.

๛ ✦ ๕

Batu led Masalta and his party to the eastern border. Some traveled on horseback. Others rode in wagons filled with provisions. Most of Masalta's court, his senior officers and those soldiers and merchants loyal to him chose to accompany the deposed king into exile.

A flat plain stretched before them. Steady winds blew wisps of dust across their path.

Batu saw a shape on the horizon, a statue of a dragon. It faced east with its right foreclaw raised, as if to ward off any invaders.

The figure stood atop a huge pedestal. A stone wall ran north and south from it. The statue was as tall as the towers of the palace at Meth.

All in the party were awe-struck, even Shara, who carried herself with arrogance.

An archway through the base led to the eastern lands. These consisted of jagged hills covered by brambles. A narrow path extended through them and vanished behind a hill. No bird or beast were seen. The only sound came from the constant wind as it blew through bushes filled with thorns.

The air around the statue was lighter and crisper than that of the plain. Batu felt a sense of alertness. It heartened him and the Fadella in his command.

Masalta and all his household averted their eyes.

Batu and the Fadella stopped at the archway.

Masalta and the wagons continued on.

Shara was the last to cross. She looked back at Batu. There was a crooked smile on her face.

Batu wondered what a fallen princess could smile about in her moment of defeat. "We're done here. Let's return to the land of the living."

Masalta rode back to his daughter. "You got us into this, so come along and share in the spoils of your treachery."

She continued to stare into the west. "I loved him. I would have been his queen."

"Well, would buys a sack of air without a string to tie it, girl. Your lover is consumed with your rival. By this time, he has forgotten you."

"Perhaps for now. He will come to face me again." She placed a hand on her belly. "I carry his child."

She rode down the path.

❧    ✦    ☙

A terec landed on the saddle of Baron Dek's horse as he prepared to mount for a patrol. He hoped it was from Jea.

The bird allowed him to take it into his hands. He looked into its eyes. They changed from hazel to green. He heard Ryckair's voice in his head and nearly dropped the terec.

"*Find ships. Bring them to the mouth of the Great River. Sail north until you reach a ruined city on the coast. I'll meet you there.*"

Dek smiled and went to find Quib.

She sat on a fallen log with a bowl of venison stew and a sour look on her face. The baron patted her on the back. "How is the fare?"

She looked up at him in irritation. "Not as bad as last night. At least someone found some flavoring. If I had my staff it'd be edible."

"That time may not be far off. Some of the clerks who escaped with us appraised your jewels. We could buy many ships and still leave a tidy sum."

"I don't know of any shipwrights in this wretched forest."

"Of course not. They're in ports like Gelalan and Meth. We need ships, Quib. Many ships. You still have contacts in Gelalan interested in profit who ask no questions."

"If you think I could walk into any Carandirian port and buy a fleet of ships, think again. My contacts, as you say, would happily turn me over to the Barasha to increase their profit after the transaction."

"That's why I'll send some of our people, each with a part of the gems, to make discreet purchases of individual ships. They can say they're open-ing new trade with the east. You just have to give the names those we can deal with discreetly. We've sailors among us who can appraise the worth of good vessels."

"And where are you going with these ships?"

Dek smiled. "Let's just say that you're about to become a patriot."

Quib grimaced as Dek laughed.

Before she was captured by the mercenaries, Baroness Quib intended to skirt the western border of Karaken and travel as far from the Barasha as possible through the southern nations to the monarchy of Hura. Although she'd never been there herself, she traded with its merchants for rare and exotic items.

It was called paradise by most. The weather was tropical. Rain showers were gentle. The people were friendly and welcoming. They had skin that ranged from black to light ebony, curly hair that many shaved, both men and women, and eyes of deep brown. They loved clothing with bright colors, smiles and laughter. Yet, in a crisis they were serious and quick to act.

Water clocks were first devised in Hura. The design spread to Carandir and Xinglan where they established the official standard for time keeping.

The capital city of Vabesoo was located on a sandy coast of the Western Ocean. Buildings of stone and wood spread along the shore. Piers extended out into the sea where many fishing boats and ocean-going sailing vessels moored.

A wizard tower stood on a hill a short walk from the city. Few took notice of it and fewer yet knew its purpose.

At brightnail, Jarat and Nissor emerged from the tower door. The garat wore the semblance of a young boy.

Jarat knew this place well, for it was her land before she was summoned by Ilidel to become a wizard.

It was the Festival of the Sea, a celebration of the bounty from the ocean. All manner of seafood dishes were prepared. People played music on flutes and drums and bells. The mood was merry with much laughter and dancing.

Jarat and Nissor walked to King Tolay's palace. His wife, Queen Malah, died years before. His son, Prince Udalla, was a young man of twenty-four.

By tradition, the king opened the palace at festival time to greet his subjects. This was a complex of buildings in the center of the city. Walls enclosed grounds to the north, south, east and west. The east wall faced on a main boulevard where tall double doors admitted visitors.

Jarat and Nissor stood in line with others to await an audience. When she came into the presence of the king she knelt. "Great festival day, Highness. Many long years of success to you and your house."

Tolay smiled. "Rise. What are your names?"

"I'm Jarat. This is Nissor."

"What favor can I offer?" It was a custom for the king to give presents to his subjects on festival day.

The room faded around Tolay. He saw, in his mind, the Barasha, the demons they called and the crown they sought to release Baras. He saw Ryckair's quest and Dek's fight against evil. Words came to him. "The true heir of Carandir, Ryckair Avar, needs the help of all free peoples. Send ships with armed troops and horses north. Sail into the Great River to this spot. Seek Baron Dek." A clear picture of the location formed in Tolay's mind.

The king blinked. The room fell back into focus. "I'm sorry. I seem to have wandered for a moment. Here are two silver coins for you and your child. Great festival to you."

Jarat bowed. "And to you, Highness."

Dek watched a rowing ship his agents were able to purchase approach shore. He now had two galleys and three deep water sailing ships. He expected twenty vessels.

The captain reported questions were raised as to where the jewels came from and who the boats were for. "We saw Barasha priests. I fear this is the last ship we can openly purchase. We could sail to the port of Au and try again."

Quib shook her head. "They value their trading ships more than their children. They wouldn't sell any ship."

Dek sighed. "Sadly, it's true. Can we build ships, captain?"

"There is timber, but we have no shipwrights."

A sailor shouted, "Ship ahoy upstream."

The first thing Dek thought of was Reshna. "Colonel Herrik, prepare for battle."

Over one-hundred ocean going vessels approached.

Herrik set her troops ready.

The first ship dropped anchor. A launch was lowered.

Dek drew his sword, then a broad smile spread across his face when he saw Baroness Jea at the prow of the small boat. Two men with monolided eyes sat behind her.

When she reached the bank, the three disembarked.

Jea ran and embraced Dek. "I so prayed to Ilidel for your safety."

"And I to Jorondel for yours."

"May I introduce His Excellency, Ambassador Exor of Xinglan.

Exor bowed. "Queen Quanto sends her compliments along with these ships and troops to fight the Barasha."

He indicated the other man. "This is Major Telarha-Tey,"

The major saluted. "My troops are ready for your command, Baron Dek."

Dek shook the two men's hands. "Now, we have more than hope."

Again, a call came. "Ship ahoy, to the west."

Dek saw another fleet approach.

Herrik signaled her soldiers to be ready.

The ships anchored. A single launch came ashore. A tall man with dark ebony skin stepped onto the bank of the river. "I am Prince Udalla, son of Tolay, King of Hura. We seek Baron Dek of Rascalla."

"I'm Dek."

Udalla touched his right index finger to his head between the eyebrows and nodded. "My father had a vision of a terror that will consume all. He commanded me to seek you. I bring one-hundred ships and twenty-five-thousand mounted troops armed with bows, swords and spears to battle against the Barasha."

Dek took Udalla's hands in his. "Well met, friend of the south. Praise the dragons."

Over several weeks, Ryckair led his army of men and women, now over thirty thousand strong, to the gates of the ruined city. Against his protests, Batu was appointed narech. He grumbled and said he had no more temperament for being a soldier than he did when they first entered the city. Still, he handled the day-to-day operations of the host with ease and efficiency.

Ryckair thought constantly of Mirjel and the target poison. He tried to force the images to the back of his mind only to have them reemerge.

These worries he expected. What surprised him were thoughts of Shara. Her betrayal filled him with a rage he'd never known. After the banishment, he thought all memory of her was erased.

Still, at times, images of her face appeared unbidden, along with the recollection of a smile or her body nestled into his. He recalled secrets shared and plans made. Even through his anger, sorrow for those things lost remained.

The company reached the ruined city.

Batu moved his horse up to Ryckair's side. "Highness, the Fadella are afraid to enter. They call it the forbidden place and say the dragons will strike dead any who pass its gates."

Ryckair surveyed his army. It filled the slope of the hill and spread down into the valley below. "Their fear comes from an ancient liturgy."

He looked to the city, then back to the Fadella. "Of course. That's what this place is. Now I understand why Jarat instructed me to come here."

"Highness?"

"Gather the troops along the side of the hill."

The army was marched into position. Most of the troops looked warily at the city walls.

Ryckair bared his chest to expose the dragon mark. It glowed in the sun. "Hear me, Fadella, the Wandering Sorrow. Hear me exiled ones."

Whether by the force of his will or some magic of the dragon mark, each heard the words clearly.

Ryckair raised his hands toward the ruins. "I've walked the streets of this city."

There were hushed whispers.

Ryckair let them pass. "I come to you with the sign of Ilidel. The three trials are accomplished. Yet, you still doubt the prophesy has come to pass. The wrath of the dragons is ended. Ilidel's promise is fulfilled. You've come home. No longer are you Fadella. Know once more your true name."

He spread both hands out to the crumbled buildings. "Behold. Amblar. City of Avar the Great. This is your home, your name. Say it now and know its power."

A few voices timidly said, "Amblar." More followed in stronger chants until a deafening cry of "Amblar" sang out. The din continued for a tespan.

A ray of sun broke through clouds to illuminate Ryckair in golden radiance. "Now, Amblar, come home, never to wander again."

The troops marched through the gates and down wide streets. Some showed a sense of trepidation. Most gawked in wonder. The city was ten times the size of Kackar. They marched on to the wizard towers at the western wall where the ocean crashed against a sandy beach.

Ryckair climbed the steps to the tower along with Batu and Telasec. He stood on the threshold where a door should have been but where there was only stone.

Batu rubbed his beard. "Perhaps the wizard awaits us somewhere else in the city."

Ryckair touched the stone. "This is the door, though you don't believe it. I wouldn't have believed before I saw who the warrior of the mountain really was. We must pass belief to find the truth. Batu, you're in command until I return." He pressed his hands against the stone of the tower and walked through.

# CHAPTER SIX

Ryckair stood in a room wider than the outer appearance of the tower. It was barren of furnishings. Above was a ceiling with wooden beams. A soft glow illuminated the scene, even though there were no torches or lanterns.

Near the door, which now appeared to be made of oak, was a set of stairs. They curved up to follow the shape of the tower.

Ryckair climbed. He counted his steps. When he reached one thousand, he realized he'd risen higher than the tower seemed to stand.

He reached doors outlined in different colors that refused to open. There was a sense of dread near each.

The prince passed two windows that looked out on strange scenes.

From one, he saw a storm churned ocean. Waves crashed at the base of the tower.

Another opened onto a desert sand dune. It came up to the window. He could've step out and walked on it. An unfamiliar city with a tall spire and towers lay in the distance.

Around the next turn, he came to a window and shielded his eyes. There was no sight of land or even a horizon, only bright blue sky and white, puffy clouds. The tower stretched both up and down with no sign of a base or top.

He was about to leave the mystery of the window behind when a glint of silver caught his eye. It appeared for an instant behind the edge of a cloud, then vanished.

He watched the spot.

Another flash of color came near the window.

He gasped. No more than ten arm lengths away loomed a silver scaled dragon.

The carvings and paintings Ryckair remembered were mere shadows of the truth. The long sinuous body had four clawed feet. The face was round, with a short snout. The massive body was held aloft by transparent wings no thicker than a butterfly's. They glowed with rainbow veins that reflected light in a myriad of changing colors.

The eyes were as bright as a child's, yet deeper than the wisest Kyar. They held him, contemplated him, then beckoned for him to come outside and play as plain as if the dragon spoke.

Without hesitation, Ryckair pulled himself up on the sill.

A trumpet sounded.

Ryckair looked down and realized he stood on the edge of a bottomless precipice. He eased himself back into the tower.

The dragon pulled its tail up underneath its belly and twisted its head.

Below, two other silver shapes moved about a cloud. One opened its mouth. Again, the trumpet call resounded.

The first dragon looked back to Ryckair. "Good-by," said the eyes. The silver creature dropped and flew toward the clouds.

The dragon outside the window reached the others below.

Ryckair was amazed to see it was only a quarter their size. His mouth turned up in a grin at the realization he'd met a baby dragon.

He reached a wooden door at the top of the stairs and walked through to a round room.

A fire blazed in a hearth. There was a woven rug, settees and several chairs. Next to one of these stood a table stacked with books. The wall to the right was covered with shelves of books, scrolls, jars and boxes. To the left, a glass double door led to a balcony.

He stepped through and saw other towers only a few paces away. Some were round like this one in Amblar. Others were square like the tower in Barta far away on the south continent. Arched bridges connected all the towers to the one he stood on so he could have walked to each in a few steps. Bright stars shone overhead. This struck him as odd as it was a span before brightnail when he entered.

He climbed a set of steps to a flat roof and beheld an extraordinary view. Spread out before him was the whole of the northern monarchy from the mountains of the Fadella to the banks of the Great River and clear to the dragon statue Batu described on the eastern border. He saw the sweep of the land and the smallest detail at once as a whole.

A woman's voice came from behind, "You stand atop the hub that connects the five wizard towers, each of which touches many worlds."

Ryckair turned to see Jarat and Nissor.

The wizard stepped forward. "Here, they are only a few strides apart. Yet, from the ground below, they are separated by vast distances."

Jarat spread her hands wide. "Look south, Prince of Carandir, and know your home."

Ryckair gazed across the Great River and saw Meth. Vapors seemed to hang over the palace. He saw the Barasha priests, the Sinkarakan guards and Craya, along with Mirjel, whom the target poison had not yet reached.

He felt the starvation of his people, both of body and spirit. "Such suffering. How can I possibly stop this?"

"Find the key that opens the crystal case."

He cast his gaze all about, even west out to sea where thick fog obscured any sight. "I've looked everywhere. I can't see it."

"To find the key you must find yourself. Think of the warrior."

"There's no phantom to fight here."

"You're in constant battle. You battle your wit, your ignorance, your hopes, your fears. Many things compete within your mind. None of them are you"

Ryckair remembered how he felt when he believed the warrior was real and he trusted his weapons. They were proof he was in a fight. It would have been foolish to give them up. Yet, he dropped the knife. It just seemed the right thing to do. The act of faith cut through his fears and doubts.

So many things he once believed to be real were wrong; the fear he wasn't a leader, his blindness toward Craya's faults, concern over whether the birthmark was the sign of Baras, the false messages Craya was king and Mirjel dead, Shara's deceits and betrayal. Faith in himself showed the truth.

He remembered how Baron Dek once told him something his father said, the strength of Carandir is in the faith the citizens hold within themselves.

The haze around Ryckair dissipated. "The power is within me." He put his hand over the dragon birthmark. It glowed brighter than the sun.

When the light dimmed, the birthmark was gone. In its place he held the dragon shaped key. It hung from a silver chain around his neck. "The key's been here all the time. It's what saved my life in the fall."

"It was you who saved your life, Highness. Without knowing it, you used the power of the dragon crest through the key."

"But how did it come to me?"

"When Craya touched it, the key saw the evil intent in his heart and felt the threat of the Barasha. It came here where it knew it was safe from both. This was the sign I'd waited for with both anticipation and dread. It meant the Servants of Baras survived and the time of the Parili had come when the Fadella would be free again to follow the heir into battle.

"I traveled with it back though time to the day of your birth. There, I placed it around your neck and disguised it as the dragon shaped birthmark."

Ryckair held the key aloft. He perceived all those assembled below in Amblar saw it as well. He heard a great cheer.

Jarat pointed out to sea. "Look to the west, heir of Avar. The time of your rising has come."

Ryckair turned to the ocean. The fog cleared to reveal a fleet of rowed galleys and sailing ships in the harbor of Amblar.

He descended the tower with Jarat and Nissor.

Batu Jumped back as the prince emerged from what seems a stone wall. He started at the key. "Highness."

Jarat and Nissor stepped out of the tower behind Ryckair. He took Batu's hands in his. "The hour has come, dear friend. Carandir rises."

He led Batu, Telasec, Jarat and Nissor across the city to a stone wharf.

One of Prince Udalla's sailing ships docked. Dek and Quib came ashore. They knelt before Ryckair and gazed upon the dragon key.

Dek raised his head with tears in his eyes. "Highness. Through concern and fear I never lost faith. Your terec message was the greatest joy I've known since Mirjel's birth. My dear wife traveled to Xinglan and formed an alliance with its people. King Tolay sent a fleet from Hura. Their troops await us in Carandir. We're ready to transport you and your soldiers."

Ryckair placed a hand on Dek's shoulder. "Never more welcome a vision is your fleet. This is Jarat, the last wizard."

Dek lowered his head. "Praise to you, great one. Praise to the dragons."

He rose and pointed to the ships. "With the help of Baroness Quib we purchased vessels."

Ryckair raised an eyebrow to Quib. "You gave of your own treasury?"

A serious look came to her face. "I must confess, I hoped to escape to the south. I've often thought of myself as a merchant rather than a noble of Carandir. Even when the Barasha rose, I worked to protect my holdings and not of the monarchy."

Her voice became ragged. "I saw Baron Dek's courage as he fought the forces of sorcery, yet still sought to turn things to my advantage. As I stand here in the presence of you and Mistress Jarat." She placed her hands over her face and wept. "I'm filled with shame."

Ryckair took her hands and kissed them. "The truth you speak holds great power. The strength of the west, east, north and south, old and new, loyal and redeemed rises this day. To the palace and the final battle."

At her home outside Au, Osba looked out a window of her cottage. The Sinkarakan guards were no longer on duty. "Garto, come look at this."

They went outside. There was no sign of the sentries the Barasha had placed. Garto hitched a horse to the carriage and they rode into the city.

There were no Barasha or Sinkarakans to be seen. People milled around streets where open doors revealed empty storehouses.

Councilor Tradas walked down the steps of a municipal building.

Garto dismounted the carriage. "What happened?"

Tradas spoke in a faint voice. "The Barasha left and took the Sinkarakans with them. They emptied the treasury vaults. The wealth of Au is gone."

It took several spans for Ryckair's army to be loaded onto the vessels. Quarters were crowded.

Ryckair stood next to Jarat as they set out to sea. "I fear it'll be a long and cramped journey, Mistress Jarat."

"It need not be." She faced east. The air in front of the fleet shimmered with a silver sparkle. An arch formed at the water's surface. Strong winds from the west pushed the fleet into a tunnel whose sides consisted of white vapor.

The fleet emerged from the arch.

Ryckair saw a riverbank. Baroness Jea stood upon it with a smile on her face."

Dek raised an arm. "Baroness Jea stands with Ambassador Exor of Xinglan and Prince Udalla of Hura."

A longboat carried Ryckair to the bank, along with Dek, Quib, Jarat, Nissor, Telasec and Batu.

Exor fell to one knee before the wizard. "Oh, mighty one, our ancestors told of your return for a final battle. We're ready to repay our debt for your protection. Long has your image been revered and long have we held faith with the dragons. I, Exor, have brought with me troops trained in the art of the pollaxe and trident. We commit our lives to defeat the Barasha and hold the evil one in sleep."

Jarat smiled. All felt the air grow lighter. "Rise, valiant Exor. I remember the gallant sacrifices of your ancestors and honor them as I now honor Baroness Jea who brought you here."

She addressed Udalla. "The faith of Hura is well known to me. We are kin. I've never forgotten my homeland."

Udalla lowered his head. "Great one."

Ryckair sketched out a plan on the ground with the tip of his sword. "Force of arms can't defeat the sorcerers, nor can Mistress Jarat do so by herself, is that not right?"

"There's much I can accomplish, and more could be done if other wizards of Ilidel still walked the earth. I alone can't defeat all the demons they can call."

Ryckair refined the drawing. "There's only one force that can, the magic of the crown. We must outmaneuver the Barasha to reach it."

Herrik studied the sketch. "I think I know what His Majesty has in mind. A distraction."

"Exactly, colonel. The ships and galleys will transport our troops upriver past the docks of Lena. Dek, you'll march the host across the mountains to the high plain before the palace and create a diversion. I'll sail into Lake Hasp and enter the palace through a secret entrance at the base of the pinnacle know only to the

Kyar and myself. From there, I'll slip into the grand audience hall and take the crown."

Dek squinted one eye. "A secret entrance?"

"Yes. It's a long story. Make plenty of noise. We want the Barasha to know you're coming and focus on your attack. Once the crown is upon my head, no force can stand before us, not even Baras."

The leaders dispersed to relay the plan to their troops.

Jarat took Ryckair to the side. "Be warned, heir of Avar. The purpose to which you put the crown will control what it will do. Think always of Carandir's good, never of personal desires. You're its steward, not its owner."

Dek and Herrik conferred next to a tent.

Ryckair approached. "Baron, let's take a walk into the woods."

The two men followed a trail through the forest. Tall trees shaded them from the sun. Ryckair had forgotten how warm the southern continent was. They came to a gentle stream.

A feeling of wholeness grew in Ryckair. He saw his own land with fresh eyes. The serene beauty of the little stream, the sharp green leaves against a bright blue sky told him he belonged here and would stay.

Ryckair stared into the forest. "Master Orane spoke many times of the demon and my parents' death. Tell me, when you wore the crown, how fast did you learn to command it?"

"That's difficult to say, Highness. So much happened. I thought instructions of some type would come. Instead, I just knew how to contain the demon. It obeyed my commands and walked into a cell under the keep. I told it to sleep. It did."

"It sounds so simple."

"There is something else. It may make no difference to you as Avar's heir. Still, be warned. The seduction of the crown was nearly beyond me. I had the power to do anything I desired. No force could stop me. The greatest challenge I ever faced was to seal the crown back in the crystal sphere."

Ryckair thought about this for a long moment. "Jarat warned me to think only of Carandir." His mind wandered to Mirjel and whether the crown would allow him to save her. He told Dek about the target poison Shara sent. "It becomes impotent at the next full moon.  That's less than a week away."

Dek  drew in a slow breath. "I love my daughter deeply, and know you do as well. Even though you both obeyed the rules of courtship, the affection between the two of you was always plain to my eyes. When I asked your father to grant her hand to the next king, I pictured someone like you. By the grace of the dragons, it happened. I'll command everyone to seek the poison and trust to the dragons."

Dek supervised the loading of felled trees onto one of the smaller merchant galleys. "Rascallan lumber comes into Meth every day from the Ulta Mountains, Highness. There'll be nothing to arouse suspicion. Still, you may be boarded for inspection."

Ryckair dressed in sailor's breeches and doublet. He rubbed his shaven chin. "I wish I still wore the beard from the Sarte mines to hide my identity."

"You'll have to busy yourself if you are stopped," said Dek.

Jarat came up from behind. "There's good reason not to be disguised. Even if I conjured a beard, the people must see your face to take heart."

"And take heart they will," said Dek. "Carandir may be a nation beaten to its knees, yet beneath the surface its strength awaits a call to rise."

Dek marched the loyal forces east through the Barony of Lena and into the Barony of Lanteler in which the palace was located. To Dek's surprise, they encountered no resistance. He felt a trap. Still, if he drew the Barasha's attention away from Ryckair his mission would succeed.

They came to the Dragon Mound. As always, there was a cold disquiet to the place. Everyone looked about nervously.

The members of the various militias loyal only to their own nobles before the Barasha seized power now marched without hesitation as a single force. Dek thought of Baron Etera and his dying wish for all baronies to pledge their loyalty to the Crown for the good of Carandir and felt a deep sense of pride in the troops.

The company moved through thick forests until they reached the edge of the plain in front of the palace. It was filled with enemy soldiers.

Dek lay behind an embankment with Batu. "We outnumber them but they're dug in."

A Huran lieutenant crawled up to the pair. A sheen of sweat on his dark skin reflected sunlight. "Lord Baron, Prince Udalla is in position."

"Good. What's your name, soldier?"

"Marawee Bedquanga, sir."

"May the dragons protect you this day, Marawee. Tell your prince I'll give the signal momentarily."

Marawee saluted and left.

Dek took a drink of water and handed the skin to the former smuggler.

Batu wiped water from his chin. "I was gonna retire from smuggling. If Quib had bought those Karaken fire stones I could've paid for a farm near Madewy, maybe gotten married."

"Nice country, Madewy."

"Good dairy land."

"Probably the best."

The two men stared across the plain.

Dek stood. "Well, let's to it."

He blew a horn.


Column upon column of mounted troops and foot soldiers engaged in mortal confrontation.

Exor led his soldiers in a flanking maneuver to the left. Some Xinglaners used their long tridents to bite into the enemy. Others finished them with their pollaxes.

Udalla and his troops rode down the mercenaries on the right flank with swords and spears. Their charge laid waste to the enemy.

In the center ranks, Ichary brought his archers forward and assailed the enemy.

Mercenary troops dropped to the ground with arrow wounds. When their own shafts fell short of the Fadella, the Barasha's forces pulled back.

Colonel Herrik led a wave of foot soldiers into the fray.

Dek drove his cavalry in a charge toward the palace. His men wielded heavy battle sabers that slashed through enemy soldiers who stood in their way.

As the Carandirian army and its allies pushed the mercenaries back toward the bridge, five hundred Karakien fighters dropped their weapons and fled. A general rout among the rest of the mercenary forces ensued.

Jarat watched as the battle move toward a quick conclusion. "I don't like this, Nissor. Where are the Barasha?"

She raised herself in the stirrups as the sight of a tall mercenary captain appeared on horseback. He wore shining armor with a white plume on his helmet. His presence stopped the rout. The mercenary army turned and charged.

Herrik's troops in front were ridden down by cavalry. Mercenary foot troops swept behind the horses to dispatch any who lay wounded. The rest of the defender's forces took heart from this and pressed forward.

The battle raged for most of the day. Both sides were exhausted. Dek ordered retreat. The same call came from the other side.

It was almost sunset when Dek slid from his horse in front of the command tent. He doffed his helmet and handed it to an aide as he stepped inside. All the other commanders along with Jarat and Jea awaited him.

Jarat studied a map with markers showing the armies' positions. "Success seems within easy grasp. Too easy."

Herrik removed her helmet. "My troops can be ready for battle after a few hours of rest, Mistress Jarat."

"That may be, but I suspect some sorcery in the waiting."

"I remember the cloud demon in the courtyard, honored one. It's all the more reason to act now before they can regroup."

Jea spread a hand over the map. "I agree. Had we broken through and killed the Barasha priests while we skirted the swamp the ice demon would never have been called."

Nissor ran into the tent. The garat jumped from foot to foot as it chirped.

Jarat's face clouded in alarm. "It's as I feared. Colonel Herrik, call the troops to arms. Our enemy attacks."

"Impossible. They're as exhausted as we are."

"We fight more than a mortal army. Come."


Ryckair's rowing galley entered Lake Hasp a span before sunset. Dozens of boats and ships sailed by. Most were fishing vessels.

A Carandir military galley raised a green stripped pennant and made for them.

The captain of Ryckair's vessel peered across the water. "They order us to come about and make ready for boarding, Highness."

Ryckair sat at the stern of the vessel and coiled rope as the war galley shipped oars.

The military vessel came along side. A Karakien in a Carandir captain's uniform boarded Ryckair's galley. "Bring me your manifest."

Ryckair glanced up to see shackled rowers on the war ship. They wore tattered Carandirian uniforms. Two other mercenary officers stood on the deck of the war galley. One was a Sinkarakan.

The Karakien walked up and down the Rascallan galley as he inspected the load of wood.

Ryckair continued to coil rope.

The prince felt a touch on his shoulder.

The mercenary officer looked down at him. "What's wrong with you? You've been coiling the same rope for a tespan."

Ryckair let his arms relax as he realized the officer didn't recognize him. "My captain demands it just so."

The captain pushed him away. "Rascallans." He threw the manifest to the deck. "Take your cargo in and get back to your wretched lands."

Ryckair looked up at the other galley again.

One of the rowers stared. His eye opened wide. "Prince Ryckair has returned."

Another sailors shouted, "Praise be to Jorondel and Ilidel."

A third cried out, "Praise to Prince Ryckair."

The mercenary officer reached for their cutlasses.

Ryckair pulled a dagger from his doublet. With a single thrust he sunk the blade into the Karaken captain's belly, then grabbed his cutlass and leapt to the Carandir ship.

Rascallans from the lumber galley retrieved the axes used to fell trees and followed. On the commandeered Carandir war ship, they broke the chains of the rowers. The freed sailors grabbed belaying pins and scraps of wood to join in the rout of their captors.

The two mercenaries positioned themselves on the aft deck.

Ryckair charged up the ladder.

The Sinkarakan slashed for the prince's neck with his cutlass.

Ryckair parried with confidence.

The Sinkarakan's blade swung wide.

Ryckair sliced open his opponent's belly.

The Rascallans dispatched the other mercenary. The freed sailors cheered.

There was only one Carandirian officer among the captives, a young man in a tattered ensign's uniform.

He knelt before Ryckair. "Highness, I've secreted this for years now, though I would've been killed for it." The officer held up a crudely sewn pennant. It was a blue field with a silver dragon against it.

Ryckair took the flag in his hands and kissed it.

Everyone on board touched their heads in the sign of the covenant.

The prince handed the flag back to the officer. "What is your name?"

"Ensign Gorsh Efra, Highness."

"No greater act of love for Carandir have I seen. Guard this for a little longer. The battle's not yet won and we require stealth."

The ensign pointed to the rest of the Carandir fleet. "Every ship on the lake is commanded by foreign officers and rowed by Carandirians in chains. Many have died at their oars. Their bodies were dumped into the lake. Some were taken by the Barasha to a fate I wish not to think about."

Ryckair handed Efra his cutlass. "Ensign Efra, I promote you to the rank of lieutenant and appoint you master of this galley. Continue your patrol as if nothing's happened. When you approach another enemy held galley, come along side and board it. Free the prisoners. Command all reclaimed galleys to take every enemy held vessel on the lake."

"It shall be done, My Prince, and may the dragons protect you."


An exhausted terec landed on top of the north tower. Without a specific location imprinted on its mind, the bird had flown through fierce storms with only the image of a face to guide it to the recipient.

A bony hand reached down and picked the bird up. The crimson-robed sorcerer dropped powder on its wings.

The terec shrieked and convulsed.

Before it died, the sorcerer was able to read its mind and determine who it sought.

He removed the canister with the target poison and walked down the tower to report to Reshna.

# CHAPTER SEVEN

In her chambers, Mirjel packed for a long voyage. Yetig only told her they must flee before the Barasha discovered Telasec was missing. She knew their plan was lost and still thought Ryckair dead. Yetig was all she had. She made him promise to bring Lek. They would all escape east up the river where there were others faithful to the dragons who might help.

She selected clothing best suited to a life on the run, jerkins, blouses and pantaloons. The finery was left behind except for jewels and coins sewn into the garments.

Lek and Yetig had left two tespans before to gather more supplies.

A knock at the door. She opened it. "Thank Ilidel you're back."

Reshna stood in the corridor with four crimson robed Barasha priests.

Mirjel tried to force the door closed.

One of the priests held it open with his arm.

She backed away toward the balcony.

Reshna stepped into the room and surveyed the tousled belongings. "You would leave your love, just as he is about to return to you?"

"I don't know what you mean."

"You lie poorly, Princess Mirjel. You think to protect Yetig, by hiding your affair. I have known of this for some time. I speak of your true love, your one love."

Mirjel took in a sharp breath. "Ryckair." She shook her head. "Don't think you can torment me with such lies."

"It is no lie. Ryckair lives. He approaches from the lake at this moment."

Mirjel wanted the words to end. She'd accepted Ryckair's death. He was gone and, in a strange way, safe. More importantly, her own pain was locked away.

Now the wounds broke open. In her heart she wanted Reshna's words to be true, though she was certain they couldn't be.

She closed her eyes. "Whatever your game, I won't play."

"You will." Reshna took the canister with the target poison from behind his back.

Mirjel felt dizzy. She tried to pull away. All conscience thought left her. She followed the sorcerers out of the room.


It was near sunset when Ryckair slipped over the side of the lumber galley as it passed near the rock pinnacle below the palace. He swam to the entrance of the secret cave while the galley continued on.

The prince reached the narrow strip of land at the entrance of the secret passage.

Yetig stepped out of the cave and bowed. "Your Highness." A dozen Carandirian soldiers stood behind him.

Orane appeared from the darkness. "Highness, there's no time to explain. Know that Narech Yetig and the Kyar now work together to eliminate the Barasha."

Ryckair stared at Yetig with contempt. "Telasec told me."

"She lives?"

"Yes."

"Then we must hurry."

"I'll form no pact with traitors."

Yetig knelt before the prince. "Highness, if any of us live to see the end of this day, you may judge me as you see fit. I make no excuses. I acted to save Carandir and guide the monarchy back to greatness, though I miscalculated the power of the sorcerers. For this I may well pay with my life, but not at your hand."

"And what would give you that protection?"

"Your word."

"That's something you'll never have."

"Not even for Mirjel's life?"

Ryckair reached for his dagger. "Where is she?"

"It's not I who threatens her. She's been taken to the north tower by Reshna. Allow me and the crew of my flagship to depart Carandir in exile. Give me your word and I'll tell you how to rescue her."

The narech extended his open hand.

Ryckair looked into Yetig's eyes. Though he was certain the officer concealed something, he saw no alternatives. The prince raised his hand, placed it into Yetig's and gave a single, short shake.

Jarat led the way across the plain. Over one-hundred Barasha priests had raised a triangular scaffolding until it towered to the height of two stories in front of the bridge. Solid platforms were arranged along the width of the first and second levels. Lit braziers sat on each.

Mercenaries carried a captured Fadella whose legs and arms were strapped to a wagon wheel. The captive twisted and pulled on the bindings. The wheel was placed in front of a brazier at the center of the lower platform. Drums beat out a low, dull rhythm.

The drums stopped. A sorcerer drove a dagger into the prisoner's chest. Flames flashed in the brazier and rose to form a vortex above the tower. The wooden wheel was set on fire. Above, the vortex glowed red. Smoke from the burning body flowed into it.

The sorcerer spoke an incantation and tossed powder into the flames. It was sucked up by the vortex and shot into the air to shower down on the mercenary army. As it descended, battle worn troops rose fresh and renewed.

Jarat raised her arms overhead. "*Sin cae aj del, hachana.*"

A screech emanated from the vortex. The mercenaries who were rejuvenated a moment before fell to their knees and screamed as they held their heads.

Dek stared in amazement. "What is this?"

"The Barasha summoned a demon and commanded it to give up its life force, a very dangerous thing to do. It now consumes those it was called to strengthen." Jarat closed her eyes and placed her hands on her forehead. "*Ava hin eer.*"

The demon vortex spun faster and faster as it folded in on itself. With a bang, it vanished. Some of the mercenary troops lay on the ground as the flesh of their bodies bubbled, then crumbled. Others dropped and tried to crawl away.

Dek drove his forces ahead. They reached their enemy and dispatched those in the front lines.

The flames of the brazier ignited anew. Five wheels were brought out, each with a Carandirian soldier strapped to it. They were hauled up to the platforms on the lower and upper levels of the tower.

Once more, the wheels were set ablaze and powder thrown into the flames. This time, five demons in the form of spinning pinwheels appeared above the tower to take in the smoke.

The mercenaries were showered with the enchanted powder. They cheered and ran forward with renewed energy. Those who were slain shuddered, then their reanimated corpses rose to follow their comrades. The silver armored mercenary champion came forward and the charge was on.

Jarat staggered back. "I can't defeat such forces. Our troops must hold their ground and wait for Ryckair to take the crown."

Dek mounted his horse. "All commanders. We fight for our lives."

Ichary's archers fired on the charging enemy. The arrows struck the advancing troops. Shafts protruded from their necks, arms and chests. No blood came from their wounds as they continued forward

Dek, Exor and Udalla found the same to be true. Saber cuts, tridents and spears failed to stop the advancing horde. Only when an enemy soldier's legs were hacked away would the attacker fall. Even then, the body clawed its way forward with its hands.

Dek waved his sword overhead. "Pull back, but keep them engaged."

In the cave, Yetig handed Ryckair a sword and scabbard. "Reshna took Mirjel to the roof of the north tower."

Ryckair strapped on the sword. "I'll go to the throne room and take the crown. Then, I'll deal with Reshna. All of you wait here. I can travel faster alone."

Yetig buckled on his own sword. "You'll need my help to get past the guards. We'll pretend you're my prisoner."

"With a sword in my hand?"

Yetig held his gaze on Ryckair. "You need me, Highness."

Ryckair looked to Orane, then to Yetig. "Very well. Let's go."

The prince led the way up the secret corridors to the vaults of the Kyar and into the hallway connecting the north and south towers. They entered the throne room and stopped.

The crystal sphere and the crown were missing.

"Where is it, Yetig?"

"Reshna still plays his games, Highness."

They ran to the north tower and up the grand staircase. There were no guards or Barasha. Ryckair mounted the stairs to the tower roof with Yetig behind.

A low parapet ringed the flat top of the tower. Reshna stood on a raised platform at the west end. His red robes were silhouetted by the setting sun.

A fire burned in a brazier in front of him.

To his left, Mirjel sat chained to a ring. Her eyes stared ahead.

To his right was Commander Petstra.

In front of him, sword in hand, stood Craya next to the wooden pedestal with the crystal sphere and the crown.

Reshna tilted his head, like a bird of prey. "Greetings, son of Haram. Across deep waters and past lonely wastes our paths have run."

Ryckair looked to Mirjel, then to Reshna. "Your time is ended, sorcerer." He took out the dragon key. "The crown will deal its terrible justice."

"The game is not over yet." He raise the canister of target poison.

Mirjel crawled toward it. Her hands and feet still moved when she reached the limits of the chain.

Reshna toyed with the canister. "It is a crude bane whose potency ends with the rise of the full moon tonight. At the moment it is the deadliest threat possible to Princess Mirjel. The moon holds your destiny as well." He indicated Petstra who held a leather pouch in his one hand.

Ryckair drew his sword and took a step toward the case.

Craya raised his sword and blocked him. "I can't allow that, brother."

Petstra threw the pouch. It hit Ryckair and covered him with red powder.

Craya and the commander attacked in unison.

Yetig joined in and beat Petstra back as Craya advanced.

Ryckair deflected his brother's blows, yet held back on his own attack. Images of the twins in their youth when they laughed and played and shared secrets swam in his mind. "Craya, don't do this. We can defeat Reshna together."

For an instant, Craya dropped his guard. Pain strained his face. He looked into Ryckair's eyes. Then, with a guttural cry, he attacked.

Craya circled to bring the glare of the setting sun into Ryckair's eyes.

Ryckair feigned to the left and came round for a thrust.

Craya easily parried the blow and returned a riposte.

Ryckair pressed Craya back as he prayed to Jorondel for his brother to yield before he was forced to kill him. He threw himself against Craya.

Their swords clashed.

Craya shoved his brother away. He nearly tripped as he lost his footing.

Ryckair pressed his attack.

Craya gave ground.

They moved toward the crystal sphere.

Reshna dropped powder in the brazier and spoke the words of a spell. A flash momentarily blinded everyone on the tower.

When Ryckair's eyesight recovered, he saw, twelve exact duplicates of Craya. As one moved, so all thirteen moved together in unison.

The mirror image army raised their swords and charged.

Ryckair parried.

His opponents' swords were hard as steel. Their bodies were like smoke. Each time he attacked, his sword passed through their images.

Yetig knocked Petstra's sword aside and stabbed the commander through the abdomen.

Petstra dropped to the roof top.

Reshna was too absorbed with the phantoms to take notice of anything else.

Yetig dropped to his knees next to Mirjel. As the brothers fought, he took a set of keys on his belt, one of which would unlock the chains holding Mirjel. If he guided her down the stairs in her dazed state, he could take her to the waiting galley and flee into the east while Ryckair and Reshna were occupied. He would tell her  Ryckair opened the sphere but Craya killed him and took the crown.

Ryckair concentrated on the thirteen images. One moved its hand slightly ahead of the others. He pushed all thoughts and emotions from his mind and struck.

The blade drove hard into Craya's chest. The phantom images vanished. Craya stared at the red stain on his doublet as though he tried to recognize what it was. He looked up to Ryckair, then fell.

Reshna's trance broke. His first sight was that of Narech Yetig. "Insulant fool. I will take from you what you hold most dear." He tossed the canister to Mirjel.

Yetig grabbed it in midair and jumped on the parapet wall. His chin quivered. "I'll keep what I hold in my heart."

He looked to Mirjel. Tears came to his eyes, then he leapt from the tower with the canister in is grip.

As the target poison receded, Mirjel's mind cleared. She tried to make sense of the scene. The ring of keys lay before her. She struggled to find the right one to unlock her chains.

Ryckair ran to the box, inserted the key and turned it round once. The crystal formed a line in its center. The top half opened like a lid. He placed the crown on his head just as the full moon rose.

On the plain, the animated corpses shuddered and fell. The Barasha's brazier went out. The spirals above the tower imploded.

Dek's troops felt a spontaneous and unexplainable joy.

The mercenaries who still lived dropped their weapons and fled.

Jarat raised her heads to the palace. "The crown is once more focused and the foes of Carandir can't stand before the power of the rightful monarch."

Batu raised his sword. "Then, we've won."

"Not yet. We have to reach the north tower before the greatest danger strikes. First this filth must be cleared."

Jarat raised her hands overhead and clapped them together. Dull thunder rolled across the plain. The scaffolding where the sorcerers stood shook. Screams rose from the Barasha priests.

The ground opened. Flames reached up from beneath and engulfed the scaffolding. It and the Barasha priests fell into the abyss.

Jarat spread her arms apart once more and slapped her hands together. The hole closed with a crack. "We must reach the tower at once."

 formula ∽ ✦ ✍

Ryckair was flooded with the minds of all his ancestors back to Avar. He saw his mother Araney through his father's eyes and knew the love he held for her. Within a heartbeat, he saw former kings and queens, their reigns, their battles, their mistakes and their triumphs.

Craya moaned. Ryckair knelt at his brother's side, took Craya in his arms and held him as he had when they were boys.

Craya's face was relaxed and calm. He reached up and grasped Ryckair by his sailor's jerkin. "Of all the people in the world, only you loved me enough to come back and free me." He smiled. "Things are supposed to get black when you're dying. Strange. Everything seems so very crisp and clear. I almost..." He stopped; his face serious. "Ryckair, if I did something really terrible, really awful, would you still love me?"

Ryckair nearly choked as he answered. "Of course."

"Forever."

"Forever and ever."

Craya relaxed, then died.

Ryckair kissed his brother on the forehead and lowered his body, then stood and advanced on Reshna.

Mirjel opened the lock and dropped the chains holding her. Before she could move, the sorcerer drew a dagger, grabbed her by the hair and held the blade to her throat. "Can you evade a demon yet, Ryckair Avar? This fresh blood will call your death."

Behind him, Jarat burst through the door and onto the roof. "Highness, stay your hand." The others rushed onto the roof behind her.

Ryckair thought of nothing beyond Mirjel's life and his hatred of Reshna. He formed an image of the sorcerer burning with fire. Blue flame sprang from the dragon crest to engulf Reshna in a brilliant glow.

He released his grip on Mirjel and stumbled against the parapet. His form was engulfed in flames. The features on his face showed horrific pain. When he spoke, his voice was harsh and cracked. "Fool. You have used the crown for personal gain to save one most precious to you. When it is not used in the name of all Carandir its power is corrupted. You have played your part well. The wizard has destroyed the other Barasha, yet they played their part in delaying her. Now, I play mine." Reshna swung around to the west as the last rays of the sun touched the horizon. "Awake."

The blue flame changed to bright red. It poured out of Reshna's fingers and struck the Dragon Mound. The top of the hill glowed in the twilight. The Barasha priest laughed as his body vanished in a haze of smoke.

The earth rumbled and shook the foundations of the palace. Birds leapt into the air. The top half of the Dragon Mound shifted as dirt and boulders fell away. A shrill bellow cut through the air followed by a deep base voice. "*Nuava. Ata laney.*"

Where once a hill stood, a sinuous shape covered in red scales now rose on four legs. Nearly transparent wings, each as large as a dozen sails, spread wide. The rays of the dying sun sparkled though them.

Jarat made the sign of the covenant. "Baras has risen."

The red dragon climbed into the air and swept across the plain. Soldiers fell to the ground. Others ran in circles.

Ryckair shouted, "Baras. You will yield to me."

The dragon gave a great bellow. All on the tower were knocked down save Ryckair. He stood steadfast as the crown's dragon crest glowed.

Baras flew straight for the palace with his talons extended outward.

Ryckair focused on the approaching dragon. "Baras, you will yield." He searched back through the ages for spells locked in the crown to attack the dragon. Images came to his mind. He couldn't understand them. In frustration, he raised a hand. "Yield."

The great dragon slowed, then stopped a stone's throw from the tower and eyed the crown.

Ryckair felt certain he'd subdued Baras.

Jarat leapt between Ryckair and the dragon just before the air ignited into flame.

The wizard stretched out her arms. The fire reached them with a roar but was deflected from their bodies and shot away harmlessly. "Highness, don't..." Before the wizard could say another word, Baras was upon her.

He grabbed Jarat in one claw and carried her aloft.

Nissor chirped wildly. The garat leapt into the air and assumed the shape of a golden dragon. It flew straight for Baras with such speed it appeared to be no more than a streak of light. With talons extended, Nissor flew into Baras' face.

Ryckair fought to find a spell to defeat the evil one.

Thunder echoed in the sky as lightning sparked. The two dragon forms writhed in the air.

Above the din, Ryckair heard Jarat's voice shout, *"Lan cheha."*

Baras' great bulk shuttered. He released the wizard.

In the same instant, Nissor flew down and caught Jarat in its own claws. The pair descended toward the tower roof as Baras flew aimlessly in a circle.

Ryckair felt elation at first, until he saw Baras recover from his stupor and dive for Nissor. He struck the dragon shaped garat in the left wing.

Nissor dropped Jarat.

Baras swooped down and captured Jarat once more. He crushed the wizard in his claw and threw her body to the tower's roof.

Ryckair ran to Jarat and knelt at her side.

Nissor landed, returned to garat form and took the wizard's hand.

Ryckair expected Nissor to coo. Instead, it remained silent.

Jarat took in shallow breaths as she opened her eyes and coughed. "Remember the warrior in the mountain and the strongest weapon of all. That is the key to unlock the spell..."

She closed her eyes and fell unconscious.

Nissor rested its head on the wizard's chest and closed its eyes.

Mirjel ran to Ryckair's side.

Together, they faced the approach of Baras as he dove on the tower.

Ryckair and Mirjel clasped hands. He called up a blast of lightning and sent it skyward.

It struck Baras full in his chest and knocked him back.

The dragon raised a claw and double the number of lightning bolts flew back at Ryckair and Mirjel to strike the walls of the tower and blast large sections of stone away.

Ryckair willed a ball of fire to entomb Baras.

This time the dragon fell from the sky and crashed onto the plain. The fire burned so hot it was felt from the top of the tower.

The fireball expanded, then exploded.

Baras took flight once more and charged directly for Ryckair and Mirjel.

The prince called up boulders and hurled them at the dragon. They bounced off his red scales as though the rocks were snowflakes.

Ryckair summoned a tornado, acid fog, a thousand spears. The more he attacked Baras, the stronger the dragon became.

Baras reached the tower and blew a cold wind that enveloped and chilled all present. The visions from the crown vanished from Ryckair's mind. The spells he understood a moment before were now jumbled.

The dragon grabbed Ryckair and Mirjel in one of his massive talons and flew north over the Great River. "Your torment will be long, Avar. In the end, you will both bow down and pray to me for death. All humankind will pray to me."

Baras studied the prince. "No, not Avar. Merely a descendant."

Ryckair tried to focus his thoughts on the spells.

Baras laughed. "Fool. You think you have the strength to challenge me? What lies have the wizards told you? Drop the crown. I'll do you no harm. Can't you see you are but their instrument? We're not enemies."

"Jorondel, protect me."

"Jorondel and Ilidel use you. You don't know the truth of the Dragon Wars and the role of the wizards. They conspired against me out of jealousy because I was the best teacher and the people loved me better."

Ryckair felt the presence of Baras his mind.

The dragon was soothing and sympathetic. "As I see your own brother conspired against you. We are kindred spirits."

"No. I have read the histories."

"Histories are written by the victors. The wizards use you. Bring a new age. Be my voice to humanity, the emperor of the world. Drop the crown. It inhibits you. Join me."

Baras' words filled Ryckair with calm and reassurance. They made sense. He reached up to remove the crown.

Mirjel squirmed against the dragon's claws and managed to place a hand on Ryckair's cheek. "I have faith in you."

Ryckair returned her gaze. He remembered how Jarat spoke of faith when she took the form of Maganda in the cave. For years he had dreamed of Mirjel, longed to return to her as he had vowed in the palace gardens so long before. He realized since their meeting in the woods, she had become a part of him and he a part of her. "I have faith in you."

The power of the dragon crest embraced Mirjel. She, too, saw the generations of kings and queens, and understood the workings of the crown and the power within.

Through it, each of them saw the trials the other had endured over the last years, understood the pain and the triumphs.

In unison, they each said, "The warrior of the mountain."

The spell Baras wove evaporated. The world snapped bright and clear before their eyes.

The binding command came instantly to their minds. They pictured the dragon as he rested unfettered by the cares of the world. In their minds there was no resistance to attack, no revenge, no anger.

Ryckair felt strength flow back into him.

Baras gave a shrill cry and twisted in the air. His talons relaxed. He almost dropped them. "I'll crush you. I'll destroy all you hold dear. I'll bring flame and death everlasting to your lands."

Mirjel and Ryckair cleared their minds of the anger they held. They had but to finish the binding spell together to drive Baras back into sleep. They both realized they would be dragged to the bottom of the river with the dragon. He wondered if they would die in the fall or be trapped to duel in hellish dreams with Baras until the end of the world.

Ryckair spoke in soft, calm words. "There is no conflict, only peace."

Mirjel continued the spell. "Find now peace and rest until the world is unmade."

Baras cried a long wail. He curled into a ball and fell from the sky.

Ryckair blocked all thoughts from his mind except for the spell, even those of his own impending death.

Before Ryckair could speak the last words of the spell, the image of Jarat on the tower roof raised anger inside him. It lasted an instant, yet the spell was disrupted enough for Baras to break free.

He released Ryckair and Mirjel from the grasp of his claws and flew off eastward in an erratic pattern.

The prince and princess dropped toward the river. They knew they fell to their deaths, yet said nothing. No words would suffice. They wrapped their arms around each other as they plummeted.

Something fluttered against Ryckair's cheeks, then his arms. It was a bird, a terec, a dozen terecs, a hundred, a thousand. They flew around and beneath him and

Mirjel to support their bodies. The birds carried them across the river toward the palace.

Ryckair wondered where they came from.

A thousand small voices in his mind echoed the thought, "You both called us, of course, great monarchs."

The terecs lowered them to the top of the north tower.

Cheers erupted from everyone.

The wizard lay on her back.

Nissor stroked her hand.

Ryckair and Mirjel ran to her side and knelt.

He lowered his head. "Mistress, I faltered. The subduing spell was incomplete. Baras flew off."

Jarat reached up and touched the dragon crest. It glowed for an instant. "Don't despair, Ryckair and Mirjel Avar, King and Queen of Carandir. The partial spell you cast weakened Baras. He must hide and regain his strength."

The wizard panted. "Seek him and complete the spell or he will rise again. You now know how to. The Barasha are truly destroyed. The time of the wizards is at an end. It's your time, the time of people."

Her expression relaxed, as one who has set aside a great burden. "You're the true monarchs. Your minds thought as one through the crown. Work together as is the plan of Ilidel and Jorondel. Have faith in yourselves and the dragons. You will prevail."

Jarat closed her eyes. A glow emanated from her and Nissor.

Ryckair heard a trumpet as he had when he saw the dragon from the window in the tower. Pure and sweet, the sound heartened him.

A silver shape appeared in the sky. It grew closer to reveal a dragon with gossamer wings. It hovered above the tower. The light around Jarat and Nissor intensified. Their bodies rose into the air.

The dragon took them in its talons, then sped off and vanished into the sky.

All on the tower stared in awe. Many cried and fell to their knees.

The sound of a trumpet filled the air again.

The feeling of loss evaporated to be replaced with great cheers and a sense of peace and relief.

Mirjel looked at Ryckair. He was so familiar yet so different. It was the same face, though hardened. The eyes held confidence and assurance as they never did before. Yet, they still reflected gentleness. She put her arms around him.

They kissed and touched and drew in the reality of each other. All the leagues, all the years, all the pain washed away.

Ryckair took her hands in his as his face grew grim. "I've seen terrible things, Mirjel, acts I never thought people capable of doing to each other. I questioned my destiny, the resolve of my friends, the strength of my enemies, even my own faith in the dragons. Yet, in all this time, I never once doubted my love for you. It's the only sanity I've known, the only thought never to dim."

Her jaw trembled.

They wrapped their arms around each other again.

Batu approached and knelt. "Father and Mother of Dragons, I never thought to see this day."

Ryckair placed his hand on Batu's shoulder. "My dearest and truest friend. Never have you failed me. Serve now your king as you have served your prince."

"My Liege." Batu took Ryckair's hand and kissed it.

Ryckair noticed Petstra's body was no longer on the tower roof. "It appears I vaporized the commander along with Reshna. Good riddance."

Arms linked, Ryckair and Mirjel walked to the western parapet. Batu stood next to them.

By the light of the full moon Ryckair looked across the plain littered with the dead.

Soldiers constructed pyres to cremate the bodies. Above them, stars shone in the sky. He closed his eyes. "Batu, ask Mistress Telasec to prepare my brother's body. He shall be laid to rest in the Valley of Remembrance with full honors."

Batu bowed. "As you command, My King." He walked away.

Ryckair opened his eyes. To the west, hills and valleys and dales stretched on seemingly forever in the moonlight. To the south, torches lit the city of Meth as celebrations commenced.

He and Mirjel would go down to the city in the morning and hold open court to commend those who fought against the Barasha.

Mirjel squeezed his hand.

He stared into her eyes. They reflected the hurt and fear she lived with for so long. Yet, she was strong; a woman who overcame the Barasha and challenged

Baras himself.

Ryckair took a step back. "On the day of my birth, our fathers made a pact that bound you to marriage without your consent. As king of Carandir, I revoke that pact and free you of all obligations therein."

He dropped to one knee. "And now, as Ryckair Avar, I ask you to be my wife, to live with me until the end of our days, to rejoice with me in my victories and comfort me in my defeats. To be my queen and rule with me. To help me find the resolve to be stern when I must and to remind me of the times I need to be gentle. To do all this and remember I will love you longer than the sun burns and the stars shine, and even when these lights fail you shall still warm me and bring me joy."

She took his hand and raised him to his feet. "I will be your wife, if you will be my husband, to rejoice in my victories and comfort me in what defeats life delivers. To tell me the truth about myself, even when it's hard. To do all this and know I love you to the root of my soul."

Ryckair smiled. "I so swear."

Mirjel squeezed his hand. "As I do."

They kissed.

Hand in hand, King Ryckair and Queen Mirjel walked down the stairs to the palace below.


Far to the east on a lonely, barren plane in the North Continent, a newborn child gave his first cry.

His mother extended her arms. "Let me have him."

Zamalatha placed the baby boy into Shara's grasp. She held the infant at arm's length.

"Ryckair Avar's son." She laughed. "I hold the heir to Carandir, do you hear me, Ryckair? The heir to your throne!"

# ABOUT THE AUTHOR

David A. Wimsett writes novels, poetry, short stories and screenplays as well as articles, columns and blogs for newspapers, magazines, corporations, and online platforms. He has appeared on radio and television talk shows and as an actor in musicals, comedies and dramas.

He became a single parent in his twenties and both raised and guided his son into adulthood.

The stories he writes follow characters as they grow and have the opportunity to examine themselves and their place in the world while they face challenges in their lives. He explores ideas and concepts through entertaining stories set in immersive worlds.

His books include fantasy, science fiction, women's historical fiction with elements of mythology , humour and children's picture books.

Mr. Wimsett graduated from UCLA with a certificate in television writing with distinction. He's a member of the Writers' Union of Canada, the Canadian Freelance Guild and the Canadian Society of Children's Authors, Illustrators and Performers.

He lives in a rural town near the sea.

His author's website is https://www.davidawimsett.com

The story continues in

# HALF AWAKENED DREAMS
## Volume II of The Carandir Saga

A wizened Zerite with wrinkled skin and closed eyes slumped on the throne. One hand rested on an arm of the throne and the other held a staff.

Sif and Tarawee signaled Ryckair to stop.

Another Zerite behind the throne spoke in a clear voice. "All bow. Pay homage to Eminence Levalat, Tabosey of all Zerites, Master of the Orb, Protector of the Root. All hail."

Everyone bowed except for Ryckair and Levalat.

They eyed each other.

Ryckair found it difficult to gauge the Zerite. Its face was nothing near human. Even its eyes were uncommunicative.

Levalat raised the staff. "All rise." The eminence looked to Sif. "Is this the one, then?"

Sif bowed. "Yes, Eminence. He would have been ready sooner if the root we were forced to take hadn't broken. We had a slight bit of trouble finding another and…"

"Enough. We are already aware of your bungling. Dropping him the way could have killed him, and then what? Humans are frail. You were told this. We imagine you have continued to err. Has he been well attended on his arrival? Are the rooms adequate?"

Ryckair stepped forward. "The rooms are adequate. Your subjects have been most attentive."

Levalat raised his gaze. "We have not given leave to be addressed."

"We have not given leave for our royal personage to be abducted, yet, we have been. If the eminence wishes to discuss a matter of state proper diplomatic protocol must be followed. Instead, we find ourselves a prisoner."

"And so you are. Forget this not. As we have exchanged dialogue, it is pointless to end the discussion. Very well. For what reason did you release Baras?"

"We did not release him."

"Trade not idle words with us. Only the magical crown could release him.

You alone possessed the crown and its power when he rose."

"We were tricked into giving the Barasha the power. It was they who released the evil dragon."

"Nonetheless, you are responsible. Baras is again loose in the world. His actions trouble us. We have no thought for the dragons and their wars. Yet, even here, we were distressed by the acts of Baras. Now, he is free once more. You must undo your actions."

"You misunderstand, Eminence Levalat. We intend to confront Baras and subdue him. We seek the evil dragon even now."

"You have no time. Baras must be contained, or Carandir will be destroyed."

"We know this."

"Now it is you who misunderstand. We cannot abide Baras in the world. You have released him, you shall contain him. If you do not, your monarchy is forfeit. The Zerites will obliterate it from the world."